Robert Goddard's first novel, *Past Caring*, was an instant bestseller. Since then, his books have captivated readers worldwide with their edge-of-the-seat pace and their labyrinthine plotting. He has won awards in the UK, the US and across Europe and his books have been translated into over thirty languages. In 2019, he won the Crime Writers' Association's highest accolade, the Diamond Dagger, for a lifetime achievement in crime writing.

T0054602

www.penguin.co.uk

THIS IS THE NIGHT
THEY COME FOR YOU

Robert Goddard

PENGUIN BOOKS

TRANSWORLD PUBLISHERS
Penguin Random House, One Embassy Gardens,
8 Viaduct Gardens, London SW11 7BW
www.penguin.co.uk

Transworld is part of the Penguin Random House group of companies
whose addresses can be found at global.penguinrandomhouse.com

First published in Great Britain in 2022 by Bantam Press
an imprint of Transworld Publishers
Penguin paperback edition published 2022

A CIP catalogue record for this book
is available from the British Library.

ISBN
9780552178471

Typeset in 9.9/13.95 pt Times NR MT by Jouve (UK), Milton Keynes.
Printed and bound in Great Britain by Clays Ltd, Elcograf S.p.A.

The authorized representative in the EEA is Penguin Random House Ireland,
Morrison Chambers, 32 Nassau Street, Dublin D02 YH68.

Penguin Random House is committed to a sustainable
future for our business, our readers and our planet. This book
is made from Forest Stewardship Council® certified paper.

'Le pouvoir est, par nature, criminel'

Marquis de Sade

A glossary of acronyms, foreign phrases and historical personalities mentioned in this book can be found at the end.

THIS IS THE NIGHT
THEY COME FOR YOU

ONE

IT IS THE MIDDLE OF A HOT AND CLAMMY AFTERNOON AT POLICE Headquarters in Algiers. Superintendent Mouloud Taleb, with no pressing business requiring his attention, is content to wait until the clock reaches a respectable hour before taking his leave. At this late stage in his career conspicuous dedication to duty will gain him nothing but the suspicion of his colleagues, so he generally tries to act even more disengaged than he feels. But, even so, 3.45 is too early by anyone's standards to be making a departure. He is going to have to sweat it out a little longer – literally so, since his office receives no cooling sea breezes and commands only an unappetizing view of the blank concrete wall of the next building.

Since coronavirus made its impact on the country in March, HQ has been more thinly staffed and there has been markedly less crime to investigate for those officers still putting in an appearance. The Hirak protests have been stutteringly revived, but they lie well outside Taleb's area of responsibility. Though he could not afford to say so at the time, he heartily approved of the organizers' demands for a root and branch reform of the government and silently rejoiced when President Bouteflika gave way to

1

pressure and resigned. Alas, many of Bouteflika's apparatchiks remain in place and Taleb is surprised they have not yet concluded that the time really has come for him to retire. It's hardly their fault he has very little to retire to, although that is in a sense an arguable point. Like so many of his fellow citizens, Taleb is as much a victim of history as a survivor of it.

Much the same could be said of his relationship with Nassim cigarettes, one of which he lights to relieve his boredom. He rises and moves idly to the window, where he gazes down into the street and discovers that very little appears to be happening in the outside world.

Glancing at a ghostly reflection of himself in the dust-filmed glass, he sees a lean, heavy-browed man with thinning curly grey hair, dressed in a crumpled brown suit and a faded yellow shirt, open at the neck. He should be wearing his tie, in case anyone calls in to see him. But no one is going to call in to see him. Friends made in earlier days in the service are all either dead or long retired. He's a forgotten man.

But not by all, apparently, since at that moment his telephone starts to ring.

With an eagerness he feels ashamed of, Taleb springs to the desk and picks up the receiver.

'Taleb?' The voice sounds unaccountably but unmistakably like that of his boss, Director Bouras, who should surely at this hour be in the arms of the mistress he's reliably rumoured to keep in an apartment in the Oliviers district. But then maybe he is in her arms. Taleb amuses himself for a fraction of a second by wondering if he will hear some purring endearment in the background.

'Yes, Director?'

'Are you busy?'

'Not if you need me.'

'Amazingly, Taleb, it seems I do.'

'Are you in your office, Director?'

2

'Where else do you think I'd be?'

'Well, since you rang in person . . .'

'My secretary is not in today.'

'Of course. Well then . . .'

'You'll be here just as quickly as your emphysemic lungs will allow, yes?'

'Yes, Director. Exactly.'

Pausing only long enough to take a last drag on his cigarette before stubbing it out, Taleb yanks open the drawer of his desk where he left his tie and makes a grab for it. He didn't untie it before removing it earlier, just loosened the loop, and now it contrives to lasso the trigger of his service pistol as it leaves the drawer, hoisting the weapon out and sending it crashing to the floor, where, to Taleb's relief and faint surprise, it doesn't go off. With a shake of the head at his own clumsiness, he carefully retrieves the gun, puts it back in the drawer and locks it safely away.

A few moments later, tie in place, he climbs the stairs to the upper floor of Police Headquarters, where the Director's lair is to be found. He wonders if the crack about emphysema is a prelude to an unrefusable offer of retirement. As far as he knows, he doesn't have emphysema, just a morning coughing routine and breathlessness on steep flights of stairs. He has no intention of asking a doctor for an opinion on the subject. Could that be it, then? A compulsory medical examination? No. That would be handled by Personnel. The Director would play no part in it, other than saying a few platitudinous words about distinguished long service at a brief farewell ceremony. A summons of this nature suggests a different kind of problem altogether. And since there's no significant ongoing case in which Taleb is involved, he's perplexed as to what the problem might be.

But temporary perplexity is at least rewarded by immersion in the air-conditioned cocoon of the Director's spacious office, with its wide view of city and sky. The less appetizing features of Algiers – the dilapidated apartment blocks, the rusting satellite dishes sprouting from roofs like mushrooms, the traffic-snarled streets, the haze of pollution – are happily absent from this vista of dockside cranes and stately tankers gliding across the placid broad blue Mediterranean. Status has brought with it for Farid Bouras a sanitized panorama of Alger la blanche.

He is a smooth-skinned, good-looking man running to corpulence and baldness. He didn't get to occupy such a post without lengthy lunches with influential figures in the hierarchy and it's beginning to show. Many moral corners have had to be cut on his path to the top and the awareness of this hovers between the two men like an unspoken reproach. If Taleb were as corrupt as Bouras, it would make their relationship a great deal easier, especially since, ironically, they actually like each other.

'Sit down, Taleb,' says Bouras, with a lordly sweep of the hand.

Seating for visitors to Bouras's office comes in the form of a buttoned-leather sofa said to have been imported from Italy. It looks expensive but is notoriously uncomfortable. The general belief is that the Director enjoys watching his underlings try to remain upright on its slippery upholstery. Taleb assumes an unabashed slump between two cushions that he knows from experience to be a secure perch.

It affords a good view of a white rectangle on the wall behind Bouras's desk, marking the spot where for twenty years hung a framed photograph of President Bouteflika. Following Bouteflika's forced resignation last year, it has not been replaced, despite the election of a successor. Its absence suggests a certain lack of confidence in the new regime, which Taleb shares.

'How old were you at independence, Taleb?' Bouras asks, as if genuinely interested in the answer.

'Seven, Director.'

'Do you remember the day?'

'I remember my father smiling. It was not a common sight.'

'Did he smile more often after independence?'

'Less, if anything.'

'So, there we have it. The history of the republic encapsulated in the history of your father's smile.' Bouras broods on this thought for a moment, then says, 'Do you believe in the existence of hizb fransa, Taleb?'

'No, Director, I don't.' Unlike many of his countrymen, Taleb gives no credence to the conspiracy theory that the French left a fifth column of saboteurs behind them when they left in 1962 – hizb fransa, the 'party of France' – dedicated to undermining the new republic in any way they could. He believes that if de Gaulle had been able to pull that off, the old fox would surely have found a way to prevent independence altogether.

'But if it did exist,' Bouras muses, 'it would account for the damage done to the state by such people as Nadir Laloul and Wassim Zarbi, wouldn't it?'

'Have you asked to see me to discuss Laloul and Zarbi, Director? If so, let me be clear. They and their kind have always been motivated by personal greed, not the service of some higher cause.'

'Didn't they start out as zealots rather than criminals?'

'Perhaps. But it didn't take them long to make the transition.'

'And in Zarbi's case he paid for that with twenty years in prison.'

'Yes. He paid the price. But Laloul did not.'

'Which still rankles with you, I see.'

'I would be happy to bring him to justice before I retire.'

'Well, then . . .' Bouras beams at him. 'I have good news for you, Taleb. You may be able to do just that.'

Taleb feels a stirring of professional pride deep within him. It is disquieting, but also reassuring, as he imagines it would be to rediscover his libido in the wildly improbable event of some sultry temptress attempting to seduce him. Laloul, embezzler of billions from the national oil company, Sonatrach, left his old confederate Zarbi to face the music when he fled the country shortly after Bouteflika's takeover in 1999, with his stolen fortune already squirrelled away in secret offshore bank accounts. Taleb was part of the team put on the case. Beyond Zarbi, who was handed to them on a plate, their investigations led nowhere but dead ends and walls of silence, as was entirely predictable – and was indeed predicted by most of the officers involved. That was simply the way it was. That was Algeria.

'We have a lead on Laloul, Director?' Taleb asks hopefully.

'Not exactly. We haven't found Laloul. But we have lost Zarbi.'

'Lost him?'

'A condition of his release late last year was that he couldn't spend a night away from his villa without official permission. But earlier this month . . . he went missing.'

'I heard nothing of this.'

'The DRS kept it to themselves.' Ah, the DRS: Algeria's secret intelligence and security organization, viewed by all – including Taleb – with a mixture of fear and suspicion, capable of anything, accountable for nothing. He is unsurprised by their reticence. Zarbi worked for the DRS – and its previous incarnation, the Sécurité Militaire – for more than thirty years. His complicity in Laloul's fraud was an embarrassment to the organization and Toufik, its notoriously ruthless director, didn't hesitate to throw him to the wolves. The episode's still an embarrassment twenty years later and a serious surveillance failure isn't something the DRS's current leadership will have wished to advertise.

But Bouras has overlooked a nicety that might cause him embarrassment in some circles and Taleb decides gently to point it out. 'That would be the DSS, Director?' Not long after

6

Toufik's removal from its helm, the intelligence service rebranded itself with a subtle change of initials and some opaque reorganization that supposedly rendered it more accountable – though to whom was not entirely clear.

'Yes, of course.' Bouras appears annoyed with himself. 'How could I have forgotten? The DSS.'

'Do they know where he's gone?'

'No. At least, they claim they don't. But out of the country. That much seems certain. A seagoing launch believed to have been leased on Zarbi's behalf has vanished from its berth at Sidi Ferdj.'

'Does he have his passport?'

'Not his real one, no. But with his background I don't think he'll have had too much trouble acquiring one, do you?'

'All the more reason for the DSS to have kept a close eye on him,' Taleb grumbles.

'I would have gained little by emphasizing that point. What I have gained is an agreement for this department to be involved in the search for him. The DSS's incompetence left them poorly placed to argue. And our new president is not as enamoured of them as his predecessor, hence this opportunity. The search for Zarbi may lead us to Laloul, Taleb. If I'd been abandoned to a twenty-year jail term by a supposed friend – who's led a life of luxury ever since – I think I might want to . . . pay a call on him.'

'That could be so,' Taleb agrees.

'Yes. And perhaps you can do better than the DSS in following whatever clues there are to follow. As the only senior officer involved in the original inquiry who's still on the active list, you're the obvious choice. You're also an assiduous detective. No one has ever doubted that.' Bouras's tone suggests this is a quality to be set against several other deficiencies which mercifully he's not about to list. 'I've arranged for you to meet a DSS agent at Zarbi's villa in Hydra at eight tomorrow morning. You'll be working together on this. Her name is Souad Hidouchi.'

'Her?'

'Yes, Taleb. She is a woman. You remember them?' Bouras's expression suddenly freezes. He raises his hands apologetically and runs one of them over his forehead. 'I am sorry. Forgive me. I intended no disrespect to you or the memory of your late wife.'

Taleb composes a rueful smile. 'It's all right, Director. It's been a long time.'

Bouras sighs. 'Still . . .'

'I didn't know the DSS had started using female agents.'

'Oh yes. There are new brooms everywhere, sweeping out the old ways. We must adapt or be cast aside. Learning to work collaboratively with another department will be good for you, Taleb.'

'But will their objectives be the same as ours, Director?'

'That will be for you to find out. It is our objective – apprehending Laloul – that I expect you to pursue, whatever the DSS's priorities may be.'

'Understood.'

'You will report progress to me and me alone. This is a highly sensitive matter.' Bouras lowers his voice and leans forward across his desk. 'Le pouvoir has not ceased to exist simply because the younger generation insists it should.'

Ah, le pouvoir. Unlike hizb fransa, there's good reason to believe, as most Algerians do, that some power over and above the republic's constitution – some authority that is almost inhuman, despite humans being its ready and willing accomplices – has always had and always will have the final word in the nation's disputes. And that authority is known to all simply as . . . le pouvoir: as tireless as it is merciless, always ready to crush any organization – any citizen – who dares to dream of a free and uncorrupt Algeria; the ultimate arbiter of all their fates, that will not be defied and cannot be defeated.

Taleb nods. 'Superintendent Meslem always said our difficulties in the case were caused by the actions of those far above

8

Laloul and Zarbi in the hierarchy who were protecting themselves.' Meslem was the lead officer in the inquiry, long since retired and deceased. But Taleb knows Bouras will remember him, as he does, as one well familiar with the machinations of le pouvoir.

'Just do your best, Taleb,' Bouras says with quiet emphasis. 'Don't take any unnecessary risks. And don't do anything you know I wouldn't approve of. Is that clear?'

'Absolutely.'

Bouras takes a mobile phone out of one of the desk drawers and slides it towards Taleb. 'Keep me apprised of progress by standard means. But use this for emergency communications. It has a number on it where I can be contacted. But in an extreme emergency only. It would be best for both of us if you never needed to use it at all.'

'Then I hope I never will.'

'So do I, Taleb, I assure you.'

A brief silence falls, broken by a faint squeak emitted by the sofa as Taleb stands to pick up the phone.

'You'll want to look through the files on the case, no doubt.'

'Such files as there are, Director, yes.' As he recalls, the Ministry of the Interior requisitioned the files, but Meslem, as he also recalls, contrived to hold some material back.

Bouras flaps his hand in a gesture of dismissal in which there's also a hint of a blessing. 'Then I won't detain you any longer.'

On the way back down to his office, Taleb pauses on a half-landing to light a cigarette and gaze out through the grimy window at the no less grimy city, some seedy tracts of which are visible from this vantage point. He knows these crumbling steps and winding streets and malodorous back alleys from long and often bitter experience. They are the map of his career and his life. He also knows their inhabitants, possibly better than they

9

know themselves: hard-pressed, dry-humoured, trapped together in a struggle to thrive, or, if not to thrive, at least to survive. Such is the city of his birth and such are its people.

Taleb feels an unfamiliar lightness of heart as he stands there. He should have found some excuse to refuse the Director's assignment. No good can come of seeking the truth about how Laloul was able to embezzle so much money over such a long period without being detected. Too many people had and still have too much to lose for such a quest ever to be allowed to succeed. And yet . . . and yet. He is actually keener to take on the challenge than he would ever have imagined. What is he looking for? Kudos? Redemption? Excitement? The truth – the real truth – against all the odds? He's not sure. But something more than his existence has supplied him with for far too long. Yes, that's what he's looking for. A purpose, a meaning. A last shot at . . .

'Still with us, Taleb?' comes a voice from behind him.

It's Megherbi from the vice division, obsequious to his superiors, contemptuous of those he considers beneath him.

'It seems they still have a use for me,' Taleb responds as Megherbi starts down the next flight of stairs.

'Hard to believe.'

'But true nonetheless,' Taleb murmurs under his breath.

And as he watches Megherbi go, he takes a long draw on his cigarette . . . and smiles.

TWO

THE HAZY SUN OF LATE JULY FALLS GENTLY ON THE FIELDS AND FOLDS of Hampshire. From the roof of Litster's Cot, where Stephen Gray is making slow progress with retiling, the view is wide and tranquil, dark green patches of hilltop woodland dotted amongst the paler green of the sloping meadows. The lane below him is quiet, the air still. The only sounds when he isn't driving a nail home are the sleepy cooing of doves and the occasional barking of a dog half a mile away.

Gray is a stocky, broad-shouldered man in his mid-sixties, hair and beard as grey as his name. He's gained some muscle and lost some fat in the months he's been refurbishing his father's cottage – the long, empty months of national paralysis that to him have been little different from the solitary life he's led for the past few years. His father died less than a year ago, but he'd been in a care home in Basingstoke for most of the previous decade, leaving Litster's Cot to moulder gently and refusing to let his son or anyone else do more than pick up post, prune the shrubbery and mow the two pocket-handkerchief lawns.

Gray pauses and mops the sweat from his brow. He leans against the chimney stack and gazes around, savouring the picturesque surroundings. Familiarity has bred a degree of indifference. He knows what he sees is beautiful. But it's also simply the world he's part of.

And he's alone. He can't see another human wherever he looks. Signs of them, yes. Farmhouses, church steeples, gateways, a rare jet-trail in the sky. The marks of humans, certainly. But not their physical presence. It's just him out here, enclosed by the heat-stunned afternoon, with the warmth of the sun-baked bricks of the chimney stack beneath his palm.

And then he hears a familiar sound that's become relatively unfamiliar of late in this corner of the countryside. A car engine.

He listens, wondering how long it'll be before the car comes into view round the hedge-screened corner of the lane. Then, marginally sooner than he expects, it appears. And somehow he knows at once it's not going to drive on past.

The car's a Renault, with a French numberplate. It pulls in by the front garden wall. It's left-hand drive, of course, so the driver can look straight up at him as she lowers her window. Gray glimpses a narrow face framed by long dark hair, eyes obscured by sunglasses.

'Is this Litster's Cot?' she calls up. The accent is undoubtedly French, but her enunciation is perfect – this, not zees, he notices.

The only reply he gives is an affirmative nod. He's already apprehensive. Who is this woman? What does she want?

She frowns up at him. 'Are you Stephen Gray?'

He nods again, reluctantly, suspiciously.

'Yes?'

'Yes,' he admits, feeling forced to speak at last.

'Très bon.'

She turns off the engine. The silence of the afternoon is instantly restored.

She opens her door and climbs out. She's quite tall, slim and somehow typically French, dressed plainly but stylishly in pale linen top and trousers. Forty, maybe, with long, slender fingers, round which she winds the cord of the key fob. The gesture hints at nervousness. So does the slight breathlessness in her voice.

'It was not easy . . . to find you,' she says.

'Why were you trying?'

'You were not . . . expecting me?'

'No. Why would I be? I don't even know who you are.'

'Ah. I thought . . . your sister would have telephoned.'

'My sister?'

'She gave me your address. And she said she would call you . . . to let you know I was coming.'

He wishes then he'd turned on his phone at some point today. But he's got out of the habit. And he wanted to get on with the retiling uninterrupted. Generally, no one wants to speak to him anyway. But he wishes he'd spoken to Wendy. At least then he'd have had some warning of . . . whatever this is. The fact that his visitor is French is already disturbing him. 'Who are you?' he asks directly.

'Suzette Fontaine. But you would know me as Suzette Dalby.'

Suzette Dalby. She would have been about ten when Gray paid his third and final visit to the Dalby household in Algiers. A quiet, watchful girl, with large brown eyes that seemed to see everything – and to follow him wherever he turned. Gray knows he'll be met by those eyes again if she removes her sunglasses. He knows with utter conviction that her gaze will be just the same – and just as inescapable.

'Can we talk, Mr Gray? I've come a long way.'

'Haven't we all?' He's not sure why he's just said that. But undeniably Madame Fontaine, the woman he last met as a young girl in Algiers more than thirty years ago, has come a long way. And to hunt him down here, when international travel is so fraught, suggests a compelling motive. 'I'll come down,' he says decisively.

13

He moves carefully across the slope of the roof, steps on to the ladder and begins to climb down, more slowly, strictly speaking, than he needs to. He's playing for time, wondering exactly what's prompted this visit. It's not something he's foreseen. And it's not something he welcomes.

He reaches the bottom, walks round the side of the house and follows the cracked concrete path around the edge of the lawn to the rusted sunburst front gate. His visitor hasn't opened it. She's waiting on the other side.

'Come in,' he says. The gate spring squeaks as he holds it open for her.

She pulls off her sunglasses and looks at him. 'Hello again,' she says, with a disarming smile.

He meets her gaze glancingly and finds it as disturbingly unaltered as he expected. 'How long has it been? Thirty-two years?'

'You are good on dates. But yes, that is when it was. The spring before things went bad. Eighty-eight. Most of my lifetime ago.'

'How did you track me down?'

'You were in Papa's address book. I still have it.'

'Ah.' But the address Dalby had was the house in Guildford. So . . . 'My ex-wife must have put you on to me.'

'She put me on to your sister. She thought you were living with her.'

'Well, Madame Fontaine, the thing is—'

'Please, call me Suzette. I'm sure that's what you called me when we last met.'

'OK. Suzette. What's brought you all this way? It must be something important for you to go to such an effort.'

She nods. 'It is.'

He looks at her inquisitively. But she doesn't continue.

'Could we . . . talk inside?' She nods towards the house. 'There is . . . quite a lot to explain.'

14

'Sure.' He thinks he still sounds nonchalant and untroubled, though he can't be sure. 'Actually, why don't we go into the back garden? We can talk there. I could make tea . . . if you'd like some.'

She smiles. He realizes he has no memory of her smiling as a child. She was a grave and silent little girl. A different person, perhaps, in a different place, at a different time. 'That would be nice.'

He leads her round through the honeysuckle-draped side gate to the back garden, where there's a wrought-iron table and a couple of chairs.

'I'll be right back,' he says, leaving her there and heading indoors.

He goes into the kitchen, washes his hands and sets the kettle to boil, then hurries into the sitting room, finds his phone where he left it on the windowsill and turns it on. There's just one message – from Wendy.

'Hi, Stephen. Wendy here. I've sent someone on to you at Litster's. Hope you don't mind. She seems . . . anxious to see you. Suzette Fontaine. Dalby, as was. Pretty weird, her showing up after all these years. She had to explain to me who she was, of course, but you've met her, so maybe it makes more sense to you, her coming to see you, I mean. Anyway, I wanted to warn you she's on her way. I hope you get this before she arrives, but since your phone never seems to be on . . .' She sighs. 'Give me a call when she's gone. I'd like to know what it's all about. And how you're getting on there. So . . . Hope to speak to you soon. 'Bye for now.'

Why couldn't Wendy just have said she had no idea where he was? Because she wasn't a natural dissimulator, for one reason. And because he didn't ask her to cover his tracks. But then, why would he have? There was no reason to expect Suzette to burst out of the past.

15

But now she has. He casts a glance out through the window as he loads the tray and sees her circling the lawn, arms folded, head down, thinking. Yes, she's thinking. But what about?

He heads out into the garden with the tray and a synthetic smile. 'This is quite a surprise . . . Suzette,' he says as he sets it down on the table.

'I know. Sorry.'

'Please. Do sit down.'

They sit a little awkwardly, either side of the table, Gray in the sun, Suzette in a shadow cast by the oak tree at the end of the garden. He pours the tea, offers milk and apologizes for the lack of sugar.

'I was sorry, you know,' he says hesitantly, 'to hear about your father.' His condolences are twenty-six years late. He's aware – and aware she's aware as well – that he could have found some way to express them to her and her mother at the time had he made the effort.

'He should never have stayed in Algiers,' she says, dolefully but matter-of-factly. 'He was a marked man.'

'What have you done with your life since then?'

'Nothing remarkable. I live near Paris. I have two children. The usual stuff. You?'

'No children. No marriage either now, as you've discovered. This place belonged to my father. He died last year. I'm doing it up. And living here while I'm about it. Now, are you going to tell me—'

'Why I'm here?'

'I'm guessing it must be something to do with your father.'

She nods and sips her tea. 'Yes. It is.'

'So . . .'

'And also your sister.'

She doesn't mean Wendy, of course. She means Harriet. She can only mean Harriet. Harriet was what took Gray to Algeria. She was the link with Nigel Dalby, Suzette's father.

16

She sighs. 'It is a strange thing.'

'What is?'

'According to my mother, Papa always said he had no idea what actually happened to your sister Harriet. That's what he told you, isn't it?'

'Basically, yes.'

'Well, it seems that may not be true.'

Gray frowns. 'No?'

'A few weeks ago, I received a letter from Coqblin and Baudouin, a firm of Swiss lawyers based in Geneva, acting on behalf of an Algerian client. A man called Saidi, although that must be about the commonest surname in Algeria, so I'm not sure it's genuine. The lawyers said Monsieur Saidi had found a document hidden in our old apartment in Algiers, apparently written by my father.'

'What sort of document?'

Suzette hesitates. She seems to be struggling to find the right words. Then she says, 'I suppose you could call it a confession.'

'A confession?'

'Of what actually happened in Paris at the time of Harriet's . . . disappearance. Of what Papa did that . . . led to her disappearance.'

Gray sets down his cup and looks intently at Suzette. 'What did he do?'

She closes her eyes for a moment. 'This is very difficult for me, Stephen. Monsieur Saidi is asking me to say whether I think the document is genuine. It is typewritten, you see. They have sent me a photocopy. It looks like it was typed on the kind of old manual machine that Papa used, but I cannot be sure. Even so, everything in it suggests to me Papa wrote it. It's not all about Harriet. There are . . . other things. I think Monsieur Saidi hopes to sell the document to the French press. You will understand why when you read it.'

17

'You have it with you?'

'I made another copy for you. I want your opinion . . . before I give him an answer. Technically, if it is genuine, the contents should belong to me and my mother, although Papa never made a will and I don't know exactly what the situation is under Algerian law. And there is an implication Monsieur Saidi will pay us to let him use it. I thought . . . maybe there were things you found out about Harriet that would mean you could . . . verify some of what Papa says.'

'Maybe.'

'But you need to read it, of course. And decide for yourself.'

'I'll be glad to. I've spent a lot of my adult life trying to learn how Harriet died. This is, in some ways, an answer to a prayer.'

Suzette bows her head. 'I doubt you'll think that . . . when you've read it.'

'To be honest with you,' Gray says hesitantly, 'I always suspected your father knew more than he was willing to tell me.'

'You should remember that even before the Terror it was dangerous to speak about . . . people close to the regime.'

'Are you saying "people close to the regime" were involved in Harriet's death?'

'Did you know about her connection with a man called Zarbi?'

'Wassim Zarbi? Yes. When I asked your father about him, he said he worked for the security service.'

'Yes. The Sécurité Militaire. It would never have been safe for Papa to . . . make any kind of allegation against such a man.'

'But he does make an allegation against him . . . in this document?'

'I wondered for a long time what to do about this, Stephen. Whether to contact you or not. It is all so long ago. My mother would like it to be forgotten.'

'You've discussed this with her?'

'Not coming to see you, no. I knew what she would say about

that without needing to ask her. But she's read the confession. She's told me what she thinks we should do.'

'And that is?'

'Maman's opinion isn't relevant. I want your opinion.'

'Well, you can have it, obviously.'

They study one another across the table. There's an existential strangeness to their encounter. Gray feels sure Suzette senses this, just as he does. She was a child when they last met and he was in his early thirties. Now she's older than he was then and he's in his mid-sixties. But Harriet's for ever young, plucked from life at twenty-three. And Nigel Dalby never made it to his mid-sixties. A Hampshire cottage garden on a summer's afternoon is no place for a haunting. But Gray's lost sister and Suzette's dead father haunt them nonetheless.

Suzette stands up then and says simply, 'The copy's in my car. I'll go and get it.'

As she walks away across the lawn towards the side gate, Gray tops up his teacup and tries to order his thoughts. Bees are buzzing around the nearby lavender bush. A cabbage white butterfly is fluttering over the patch of weeds where his father once grew vegetables. And the doves are still cooing. But he doesn't feel the peace that seems to ooze from his surroundings. He feels doubt and uncertainty. What to say to this woman? How much to tell her? All he knows for certain is that there are no good answers to those questions. Not in this situation.

A few minutes slowly pass. Then she's back, smiling cautiously as she lays an A4 buff envelope on the table in front of him. 'Here it is.'

He moves to pick it up, but she keeps her hand resting on it.

'I'd prefer it if you didn't read it until I've gone. I want you to study it carefully. I want you to give me your . . . dispassionate response.'

'You think that'll be possible? We're talking about my sister. And how she died.'

'I know this is hard for you. It's hard for me too.'

'I'll tell it how I see it, Suzette. Is that good enough?'

She sits down again and takes her hand off the envelope. But he makes no further move towards it.

'Do you mind if I smoke?'

'Go ahead.'

She lights a low-tar Camel. The first draw she takes suggests it's badly needed.

'Monsieur Saidi seems to think someone might have forged my father's confession, Stephen. I don't know why. Do you have any ideas?'

'I don't see what anyone would have to gain from that.'

'Neither do I.'

'Does it read to you like his work?'

'Yes. But . . . I have nothing to compare it with. The letter E is misaligned, though. And it was like that on Papa's typewriter. I used to look over his shoulder as he typed letters and invoices and smell the smoke from his cigarette propped on the ashtray by his elbow. Imported Rothmans. The ashtray was Bakelite. It had a picture of Cagayous in the saucer. A cartoon character from Algerian newspapers back about a hundred years ago. It must already have been an antique when Papa first got hold of it. He liked things like that. He liked the past. Well, parts of the past.'

She's been speaking in an increasingly dreamy tone. But now, with an almost physical effort, she focuses her thoughts. 'Who told you my father had been killed, Stephen?'

'Er . . . I got a letter from his assistant in the bookshop.'

'Riad Nedjar?'

'That's him.'

'Did you ever hear from him again?'

'Nedjar? I can't say I did. Are you in touch with him?'

'No. He emptied the apartment after Papa was killed and sent us some of his possessions. They didn't include the typewriter. Too bulky, I imagine. And there would have been no reason for him to think we wanted it anyway. I don't remember the details of it all and Maman doesn't seem to either. We were both . . . very upset.'

'Naturally.'

'Anyway, I'm wondering if Nedjar knew anything about Papa writing this . . . confession.'

'I thought it had been hidden.'

'According to Monsieur Saidi, yes. He didn't say where exactly. Under the floorboards, maybe. I don't know. But Nedjar was the only friend Papa had left by the end. So . . .'

'Does he still live in Algiers?'

'Apparently not. I made enquiries. It seems he left the country a few months after Papa was killed.' She shrugs. 'Everyone who could leave was leaving then. The nineties in Algeria were . . . madness.'

'Do you know where he went?'

'France is the obvious answer. But he speaks English as well as French. Papa taught him the language. He speaks it well. So, he could be in this country. Or the US, maybe. He could be any-where. But as for how Papa was living in those months after Maman and I left . . . he's probably the only one who could tell us. And there's not much chance of finding him.'

'I guess not.'

'I'm not sure I want Monsieur Saidi making money out of my father's confession, Stephen, even if he shares it with me. And especially not if there's any doubt about whether the confession is genuine.'

'I'll read it, Suzette. And I'll tell you what I honestly think. That's really all I can do.'

'Of course.' She stubs out her cigarette. 'Can you phone me . . .

as soon as you've been through it? I'm staying at a hotel the other side of Basingstoke. Tylney Hall. You know it?'

'I know of it.' Gray picks up the envelope and prises back the flap, gauging the number of sheets it contains. 'I'll aim to call you in the morning.'

She nods. 'OK.'

They go out through the house, Gray fetching his phone so they can swap numbers. He notices her noticing how dilapidated the interior is. 'It's a work in progress,' he says with a rueful smile.

'Did your father live here alone?'

'Yes. My mother died many years ago. She never recovered from losing Harriet.'

'I'm sorry. I think Papa may have mentioned that.'

'Don't worry.'

'Did your father . . . ever recover . . . properly?'

'He . . . coped, I suppose you could say.'

'And you?'

'Things happen to you in life, Suzette. You can't make them unhappen. I'm sure you don't need me to tell you that.'

'No. Of course. I understand.'

And about that at least Gray is in no doubt.

THREE

AN HOUR LATER, SUZETTE FONTAINE IS GAZING FROM THE WINDOW OF her room at Tylney Hall, out across the orderly parkland of the hotel's grounds. All is green and somnolent in the golden late afternoon light. The contrast with the clamour and stridency of her native Algiers couldn't be greater. It's such a different world it could be a different planet. But it's very much the planet she lives on, more than a quarter of a century after abandoning her homeland for the comfort and safety of France.

And comfort and safety are, she's well aware, what she should be governed by. As far as she is concerned, her meeting with Stephen Gray went as well as she could have hoped, allowing for her ambivalence about what conclusion she wants him to reach regarding her father's confession. She didn't tell Stephen Gray that Saidi's lawyers have made it as obvious as lawyers can that their client actually wants her to say the confession is a fake – and for this she will receive 'compensation' much greater than her theoretical share of the proceeds from selling it to the media. Theoretical, because, of course, it won't be sold. That's as clear as day to her. She's effectively going to be paid to deny her father wrote the document. It's basically as simple as that. Though as to why . . . there simplicity gives way to a tangle of speculation.

She can't help wondering whether her current financial difficulties are known to Coqblin & Baudouin's client. The insolvency of Vincent's gallery business, coming hard on the heels of the accusation that he was acting as a high-class fence for forged artworks, attracted a slew of lurid if short-lived publicity. Their separation is probably known as well, though the scale of the debts she's run up trying to sustain herself and her children probably isn't. It could be guessed, though. It could be surmised by anyone with an interest in calculating how susceptible she'd be to a certain kind of offer: just the kind of offer, in fact – implicit, discreet and hedged about with well-turned legalese – that she's recently received.

She knows what her mother thinks she should do. She can still hear the exact note of exasperation mixed with insistence in Maman's voice when they last spoke. 'It is not important why Saidi wants you to agree the document is a forgery, Suzette. Look where asking that kind of question got your father. Focus on what is best for you and the children. That is all you should be thinking about. Say what Saidi wants you to say and let him compensate you.' The policy of not asking awkward questions has served Maman well in her marriage to Kermadec. (Suzette only ever thinks of her stepfather by his surname, and refuses to call him Papa or Gérard when they meet, which is seldom. She suspects he's not just a shady businessman, but probably an out-and-out crook. She dislikes him intensely and, worse still, he knows it. Indeed, he seems to take some perverse pleasure in it.) 'This is actually good news, ma chère. Surely you can see that? It will make things easier for you. And for Timothée and Élodie. You should be putting them first. Besides, I do not believe for an instant your father wrote the document. So, there really is no problem, is there?'

No problem? If only that were so. Her mother is an expert in reinvention. She remembers her appointments with her beautician and hairdresser more accurately than her own past. After they left Algiers, Suzette hoped and prayed every day her father would join them in Marseille. But he never came. And when news of his death reached them, she could see Maman was actually relieved. As a relatively young widow, she had many more options than as the wife of an absent husband. Kermadec was already waiting in the wings. It was time to move on.

But not for Suzette. It wasn't then. It isn't now. If the document Coqblin & Baudouin sent her is genuine, it's a message from her father she can't ignore. It amounts to the story of his life – and death.

What will Gray say? If he denounces the confession as a forgery on the grounds that it contains manifest untruths about his late sister, then the problem is solved for her. But if he says everything about it rings true to him, she'll have to decide what she's going to do.

That won't be easy. The name Haddad that appears many times in the document seems to her to have been substituted for a different name erased from her copy. It doesn't contain the letter E, of course, which is consistently misaligned elsewhere, and may have been chosen for that reason. Even without that to go on, though, the letters in Haddad are just a fraction more sharply defined than in other words. But if it is a substitution, whose name isn't she supposed to see? And why?

This is exactly the kind of question Maman cautioned her against asking. And she's tried to take her advice, she really has. She crosses the room to the bedside table, picks up her phone and checks for messages. Élodie has sent her a picture of the octopus salad lunch she's enjoying with her friends at a taverna on Mykonos. Laughing and carefree, full of holiday spirit, she knows nothing of the fragility of her future. Suzette sends a brief reply, trying to sound carefree herself.

There's no message from Timothée, which isn't surprising. Their relationship is increasingly fraught. Timothée blames her for the split with his father, doubly so because he can't actually find a reason to blame her. Vincent was the one doing deals with crooks, after all, not her. Somehow, though, that doesn't matter.

Their most recent argument happened because she made the stupid mistake of allowing herself to be provoked by his assertion that 'her kind of people' – by which he apparently meant French colonists in North Africa – were ultimately responsible for Islamist terrorism in France. The fact that it was no more her choice to be born in Algeria than it was his not to be counted for nothing.

She wishes now she hadn't ended up shouting at him. She can still see the telltale edge of a smirk at the corners of his mouth as he looked blankly at her, before shrugging and ambling out of the house.

Suzette sighs and puts the phone back down. Lying on the bed is the envelope containing her copy of her father's confession. His supposed confession. 'Oh, Papa,' she murmurs, dreaming for a second she really can speak to him, even though the last words they exchanged were on a bad telephone line between Algiers and Marseille a few days before he was killed in February 1994. So long ago. But sharper in her memory than most of every day since.

She sits on the bed and slides the document out of the envelope. Are these pages she holds in her hands really copies of pages her father fed into his typewriter and filled with his words as he sat alone in their Algiers apartment and waited for the end? Or are they artful forgeries, produced to order to serve some sinister purpose in the present day?

She doesn't know the answer. But she knows, as she starts reading the words once again – which she can't seem to stop herself doing – what she feels.

I'm like a fly trapped in an upturned glass. I can see out, but I can't leave. I should have left with Monique and Suzette when I still had the chance. I'm not sure why I didn't. I said I had to look after the bookshop. Monique said I was crazy. She was right. Who was I kidding? They burnt me out a few weeks later. Le Chélifère up in flames. Just a shell left. The books reduced to ashes. A few scorched covers. But the pages - and the words on them - all gone.

Riad got rid of the debris. Cleared the place out and made it secure. I don't know how. I didn't ask. I'd got the message by then. Should have sooner. When they started growing their beards and dressing like Afghans the writing was on the wall. Then the killings began. They started with Boudiaf. He was the first honest leader this country's ever had. No wonder he had to go. Shot dead on live television by one of his bodyguards. Next came the intellectuals: writers, journalists, university lecturers; and booksellers, of course. Shooting the messenger is standard practice. I really should have been able to work that out. But I didn't believe things could fall apart so quickly.

They gave me plenty of hints. Not subtle ones either. Hissing and drawing their fingers across their throats as I walked past in the street should have told me what they had in mind for anyone like me, dressed in western clothes, speaking French and English, daring to sell European books. I was in their sights.

Riad told me as much. Close Le Chélifère and clear out was his advice. Which would have put him out of a job. But he reckoned that was better than coming in one day to find me lying dead in the doorway. A less provocative window display would help, he said, if I was determined to go on trading. But what could be less provocative than Dumas and Zola? I'd even moved Camus to a high shelf in a shadowy corner. Riad wasn't sure. Tintin, maybe. Or maybe no books at all.

Well, there are no books now. And he's lost his job anyway. He's found another, though. Clerk at Hasnaoui's warehouse. Which doesn't stop him delivering food to me and stopping to chat - or mostly just listen while I talk. He's a good man, Riad. A gentle soul. But he doesn't have any illusions. Algeria's gone mad, as he sees it. Lost its collective reason. The killings don't serve any purpose. They're just a symptom of the madness.

Riad's the only person I speak to now, apart from occasional phone calls to Monique and Suzette. I can't always get a line. Or an answer. And Riad thinks using the phone at all is risky. I think he's exaggerating. I'm not the target of some kind of organized manhunt. As long as I stay in the apartment, I'm safe.

But what does safe mean? What's the difference between safety and imprisonment? Precious little as far as I can see.

So, here I am, wandering the five small rooms of our apartment - six, if you count the tiny entrance hallway. It actually seems quite big to me now I have it to myself. I sleep in Suzette's old room. I feel less lonely in her bed than in

the one I shared with Monique. When I wake,
the sun's often shining on the wall by the
door, where I can see the lines we pencilled
on the plaster to record Suzette's height as
she grew up.

I read a lot. Reread, actually. I've never
kept many books here, so the list isn't long.
Nothing highbrow. The complete Sherlock Holmes
short stories and a sizeable chunk of Maigret is
basically what it amounts to. Plus copies of Le
Monde and the International Herald Tribune Riad
buys under the counter from a contact at the
airport to keep me in touch with the outside
world.

I can tell the time now, almost to the minute,
by the way the sun works its way round the
apartment. I've become sensitive to any change
in the weather. Even variations in traffic noise
give me clues to what's going on in the city
around me.

And then there are the pigeons. I can hear
their cooing and the explosive flapping of their
wings as they take off from their rooftop
perches. Sometimes they land on the balcony. But
I don't go out there in daylight, so I just cock
my head like they do and fix their beady eye
with mine through the glass. When they realize
there aren't going to be any breadcrumbs, they
give up and fly away.

I wish I could give up and fly away.

From one end of the balcony, if I lean out
over the railings, I can see the Martyrs'
Memorial up on the southern heights above Sidi
M'Hamed. I haven't gone out there to look at it
for a long time now. The design has always

troubled me. It looks like some cloaked and cowled phantom surveying the city, waiting to devour its citizens. But they're doing a good job of devouring themselves now. They'll have to build another memorial soon, to another generation of martyrs.

No one learns anything from history in Algeria. They just keep repeating it in ever more exaggerated forms. I wish I'd never come to the country. I've had many happy times here. But the horror this place generates blots out everything else eventually. You can't survive it. You can only flee. And it's too late for me to do that.

In a sense, my fate was written before I was born. My father worked in Naval Intelligence during the Second World War. He met and fell in love with a beautiful secretary at Free French HQ in London. They married in 1941 and I was born the following year.

They were often apart in the early years of their marriage. After the war, when life was less exciting and Dad began his transition into a crusty tweed-jacketed schoolmaster, Maman started to feel bored and stifled. England in the late forties and early fifties wasn't the place for her. She left when I was twelve. Moved back to Paris. Took an Italian lover. Lived 'la belle vie'. It all sounded wonderfully exotic to the teenage me. And I missed her badly. More than I could ever tell Dad, especially after they were divorced and he married Marjorie, the school matron. I nicknamed her Margarine: a tasteless substitute for the real thing.

In Paris, Maman dressed more elegantly than she ever did in England, chain-smoked Disque Bleus, drank like a fish and spent most of her time shopping. Giuseppe was besotted and denied her nothing. He was some kind of businessman. I never worked out what kind exactly. He often had to go to Milan at short notice. He wore smart suits, drove a Maserati and smoked cigars. They lived in an apartment on the Île St-Louis. To me their life seemed impossibly glamorous, though a few overheard rows suggested it was no idyll. There was a problem with unpaid bills. And another problem called Isabella who lived in Milan.

I tried to ignore all that. Giuseppe was entertaining and generous. And I wanted to spend as much time in Maman's world as I could. My love for France, I realize now, was just a larger version of my love for her. I think I always knew, somewhere deep down, that I wouldn't have her for long.

I went up to Cambridge in 1961. To read Modern Languages. French, obviously. I already had my sights set on a postgraduate place at the Sorbonne. But I'd only been there a couple of weeks when my tutor summoned me with bad news. Giuseppe had phoned the college to say Maman was gravely ill in hospital after falling down the stairs in their apartment building. I should go at once.

I tried to call Giuseppe, but got no answer. I called Dad and was amazed to discover Giuseppe hadn't thought to inform him what had happened. Not that he seemed particularly interested. All he said was that it would probably be a good

thing if I went to Paris to 'represent the
family'. I set off early the following morning.

It was a difficult journey from London
onwards. I was so distracted thinking about
Maman I got on the wrong branch of the Northern
Line and missed my train at Charing Cross by
five minutes. The weather worsened and the next
ferry from Folkestone was delayed for hours. It
was already getting dark when we docked in
Boulogne. And it was gone nine o'clock when the
train rolled into the Gare du Nord in Paris.

This is a roundabout way of explaining how I
found myself in Paris on the night of 17 October
1961. It was just a date at the time. An ordinary
Tuesday. I didn't know it was going to earn an
infamous place in history. Or that I was going
to see that history unfold. Right in front of me.

In his call to the college Giuseppe had said
Maman was in the Hôtel-Dieu hospital on the Île
de la Cité. I still hadn't been able to speak to
him. And a call I'd made to the hospital while
waiting for the train in Boulogne had been cut
off after the phone had swallowed all my coins.
So I had no idea how she was. I was in a state
of high anxiety as well as exhaustion when I got
on the Métro at the Gare du Nord.

I should have got off at Cité, right by the
hospital. But I decided to go on to the next
stop, St-Michel. I needed to walk a little and
breathe some fresh air before facing whatever
was waiting for me at the Hôtel-Dieu.

Big mistake.

The first inkling I had that this wasn't a
normal night in Paris was the sight of a man on
the platform at St-Michel with blood streaming

from a wound to his head. He looked Algerian. So
did quite a few other people around him. They
were talking excitably. They looked . . .
frightened.

I'd followed the war in Algeria more closely
than most in England partly because my mother
was French and partly because she wasn't short
of opinions on how the rebellion should be dealt
with. It's fair to say she wasn't sympathetic to
the Algerian cause. But the general assumption
was that France would eventually grant them
independence and withdraw from the country. De
Gaulle's government was in talks with the
Algerian liberation army, the FLN. A peace
treaty was in the offing.

But there was no peace that night. I emerged
from the Métro station into a scene of carnage.
A mass of Algerian demonstrators had been hemmed
in by the police. Like me, they were trying to
cross the Pont St-Michel and as I made my way
towards the river I was immediately caught up in
something between a battle and a riot.

I turned east, thinking I could cross by the
Petit Pont further upstream. But everything got
much worse very quickly. There were sirens and
whistles and shouts and screams and the sound of
windows being smashed. There were occasional
cracks of gunfire as well. Groups of Algerians
were fleeing from attacks by baton-wielding
police. I was jostled and barged and nearly thrown
off my feet. To add to it all it was raining
heavily. We were splashing through deep puddles
red with blood, stepping on abandoned hats,
scarves, even shoes. I couldn't really believe
what was happening around me. I couldn't really

33

believe I was in Paris rather than Algiers. It was as if war had broken out around me.

There was no chance of crossing by the Petit Pont. As I tried to pick my way through the mayhem, I looked ahead and saw Algerians being literally thrown off the bridge by police officers. I saw one policeman beating the hands of a protester who was clinging on to the parapet until he let go and disappeared into the water. Glancing downstream, I saw similar scenes playing out on the Pont St-Michel. The river was high and flowing fast. The protesters who fell or were thrown in were swept away, vanishing into the darkness.

I was still stumbling towards the Petit Pont, dazed by the shock of what I was seeing, when a policeman lunged at me. He took a swing at my head with his baton, but I managed to get my arm in the way, though the pain of the blow made me think he'd broken it. Then he spat at me. I think I just stared at him, too taken aback even to run away.

And then, luckily for me, another policeman stepped between us. He shouted to his colleague that I obviously wasn't an Algerian, although the word he used wasn't 'Algérien'. I explained as best I could that I was English, trying to reach the Hôpital Hôtel-Dieu, where my mother was a patient. And he was suddenly transformed from a baton-wielding thug into something closer to my bobby on a bike vision of police officers. He took me by the arm and led me through the police lines and over the bridge, completely ignoring the vicious assaults on demonstrators

that were going on all around us, in fact
steering me gently and adroitly between them.

'Qu'est-ce qui se passe?' I asked as another
couple of hapless souls were thrown screaming and
bleeding off the bridge right in front of us.

'Un nettoyage en retard,' I remember he
replied. The phrase sounded almost innocent. An
overdue clean-up. Apparently, that was all I was
seeing. Some Parisian street-cleaning. A little
necessary housekeeping. Nothing for me to worry
about now I was in his care.

He took me as far as the hospital entrance and
left me there. I didn't realize until I went in
that there was blood on my face. I couldn't have
said how it got there. At first, I was taken for
walking wounded from the riot. I glimpsed several
figures on stretchers who looked a lot worse off
than me. Eventually, I managed to explain why I
had actually come.

A nurse consulted a list. I watched her finger
work its way down the names. Then her finger
stopped.

And I knew at once by the expression on her
face that I was too late.

It seems almost criminal that my beautiful and
cultured mother should have died because she
fell down a flight of stairs while drunk at the
age of forty-four. She could easily still be
alive today. She'd only be in her mid-seventies.
But she died that night, 17 October 1961,
without regaining consciousness.

I can't recall what happened over the next
twenty-four hours with much clarity. Various
aunts and uncles came to lend support to

Giuseppe and me. He basically disintegrated,
which somehow obliged me to cope on a practical
level, even though my emotions were in turmoil.
The gardienne of the apartment block stepped in
to manage many things that needed managing with
quiet efficiency.

I stayed in Paris until after the funeral,
which was fixed for the following Monday. As for
the violence on the streets, at first I literally
forgot about it. It was several days before I was
in any state to understand what I'd been caught
up in. And then the official version of events
seemed totally out of kilter with what I'd seen.
A few Algerians killed and wounded, several
policemen injured. I knew that couldn't be right.

The press didn't believe it either. Awkward
questions were being asked. Why had the police
fired on unarmed and peaceful demonstrators? What
was the true scale of fatalities? On the TV I saw
hundreds of arrested demonstrators being loaded
on to planes at Orly airport for deportation back
to Algeria. I started to tell Uncle Benoît - my
mother's older brother - what I'd witnessed being
done to them on the streets and he exploded with
rage, saying deportation was too good for them.
The FLN had been murdering police officers on
their way to or from work for the past two months.
There had to be retribution for that. When I
suggested it wasn't FLN gunmen the police had
attacked on the night, just ordinary Algerian
immigrants, he grew angrier still and demanded
to know whose side I was on. If we'd been in his
house rather than my mother's apartment, I think
he'd have thrown me out.

But that was Uncle Benoît. He had a softer side. I remember him putting his gigantic arm round me at Maman's graveside as brown leaves skittered across Père-Lachaise cemetery beneath an autumnally grey sky and tears welled in my eyes. They were welling in his as well. He didn't say a word and he didn't need to. He was always a better communicator when he didn't speak.

When I got back to England, I discovered no one knew anything about the events of 17 October 1961. They weren't much interested either. France's 'Algerian problem' barely registered in the public mind. To most of my contemporaries at Cambridge it meant nothing at all.

As I adjusted to life back in Cambridge, it meant less and less to me as well. I read a few newspaper reports on the build-up to Algerian independence and the moment of its arrival in July 1962 - the flight of French colonists, the lowering of the tricolore, the formal handover, the wild celebrations on the streets of Algiers. I amused myself imagining Uncle Benoît's apoplectic reaction. Otherwise, as far as I was concerned, that was that.

I didn't know then - few did - just how many Algerians that night of 17 October 1961 had been shot on the streets, taken by van to the Bois de Boulogne and beaten to death, thrown unconscious into the Seine to drown, murdered in the detention centres the police set up. I didn't know. And I wouldn't have believed it.

Belief was to come later. And with it the conviction that someone should be made to answer for it.

FOUR

My plans for a first at Cambridge, followed by a
move to the Sorbonne, didn't quite work out.
That's putting it mildly. I could blame losing
my mother young, but there's no one to blame
really except myself. Although the money she
left me didn't help. I developed a taste for
excess and, while the money lasted, I was able
to indulge it. Let's not waste time on the sad
story of my frittered away opportunities. I
ended up with a Third and was lucky to get that.

I didn't know what to do after Cambridge.
Going home to Dad and Marjorie wasn't an option.
I drifted to London and a circle of equally
drifty friends. This was 1964. The Swinging
Sixties were only just getting into gear. There
wasn't anything very decadent about our lives.
Or glamorous, come to that.

I found a job - in the foreign languages
department at Foyle's bookshop. That's where I
first met Harriet Gray one late November
evening. I was entranced the moment I set eyes

on her. More accurately, I was entranced the moment she spoke. Her gentle but precise voice elevated the sparkle in her gaze to some level of inner as well as outer beauty. And her search for a dictionary of French slang was my chance to get to know her. It was raining outside. Water was streaming off her brolly. I remember her apologizing for that. And then for some reason we both laughed. It was a strangely wonderful way to begin a relationship.

Before she'd left, I'd secured a date for the following evening. Whether she was as attracted to me as I was to her I wasn't sure, but already she seemed to find me amusing, which was a good start.

Christmas and the New Year were a romantic whirl. I'd never felt so happy with someone as I did with Harriet. She made me want to be a better person. And for quite a while I actually was. We seemed to belong together.

She'd come down from Oxford the previous summer and was working as a junior assistant at a casting agency in Soho. Her sights were set on making a career for herself in the film industry, which, so she told me, hadn't impressed her parents at all.

I found that out for myself when I spent Christmas with her at her parents' home in Basingstoke. Her father didn't say much, but her mother quizzed me on several occasions about my family and job prospects and harped on the need for Harriet to 'settle down', though it wasn't clear she wanted her to settle down with me. A dowdy younger sister, an Airfix-mad brother and a bouncing Labrador added to the general impression

of middle-class conformity Harriet was determined
not to be governed by.

It was only after we'd got back to London that
she revealed her breakthrough in the film
industry. She'd wangled the offer of a job
working for the legendary comic film-maker
Jacques Tati on his latest project. Tati, she
told me, had built a huge outdoor set on the
outskirts of Paris for the production and needed
someone who could speak French and English to
handle the administration thrown up by a horde of
extras. Not all of them were French, so there was
going to have to be a lot of bilingual
communication. She'd expected to start in
January, but bad weather had delayed the project.
She was now expecting to take up her post -
poorly paid but perfect for her CV - in April.

It was a juicy opportunity for her. I knew she
had to take it. But what about me? What about
us? She'd already thought about that. 'Why don't
you come too, Nigel?'

Yes. Why didn't I? It wasn't as if I'd be
turning my back on much. And I knew for certain
I didn't want to turn my back on Harriet. Paris
in the spring with the girl I loved. Who was
going to say no to that? Not me.

I'd seen Les Vacances de M. Hulot and Mon Oncle,
so I knew Tati was a comic genius and Harriet was
lucky to have landed a job working for him. As to
what I was going to do in Paris, I had no clear
idea when we set off at the end of March, 1965.

Specta-Films, Tati's company, had found a flat
for Harriet near the Place de la Bastille. It was
a tiny fifth-floor eyrie from which you couldn't

just tell the time from the clock on the Gare de
Lyon, you could see the movements of its minute
hand. Naturally, the plumbing was a law unto
itself and the windows leaked whenever it rained.
But they were also huge and full of Paris whatever
the weather. And when we opened them and made love
with our Françoise Hardy LP playing on the
Dansette, there was nowhere we'd rather have been.

Giuseppe had long since gone back to Milan to
dodge his creditors, so there was nothing
connected to my mother to haunt me in the city
apart from her grave at Père-Lachaise, which I
visited just the once, with Harriet. Paris felt
new to me that spring - the start of something
unknown but exhilarating.

Tati's outdoor set was on a windswept plateau out
beyond the Bois de Vincennes. An advantage of the
flat's location was that Harriet could travel
there by train from the Gare de la Bastille, a
stone's throw from the flat. Her early accounts
of working arrangements suggested a production
mired in dither and delay. Tati had leased the
site from the city council so he could build a
fake contemporary cityscape as the setting for
M. Hulot's latest misadventures. Most of the cast
were amateurs. The skyscraper facades had a habit
of blowing over in a gale. And Tati kept changing
his mind about how to tell the story.

To make matters worse, the site was earmarked
for a gigantic cloverleaf interchange on the
Autoroute de l'Est, which was already under
construction. The authorities weren't going to
wait for Tati to resolve his creative difficulties
before moving in with the cranes and bulldozers.

So Tativille - as it was dubbed - had a limited lifespan. Playtime, the film ended up being called. No one knew that then. Except Tati, maybe, who presumably also knew he had only a certain amount of time to play with.

Harriet's main job was corralling and pacifying extras who often had nothing to do, including a platoon of American service wives who'd been cast as tourists. She didn't always have much to do herself and soon succumbed to my requests to get a look at Tativille from the inside.

It was every bit as bizarre as she'd described: a vast, windblown arena of fake high-rise buildings where the comedy was supposed to play out, but where all that seemed to happen was that carpenters and electricians fussed over hinges and light switches and a tall, glum, raincoated figure in the distance identifiable as the great man himself shambled from one inconclusive deliberation to another.

But he liked Harriet. That was obvious when he wandered into the Portakabin where she worked and smiled in delight at the sight of her. 'La rose anglaise', he called her. He seemed to take to me as well and thought I'd be ideal as a faceless functionary in one of the office scenes he was planning. And so, for the princely sum of seventy francs a day - about five pounds - I was hired to play my small part in the production - when and if the time finally came.

That's how I came to join Harriet at Tativille, on days when I was likely to be required, although even then I usually ended up doing nothing but drink coffee, read a Maigret and wander the site. It was boring, but at least I was being paid to be bored. Harriet was no longer the only one of us bringing in some money.

It was on one of my site wanderings that I met and fell into conversation with Wassim Zarbi. I'd seen him around, but knew little of his role in the film other than that it required him to wear a loudly striped suit and flamboyant fedora. His dark complexion suggested he was North African. He was tall and good-looking, with a luxuriant moustache. We introduced ourselves to each other over a cigarette.

Zarbi mentioned he was Algerian. He could speak English as well as French and conveyed the impression of someone who'd already experienced a lot in his life. He looked about thirty and implied he'd seen more than his share of action during the War of Independence.

That meant he'd served in the FLN. He was mildly impressed I'd even heard of it. He'd come to Paris to make a living, but he'd left his heart in the country he'd fought for. 'Most English people know nothing about Algeria. They think it's all sand dunes and camels. But that's the Sahara. The Algeria most people live in is more like Spain or Italy.'

He was even more impressed when I revealed I'd been in Paris on 17 October 1961 and witnessed the police attacking Algerian demonstrators. A massacre, he called it: more than a hundred killed. And the world merely shrugged. France still refused to acknowledge what had happened. 'They slaughtered our people and they treat it like nothing.' He hadn't been in Paris himself at the time, but he'd spoken to many who had. 'They will never forget le dix-sept octobre.'

I told Harriet about our conversation later. I'd never described that night to her in any detail before. She was horrified, but also incredulous. How could so many deaths have gone unreported? Zarbi must be exaggerating. She didn't like him - or trust him. He'd made his disdain for her very obvious whenever they'd had any dealings at Tativille. His attitude to women was patronizing and dismissive. He couldn't be relied on to tell the truth about anything. But if he was exaggerating, so, by implication, was I. Her refusal to back down on the point led to our first argument. We patched it up quickly enough. But the realization that she could doubt me lodged in my mind and wouldn't go away. I didn't like how it made me feel.

Next time I saw Zarbi, we soon got on to the same subject. He asked me if I'd like to meet a survivor of one of the worst episodes of 17 October. I said I would. So, one afternoon when neither of us was needed at Tativille, he drove me in his beaten-up old Citroën to a back-street café somewhere near the Gare du Nord. Most people in the area and everyone in the café appeared to be Algerian. They spoke to each other in a language Zarbi told me wasn't Arabic but Tamazight - the Berber tongue.

A limping, one-eyed man in greasy whites emerged from the kitchen and joined us at a table. He gave his name as Hamed Kaddour. He wasn't inclined to be talkative, but Zarbi persuaded him to reveal why he limped and how he'd lost an eye.

Kaddour joined the protest march on 17 October 1961 because police Z squads, as they were called, had started raiding the shanty town where he lived in Nanterre, wrecking homes and arresting anyone who got in their way. He was one of many arrested near the Pont St-Michel and taken to the nearby Préfecture of Police, where they were held in the courtyard and subjected to brutal beatings. A blow to the head took out his eye and a savage kicking caused him a permanent groin injury. It was when they started garrotting him with a belt that he thought he really was going to die. But they tired of that and threw him into the Seine instead.

He wasn't the only one. 'The river was full of bodies,' he said. By some effort of will, he stayed afloat and breathing, eventually crawling out up a ramp in the Port de Javel. A nightwatchman found him and called an ambulance. 'I was lucky,' he said, smiling grimly.

'Like I told you, Nigel,' Zarbi said. 'It was a massacre.'

Another man joined us as Kaddour limped back to his kitchen: a friend of Zarbi's, a fellow FLN veteran called Nazim Haddad. Shorter and less imposing than Zarbi, Haddad looked slightly older, with thinning hair and a frowning expression. He spoke quietly, but seemed to weigh every word. Like Zarbi, he spoke good English. I had the impression they'd arranged to meet there. 'Wassim tells me you saw some of the things our brother Kaddour suffered that night, Nigel. Do you know who is to blame for them?'

'The police, obviously,' I replied.

'They obeyed their orders, that is all.'

'Then who gave the orders?'

'Papon, préfet de police then and now. And de Gaulle, Monsieur le Président . . . then and now.'

'I can't believe-'

'But it is true.'

'Look, the police went on the rampage, no doubt about it. But you seem to be suggesting it was orchestrated . . . at the highest level.'

'Yes, Nigel,' Zarbi intervened. 'That is what we are suggesting.'

'That's just not . . .'

'Not possible?'

'Well . . .'

'Oh, it is very possible. And we are getting close to proving it.'

It was then I realized Zarbi wasn't really a jobbing actor at all. And he hadn't come to France just to make a living. He and Haddad were men with a mission. There was an underlying seriousness to them - an intensity of purpose. And a slight but palpable air of menace I found both disturbing and enticing. They looked at each other. And then they both looked at me.

'We need your help,' said Haddad.

'Sorry, but-'

'There would be no danger, mon ami,' said Zarbi. 'We think this would work. But if it didn't you could walk away without a problem.'

'Still, I . . .'

'All it would be is a little acting. Like Tati pays us peanuts for.'

'Why do you need me?'

'Because you are a white European, Nigel,' said Haddad. 'And as you see . . . we are not.'

'What's that got to do with it?'

'We cannot say more unless you commit to doing it.'

'How can I commit to something when I don't know what it is?'

'We understand. Think about it. Take a few days.'

'Remember, Nigel,' said Zarbi, grasping me by the shoulder in a powerful grip, 'there would be no danger for you.'

'And it would get us the proof,' added Haddad.

'Which would be something, no?' Zarbi relaxed his grip and smiled at me, urging me with his gaze not to let them down. 'You can do this. I know you can.'

Zarbi didn't drive me all the way back to the flat. He dropped me on the Boulevard Beaumarchais, claiming he had to be elsewhere and couldn't take me any further. His parting remark, as I climbed out of the car, suggested to me this was actually a precaution to avoid our being seen together. 'Don't tell Harriet about our visit today, Nigel. Just between us, OK?'

I'd already decided, after the row we'd had, not to mention it to Harriet, fearing she'd make up my mind for me about helping Zarbi and Haddad, whereas I very much wanted to make up my own mind. I'd proclaimed disbelief of Haddad's allegation that police violence on 17 October 1961 had been approved at the very top of government. But I was secretly excited as well as appalled by the idea that it might have been - and that I could be instrumental in proving it.

I was careful to give Harriet no sign that I was mulling something important over. And she didn't seem to notice anything amiss.

*

That weekend, we had an invitation to Sunday lunch with Viviane Labbé, deputy wardrobe supervisor at Tativille, and her husband Alain, an academic. The party was a dozen or so, at their riverside house in St-Maur-des-Fossés. The atmosphere was relaxed and self-satisfied: well-fed Parisian intellectuals arguing the finer points of film and literature in a spring-prinked garden, with an occasional seasoning of left-wing politics. I decided, after a few drinks, to test just how left-wing they really were. I raised the dreaded topic: 17 October 1961.

The reaction was strangely schizophrenic. They deplored Papon as basically a fascist - an enthusiastic collaborator with the Nazis during the war. They didn't doubt there'd been police brutality on the night. But they did doubt there'd been many fatalities, or that dozens of Algerians had been thrown into the Seine. The bodies would have been found downstream, they reasoned - and they simply hadn't been. There was an arcane debate about where such bodies would have ended up. The lock at Suresnes, maybe? Rouen, even? This began to exasperate me. Why, I asked, would de Gaulle put a Nazi collaborator in charge of the Paris police? Not his decision, I was told. He wasn't president when Papon was appointed. OK, but why would he leave him in post? Because, on some level they didn't want to acknowledge, he got the job done. And it was a job, I sensed they secretly felt, that needed doing. There were still too many outlying districts where the police didn't dare to go except in force. Had any of them ever been to these districts? Apparently not. They didn't need to. They knew what they were like. Besides, why

were the Algerians still complaining? They had
what they'd fought for: their independence. That
story was over, consigned to the past and best
forgotten.

I dropped the subject before it turned into a
full-scale argument. Harriet agreed with me as
we made our way home that I'd hit a nerve. But
it was fundamentally their problem, she pointed
out, not ours. 'Algeria's got nothing to do with
us, has it?'

I suppose on one level she was absolutely
right. And I wish now, more than I wish anything,
that I'd left it there.

But I didn't.

✣

Gray breaks off from reading and drains his whisky glass. He
wonders if Suzette harbours any genuine doubts about the
authenticity of the document. Every word seems to him to have
the ring of truth. Except the name of Zarbi's friend, Nazim
Haddad. When Gray peers closely at the page, he feels sure he
can make out something suspect in the appearance of those two
words. They're just a fraction of a fraction more distinct than the
others around them. And the name couldn't have been better
chosen, avoiding as it does the letter E, which is consistently misaligned elsewhere.

What should he do? What to say to Suzette is an easy question
to answer. But there are considerations beyond that. He has to
protect himself against future actions by whoever sent her the
copy of her father's confession. And he should do so sooner rather
than later. Because there's no telling what they have in mind.

Gray rises and goes from room to room, drawing curtains and
switching on lights. It's nearly dark outside. The night's crept up

on him across the silent fields. The owls will be calling soon. He hears them every night, but he never sees them. A man in a lamp-lit window is never more visible than here, in the heart of the countryside. Solitude is a peaceful state. But sometimes it's also a vulnerable one.

He dismisses the thought that he might be in danger as an overreaction. There's no one out there, watching him. Still, he can't afford to ignore the possibilities that have opened up. There's one obvious precaution he can take. The only question is whether he should take it now, or wait until morning.

Akram, the more talkative of the two brothers who run the gar-age near Taleb's apartment where he rents a parking space, registers his unwontedly late return that evening with a slight cock of the head as he opens the gate for him to drive in. Taleb normally arrives well before the gate is closed, but a lengthy perusal of the files he inherited from Superintendent Meslem relating to the Zarbi/Laloul case delayed his departure from Police Headquarters by several hours.

Meslem circumvented the Ministry of the Interior's removal of sensitive material by storing some of it in unlikely places, knowing ministerial officials to be lazy as well as arrogant: a show of subservience to them could buy any amount of negli-gence. Sifting through what Meslem left behind when he retired reminded Taleb of all the loose ends not tied up in the case, the suggestions of corruption running deep within state organiza-tions, the connivance of numerous others Laloul must have relied upon to perpetrate and sustain such a fraud. It was a case study in everything that was wrong with Algeria at the time – and, as he knows only too well, is still wrong with it.

Taleb has rented a space in this garage since the early 1990s, when it became too dangerous for a police officer to park his car on the street. Arguably, he could safely revert to street-parking now. But he is a creature of habit. Akram and his brother are in no danger of losing his custom. Their facilities, such as they are, comprise a large courtyard, hemmed in by neighbouring buildings and only partly roofed over. Parking spots under cover are at a premium, although Taleb has one of them, testament to how long ago he secured it.

After parking his car, he climbs out into an echo chamber of roosting pigeons cooing and flapping on shadowy perches and walks back to the gate, which Akram is holding open for him.

'Working late, Inspector?' Akram asks. Taleb has never bothered to inform him of his promotion to superintendent.

'It is the policeman's lot, Akram.'

'I keep expecting you to tell me you are retiring.'

'Not yet.'

'That is good.'

'You think so?'

'Certainly. Every man must have a purpose in life. Mine is this garage. Yours . . . is the suppression of villainy.'

'And how do you think I'm doing?'

'That is like asking me to judge whether independence from France has been a success.'

'What's the answer?'

Akram smiles. 'It's too soon to say.'

Gray doesn't have to think long before deciding he should wait. Surprising Wendy at this hour wouldn't be a good idea. In fact, it would probably be disastrous. As it is, though, sleep doesn't seem likely to come easily. He feels physically tired but mentally on edge. The ramifications of Suzette's visit won't stop whirling around inside his head.

In the end, there doesn't seem to be anything else for it. He goes back to the armchair and starts reading again from where he left off.

FIVE

Next time I saw Zarbi at Tativille I told him
I was game for whatever he and Haddad had in
mind. I told myself I could still back out if
I wanted to. I'd just find out what they wanted
me to do and decide whether I was willing to
do it.

The following day, Zarbi took me to meet
Haddad again at the café near the Gare du Nord
where we'd spoken to Kaddour. I glimpsed Kaddour
through the kitchen doorway and I think he
recognized me, but he gave no sign. There was a
muttered conversation between Haddad and Zarbi
and we climbed some narrow stairs to a small
upper room.

It was there, with the thin half-drawn
curtains muting the light, that they set out
their plan. Haddad showed me a cutting from
Paris Match, featuring several photographs of a
reception at the Elysée Palace. He pointed to
one in which de Gaulle was shaking hands with a

visiting dignitary. Standing next to de Gaulle
was a short, slightly built, dark-haired young
man with a pale, alert face and a nervous edge
to his smile. He appeared to be some kind of
assistant to the President.

'That,' said Haddad, 'is Guy Tournier, special
aide to Monsieur le Président. He is our target.'

Tournier, he told me, was de Gaulle's go-
between for matters he wished to oversee without
seeming to do so. During the War of Independence,
Tournier had served on a secret committee whose
function was to approve assassinations and
violent actions against the FLN and other
Algerian groups in France. Also on the committee
were representatives of the Prime Minister, the
commander of the special operations wing of
the counter-espionage agency, the SDECE, and of
course Papon. According to Haddad, this was the
group that had approved the actions of the police
on the night of 17 October 1961, as well as the
bombings of Algerian cafés and executions of
FLN sympathizers by SDECE personnel in previous
weeks. The objective, he said, was to give the
French government the upper hand in its peace
negotiations with the FLN that were by then
under way. It was an objective formulated quite
deliberately by de Gaulle and articulated to the
committee by Tournier.

Haddad and Zarbi had no proof of that, of
course, no set of minutes they could send
anonymously to the newspapers. Conveniently for
de Gaulle, he could let it go on being assumed
that Papon was solely responsible for what had
happened.

'We are going to change that, Nigel,' Haddad proclaimed. 'And you are going to help us do it.'

Then he set out precisely what they had in mind. A full account of the committee's work would be extracted from Tournier, ideally accompanied by documentary evidence. Haddad and Zarbi were ready and willing to do the extracting. But Tournier wasn't an easy man to get close to. He lived alone, moved in limited circles and when he wasn't at home or at work was generally accompanied by a bodyguard. His only vulnerability was his interest in the company of good-looking young men. But they couldn't be Algerian young men. They had to be white European. Like me.

I thought about refusing there and then. But something about the atmosphere between us in that airless little room deterred me. I sensed there would be consequences if I turned them down. And I wouldn't like those consequences. These weren't men to be trifled with. I'd said I was willing to do what they wanted. Now they told me what that was. And they expected me to do it.

De Gaulle's role in what had happened on 17 October 1961 needed to be exposed. I'd seen for myself the horror of what had been done. And all I was being asked to do was manoeuvre Tournier into a situation where he could be forced to admit that. Zarbi assured me they wouldn't hurt him. Because they wouldn't need to. 'He is a timid little homo, Nigel. When we have him on his own, without his macho bodyguard to protect him, he will sing like a bird.'

'And we will record every word on tape,'
Haddad added. 'We will have him. And we will
have Monsieur le Président.'

I knew when we left the café that I was already
out of my depth. It was one thing to condemn what
had been done to those Algerian demonstrators,
quite another to lure a special aide to the
President of the Fifth Republic into a trap. But
I was certain Zarbi and Haddad would react badly
if I pulled out now. When I thought about what
they might actually do to me, I knew I had to go
through with it. Besides, I'd seen what I thought
was a safe way out of the problem. They wouldn't
be present when I tried to chat up Tournier. I
could make sure our encounter went nowhere and
claim later I'd done my best but my best just
wasn't good enough. They'd have to think of some
other way to get to him, using someone more
likely than me to succeed.
    It was a good plan as far as it went.

Harriet noticed how distracted and anxious I was
over the next few days. I repeatedly assured her
nothing was wrong, of course. But I'm sure that
only made her worry about me all the more. I was
worried about myself, come to that. All I could
do was wait for the signal from Zarbi that they
were ready to act. And then play my part as
badly as I intended to.
    They'd been discreetly tracking Tournier's
movements for some time. They knew him to be a
man of fixed habits and routines. If he wasn't
needed by the President, he dined alone on
Mondays, Wednesdays and Fridays at a restaurant,

55

Le Doge, not far from his apartment off Avenue Montaigne in the eighth arrondissement.

It was the Wednesday after our meeting at the café that Zarbi told me this was to be the night. They'd made a booking for me at Le Doge under the name we'd agreed - Davidson. He was confident I could charm Tournier into sharing his table with me. If I made the right overtures, with any luck he'd invite me back to his apartment, shedding his bodyguard along the way. There was an entryphone system controlling the main door into his building, but Zarbi said that wasn't a problem. All I had to do was open the door of the apartment for them.

There was no way out, then. I had to go through with it - to the extent that I meant to. It was yet another quiet day at Tativille, so I was able to leave well before Harriet. I dropped by the flat long enough to scribble her a note saying I'd had to go out and might be back late. Then I took the Métro to Franklin D. Roosevelt and walked down through the early evening streets to Le Doge. A man sitting in a car parked near the restaurant, reading a newspaper, had bulky enough shoulders to be a bodyguard. He didn't seem to pay me any attention as I walked by.

Tournier dined early for a Frenchman. He was Le Doge's only customer when I arrived, seated at a corner table that I imagined they always gave him. He had the menu in front of him, along with a Martini and a cigarette. He looked even paler in the flesh than he had in Paris Match. He was wearing an expensive dark suit. There were deep shadows under his eyes. He looked tired. Maybe de Gaulle worked him too hard.

Whatever the case, he was here now, free and
alone, with the evening at his disposal.

I was given a menu. I ordered a glass of
champagne. I looked out of the window. I could
see the bodyguard in his car, absorbed in his
newspaper. Maybe he was bored with nursemaiding
Tournier. Maybe he didn't like Tournier.

I began to consider how I could set the ball
rolling, as clearly I had to. I could walk over
to his table and politely propose we dine
together. I could smile a lot and try to catch
his eye. I had no expertise in such encounters.
I really had no idea how it might go. With any
luck-

I hadn't seen him talk to the waiter. But
suddenly there the waiter was at my elbow,
informing me that the other gentleman dining in
the restaurant - he didn't name him - wondered
if I would care to join him. I looked across to
Tournier and he smiled at me - invitingly,
encouragingly. This wasn't the first time he'd
done this. That much was clear to me. What
wasn't clear to me was quite how our dinner à
deux was going to end.

I returned the smile and rose as the waiter
pulled my chair back for me. I crossed to
Tournier's table. He rose and greeted me with a
handshake and something close to a bow. We sat
down and exchanged some small talk about the
obvious desirability of two solitary customers
dining together.

Zarbi had called Tournier timid, but he
didn't seem in the least timid to me. Self-
assured, albeit stiff in his manner, with a lot
of vulnerability buried beneath the haughtiness,

I sensed he could be intimidating if he wanted to be. But he didn't want to intimidate me. We were playing a very different game. And he knew its rules much better than I did.

We ordered our meals. Tournier insisted on dealing with the wine and paying for it. 'I like the best,' he said. And I could believe that. He complimented me on my French, but we settled for speaking English, in which he was fluent. He appeared to accept my cover story - I was Christopher Davidson, trainee editor at a small publishing house, holidaying alone in France - and described himself as a civil servant, which I knew to be technically true.

I was nervous and drank too quickly as a result. The waiters topped up my glass with remarkable celerity, even when other diners arrived: Tournier was obviously a valued customer. I had no doubt my nervousness was apparent to him, but I hoped he would misinterpret what I was actually nervous about.

Since I'd claimed to work in publishing, it wasn't surprising our conversation turned to literature. I described paying homage at the grave of Oscar Wilde earlier in the day, calculating this would be a not so subtle sign. It seemed to work. His eyes rested on me a lot. He derived obvious pleasure from my attempts to describe just how good the wines he chose were. That evening remains the only occasion I've drunk Grand Cru Montrachet.

I kept telling myself I was in full control of what would happen and I was going to make sure nothing did happen, but somewhere in the course of the meal I drifted away from that determination.

The problem wasn't that I was getting rapidly drunk, or at any rate that wasn't the only problem. What started to push me off course was the realization that I seriously disliked Guy Tournier.

He was reeling me in, as he thought, but in the process he was revealing quite a lot about his own nature: arrogant, manipulative, egotistical. A case in point was when I mentioned Camus for some reason. His face darkened. Had I read the man's work? I said I'd read L'Étranger and La Peste. Asked for my opinion, I hesitated. As a French Algerian, Camus would represent failure for Tournier. And as a student of the tragic absurdity of life, he'd be philosophically repugnant to him as well. I decided to tell Tournier what I suspected he wanted to hear.

'I think he's overrated,' I said after a judicious swallow of wine. 'He mistakes weakness for misfortune. He fails to understand that without belief in something . . . we're nothing.'

Tournier looked impressed by me for the first time since we'd met. 'Exactly so, Christopher. That is Camus on a skewer.'

I couldn't put a foot wrong after that. He found me intellectually stimulating as well as physically desirable. He certainly didn't want our acquaintance to end with dinner.

'You've been fascinating company, Christopher,' he said over brandy. 'This evening's been a delightful surprise.'

'For me too, Guy.'

He glanced at his expensive wristwatch. 'It's still relatively early. Would you like to come back to my apartment, perhaps? It's not far.'

What could I do, after coming so far, but agree?

'I have my driver outside. He's sometimes a little too inquisitive for my liking. If I went back with him and you made your own way there . . .'

'I quite understand.' This too was clearly a stratagem he was practised in. For a man in his position, discretion was all.

He told me his address. I knew where he lived, of course, but I tried to look attentive as he gave me directions. 'Apartment six, Christopher. There is, ah, I'm not sure of the English word, a . . . un interphone.'

'Entryphone?'

'Yes. Entryphone. You will see what to do. I will await you.'

We left separately, Tournier going ahead after paying for both of us, which I was glad to let him do when I glimpsed the size of the bill. He climbed into the car I'd spotted earlier and was driven away.

I stepped out alone into a fragrant late spring night. I began to follow an indirect route to his apartment. Coming to Avenue George V, I saw the Métro sign down by the Pont de l'Alma and stood there, as the traffic surged past, realizing this was my chance to bail out.

Then, from nowhere, Zarbi appeared alongside me. And the chance was gone. 'What is happening, Nigel?' he demanded.

'Tournier's making sure the bodyguard won't be on hand to see me going into the apartment. I'm to call round when the coast is clear.'

'Ah, good. You have done well. But you should not wait too long. Let us walk there together.' He wasn't letting me out of his sight now.

We set off. The night air was clearing my head. I could smell the cheap tobacco from Zarbi's cigarette. In one part of my brain I knew I would regret going through with this. But in another part I knew I couldn't bear to let slip the opportunity to see the supercilious Guy Tournier brought to book, not now I'd seen and listened to him at close quarters. He deserved what he had coming.

Nothing more was said until we reached the apartment. Haddad was standing in a nearby doorway, smoking a cigarette. He had a bag looped over one shoulder. We looked towards him as we moved along the pavement on the other side of the road. He nodded. 'The bodyguard is gone,' Zarbi murmured. 'Go ahead.'

He peeled off and crossed the street to join Haddad. I carried on until I was opposite Tournier's apartment building - mansarded and grey-stoned, with decorative balconies and high windows. I walked slowly across to the door.

There was a row of buttons, labelled with the corresponding apartment numbers, in a brass panel on the pillar next to the door and, above the panel, a separate button, labelled with the number of Tournier's apartment, beside an Entryphone speaker. It appeared he had an extra layer of privacy just for himself.

I glanced over my shoulder and saw Zarbi and Haddad approaching in single file, hugging the frontage of the building so they wouldn't be visible if anyone was watching from above. Then I pressed the button for apartment six.

There was a slight crackle from the speaker and I heard Tournier's voice. 'Christopher?'

'Yes,' I replied. 'I'm here.'

'Good. Come in. I'm on the second landing.'

There was a click as the door lock released. I pushed against it and entered.

I held the door open for an extra few seconds, then let it swing back. Zarbi and Haddad stepped in adroitly behind me before it closed with a solid clunk. Neither of them spoke. Zarbi simply nodded. I was to proceed. And they would follow.

I opened a second door, leading to a marbled hallway. The stairs were also marble, climbing in an elegant curve round the caging of a lift. I moved towards them. There was still time to stop whatever this was going to turn into. But I wasn't going to stop it. Not now I'd come this far. I started up the stairs.

I could hear my own footfalls on the treads, but none behind me. Zarbi and Haddad were moving with practised stealth. I didn't look round, but I glimpsed their shadows from the corner of my eye as I climbed. Would I have to ring another bell for Tournier to open the door of his apartment for me? Or would he be holding it open, awaiting my arrival?

Neither was the answer. I reached the second landing and saw the broad, high, closed door of apartment six ahead of me, the lamplight falling lustrously on its lacquered wood. There was a spyhole in the door and Tournier must at that moment have been looking through it, because the door opened as I approached.

I wondered just how close behind me Zarbi and Haddad were. There was quite a stretch of landing between the top of the stairs and the door for them to cover. It was fully open now. And Tournier was standing there, smiling at me in greeting, extending a lordly arm to usher me in. 'There you are,' he said.

'Yes.' I returned the smile. 'Here I am.'

Then I heard hurrying footsteps behind me. Tournier heard them too. And almost immediately he realized I hadn't come alone. His smile vanished. He stepped back and swung the door towards me, hoping to slam it in my face.

But I got my foot in the way and then my shoulder, pushing hard to hold the door open. And in the next moment Zarbi and Haddad were behind me. Zarbi shoulder-barged the door with all his considerable force and Tournier was knocked clean off his feet. I saw him fall backwards on to an ornately patterned hall rug. Zarbi charged into the apartment, with Haddad close behind.

Zarbi hauled Tournier up as easily as if he were lifting a mannequin, propped him against the wall and pinned him there with his forearm. He clapped a hand to Tournier's mouth to prevent him calling out. Tournier shot a glare in my direction. Then Haddad swung the door towards me, blocking my view, and stood directly in my path.

'You can leave the rest to us, Nigel,' he said, looking me in the eye.

'But I thought-'

'We will let you know what we get from him.' I could hear Tournier's muffled protests, then a gurgling, choking sound.

'Yes, but-'

63

'Go.' Haddad nodded to me meaningfully. 'Go now.'

I could have raised the alarm. I could have asked one of the other residents of the building to call the police. I could have done many things. What I actually did was creep back down the stairs and out into the street, telling myself strong-arm tactics were probably necessary to wring a confession out of Tournier and that the less I knew of them the better. The ends would justify the means. It was the classic cop-out. And I was definitely copping out.

When I got back to the flat, I told Harriet I'd had a message from Giuseppe saying he was in Paris and suggesting we meet. The rendezvous was a bar off the Champs Elysées. We'd gone on from there to a bistro. Then he'd headed for the Gare de Lyon and an overnight train to Milan. I was sorry there hadn't been time for her to meet him.

Harriet didn't say anything openly doubtful, but I could sense she wasn't entirely certain I was telling her the truth. She probably thought my slightly shaky state wasn't how an evening with Giuseppe would have left me. It wasn't nice knowing she thought I was lying to her. But at least she could have no conception of what I'd actually been doing. That much was certain.

I wasn't needed at Tativille next day. I hung around the flat all morning, wondering if Zarbi would call by to report on what they'd got from Tournier. But he didn't.

By early afternoon I'd had enough of waiting for news. I went to a nearby bar and had a few drinks, which settled my nerves but not my thoughts. I needed to know what had happened. I couldn't just sit around, pretending I really had spent the previous evening with Giuseppe.

I took the Métro to Franklin D. Roosevelt again and walked down to the street where Tournier lived. I wasn't sure what I was going to do when I got there. I suppose I wanted to reassure myself all was quiet and normal at his apartment building.

It wasn't. There were a couple of police cars drawn up outside and a dozen or so local residents and passers-by craning for a view in through the open main door. There was a lot of muttering and shaking of heads.

I asked a middle-aged woman with a tiny dog on a lead if she knew what was going on. No one knew for certain, she replied, but there'd been a death in the building and the police had been called. The man standing next to her was more forthcoming. It was a murder. How could he be sure? Easy. He'd recognized one of the detectives who'd gone in from his photograph in the newspaper. He was the head of the murder squad. Which meant this was no ordinary murder. We'd be reading about this one in all the papers by morning.

I felt sick. In fact, I must have looked sick, because the middle-aged woman clasped my wrist in concern. 'Vous êtes souffrant, monsieur?' she asked.

'I'm fine,' I said, detaching myself from her and moving away.

But I wasn't fine, of course. I was very far from fine.

SIX

TALEB ADJUSTS HIS SUNGLASSES AS HE PULLS UP OUTSIDE THE entrance to Wassim Zarbi's villa. The sun is low in the cloudless early morning sky. The drive there was a battle between his ageing eyes – not assisted by the many scratches on the lenses of his glasses – and dazzling shafts of sunlight that blinded him whenever he turned a corner or crested a rise. Fortunately, he's feeling more than usually alert, thanks to a power cut in his apartment building which obliged him to take a cold shower that morning. He and his Renault have made it here in one piece, though in both cases that is something of an exaggeration. Neither of them is in what could be called showroom condition.

The villa is concealed by a high stone wall topped with razor wire. Visitors are obviously not encouraged. The gates are closed. Through the door of a small lodge to the right of them a guard emerges, dressed in DSS uniform. He's typical of his kind: large, muscular, shaven-headed and expressionless. He ambles over to Taleb's car with exaggerated slowness.

'I'm here to meet Agent Hidouchi,' Taleb explains, showing the man his police ID.

'You're too old for her,' the guard responds.

'Am I also too early for her?'

'She was here while you were still shaving.'

'Then we shouldn't keep her waiting any longer, should we?'

The guard can't seem to find a riposte to that, so he slouches back to the lodge and a moment later the gates swing open.

Taleb drives through and pulls up in front of the villa beside a sleek black motorbike that he assumes belongs to Souad Hidouchi. The villa is vast, multi-roofed and decoratively balconied, its walls dazzlingly white, relieved by inlaid columns of grey marble. Most of its windows are shuttered. The languidly stirring topmost fronds of a few palm trees are the only sign of the garden that lies somewhere within the complex.

Taleb clambers out of his car and goes up the wide steps to the double front doors. The brass knocker in the likeness of an elephant's head currently gleaming in the sunshine is entirely redundant, of course. No one who needed to knock for entry would ever have got past the gate.

Taleb is expected. One of the double doors is ajar. He steps in through it to a cool hallway of cream marble. He notes the soaring staircase and the big empty rooms to either side that he glimpses through half-open doorways. He listens for some sound that will give him a clue to Hidouchi's location. He hears nothing.

He wanders through a succession of still larger but barely furnished reception rooms to a wide space from which stairs descend to some lower level of garaging and basements. Ahead of him, through a vast open sliding door, is a swimming pool looking north-east towards the sea.

The sprawl of Algiers is invisible from this position. Taleb can see only the pool and the Mediterranean meeting in an expanse of blue that merges with the sky. In the distance there's a tanker bound for the port and beyond that the lighthouse at Bordj el Bahri. At such times and in such places the city he calls home is a beautiful place. He pauses to savour the view and the bracing hint of ozone in the air.

Then a figure enters his line of sight, moving along the edge of the pool. By an optical illusion Agent Souad Hidouchi appears to be walking on water. Only as Taleb moves out into the terrace do the flagstones around the pool reveal themselves. And only then, by the same token, does he reveal himself to Hidouchi.

She strides round the pool towards him, a slim young woman of thirty or so, he'd guess, dressed in biker leathers, her long, dark hair falling to her shoulders. There's a challenging tilt to her head. She holds herself proudly, uncompromisingly, as befits, of course, a representative of state security. But there's more to it than that. She clearly doesn't think she needs or can be expected to make any concessions to old traditions. Recalling the horrors of the 1990s as he often does, Taleb wonders if Hidouchi has any conception of what would have happened then to a woman dressed as she now is. Probably not, he supposes. Probably she wouldn't believe him if he told her. Which of course he has no intention of doing, generally finding as he does that the younger generation has no interest in anything he has to say. The fact that he carries within himself an encyclopaedic knowledge of the sufferings of Algiers and its inhabitants over the forty-seven years that he has patrolled its streets and inspected its many scenes of murder and mayhem counts with them for precisely nothing.

'Superintendent Taleb?' she enquires with the faint suggestion of a smile. Her eyes are concealed by sunglasses, though he knows they're resting on him.

'Yes.' He offers her a more open smile. 'Agent Hidouchi?'

'I am. You found your way here, I see.'

'Actually, I've been here before, so I knew the way.'

'When was that?'

'A long time ago. Shortly after Nadir Laloul fled the country.

I hoped Zarbi could help us track him down. But he couldn't. Or wouldn't. And then he was arrested.'

'But not by you?'

'No. That was a Ministry of the Interior decision.'

'And you were just a humble policeman.' Is she satirizing him? Or merely stating a fact? It's already apparent to Taleb that working with her is going to test his mental agility.

'I'm still a humble policeman, Agent Hidouchi. It's my lot in life.'

'And it's why you're here, of course. So my department and yours can be seen to be cooperating.'

'Are we going to cooperate?'

'I hope so. Shall we go inside?'

'Where you lead I will follow.'

Hidouchi doesn't give any sign of finding this remark amusing. But she does lead the way back into the villa. And he does follow.

'Could I ask—'

'How we managed to allow an eighty-five-year-old man with a heart condition to escape house arrest and slip out of the country?' She glances over her shoulder at him to judge his response.

'Well, I . . .'

'I wasn't in charge of monitoring the situation. The person who was has now been transferred to duties on the Libyan border.'

'How nice for him.'

'You are correct. It was a man.'

She starts down a wide corridor that leads, so far as Taleb remembers, to the study where Zarbi received him with a grand show of arrogance back in the late spring of 1999.

'Do you notice any differences from your earlier visit, Taleb?'

Taleb. Not Superintendent. So, he concludes, this is how it's going to be. Hidouchi is laying down the ground rules of their cooperation. 'There's much less furniture. Much less of everything, in fact. I seem to recall a thick and richly patterned rug along here. And expensively framed Sahara vistas on the walls.'

'It seems Zarbi's wife sold most of his possessions shortly before he was released.'

Ah, Zarbi's wife. A former nightclub singer, if Taleb's memory serves him correctly, about thirty years his junior. 'Did she live here throughout his imprisonment?'

'Yes. But she hadn't visited him in many years. And she moved out before he moved back in.'

'Do we know where she is now?'

'Tunisia. With her Tunisian boyfriend.'

'Poor old Zarbi.'

'Technically, you are correct. He is poor. And he is old.'

They reach the study. It overlooks the garden, its greenery visible through the tilted wooden slats of a blind. Zarbi's desk is still in place, along with a leather-upholstered swivel chair and a filing cabinet. On the desk stands a computer. On the opposite wall hangs a framed black and white photograph of Zarbi shaking hands with the late President Boumediene some time, Taleb would guess, in the mid-1970s. The room is otherwise bare.

'The filing cabinet is empty,' says Hidouchi. 'There was a lot of ash in the fireplace. It appears Zarbi was feeling cold during the hottest month of the year.'

'What about the computer?'

'He wasn't allowed an internet connection. The hard drive contains nothing more recent than his wife's numerous website searches for Italian swimsuits for the fuller figure.'

'You said he was poor.'

'All his funds were confiscated in 1999. He owned this villa. Otherwise, he has no assets and no capital. Though he does have creditors, some of whom have been adding interest to their loans for the past twenty-one years.'

'So, he had many good reasons to leave the country.'

'And we had many good reasons to prevent him.'

'Are you sure about that?'

She's taken off her sunglasses now. Her teak-brown eyes dwell on him for a moment. He can't decide whether the sensation is pleasurable or not. 'What point are you making?'

'Well, in my experience—'

'Ah, your experience. What does that tell us?'

'That those who decide such matters sometimes say they want one thing when actually the opposite suits them better.'

'You think they were happy for Zarbi to leave the country in order to avoid any embarrassment he might cause them?'

'It wouldn't be unknown.'

'Your experience is out of date, Taleb.' So there it is. His experience is out of date. And so, Hidouchi clearly believes, is he. It would be useless to point out to her that the past determines everything that happens in their country and that experience is one of the few protections against its ravages. She will have to learn that for herself. 'The current leadership has no interest in protecting the reputation of former regimes,' she continues. 'Rather the contrary, if anything.'

'But if, as you say, Zarbi had no access to funds, how was he able to lease a seagoing launch?'

'We're not sure.'

'Ah. I see.' He lets his own gaze dwell on her. Her mouth curls ominously. 'Look, I'm here to help.' And he's going to try to help. He really is. 'Let's begin at the beginning. How extensive was your surveillance of the villa?'

'We had a camera covering the gate, monitored at HQ.'

'But no one on site?'

'Zarbi wasn't considered worth the manpower.'

'I assume the camera didn't show his departure.'

'No.'

'How did he get out, then?'

'There's a tunnel connecting the garage level with an exit on a lower road. We didn't know about it.'

'An emergency exit is fairly standard for the home of someone like Zarbi. In my experience.'

She draws a deep breath and gives him a hard stare. 'My orders are to find him, Taleb. I don't believe anyone in my department assisted him in his flight. There's no one left there who worked with him. He was released from prison because he was old and powerless and posed no threat to anyone. As far as we knew.'

'Who was he in contact with after his release?'

'Hardly anyone. We tapped his phone, obviously. He visited his doctor regularly for check-ups. He had a few meetings with his lawyer. That was it.'

'Who came to the villa?'

'The housekeeper. The gardener. An old friend Zarbi played backgammon with a couple of nights a week.'

'What do we know about the friend?'

'Razane Abderrahmane. Aged seventy-two. A former mistress, maybe?'

Taleb has an advantage now. Being older than Hidouchi gives him a longer memory to draw on. 'There was an Abderrahmane who ran a nightclub back in the eighties. It may well be where Zarbi met his wife. She certainly sang there. As for his relationship with the proprietress . . . who knows? Did she visit him in prison?'

'His only visitor in recent years was his lawyer.'

'You've checked the log?'

'Not personally. The prison supplied the details.'

Taleb allows himself a sigh, which Hidouchi receives with narrow-eyed resignation. 'I will check it personally now,' she says levelly.

'Can I see what you have of Abderrahmane on the security camera?'

'Not here. But you can view the footage at HQ.'

He grimaces. He prefers to avoid visiting rival departments. Doing so always depresses him on account of their superior facilities. But there are even better reasons for avoiding the premises of the DSS, as every Algerian knows. They might have changed their initials, but no one really believes they have changed fundamentally. SM, DRS, DSS – it's all the same, once you're in their power.

'What's wrong, Taleb?' Hidouchi looks relieved to have regained the upper hand in their exchanges. 'Worried we won't let you out once we've let you in? Don't be. You're with me.'

Yes. He's with her. And the DRS or the DSS, whichever they choose to call themselves. They have their hooks in him now.

Fifteen hundred miles to the north, on a soft early morning in Hampshire, Wendy Baker, wearing a dressing-gown over her nightie, is making coffee in the kitchen of her house on the outskirts of Odiham. She doesn't feel as if she's had enough sleep, which is nothing new. She's been semi-permanently exhausted since her husband Oliver contracted coronavirus earlier in the year. He's still struggling with the after-effects, which has obliged Wendy to keep their wine merchant's business afloat single-handed.

She pours boiling water into the cafetière and is about to cut a slice of bread for the toaster when she hears a noise outside. Clunk.

She walks into the utility room and looks out through the window into the rear courtyard. To her surprise, she sees her brother Stephen's car parked in front of the double garage. Stephen himself is nowhere in sight, but one of the garage doors is open. Some of his belongings, which he removed from the house in Guildford after his divorce from Catherine, are still stored there, well beyond the time he initially said he'd need to impose on them. She assumes he's come to fetch something, though this also gives her the chance to find out more about his visit from Suzette Fontaine.

At that moment, Stephen emerges from the garage, empty-handed. She taps on the glass and waves to him. Stephen turns and waves back. His smile doesn't fool his sister for a moment. He was hoping to come and go unnoticed. She signals for him to come into the kitchen.

'Do you want a cup of coffee?' she asks as he enters. 'I've just made some.'

'Well, it does smell good, so . . . thanks.'

'What brought you here at this hour, Stephen?'

'Oh, I . . . didn't want to disturb you. I was just . . . looking for something.'

'Find it?' She pours coffee for them both and sits down at the table, where Stephen joins her. 'Find what you were looking for?' she presses.

'Ah, no, I'm afraid not. How's Oliver?'

'Getting there slowly.'

'Give him my regards, will you?'

'You're not staying long enough to see him?'

'No, no. I, er . . . have lots to get on with at Litster's while the weather holds.'

'No doubt Suzette Fontaine held you up.'

'Ah, Suzette. Yeah, I was going to . . .'

'Call me?'

He swallows some coffee and smiles guiltily at her. 'Sorry. I was planning to phone tonight, when I'd finished the tiling. There's nothing much to report, to be honest.'

'She came all this way to discuss nothing much?'

'Well, it's a big deal to her. It seems her father wrote some kind of memoir and left it with her mother, who's only recently revealed its existence to her. There's a possibility of publishing it, apparently. An account of working with Tati on the *Playtime* set, plus running a bookshop in Algiers and meeting various famous writers, not to mention the Black Panthers—'

'The Black Panthers?'

'A lot of them spent time in Algiers in the sixties and seventies. You know, Stokely Carmichael, Eldridge Cleaver . . .'

'Who?'

'Never mind. The point is the memoir could have commercial potential. And Suzette wanted to give me some notice – give us some notice, I suppose – that it might come out.'

'Why? What's it to do with us?'

'The part that deals with *Playtime* mentions Harriet.'

Harriet. Of course. Suzette could have told Wendy that herself. But they don't know each other, whereas Suzette knows Stephen from his visits to Algiers. 'What does he say about her?'

'Only that she was his girlfriend and they both worked at Tativille. And that her disappearance led to his move to Algiers.'

'You've read the memoir, then?'

'Suzette only showed me some of it. I'm afraid I don't have a copy. She took hers away with her. But there's nothing for us to be concerned about.'

'Still, I'd like to know what he says.'

'Naturally.' Stephen drinks more of his coffee. 'I'm going to call Suzette later and ask her to send me a full copy. Then we can both read it at our leisure.'

Wendy considers for a moment asking him for Suzette's number and speaking to her herself. Then she reconsiders. Whatever precisely Nigel Dalby wrote about Harriet, the events he recounted must have taken place more than fifty years ago. She realizes with a shock she can no longer recall the exact tone of her sister's voice. It's just too long since she last heard it. 'That's a good idea,' she says mildly. But she doesn't propose to let her brother off quite so lightly. 'What were you looking for in the garage?' she asks.

'Oh, a DVD of *Playtime* I bought a few years ago when they released a restored version. Amongst the bonus features there was a TV documentary about the making of the film produced at the time. In the memoir Dalby refers to Harriet working with the extras, including a group of American army wives. I seem to remember they were in the documentary and I wanted to check whether Harriet appears at any point, in the background. I wasn't paying close enough attention when I watched it before and, besides, there were a lot of talking heads I fast-forwarded through. So, I just wondered if . . .'

'She was there?'

'Yeah. At the edge of the frame, maybe, half in the picture, half out, but . . . still moving, still . . .'

'Alive?' Wendy sighs and Stephen catches her eye. It's a poignant thought: a moving image of the sister neither of them has seen since 1965. Wendy was seventeen then, Stephen just ten years old. He should have been better able than her to move on with his life. Instead, he carried an obsession with uncovering the truth about Harriet's fate through his adolescence and into adulthood.

'I couldn't find the DVD,' Stephen says. 'It may have been thrown away by mistake. Or maybe I just didn't look hard enough.'

'Well, there's a lot there to look through.' She raises her eyebrows meaningfully.

'And you'd like to be rid of it?'

'I didn't say that.'

'No. But you were thinking it.'

Wendy smiles. She has thought it, many times. But it isn't what she's thinking now. What she's thinking now is more serious. And much more disturbing. She has a sister's sense where her brother's concerned. Others might swallow his cover story. Not her. She knows he wasn't looking for a lost DVD of *Playtime*. She knows he's lying to her. What she doesn't know is why.

He drains his cup and smiles at her. 'I ought to be going. Thanks for the coffee.'

Once Stephen's left, Wendy takes a cup of coffee up to Oliver. 'Was that your brother's voice?' he asks as he sits up in bed.

'Yes. He was looking for something in the garage.'

'Not an extra corner to fill with his rubbish, I hope.'

'No.' She smiles. 'Not an extra corner.'

'What, then?'

'To be honest, I'm not sure.'

'Nothing new there. I've never been sure about him.' Oliver sips his coffee. 'Mmm. My taste really is coming back, you know. This is really good.'

'I'm glad to hear it. I'll leave you to enjoy it.'

'Where are you rushing off to?'

'I'm going to get dressed. And then I'm going out to the garage.'

'What for?'

'I need to check up on my baby brother.'

Oliver nods. 'Story of your life, Wen.'

Stephen's boxes are piled against the rear wall of the garage: some big, some small, some with clues to the contents written on them in felt-tip pen – LOUNGE CABINET, DEN, CLIENTS, TRAVEL, SUMMER CLOTHES, WINTER CLOTHES, ACCOUNTS. Surveying them, Wendy wonders whether he really needs any of this now. He seems to have managed quite well without. And she and Oliver could certainly manage quite well without it as well.

There's no indication which boxes Stephen may have opened.

They all look, in fact, oddly undisturbed. She doubts his ability to leave so little evidence of a search, so much so that she begins to doubt he's undertaken one at all. But if he hasn't . . .

Then she notices something. The topmost box on one pile was a wine-box cadged from them, which originally held a dozen bottles of Grand Cru Chablis. The name and coat of arms of the vineyard were printed on the side. Wendy has happy memories of visiting it with Oliver ten or more years ago. But now that box is no longer the topmost. There's another box wedged between it and the tie beam.

Wendy hauls over the stepladder and climbs up to take a look. The new box is relatively small, but stoutly constructed. She's sure she hasn't seen it there before. Stephen must have brought it with him this morning. He wasn't there to look for something. He was there to hide something.

She lifts the box off the pile and rests it on the frame of the stepladder. It's quite heavy, sealed with brown tape. Whatever it contains is slightly smaller than the box. It slides down against the lower end as she moves it. She has no idea what it could be. Stephen hasn't written anything on the side.

But he has written something on the lid. His name. STEPHEN GRAY. In black ballpoint, straddling the strip of tape. Which means that if anyone opens the box his name will no longer be intact. And he'll know it's been tampered with. It's a precaution he's never taken with any of the other boxes.

Wendy studies the box long and hard. She's tempted to tear off the tape and find out what it contains that's so important to Stephen. But why, if it is important to him, doesn't he keep it at Litster's Cot, where presumably it's been until now? Why move it here? And why lie about it?

She stands where she is, pondering the questions and finding no answers. What is he doing? What is he thinking?

She doesn't know. She's never known. Except that Harriet's

never left his life as she has Wendy's. 'Oh, Stephen,' she sighs as she slides the box back into place and starts down the ladder.

A few miles away, at Tylney Hall, Suzette sets off for a walk in the hotel grounds after breakfast. She didn't sleep well and she's already drunk more cups of coffee and smoked more cigarettes today than are good for her. She's heard nothing from Stephen Gray and she doesn't know when she will, though he said it would be this morning. That was before he read her father's confession, of course. That was before he discovered the role her father played in his sister's death. The role he played, that is, if you believe the confession is genuine. As secretly she does. There are many good reasons for her to say otherwise. But none of them can change the way she feels. And now all she can do is wait for Stephen Gray to tell her how he feels – now he knows the truth.

SEVEN

The murder of a close aide of the President was
the front page headline in every newspaper and
must have led every TV news bulletin, though
fortunately we didn't have a TV in the flat.
Everyone at Tativille was talking about it.
Except me, of course. I tried to dodge the
subject whenever it was raised, particularly by
Harriet. I kept my head down and tried not to
contemplate just how big a fool I'd been taken
for by Zarbi and Haddad. Zarbi didn't show up on
set that day, though whether because he wasn't
required or simply hadn't turned up I didn't ask.
I had a pretty good idea I was the reason anyway.

Everything got worse the next day when further
details of the murder scene at Guy Tournier's
apartment came out. Initially, there'd been no
consensus about whether he'd been the victim of an
assassination or a burglary gone wrong. But at a
sensational press conference the police revealed
there'd been no burglary and no break-in. Tournier
had been strangled by someone he'd let into his

apartment and a message from his killer or killers had been daubed on the wall above his body: POUR LES MORTS DU 17 OCTOBRE 1961.

The press were puzzled as to why Tournier should have been singled out for such an act. They didn't seem to know anything about the secret committee he'd served on. More generally, though, revulsion was expressed at what had been done to him. Whatever had or hadn't happened on 17 October 1961, the argument ran, there could be no justification for such a horrific crime. As to who was responsible, there could be only one answer. Les Algériens. They'd been given their independence. And this was how the French people were thanked for it.

The police backed this up by saying the murder bore all the hallmarks of the FLN. This implied a connection with the Algerian government, which, naturally, was hotly denied in Algiers. But the police also appealed for a young Englishman by the name of Christopher Davidson to contact them. He'd dined with Tournier at the Le Doge restaurant a few hours before the killing. It was emphasized he wasn't a suspect in the case.

Suspect or not, they weren't going to hear from Christopher Davidson, of course. And I could only hope the waiting staff at Le Doge wouldn't be able to supply a useful description of him. I'd have happily left Paris and gone straight home to England to escape the nightmare I'd been lured into. I had a dead man on my conscience and the wrath of the French authorities to fear if I did anything to draw attention to myself.

As for Harriet, she already had doubts about my account of what I'd done on Wednesday

evening. She'd reiterated on more than one
occasion that she thought I should avoid Zarbi
and I began to worry that she'd wonder now if I
was somehow implicated in what had happened to
Tournier. Yet she said nothing.

Friday was an unusually busy day at Tativille,
with elaborate stagings and restagings of a scene
at a bus stop in which I was one of the passengers
required to get on and off the bus while Tati
choreographed everyone's movements to his exacting
satisfaction. Zarbi, I suddenly realized, was also
a passenger, but I never got the chance - or he
never gave me the chance - to talk to him. The
ghost of a smile as I caught his eye down the
aisle of the crowded bus was all I got from him.
He slipped away as soon as we'd finished. When I
tried to find him later, someone told me he'd left
for the day.

The weekend came, extended by the Whitsun
holiday. It passed in a slow motion torture of
apparent normality. Harriet continued to say
nothing about Tournier, even though a fleeting
reference to the big news of the moment would
have been entirely natural. It was still all over
the newspapers. I said nothing either. We shopped.
We strolled by the Seine. We saw a film. We ate
at a bistro. We fumblingly abandoned an attempt
to make love. We talked about very little beyond
everyday practicalities. I couldn't decide whether
she was tormenting me or I was tormenting myself.
I was so tense I felt sure it must be apparent
to her.

Then, late on Whit Monday afternoon, she
finally broke her silence. We were sitting on a
bench in the Jardin des Plantes, with closing

time approaching and neither of us, I think, eager to return to the flat.

'I'm sorry I missed Giuseppe last week,' Harriet said suddenly - and so disingenuously I knew it was an ominous opening.

'Well, it was only a flying visit,' I countered, trying to sound relaxed and reasonable.

'I ought to phone him and introduce myself.'

'Really?'

'You've got a number for him in Milan now, right?'

'Er, no. Actually, I haven't.'

'An address, then.'

'Not . . . as such.'

'The message you got from him. Did he leave it with Marthe?' Marthe was the gardienne of our building.

'I never asked him. Someone must have let him in, though. He slipped a note under our door.'

'And how did he know where we lived?'

I was getting in deeper and deeper with every evasion. 'Er . . . I never asked him that either. I suppose . . . he must have phoned Dad.'

'OK. So, maybe he gave your father his number.'

I couldn't fashion a response to that beyond a mumbled 'Maybe.' She'd forced me into a corner. I could stop her checking my story with Giuseppe by denying I knew how to contact him (which happened to be true). And I could argue Marthe out of the picture. But I couldn't prevent her phoning my father, who'd tell her he certainly hadn't heard from Giuseppe. And then . . .

I reached for her hand, hoping somehow to defuse the moment. But she pulled her arm away and made a show of looking at her watch. 'We should be going, don't you think?' And she stood up without waiting for my answer.

I slept soundly that night, maybe because I'd slept badly for several nights previously. Evidently, even anxiety can be exhausted. But I was woken early, by the sound of Harriet showering. The Gare de Lyon clock gave the time as barely past five.

She came into the bedroom a few minutes later, her hair still damp, and started getting dressed. 'What's going on?' I asked.

'Didn't I say?' she replied, avoiding my gaze as she hurried into her clothes. 'I have to be at Tativille early today.'

'What for?'

'Can't stop to explain.' She gave me a cursory kiss on the cheek. 'See you later.'

And with that she was gone.

I left an hour and a half or so later, wondering when or if I'd be given the promised explanation. She'd gone without breakfast, without even a cup of coffee, which was unheard of. And I couldn't imagine why she'd be needed so early at Tativille. It seemed certain to me she'd lied about that. But why? What was she trying to accomplish? I'd have rather she told me outright she knew my story about Giuseppe was nonsense than play whatever game this was.

When I reached Tativille, she wasn't at work and no one knew why. Even stranger, she'd evidently been there briefly before anyone else showed up, according to the nightwatchman, who'd

seen her as he was leaving at the end of his
shift. Not unnaturally, several people thought
I'd be able to explain what was going on and
became exasperated with me when I couldn't.

Viviane Labbé wasn't one of them. She was
surprisingly sympathetic and assumed we'd had a
lovers' tiff. I played along. In a sense, after
all, it was true. And Viviane got even closer to
the truth when she said she hoped I wasn't upset
about the Tournier case. I stumbled out
something along the lines of 'Why should I be?'
And she reminded me I'd raised the vexed topic
of 17 October 1961 at her lunch party the
previous weekend, followed within days by a
murder explicitly tied to it. 'Une coïncidence
horrible, Nigel,' she said. 'Rien de plus.'

Nothing more than a horrible coincidence? If
only she'd been right.

We were back on the bus that day, and off, and on
and off again, as Tati went through his painstaking
routines. Zarbi was nowhere to be seen. I didn't
ask where he was, fearful of appearing curious
about him. I was frightened of incriminating
myself. Most of all, though, I was frightened by
the thought of what Harriet might have decided to
do to break the deadlock between us.

I left as soon as we'd finished for the
afternoon, caught the next train to Bastille and
made a beeline for the flat, hoping Harriet
would be waiting for me there.

But she wasn't. As far as I could tell, she
hadn't been back to the flat since walking out
early that morning. I bounced off the walls for
an hour or so, then headed for a local bar we

knew. I left a desperate note for her. 'Please please join me at La Pouliche.'

She didn't.

Self-pity, sitting alone on a bar stool at La Pouliche, gradually got the better of me. I lost count of how many beers I drank, but it was definitely too many. I was well gone when I got back to the flat. In my fuddled state, I thought that might actually make facing Harriet easier.

But she still wasn't there.

I collapsed on the bed still fully dressed and fell asleep.

I was woken by the sound of the key turning in the lock. My first thought was that she'd returned at last. It was already light, so she'd stayed out all night, but I didn't care. I just wanted to see her face and hear her voice. I rubbed my eyes, tried to ignore the headache that seemed intent on splitting my skull open and scrambled to my feet.

'Harriet?' I called as I staggered into the lounge.

'Not Harriet,' came the gruff answer.

Zarbi was standing there, smiling slightly as he assessed the state I was in. His leather jacket creaked faintly as he took a pack of cigarettes and a lighter from the pocket of his jeans and lit up while I stared at him, too amazed to speak.

'Smoke?' He held out the pack for me. 'Or maybe coffee? You look like you need it.'

I managed to get some words out at last. 'What the hell . . . are you doing here?'

'I came to see you, Nigel.' He went on smiling at me.

'How did you . . . get in?'

'I used Harriet's key.'

'What?'

'You won't be seeing her again.'

'What do you mean?'

'I mean you won't be seeing her again. No one will. Ever.'

'What have you done to her?'

'She came to my place yesterday morning, early. She got the address from the files at Tativille. She accused me of killing Tournier and threatened to go to the police. I couldn't let her do that.'

'Are you saying . . . you killed her?'

He didn't answer, just drew on his cigarette and gazed calmly at me. I wrestled for a second with the horrifying realization that Harriet had died at his hands. Then I made a dash for the door. I had to get away from him. I had to report what he'd done.

But he reached the door before me and punched me in the throat. I never actually saw his fist coming until the blow hit me and I went down in a choking heap.

Before I could recover, he'd dragged me across the floor into the kitchen, where he pulled me upright and propped me against the stove. 'Breathe, Nigel,' he instructed. 'Breathe.' He waited while my coughing and spluttering subsided, then poured me a glass of water from the sink. 'Sit down and sip that while I make coffee. We can talk everything over, you and me. We can be reasonable. That was Harriet's mistake. She just wasn't reasonable. You understand, don't you?' He slapped me gently round the face. 'Tell me you understand.'

I nodded and mumbled, 'OK, OK. I get it.'

'Coffee, yes?'

'Yes.'

I took the glass of water from him and sat down at the tiny kitchen table while he opened drawers and cupboards to find what he needed before setting the percolator to heat on the stove. Then he leant against one of the cupboards, finishing his cigarette and lighting another while he smiled down at me. I was in his power. I didn't doubt he could kill me if he wanted to. What had Harriet hoped to gain by confronting him? Threatening a man like Zarbi was like goading a tiger. It could only ever end badly.

'She told me I had to leave Paris - leave France - right away,' he said as the percolator started to boil. 'Otherwise she'd report us - you and me both - to the police. I suppose she was trying to protect you, by getting me out of the picture. But I can't go back to Algeria. Not while Ben Bella is president. When he's been dealt with, it'll be different. But I have to stay here for now. So there was no way I could do what she demanded. She gave me no choice, Nigel.'

I sipped the water and looked at him warily. A minute or more of silence followed. I was trembling uncontrollably and breathing shallowly. I didn't know what to say. I didn't want to think too much about what he'd done to Harriet.

'It was quick,' he said, guessing what was on my mind. 'Not like Tournier. We made sure he knew what was happening to him. And why.'

'Did you . . . record him?' I asked, managing to speak at last.

88

'He denied everything. He tried to bribe us to let him live, but we were never going to do that.'

Which didn't seem like an answer to my question.

'You always meant . . . to kill him?'

'Of course. Ben Bella has been trying to build bridges with the French so they'll help him stay in power. Killing Tournier blows up those bridges. Ben Bella's denied responsibility, but the French don't believe him, so they won't come to his rescue when we move against him.'

'You're saying . . . you used me to stage an assassination . . . as part of a . . . coup in Algiers?'

'You did well, Nigel. You played your part perfectly. We're grateful. That's why I'm helping you.'

'You're . . . helping me?'

'For sure. Going to the police would be crazy. They'll never get Nazim and me. We have lots of places to hide in this city. And escape routes if we need to use them. So, they'll just have you. And a story they won't believe. They'll probably charge you with Harriet's murder as well as Tournier's. You'll end up in prison. Or maybe you'll even get the guillotine. They'll want revenge for the killing of de Gaulle's little pet. So, yes, I'm helping you. And you'd better believe it. Because no one else is.'

I was dimly aware the coffee had stopped percolating. Zarbi noticed too. He fished two cups out of the cupboard and filled them.

I sat there, watching in what felt like a half-disembodied state as he added two spoonfuls of sugar to his cup and, without asking, two to mine as well before plonking it down in front of me.

'What did you do . . . to Harriet?' I asked
eventually.

'You don't need to know, Nigel.' He sipped his
coffee. 'She's gone, that's all. She's gone. But
you haven't. You're still here. You're still
alive. And I want to help you stay alive. You
understand?'

'Not really, no.'

'I told you. You've been useful to us. I can
see you being useful to us again. In Algiers,
after our lot take over.'

'Algiers? I'm not . . . going there.'

'We'll set you up nicely. I already have some
ideas about what you can do for us.'

'No, no,' I said, recoiling from the future
he'd mapped out for me. 'No, no.'

Suddenly, he reached behind his back and
pulled a gun out from the waistband of his
jeans. He laid it on the countertop close to
where I was sitting. He took another sip of
coffee and nodded at the gun. 'If you want
revenge for Harriet, try to take it.'

I looked at the gun. I looked up at Zarbi. But
I didn't move. I knew deep within myself that
he'd be too fast for me, even with the coffee cup
in his hand. Harriet was self-confident enough to
have believed she had the measure of Wassim
Zarbi. But she was wrong. And now she was . . .

I hated myself in that instant, detested my
lack of courage. I was going to do whatever he
told me to do. Because he was offering me a way
out of something I couldn't escape on my own.
Like he'd said, the French authorities probably
wouldn't believe he'd tricked me. Even if I made
a run for it back to England they could still

come after me there. I'd been seen with Tournier
shortly before his death. And the most obvious
explanation for Harriet's disappearance was that
I'd killed her because she was threatening to go
to the police. But if I remained unconnected
to Tournier's murder, there was no reason to
assume she was dead as long as her body went
undiscovered. All that was in Zarbi's gift, so I
had to fall in with his plans. I was trapped.
I'd become his creature.

Zarbi retrieved the gun and put it back out of
sight. 'Drink your coffee, Nigel,' he said.
'It'll stop you shaking. Then write a note to
Specta-Films saying Harriet's gone away and
you're going too, so neither of you will be
working at Tativille any more. I'll post it for
you later. After that pack a bag and go down to
the street, where Nazim's waiting for you. I'll
clear up here. You two are going to Marseille. We
have a place there where you can wait until I
join you. I'll work on at Tativille for a while
so there's nothing to connect me with you and
Harriet leaving. How long depends on how fast
things move in Algiers. But they will move, trust
me. Then your new life can begin. Exciting, no?'

I stared up at him, helplessly and
despairingly.

'Don't look so worried.' He grinned at me.
'It's not going to be as bad as you think.'

I've asked myself so many times since then what
I should have done, how I could have outwitted
Zarbi and brought him to justice for Harriet's
murder as well as Tournier's without ending up
in prison - or worse - myself. I've never found

a convincing answer. Which doesn't excuse my
betrayal of Harriet's memory one bit. I should
have gone to the police, told them the truth and
accepted the consequences. I should have stopped
lying and evading and running and hiding. I
should have faced the reality of what had
happened and what I'd been part of.

God knows how that would have turned out. But at
least I wouldn't be here, alone in this crumbling
apartment, in this city of heat and hatred, in
this present I can't seem to find a way out of:

✛

There is no more. The extract ends there, at the bottom of a page.
According to Coqblin & Baudouin, what they were sending
Suzette would be sufficient for her to make up her mind about its
authenticity. Why they weren't sending her the whole thing they
didn't explain. She wondered what the reason might be every time
she looked at that last line – the abruptly severed sentence, the
story suspended just as her father was about to leave Paris in 1965.
She wonders it still, as she slides the pages back into their envelope. Does his account of his life in Algiers – and the things he did
there at Zarbi's bidding – reveal secrets that can't be divulged to
her? Does Monsieur Saidi have something sinister to hide?

If he does, it would go some way to explaining why he's trying
to induce her to denounce the confession as a fake. It's the easy
course for her to take. It would avoid facing up to her father's
role in Harriet Gray's death. And it would solve many of her
financial problems at the same time.

She can still do that, of course. It doesn't really matter what
Stephen Gray says. The decision is hers to take.

But she hasn't taken it yet.

EIGHT

TALEB LEANS BACK IN THE COMFORTLESS PLASTIC CHAIR AND RUBS HIS eyes. He feels rather pleased with himself, which lightens somewhat the oppressiveness of the windowless matt-grey-walled room where he has spent the last few hours. He thinks he's done well, despite having to spend most of the first hour mastering the temperamental slow rewind system on the disc player he's been allotted. Before heading off to El-Harrach prison to examine the visitors' log, Agent Hidouchi apologized for not being able to give him access to the DSS computer system, which would have made reviewing the surveillance footage of Zarbi's villa a great deal easier and quicker. 'You are not one of us, Taleb. You are not trusted here. So, you will have to do it the hard way.'

Well, the hard way he's done it. And the answer he's found. He's looking forward to Hidouchi's reaction to his discovery. And having something to look forward to is important for someone consigned to the bowels of DSS HQ, whatever their status. It's a brighter, whiter, less obviously oppressive building than the old DRS nerve centre at Ben Aknoun, but there are still the same rumours about what goes on there.

Mission accomplished, he feels a celebratory cigarette is in order. Hidouchi will undoubtedly object if he smokes one in this unventilated room which he suspects may have been used for interrogations in the recent past – the ceiling hooks are a design feature he doesn't care to dwell on – so he decides to head out to the small courtyard he glimpsed through the windows of the corridor she led him along earlier.

He sets off with something of a spring in his step. In the game he and Hidouchi are playing, he reckons he's ahead on points, though it'll only stay that way if he keeps his wits about him. The corridor is empty and silent. Wherever the action currently is in DSS HQ, it isn't here.

About halfway along there's a door. The gravelled courtyard it leads out to is canyoned in by high mirror-windowed walls. Taleb neither knows nor cares who may be looking out of any of those windows. Watching him smoke a cigarette isn't going to be a highlight of anyone's day. He turns the door handle.

But before he can actually push the door open and step out an ear-splitting alarm starts to blare. His cigarette break has suddenly turned into something else.

It can be only a matter of seconds, he estimates, before armed DSS guards arrive to investigate. Making a run for it would be acutely unwise. He lights his cigarette, then raises his hands above his head to ensure there can be no misunderstanding about his willingness to surrender. He doesn't want to become yet another guest of the DSS to be shot while trying to escape.

It's possible, he concedes, that his points lead over Hidouchi has just evaporated.

'Hello?'

'Suzette? It's Stephen Gray here.'

'Oh, Stephen. I was beginning to wonder when I'd hear from you.'

'Sorry. A few things . . . cropped up.'

'Never mind. You finished reading . . . the pages I gave you?'

'Yes.'

'And?'

'Well, there's no doubt in my mind your father wrote the document.'

'I see.'

'Why don't we meet and talk it over?'

'Good idea. Shall I come to you?'

'Fine by me.'

'I'll be there in an hour.'

'OK. See you then.'

A chastened Taleb is seated in front of the disc player, sipping from a styrofoam cup of DSS coffee – predictably superior to Police HQ's offering but still far from the stuff of coffee-lovers' dreams – when the door opens and Agent Souad Hidouchi makes her entrance. The expression on her face tells Taleb nothing beyond the fact that her natural hauteur is still intact.

'You should give up smoking, Taleb,' she says without the slightest flicker of a smile. 'It's bad for your health.'

'So it appears,' he responds with a weary grimace.

'You assured me before I left that you'd be on your best behaviour.'

'I'm afraid I got over-excited. You'll have to blame the film I was watching.'

'Some memorable scenes?'

'There were.'

'You'd better show me.'

'Draw up a chair. Anything to report from El-Harrach?'

Hidouchi pulls a chair over to the desk and sits down next to him. She sighs. 'The administrative staff there are idiots. Zarbi had a regular visitor other than his lawyer, but because she also visited another prisoner, she was recorded against his name rather than Zarbi's.'

'And this visitor would be Razane Abderrahmane?'

'Correct.'

'I wouldn't assume idiocy is the explanation for the discrepancy, then.'

'No?'

'I trawled through all the recordings of her visits to Zarbi's villa. Look at this.'

Taleb activates the disc player. The screen shows a fish-eye-lensed view of a battered white Peugeot drawing up in front of the gate of the villa. It's after dark. The date log in the corner of the screen reads 19:54 04.02.20. A woman of some age dressed in a coat and shawl is seated behind the wheel of the car. She has a lot of grey-white hair secured in a bun and a cigarette drooping out of the side of her virtually lipless mouth. The scowl she gives the camera is hardly endearing, but evidently does the trick, since the gates swing open and she drives in – and out of the camera's range.

'That's her?' Hidouchi asks.

'It's quite a few years since I last saw her and it doesn't look as if those years have been kind to her, but, yes, that's Razane Abderrahmane.' Taleb fast-forwards to the white Peugeot's departure two and a half hours later. As he does so, stray memories of visits to Abderrahmane's nightclub during the relatively carefree 1980s tumble into his mind. He would have cherished those times so much more if only he'd known the dark days that were destined to follow. 'There she goes,' he announces.

'What am I supposed to notice?'

'Nothing. This time.'

'But some other time?'

Taleb fast-forwards again. 'Who was the other prisoner she went to see?'

'A guy called Bahlouli. Sami Bahlouli.'

'Bahlouli the crooner? He's in jail? What for? Excessively sentimental lyrics?'

'Tax evasion.'

'I'm surprised he's earned enough to make that worth the effort.'

Hidouchi sighs. 'I suppose you'll tell me Bahlouli also performed at Abderrahmane's nightclub.'

'He did. A long time ago.'

'Were you a regular customer there, Taleb? A long time ago, when you were younger?'

Taleb ignores Hidouchi's sarcasm and plays another scene of Abderrahmane arriving at the villa. 19:46 18.02.20. It all looks remarkably similar: the way she's dressed; the pendulous cigarette; her milk-curdling glare at the camera. 'Look at the back seat of the car.' Taleb points to a blurred expanse of threadbare fabric.

'I'm looking,' says Hidouchi. 'I don't see anything unusual.'

'Neither do I. But let's try another night.' He fast-forwards to 19:57 09.03.20. Here comes Abderrahmane in her beaten-up Peugeot again. He freezes the picture as she drives in through the gates. 'Look at the back seat again.'

Hidouchi leans forward, a strand of her hair brushing distractingly against Taleb's cheek as she does so. 'She's covered it with a diamond-patterned rug. And . . .'

'Yes?'

'There's something bulky beneath the rug.'

'Bulky enough to be a person, do you think?'

Hidouchi sits back. The strand of hair goes with her. She turns and looks at Taleb. 'She smuggled someone in.'

'I believe she did.'

'And out?'

'Yes.' He fast-forwards and plays Abderrahmane's departure

some three hours later. The rug's still in place, as is whatever – or whoever – is hiding beneath it. 'Perhaps Zarbi felt he needed the services of a backgammon tutor.'

'Has irony helped your career, Taleb?'

'Not at all. But it has helped my sanity.'

'Mmm.' Hidouchi stands up decisively. 'We'll bring Abderrahmane in for questioning straight away.'

'Could I suggest an alternative way of proceeding?' He looks up at Hidouchi, smiling in an effort to appeal to her better nature.

She doesn't return the smile. 'What alternative?'

'We go to her rather than bringing her to us.'

'Why? She clearly needs to be reminded of her obligations as a citizen.'

'We could waste a lot of time doing that, Agent Hidouchi. I recommend—'

'Yes? What do you recommend? A quiet chat with your old nightclub hostess in the comfort of her home?'

'Exactly. My experience is that you learn a surprising amount from people if you ask them nicely.' He holds his smile, willing her to give in.

And she does. 'All right. We'll try it your way. But if it doesn't work . . .'

'Then I'll hang her from the ceiling myself.'

NINE

THE WEATHER HOLDS, WARM AND CLEAR. SUZETTE PULLS UP OUTSIDE
Litster's Cot in the middle of a sleepy summer afternoon. Every-
thing looks much as it did the previous day, though this time
Stephen Gray isn't on the roof.

As she climbs out of the car, Gray appears at the side gate. He
waves and signals for her to come straight into the garden, then
retreats.

He's waiting, seated at the wrought-iron table, when she
catches up. The envelope containing her father's confession is
lying on the table in front of him. 'Sit down while I get the tea
ready,' he says, smiling at her as if this is just a casual social
occasion.

She doesn't try to stop him, even though she'd prefer to hear
what he has to say without further delay. Some niceties have to be
observed. As it happens, she doesn't sit down while he goes into
the house. She paces the lawn, smoking a cigarette. One part of
her wants to acknowledge the document as her father's work just
as another part preaches caution and the soft option of allowing
Monsieur Saidi to compensate her for pronouncing it a fake.

Sooner than she expects, Gray's back with the tea tray. He sets it down and pours the tea. There's a plate of biscuits that neither makes a move towards. She finishes her cigarette and lights another.

'Sorry,' she says, smiling uneasily. 'I'm a little nervous for some reason.'

'Well, what we're discussing is no small matter, is it?' Gray looks at her seriously. 'Maybe a little nervousness is in order.'

'You said you were convinced this was my father's work.' She taps the envelope with her fingers.

'I'm convinced, yes. But you're not?'

'Tell me what convinced you.'

'Well, it ties in with everything I know about Harriet, basically. It answers all those questions her disappearance left us with. Look, I understand you may be reluctant to accept the things your father did in Paris. This isn't exactly a flattering portrait. But it is a self-portrait. He had the decency to admit his role in what happened, even though he didn't intend it to happen. It took him a long time, but he faced up to it in the end. It seems to me you can be proud of him on that account.'

They both take sips of tea. She still doesn't know how to steer their conversation, partly because she's not quite sure where she wants it to go.

'Look, Suzette, I'll be honest with you. Your father's finally given me – albeit posthumously – the truth I've been looking for most of my life. Now, am I saying that because what I suspected has turned out to be remarkably close to the way it was? Of course. But I'm genuinely convinced anyway. You remember what he wrote about coming to our family home in Basingstoke with Harriet for Christmas in 1964? He refers to my Airfix obsession. It's true. I had model Spitfires and Hurricanes hanging all over my bedroom ceiling. How would anyone who'd forged this document know that? And our Labrador, Benjy. He mentions him as well. No one could fake that.'

'Unless my father gave them the information. We have no way of knowing what pressure he may have been under during those last months in Algiers.'

'Do you have any idea who might have applied this pressure?'

'No. But Algeria's a hotbed of conspiracies. It always has been. Remember, I don't know who Monsieur Saidi is or what his agenda may be.'

'What purpose would faking this document serve? It's all ancient history.'

'There's no such thing in Algeria, Stephen. Everything since 1962 happened yesterday.'

'How old were you when you left the country?'

'Fifteen.'

'And you've never been back since?'

'Never.'

'So . . .'

'I don't know what I'm talking about? Is that what you're saying?'

'No. No, no. I'm not saying that. Not at all. But . . .'

'Had you ever heard of Nazim Haddad before you read the confession?'

'No,' Gray admits with a shrug. 'I hadn't.'

'But you looked pretty closely into Wassim Zarbi's affairs, didn't you?'

Gray smiles. 'Sounds like you listened in on some of my conversations with your father when I visited him in Algiers.'

'Well, I did, yes. I was trying to make sense of what you wanted from him. And it was a small apartment. Besides . . .' She smiles naturally for the first time that afternoon. 'What child doesn't find a mystery intriguing?'

'What did your father tell you about Harriet?'

'Not much. I got more out of my mother. She said Harriet was an old girlfriend of Papa's who'd disappeared in Paris and was supposed to have drowned in Amsterdam – an accident or suicide.'

'Ah. The Amsterdam theory. It suited quite a lot of people to go along with that.'

'What evidence was there to support it?'

'Well, remember I was only ten when Harriet disappeared, so everything was very confusing for me at the time. I did a lot of listening in too while adults held sombre conversations. I got most of my information third-hand from Wendy. The story was that Harriet had vanished and so had her boyfriend, Nigel Dalby – your father. Eventually, Nigel contacted his family to say he'd moved to Algiers and would be staying there indefinitely. He said he was surprised Harriet hadn't gone back to England. He'd assumed that was her intention when they broke up. We never spoke to him directly. Dad went to Paris and did his best to find out what had happened to Harriet, without success. He was a quiet, reserved man, respectful of authority. He wasn't really equipped to get much out of the French police. I think it was probably the British Embassy that prevailed on the French to issue an Interpol alert. That led to a report from the Dutch police that a bag containing some of Harriet's personal possessions, including her passport, had been found on a Brussels to Amsterdam train a few days after she'd last been seen in Paris. Some weeks later, Dad was asked to go to Amsterdam to identify a young woman's body pulled out of one of the canals. The body had been . . . damaged by boat traffic. It was all pretty horrible, apparently. He never did identify the body as Harriet's, although the authorities were keen he should. So . . . inquiries petered out. Dad went as far as trying to visit Nigel in Algiers to ask him if there was anything more he knew but hadn't mentioned. But that never happened because the Algerian Embassy wouldn't give him a visa.'

'Do we know why?'

'We didn't then, but we can guess now, can't we? Harriet was last seen by the nightwatchman at Tativille early on the morning of Tuesday the eighth of June, 1965. Eleven days later, there was a coup in Algiers. On the nineteenth of June Ben Bella was deposed and replaced by his Defence Minister, Boumediene. The new government obviously wouldn't want any details to emerge about Zarbi's activities in Paris. It was important the previous regime should take the blame for Tournier's murder. So, they were never going to allow my father to enter the country. They probably did him a favour, actually. I can't imagine Dad in Algiers. He'd have been out of his depth as soon as he got off the plane. There's no knowing what trouble he might have got himself into.'

'Was he certain the body in Amsterdam wasn't Harriet's?'

'Certain? At the time, yes. Later, he began to doubt himself on the point. When months and then years passed and we had to accept that Harriet wasn't coming back, the only explanation that made sense was that she was in fact dead and he started to wonder if the young woman on the mortuary slab in Amsterdam might actually have been her. The doubting and the wondering ate away at him. And at my mother too. Neither of them was ever the same again. Mum retreated into herself. She just . . . stopped communicating. As for Dad, well, he did his best to keep life running normally for Wendy and me, but the effort told on him, it truly did. I suppose we've both been marked by the tragedy, you and I. And look, here we are, still struggling with it, more than fifty years on.'

'You could have dropped it, though, couldn't you, Stephen? No one forced you to start looking for the truth when you grew up. Your sister Wendy didn't, after all.'

'Wendy's always been more level-headed than me. You're right, of course. No one forced me to do anything. But it became an obsession. I'd look at snaps of Harriet in the family photograph album – on summer holidays in Cornwall, in her graduation robe at Oxford – and turn over in my mind what could possibly have happened to her and what I could do to find out. Had she just run away from us all? Was she still alive somewhere? Then there were my parents. I convinced myself the truth, whatever it was, would help to heal them. They stopped talking about Harriet, but I knew they didn't stop thinking about her. In late sixty-seven, just before Christmas, Dad went away on a business trip. The company he worked for made electronic components. The explanation I was given was that he was sounding out a French company about a joint venture. Only later did I learn he'd arranged the trip to coincide with the cinema release of *Playtime*. I found a ticket stub in his raincoat pocket from the Empire cinema in Paris that showed he'd been to see it during the week it opened. I knew at once why. And why he didn't want us to know. He was hoping he might see Harriet in one of the crowd scenes.'

'And did he?'

'No. I don't think she was ever drummed into service as an extra. Or, if she was, the scenes featuring her never made it to the final cut. When the film came out in this country a few months later, I went to see it with Wendy. We didn't tell Mum and Dad. It was a secret afternoon visit when Wendy was home from university. We were all keeping secrets from each other by then, you see. I'm pretty sure I'd have been bored rigid if I hadn't been looking out for Harriet all the time. *Playtime* didn't have a lot in it to appeal to the average thirteen-year-old boy. Anyway, we never spotted her. Your father, on the other hand? Oh yes. He was there. I recognized him from his Christmas visit in sixty-four. I remember digging Wendy in the ribs and whispering, "There's Nigel Dalby." And I remember Wendy's shocked response. "Oh my God. It is him, you're right."'

'Hold on.' Suzette can't quite believe what she's just heard.

Her father appears in a scene in *Playtime*? This is news to her. 'Papa told me all his scenes in the film ended up being cut.'

'No. He's easy to miss, but he is there.' Gray smiles. 'Do you want to see him?'

Suzette hesitates, though she's not sure why. She should jump at the chance to see a moving image of her father as a young man. But somehow the prospect frightens her.

'I've got the DVD indoors, Suzette,' Gray prompts her. 'It's the easiest thing in the world to play the scene for you.'

She drains her tea. There's no way round this. 'OK,' she says. 'Let's go.'

Gray leads the way into the cottage. As she follows him into the small sitting room, Suzette notices his deft removal of the whisky bottle from the low table beside the armchair. He deposits it on a bookshelf with one hand as he plucks the DVD of *Playtime* from further along the same shelf. 'Take a seat,' he says, gesturing to the armchair.

He turns on the TV and loads the DVD into the player. There's a second chair, pushed back in a corner of the room, but he makes no move towards it and leans against the bookcase as he thumbs the button on the remote.

The TV screen lights up and action from some part of *Playtime* unfolds in front of her. This is evidently where Gray stopped watching last time he played the disc. He rewinds by five minutes or so and lets it play again.

Jacques Tati, accoutred in his familiar Monsieur Hulot garb of raincoat, narrow-brimmed hat and half-mast trousers, is exiting a travel agency at closing time, shooed out by an assistant eager to lock up. Distracted by the clunk of the door being secured behind him, Hulot collides with a passer-by, a smartly tailored man in dark suit and trilby carrying a briefcase. A second passer-by, identically dressed, narrowly avoids the collision and hurries on.

Gray freezes the frame just before the second passer-by departs the scene. Suzette stares at him – a young, slim, dark-haired man in a suit and hat, moving fast. His face is slightly blurred. 'Can you replay it?' she asks.

Gray replays it. She sees the second passer-by's face clearly now. She fixes her attention on his features for the few seconds of the action. And catches her breath just before Gray freezes the frame again. It's her father. A younger version of her father, in fact, than she's ever seen before. It's the twenty-three-year-old Nigel Dalby.

'I don't believe it,' she murmurs.

'You don't?'

'I mean, I do. It's him, no question. It really is.' Unconsciously, she raises her hand to her mouth. There's something profound as well as moving about what she feels. It's as if time is folding over on itself, revealing a part of herself lodged in her father before he became her father.

'He appears again, a few minutes later,' says Gray, fast-forwarding to a scene of people boarding a crowded bus. Hulot's one of them. Gray freezes the frame. 'There,' he says. 'To the right of the door.'

'My God. Looking at him like this . . .' She laughs nervously. 'It's given me . . . la chair de poule.'

'Goosebumps?'

'Yes. Sorry. That's right. Goosebumps.'

'I understand. It's a strange experience. Eerie, almost.'

'Is it just these two scenes?'

'As far as I can tell. But there are lots of men in suits moving around in the film. He could crop up in other places where I haven't spotted him yet.'

'Why did he never tell me?'

'He had good reasons for wanting to forget his time at Tativille.'

106

'Yes. Of course. But why did Maman never tell me either?'

'She's your mother, Suzette.'

Yes, she is. She must have known. Suzette feels certain of that. And wholly unsurprised that she never breathed a word about it.

'There's something else,' says Gray, rewinding the disc. 'Or I should say someone else.'

He plays another scene. People are leaving an office building at the end of a working day. One of them bumps into a glass door he believes to be open. While he's grasping his bruised nose and receiving the sympathetic attention of some of his colleagues, a tall, dark-complexioned, dramatically mustachioed man – wearing a pale suit and a fedora rather than a dark suit and trilby – pauses briefly to cast a scornful glance at them before striding out on to the street and away.

'Zarbi,' says Gray simply.

'Zarbi?'

'It's him. I've seen a few photographs over the years. Not many, but enough. That's Wassim Zarbi.'

'My God. Both of them.'

'It's quite—' Gray's interrupted by the chirruping of a mobile phone in another room. 'Sorry. I'd better get that. I'm expecting a call.' He hands Suzette the remote and hurries out.

Suzette sits back, rewinds the disc and lets the scenes play out naturally in front of her. The collision outside the travel agency; the exit from the office building; the boarding of the bus. She watches her father's movements and expressions. They're his. They absolutely are.

She takes another look at Zarbi. She saw him once at Le Chélifère. And on one other occasion, when he came to their apartment. It wasn't a welcome visit. The air was thick with unease the whole time he was there. Suzette remembers his voice: deep, harsh, grating. And his face: flashing eyes; a characteristic curl of his lips that lifted one side of his moustache. She

107

remembers how powerful he seemed. As if he could pick her up and crush her in one hand if he chose. She wonders if his contemptuous glance at the other figures in the scene in *Playtime* was acting or just his natural reaction. Contempt, she feels sure, came easily to him.

Gray comes back into the room. 'How are you getting on?' he asks.

'I'm all right,' she replies. 'Really. I'm fine.'

'Sorry if it was a bit of a shock.'

'Don't be. I'm glad to have seen it. Tell me, how did you first hear of Wassim Zarbi?'

'Ah, Zarbi. Shall we go back into the garden? It's quite a story.'

The sun has moved a deep shadow across the table while they've been indoors. Gray offers to make more tea, but Suzette says no. She wants to hear what he has to say. She wants to hear it now.

'I made a serious attempt to get to the bottom of all this during my first summer vacation at Bristol University,' he begins. 'Seventy-four, that would have been. I began by contacting Nigel's father. But he was gaga following a stroke and Nigel's stepmother – the formidable Marjorie – didn't want to know anything about her stepson. She claimed they'd lost touch. He was still in Algiers, apparently, but she had no address for him. I fell back on a film buff friend at Bristol. He knew someone in Paris who'd worked on *Playtime*.

'So, off to Paris I went. The guy who'd worked on *Playtime* was happy to ply me with anecdotes about Tati as long as I plied him with drinks, but he couldn't remember Harriet or Nigel. "A lot of people came and went, mon ami," he told me. "Tativille was like ... la gare de Lyon sans trains." So much for that. But he put me on to someone he thought might be better informed: Viviane Labbé, deputy wardrobe supervisor. Yes, the woman mentioned in *J'avoue*. I visited her at her house in

St-Maur-des-Fossés, the same house Harriet and Nigel were invited to for lunch, though she never actually mentioned that. She remembered them both well, though. She'd liked them, Harriet in particular, and had been surprised and baffled by their sudden departure. There wasn't much more she could tell me, though she was gushingly sympathetic about Harriet's death in Amsterdam, which was the version of events she'd heard. It was all "une grande tragédie". And it wasn't the only tragedy, apparently. Specta-Films had gone bust and you couldn't see *Playtime* even if you wanted to. That seemed to depress her immeasurably.

'It was just as I was leaving that she mentioned Wassim Zarbi. An Algerian extra she'd seen Nigel talking to quite often. Which she thought odd, since Zarbi didn't generally socialize at Tativille. She described him as haughty. I got the impression she didn't have a high opinion of Algerians. Where could I find Zarbi? "Aucune idée!" was her response, accompanied by a massive shrug.

'It seemed like the end of the road. I went home to England and found a holiday job. Then, a few months later, I got a letter from Madame Labbé. I'd given her my address more in hope than expectation. She was writing to say she'd heard from a former Tativille colleague who'd recently visited Algiers that Nigel Dalby was running a bookshop in the city. The former colleague couldn't remember the name or address of the shop, but Madame Labbé thought I might be interested. And I was. It was something to go on at last. There couldn't be many young Englishmen running bookshops in Algiers.

'It was the following summer before I made it to Algeria. I'd seen *Pépé le Moko* and *The Battle of Algiers* thanks to my film buff friend at Bristol and I'd read a bit about the country and its history, so I thought I knew what I was doing. In reality, I didn't have a clue. I took the guided tour of the Casbah. I absorbed the sights and sounds. I climbed the steep streets. I blinked in the dazzling light and sweated in the heat. On day two, I asked the doorman at my hotel if he knew of a bookshop run by a young Englishman. Bingo! Le Chélifère. He didn't know the Englishman's name. But I felt sure I did.

'I don't need to describe Le Chélifère to you. It never changed much, did it? The piles of books, not all in possession of their covers and arranged in no apparent order on shelves, tables, floors and even the stairs. Whether the dust came in from the street or off all the old unsold books I couldn't have said. I was greeted by a young Algerian assistant – Riad Nedjar, as it turned out. This was before you were born, of course. Nigel and your mother had only recently got married and were living over the shop, as I later discovered. But it was from the tiny ground floor storeroom-cum-office at the rear that Nigel emerged when Nedjar called him. He didn't recognize me. There was no reason why he should. When I introduced myself, he must have been astonished, but he covered it well and invited me upstairs to meet his wife. Monique didn't seem pleased to meet me. Maybe she didn't welcome reminders of Nigel's dead English girlfriend. As for Nigel, he put on a good show, although he assured me there was nothing he could tell me that would clear up the mystery of what happened to Harriet. It was agreed he'd come to my hotel for a drink and a chat that evening.

'Well, he came. We chatted. He asked all the right questions about how we'd coped at the time of Harriet's disappearance. He insisted she'd simply walked out on him following a silly row about seeing him with another girl. He couldn't explain why she might have gone to Amsterdam. She certainly wasn't the suicidal type. He could only suppose she'd drowned accidentally. When I pointed out my father had said the body he was shown wasn't her, he didn't try to argue. "Who can say?" was his basic line. As for why he'd vamoosed to Algiers, he said there were too many memories of Harriet in Paris for him to remain. He'd had no wish to return to England. He'd gone to Algeria on a whim, not knowing if he'd stay long or where he might move on to. He'd worked at the bookshop for the previous owner, who'd handed it over to him before retiring to France. When I suggested he might have gone to Algeria on the recommendation of his friend from Tativille, Wassim Zarbi, he said no, definitely not. It had been all his own idea. And Zarbi wasn't a friend, just a work acquaintance. Nigel no longer had any contact with him.

'He said he hoped I'd enjoy my visit to Algiers, but explained, as delicately as he could, that he wouldn't be able to see much of me while I was there. Monique hadn't reacted well to me turning up. He was sure I understood. And I did really, though I wasn't blind to the possibility that he was using Monique as an excuse to dodge further questioning about Harriet. I implied I'd come to see the city as well as him. I'd wanted to come after watching Pontecorvo's *The Battle of Algiers*. He relaxed immediately and talked about its being filmed soon after his arrival in the summer of 1965. He said his assistant at the bookshop could tell me more about that than he could, having worked as an extra on the shoot. He offered to give Nedjar the following day off to show me round the city. Naturally, I accepted.

'Well, you know Riad Nedjar. An engaging chap. He was only a few years older than me, lively and friendly, full of fun. And he spoke good English. He turned up at the hotel while I was still having breakfast and took me out for a tour of the sights. It was eye-opening and enjoyable to be taken round the city by a native who knew it inside out. He'd played the part of a wide-eyed child in the Casbah in Pontecorvo's film and there was still something childlike about him. I remember laughing a lot that day. The only serious note came when I asked him about Zarbi. We were in a café and he immediately lowered his voice. "Advice for you, my friend," he said, leaning across the table towards me. "Zarbi is

111

Sécurité Militaire. Quite senior. It is not healthy to talk about such people. Even if you are only a tourist. You understand? You want to be just a tourist, Stephen, yes? Not a person of interest to the authorities. Trust me, you do not want to be that. So, whether Nigel met Zarbi in Paris, what Zarbi was doing there, whether they have stayed in contact since . . . do not speak of such matters. To anyone."

'It was a pretty clear warning. And looking at Nedjar across that café table with a schmaltzy chanteuse singing on the radio in the background and cigarette smoke clouding around us and glances in our direction from other tables suddenly apparent to me, I realized it was a warning I'd be wise to heed. This wasn't England. This wasn't even France. This was Algeria. And I had no idea what the rules were that Algerians lived by. But Nedjar knew. And this was one of them. A man like Zarbi was off limits. Completely.

'On Nedjar's recommendation, I took a coach trip organized by the tourist office to the Roman ruins at Tipasa the following day. I wandered round the remains of the amphitheatre and the forum. I listened to the cicadas and felt the heat on my back and squinted out at the wide blue Mediterranean. I felt pretty certain then I'd never return to Algeria. Harriet was ten years dead and I had a life to lead. Nor was I in much doubt that Nedjar's warning was well founded. I should let sleeping dogs lie. Harriet was as lost to me as the ancient Romans.

'But that's not how it turned out, as you know. I went back to Algeria twice more over the years. For various reasons, I just couldn't quite give up on the idea that there was an answer waiting out there for me somewhere. Each time I saw Nedjar, he looked disappointed that I'd returned, although he never failed to make me feel he was also pleased to see me again.'

Gray sits back in his chair. 'Well, that's the kind of man Riad Nedjar is. One of the best. You asked me yesterday if I'd heard

112

from him since your father's death and I said I hadn't. I'm afraid that wasn't actually true. I didn't feel I could give you any information about him without his permission. I contacted him last night. He lives in London now. He runs a small Algerian delicatessen in Soho. That phone call earlier was from him. He's agreed to meet you, Suzette, and tell you what he can about your father's confession.'

Suzette stares at Gray in astonishment. 'He knows about it?'

Gray nods. 'Apparently so.'

'But . . . how?'

'Why don't you ask him when you meet him?'

'How soon can that be arranged?'

'He suggests this evening. If that works for you.'

Suzette's still trying to adjust to the realization that Riad Nedjar hasn't left her life after all. Whether his knowledge of the confession is good news or bad she doesn't know. But she does know she has to find out. And the chance to do so has just been presented to her. 'That works for me,' she says emphatically.

TEN

THE APARTMENT BLOCKS OF ALGIERS, PATCHED AND PEELING, TRAILING
with wires, festooned with satellite dishes and draped with lines
of washing, sprout from the slopes of the city like Saharan buttes,
numberless and indistinguishable. Toiling up the stairs of the one
where Razane Abderrahmane lives, Taleb reckons coping with
such an ascent on a regular basis must keep her fit. The lift is out
of action, which he suspects is not unusual. As it is, he's flag-
ging already and they're not yet halfway to the top, which is to
say he isn't. Agent Hidouchi is several flights ahead of him,
casting occasional withering glances down at him through the
stairwell.

'Don't police officers have to pass a regular physical?' she
enquires ironically as he finally catches up with her.

'Allowances are made . . . for age,' he pants.

'And for smoking two packs of cigarettes a day?'

'It's only . . . one pack.'

'One too many.'

'I would never have survived the nineties . . . without my Nassims. You can't expect me to . . . abandon an old friend.'

'Try seeing less of him. Now, do you want longer to recover? Or shall I ring Abderrahmane's doorbell?'

Taleb manages to take a reasonable breath without coughing. He approaches Abderrahmane's door and rings the bell himself.

There's no response. He rings again. Still nothing.

Hidouchi, arms folded, looks at him levelly, as if it is somehow his fault. She taps the fingers of one hand on her upper arm. Then she starts ringing the bell of the next-door apartment.

She doesn't stop until it's opened by an elderly woman. Hidouchi flourishes her DSS card. 'We're looking for Razane Abderrahmane,' she says curtly.

The elderly woman looks flustered, which doesn't surprise Taleb. The DSS at your door is always bad news, even if they're looking for someone else. 'She's on her balcony,' comes the nervous reply. 'She's a little . . . deaf.'

'Please tell her we're here.'

'Oh. Yes. Right. I will.' The woman retreats nervously.

She doesn't close her door, so Hidouchi and Taleb can hear her shouting to her neighbour, although they can't make out the response she gets. She returns after a few minutes, carrying a key with which she opens Abderrahmane's door. 'She says you should go through.'

'Thank you,' says Taleb. Hidouchi says nothing.

They progress through a series of colourfully cluttered rooms to French windows standing open to the glare of the sun and the hint of a breeze.

The balcony is surprisingly large, more of a terrace really, with a vast panorama of the city and the harbour stretching away beyond the parapet. This view is partly blocked by a line of washing, which Taleb averts his eyes from for fear it comprises items of Abderrahmane's underwear.

The lady herself is draped on a lounger in the full sun, with various bronzed and wrinkled limbs protruding from a volumin-ous shift-dress. Her hair is gathered in a turban. Behind her hangs a cage containing a large, raggedly feathered parrot, who eyes the newcomers suspiciously.

Abderrahmane treats Taleb to a thin-lipped smile. Her eyes are obscured by gigantic sunglasses. 'Are you with the DSS now, Mouloud?'

He notices a twitch of Hidouchi's eyebrows at the use of his first name. 'No,' he replies, raising his voice to ensure she can hear him.

She winces. 'There's no need to shout. I'm not deaf.'

'La Samh Allah!' squawks the parrot.

Taleb does his best to ignore the intervention, though he catches himself wondering whether teaching a parrot to say 'God forbid!' qualifies as blasphemy. 'We were obviously misinformed. Anyway, I'm still with the police. Agent Hidouchi here is from the DSS.'

'Can it be true?' Abderrahmane gives Hidouchi a searching look. 'You could have worked for me as a hostess. Some men like their women mean.'

'You should take this visit seriously,' Hidouchi responds. 'It is only thanks to Superintendent Taleb that I am giving you the opportunity to volunteer the information we need in these . . . civilized surroundings.'

'Superintendent, is it? So, you made it to the top of the tree after all, Mouloud?'

'He is not at the top of any tree,' snaps Hidouchi. 'We will come to the point. Wassim Zarbi. You are acquainted with him?'

Abderrahmane chooses that moment to light a cigarette, deploying for the purpose a fat onyx lighter the size of a duck's egg. 'As I recall, this was a gift from Wassim,' she says after exhaling a first lungful of smoke. 'Ah, what it was to have a friend in the DRS. Several friends, in fact. The eighties were good to us, weren't they, Mouloud?'

They were, though they didn't seem it at the time. Taleb is personally unaware of anything in his life – or that of the nation – that has changed for the better since. But he isn't going to let himself be lured into nostalgia by Abderrahmane, who has managed to imply a closer connection between them than ever actually existed, presumably in the hope of driving a wedge between him and Hidouchi.

'You were a regular visitor to Zarbi at his villa in the months before his disappearance,' Hidouchi continues. 'You also visited him in El-Harrach prison.'

'Am I being accused of a crime?'

'La Samh Allah!'

Hidouchi glances witheringly at the parrot. 'You smuggled someone into Zarbi's villa on the ninth of March this year. That is a breach of the conditions of his release from prison. Aiding and abetting such a breach . . .'

'Would be a crime,' says Taleb.

'Ah, but there are so many crimes, aren't there?' Abderrahmane drawls through a cloud of smoke. 'It is hard to remember them all. Besides, I deny this one. I went to play backgammon with Wassim because he was lonely and all his other friends pretended they had never known him. That is all.'

'The video surveillance footage of the villa tells a different story,' says Taleb.

'This would be DSS footage?'

'Yes.'

'Faked, then. They are experts at such things. Who am I supposed to have smuggled in?'

'That's what we're here to find out.'

'Then you're wasting your time. And mine.'

'La Samh Allah!'

Hidouchi rolls her eyes. Taleb knows what she's thinking. They should just have had Abderrahmane brought in for questioning and spared themselves this performance. Her attitude would be very different in the intimidating environment of DSS HQ.

'Do you play backgammon, Mouloud?' Abderrahmane asks.

He doesn't answer. The time has come to make her understand the true seriousness of her position. He draws up a low stool he's spotted and sits down beside the lounger. He and Abderrahmane are now at the same eye level. It seems to him this renders their exchanges both more intimate and more genuine. The parrot moves a little way along his perch the better to observe them.

'You have my admiration, Razane,' he begins. 'You have conceded nothing to age or pragmatism. You lie here like a lizard on a rock and make no secret of your contempt for us.'

'I do not feel contempt for you, Mouloud.' Abderrahmane shapes a smile. 'Pity is a different matter.'

'It is a magnificent performance. If only you still had the patrons of La Girafe to join me in appreciating it.'

'I was great then, wasn't I?'

'Unquestionably. But you had to cooperate with the authorities in order to remain in business. And as it was then so it is now.'

'I am no longer in business. I have retired. I owe no one my cooperation.'

'If you do not tell us what we need to know, I will not be able to help you, Razane. Authority has many grimmer manifestations than me.'

Abderrahmane glances up at Hidouchi. 'So I see.'

'Who did you smuggle into Zarbi's villa?'

'Nobody.'

'If we do not leave here with an answer, we will leave here with you. And where we take you . . . they will crush you like a butterfly beneath a wheel. You know this. You have seen the victims of such treatment. We both have. Do not inflict that upon yourself.'

To Taleb's surprise, tears begin to trickle down Abderrahmane's cheeks. She heaves a sigh. 'How I hate this country.'

'It is the only country we have, Razane.'

'La Samh Allah!'

Another sigh. She pulls a handkerchief from one of the folds of her dress and dries her tears. 'An Englishman. White. About the same age as you. He did not give me his name and I did not ask for it.'

'This was done at Zarbi's request?'

'Yes.'

'Where did you collect the man from?'

'Another street not far away. Rue des Nénuphars. He was waiting on the corner. As Zarbi told me he would be.'

'And you returned him there?'

'Yes.'

'Did you see him enter a house on rue des Nénuphars?'

'No. He stood on the corner and watched me drive away.'

'What did he and Zarbi talk about?' Hidouchi cuts in.

Abderrahmane grimaces. She clearly prefers to answer Taleb's questions, though in truth that was going to be his next. 'I do not know. They went to Wassim's study. They left me to watch television. I was disappointed by the choice of channels. He apologized to me for that, I remember. It had something to do with the DSS blocking his internet access.'

'Describe the Englishman.'

'Sixties. Grey hair. Beard. Brown eyes, I think. He spoke quite good French. And he was polite. Which I find at my age is no small thing.'

'You're sure you didn't catch his name?' asks Taleb. 'Didn't Zarbi call him anything?'

119

'No. He didn't. He was careful not to, it seemed to me.'

'And you didn't hear anything of their discussion?'

'We were in widely separated rooms.'

'But you were bored, Razane. The television had none of your favourite channels. I can easily imagine you leaving the television on and tiptoeing along to the door of Zarbi's study.'

'Imagine all you like. I stayed in the lounge.'

'Were you surprised when Zarbi disappeared?'

'Is anyone in this country surprised when someone disappears?'

Taleb smiles at her. 'Why did you help Zarbi?'

She shrugs. 'He used to be a good customer. And everyone deserted him when he was imprisoned. I don't like people who turn their backs on their friends when times are tough.'

'He is a convicted criminal,' says Hidouchi sharply.

'The difference between convicted criminals and unconvicted ones is that the unconvicted ones run the country.' Abderrahmane stubs out her cigarette and lights another. 'Anyway, I enjoyed our backgammon games.'

'Did he tell you he planned to leave the country?'

'No. If he had, I would have asked him to take me with him. I would like to spend my remaining years somewhere more comfortable than this apartment. A villa in Sardinia, perhaps.'

'Has he gone to Sardinia?'

'I don't know. I would like to go there, though.'

'Did you ever encounter any other visitors at his villa, Razane?' Taleb enquires gently.

'No. Though I met his lawyer as he was leaving once. I met him leaving El-Harrach prison once as well. A busy man, Ibrahim Boukhatem. But expensive. Otherwise I would have called him by now for advice on how best to be rid of you two.'

'That's interesting. We understand Zarbi has very little capital to call upon. How could he afford to engage Boukhatem's services?'

'Perhaps he got a discount. In recognition of past services.'

Taleb notices Hidouchi is busy with her phone. He presses on alone. 'The last time you saw Zarbi was how long before he disappeared?'

'Don't you know?'

'Just tell me.'

'A couple of days. The first I knew of it was when I drove to the villa for one of our regular games of backgammon and was turned away at the gate by a DSS goon.'

'Did Zarbi ever mention owning a launch?'

'No. We talked mostly of the past, not the present. And certainly not the future.'

'La Samh Allah!'

Hidouchi raises her eyebrows and cocks her head at Taleb, signalling for him to join her as she walks past the lounger and across to the parapet. With a smile to Abderrahmane, Taleb hoists himself off the stool and follows her.

Hidouchi stands with her back to Abderrahmane, gazing out across the city. She shows Taleb an image on her phone. A name: Ibrahim Boukhatem. And an address in the Hydra district. 'Boukhatem owns a villa in a cul-de-sac off rue des Nénuphars,' she says in an undertone.

'You think the Englishman came from Boukhatem's villa?'

'I think we should ask Boukhatem if he did.'

'I agree. Does that mean we're done here?'

'She's getting off lightly, thanks to you.'

'Don't tell her that. I have my reputation to think of.'

Hidouchi starts stabbing numbers into her phone as soon as they are out of Abderrahmane's apartment, though this doesn't stop her talking to Taleb or setting a stiff pace as they descend the stairs.

'We should try to speak to Boukhatem before she has a chance to warn him.'

'I doubt she's in contact with him,' says Taleb.

'You'll forgive me if I don't rely on your doubts.' She raises her phone to her ear and emits a growl of frustration. 'His office number goes straight to an answering machine.'

'Are you going to leave a message?'

'No. I'm going to go there now and see what I find. I suggest you try his villa.'

Taleb suspects Hidouchi doesn't want him moderating whatever tactics she plans to use if she should be so lucky as to corner Boukhatem at his place of work. But he has no sympathy for Boukhatem's kind. Hidouchi is welcome to do her worst with him.

'Do you know this man, Taleb?'

'Slightly. He's one of those lawyers who pops up in a two hundred thousand dinar suit after a high-profile arrest to explain why his crime lord client is in fact a model citizen. I'm pretty certain he represented Zarbi back in ninety-nine.'

'But we can assume he hasn't gone on representing him for sentimental reasons?'

'Zarbi obviously had access to greater resources than your department supposed.'

Hidouchi shrugs. 'Who would this Englishman be?'

'No idea. But Boukhatem should be able to tell us.'

'Let's ask him, then.'

'If I get the chance, I certainly will.'

After Hidouchi has roared off on her motorbike in the direction of Boukhatem's office near the seafront, Taleb drives slowly and thoughtfully back to Hydra. His memory, a fallible but far-ranging organ, is beginning to string together some connections that are for the present too tenuous for him to grasp. The lawyer, the fugitive and the Englishman. They're all linked in some way, not just with the Sonatrach fraud, but, he senses, with some other deeper, darker affair, with which the history of his country is replete. Exactly what that might be remains elusive. But it will come to him. He just has to give it time. How much time is impossible to gauge. But he knows from experience that trying to hurry the process will only be counter-productive.

Boukhatem's villa presents a strikingly similar face to the world as Zarbi's: high-walled, security-gated, unwelcoming. Beyond the wall lies a walled acreage of luxury. Taleb cannot see the fountains and the courtyards, the immaculate gardens and the marbled patios. But he knows they're there. He can almost smell them. The afternoon is at its hottest, though here in Hydra the temperature is more bearable than in the centre of the city. There's no cooling breeze as such, but spaciousness and affluence somehow work their magic. Taleb stands in the shadow cast by a towering palm tree as he waits for a response to his hopeful prod at the bell-push beside the gate.

Eventually, a door set in the wall opens by thirty centimetres or so and a large, sleepy-eyed man in an ill-fitting suit squints out at him, chewing gum vigorously.

'I'm looking for Ibrahim Boukhatem,' Taleb says, flourishing his police badge.

The man peers suspiciously at the badge and appears reluctant to acknowledge that it may be genuine, although he does open the door a little wider. 'Not here,' he mumbles. 'Away on business.'

'What sort of business?'

'He's a lawyer. So, the legal sort, I guess.'

'Are any members of his family here?'

'No. His wife and children have gone away for the summer.'

'Where to?'

'They have a place in the mountains above Tlemcen.'

'Nice for them.' Taleb's phone burbles in his pocket. He pulls it out. The call is from Hidouchi. He doesn't take it.

'Something else you want, uncle?' The man's manner isn't improving.

'How long have you worked here?'

'A few years.'

'Do the family get many visitors?'

'Many or a few. I wouldn't know the difference. They're not my kind of family.'

'Did an Englishman stay with them about four months ago? Early March, it would have been.'

'March? Not sure. Maybe. Maybe not.'

'What would it take for you to make up your mind?'

'An incentive, I guess. You know, like on the TV game shows. You answer a question right, you get a prize.'

Taleb takes out his clip of pot-de-vin money and fingers a few notes. 'Was there an Englishman here in March? Five thousand for a yes or no.'

The man delivers a nod and holds out his hand.

'How long for?'

'Three nights.'

'Around the ninth?'

'Sounds right.' The man flaps his hand expectantly.

'I need a name as well.'

'Never knew it.'

'Sure?' Taleb fingers an extra few notes.

'Sure. I could make up a name if I wanted to stiff you, uncle.'

'That's true.' Taleb stuffs the five thousand into the waiting hand, which closes round the notes like a clam. On an impulse, he administers three sharp slaps on the cheek to the man, who jumps back in alarm. The cocksureness has suddenly drained out of him. 'Nice meeting you . . . nephew.'

Taleb retreats to his car, lights a cigarette and lets his memory roam for a few productive minutes. A picture is forming in his mind, indistinct for the moment, but with some shapes already discernible. It's the Englishman smuggled into Zarbi's villa by Abderrahmane who has set his recollection roaming. Zarbi and an Englishman, twenty-seven years in the past.

After a second cigarette, he phones Hidouchi. She sounds exasperated by how long it's taken him to call back. 'Is there anyone at the villa?' she asks snappishly.

'No one worth mentioning. The family's gone. Boukhatem likewise, right?'

'Right. According to his secretary – after she realized trying to fob me off was a mistake – he's in Bahrain, dealing with a dispute over ownership of an oil tanker. Likely to be tied up there for many weeks.'

'Boukhatem? Or the tanker?'

'Wisecracks aren't going to help us find Zarbi, Taleb.' She definitely doesn't sound pleased by the way their inquiries are proceeding.

Taleb decides to try to cheer her up. 'I've had an idea.'

'Is it a good one?'

'I think so. Meet me at Police HQ in half an hour.'

ELEVEN

THEY TAKE SUZETTE'S CAR TO BASINGSTOKE, WITH GRAY EXPLAINING as they go how Riad Nedjar ended up running an Algerian delicatessen in Soho.

'I had no contact with him after he left Algeria. He lived in Paris for about twelve years, but decided to leave, so he told me, after the riots of 2005. Being an Algerian in Paris just became too difficult, he said. You had to pick a side and he didn't want to. So, with his fluency in English, London seemed like his best option. He asked me if I could give him some help setting himself up and I was happy to do what I could. He'd always been helpful to me in Algiers. I ended up investing in his business. Actually, I still own a stake in it. It's been quite profitable, at least until coronavirus knocked a hole in the central London economy. But he's soldiering on. I think Riad is one of the most optimistic people I know. As for what he thinks about your father's confession, well, I'll let him tell you himself.'

'He thinks it's genuine, doesn't he?' Suzette presses.

'Just listen to him. There's nothing to be gained by anticipating what he has to say.'

'But he hasn't seen it, has he? He hasn't actually read it.'

'Well, as you'll discover, those are two different questions.'

'What do you mean?'

'I can't explain. Riad will, though.'

Gray's logic is irrefutable. But Suzette is impatient for answers to her questions now. Gray keeps stonewalling her where Nedjar is concerned, however. On the train up to London all he gives her is a fuller account of why he returned to Algeria.

'I went to Paris with Catherine, my girlfriend – who I later made the big mistake of marrying – and another couple we knew for a long weekend in the autumn of eighty-three. The French papers were full of the Marche des Beurs, an immigrant protest march against racism and police violence that was winding its way from Marseille to Paris while we were there. It's a bit before your time, but you've probably heard of it.'

'I have, yes.' Thanks largely, Suzette doesn't add, to a school project of Timothée's.

'Anyway, the doorman of our hotel was Algerian and I got chatting to him. He was pleased someone like me was taking an interest in the march. I mentioned Zarbi, who naturally he'd never heard of, although he got mildly excited when I exaggerated his role in *Playtime*. He said if I was really interested the man I should speak to was an amateur historian of the Algerian community who worked as a potter in the Ménilmontant district, where the doorman also lived. He contributed bits and pieces to a local monthly newsletter and was old enough to remember prominent figures from the sixties. The doorman offered to take me along to see the guy when he finished his shift.

'So, off we went to meet the potter, who did remember Zarbi, as an underground FLN fighter in the years before independence who'd stayed on in Paris afterwards. He knew nothing about Harriet and not much about Tativille, but when I mentioned that Harriet had vanished in June of sixty-five he was prompted to recount a rumour that Zarbi and another old FLN hand had played some part in the murder of Guy Tournier, a presidential aide, that same month.

'That was the clue that drove me back to Algeria. The following spring, remembering my visit to Tipasa in seventy-five, I signed up with a specialist archaeological tour company for a trip to see Algeria's surviving Roman monuments. Catherine had zero interest in that kind of thing, so I was able to go alone, as I'd intended all along. I opted out of a chunk of the tour to spend time in Algiers, so I could put what I'd found out to Nigel. It didn't get me anywhere. He reckoned the rumour about Zarbi and the Tournier murder had no conceivable connection with Harriet leaving Paris, as he still preferred to believe she had. And Riad just repeated his previous advice to me: lay off Zarbi and his kind if I wanted to stay out of trouble.

'Your parents had got their own apartment by then and you'd come into their lives, of course. Technically, that's when we first met. How old were you in eighty-four? Six or seven?'

'Six,' says Suzette. Her childhood in Algiers feels now so far removed from her later life that it sometimes seems to belong to someone else's life altogether. But the memory of Gray's visit is clear nonetheless, as is the effect it had on her parents. 'They were uneasy the whole time you were there, Stephen, though you probably didn't notice. Consequently, so was I. It was actually as if a cloud lifted when you left. I'm sorry, but that's how it was.'

'I'm sorry too. I hope my next visit wasn't so stressful for you. I talked up the wonders of the Roman monuments to cover my tracks so enthusiastically Catherine got genuinely interested in the subject and insisted we go as a couple.'

'You're right. That was what . . . three years later?'

'Yes. Eighty-seven.'

'I remember staring in awe at this blonde-haired English-woman who'd appeared in our apartment. She was nice to me.'

'Catherine was nice to everyone.'

'Did you go to the Mauretanian Royal Tomb as part of the tour? I mean, it's not Roman, but—'

'We went there, yes. Amazing place.'

'We drove out to it one spring evening when I was a little older. It started to get dark and Papa terrified me with a legend about mosquitoes as large as birds who might fly out and attack us if we got too close to the entrance. There's supposed to be treasure hidden inside, which the giant mosquitoes protect.'

No sooner has she said this than she regrets mentioning it all. A chasm of bittersweet nostalgia opens beneath her. They picnicked near the tomb that day, her parents and her, on the perfumed heights above the Mediterranean. The world was a wonderful place to be a young girl in. They were happy. She had no fear for the future because she had no idea what the future held. Then, as the sun slid low in the sky, red and swollen, and the shadows lengthened and the air cooled and Papa told his silly story, she shivered and suddenly she wanted to leave.

The evening seems now to have been the end of something precious. It was 1990. She was a few weeks away from her twelfth birthday. Though she didn't know it, Algeria's slide into the chaos of la décennie noire had already begun. And her father's fate had in effect already been sealed.

'You haven't asked me about the potter named as Zarbi's old FLN accomplice, Suzette,' says Gray mildly, breaking the brief silence.

'Nazim Haddad?'

'No. I don't think there's such a person as Nazim Haddad. I think the name your father recorded in his confession has been altered in the copy you've been sent.'

'Altered from . . .?' She wants him to say it before she has to.

'Nadir Laloul. The man at the centre of the Sonatrach embezzlement scandal who fled Algeria in ninety-nine and left his old comrade Wassim Zarbi to face the music. Didn't you notice anything odd about the lettering wherever Haddad's name appears in the document?'

She nods. 'I noticed.'

'The question isn't whether it was altered. I'm sure it was. And I suspect you're sure as well. The question is why it was altered.'

'To protect Laloul.'

'Yes. Which means Saidi must either be in league with him or in fear of him.'

'Both good reasons why I should tell him the confession's a fake and let him buy my silence, Stephen.'

'I know. But you should hear what Riad has to say first.'

'I'm happy to. But then I have to make a decision, don't I?'

'You do. And you should bear one other possibility in mind.'

'Which is?'

'Maybe Saidi is Laloul.'

They reach London and take a taxi to Soho through the clammy heat of late afternoon. The Maghreb Deli is still open for business. There are dried meats, jars of sauces and tinned delicacies stacked everywhere. The aroma is a heady mixture of coffee, chocolate, spices and cheese. A tiny, slim, sparkling-eyed woman dwarfed by her own visor greets them with a smile that fades when she realizes who they are and why they've come. She is Riad Nedjar's wife.

'My husband is upstairs,' she says, with a resigned sigh. 'He's expecting you.'

She points to a doorway beyond the counter and they climb the stairs to a room directly above the shop, where, in a workspace hemmed in by stacks of tinned tomatoes, chickpeas and fava beans, Riad Nedjar is sitting at his desk.

He's older than Suzette remembers, of course, older by more than a quarter of a century. But he's changed remarkably little, beyond the greying of his hair. He's thin and narrow-chested, with the same strange rubberiness to his limbs that makes him seem to bounce to his feet as they enter the room. His features are still those of a relatively young man, though he must be about the same age as Gray.

'Chevrette,' he says, smiling at her. This nickname, used only by him and inspired by her keenness as a child to show off her climbing ability, brings her instantly to the brink of tears, for reasons she can't quite comprehend.

He looks instantly devastated. 'Pardon, pardon,' he says, rushing forward to console her, then drawing back as he remembers he shouldn't embrace her.

'Ne t'inquiète pas.' She waves his concern away. 'It is good to see you again, Riad. I've often hoped to, over the years. If I'd known where you were . . .'

'After Nigel died, I felt your mother . . . did not wish for any contact with me.'

'Well, it's a long time since I lived with my mother. I'd have loved to hear from you.'

'I am sorry.' Nedjar places his hands together apologetically. 'But the circumstances . . .' He shrugs and says no more.

'It doesn't matter. Are you happy here?'

'Yes. I always loved food almost as much as books, so . . . You met my wife? Emine has a better head for business than me. Without her . . . I would be lost. She is Lebanese, which means she has known even more difficulties in her life than we Algerians.'

'You still think of me as Algerian, Riad?'

'You were born there, Suzette. Nothing can change that.'

'Do you have any children?'

'No. Which is a great sadness. But Stephen has told me you have a son and a daughter.'

'Yes. Timothée and Élodie.' She pulls out her phone. 'You want to see some pictures of them?'

Judging by the smile on Nedjar's face, the answer is emphatically yes.

131

'Why don't I leave you to it?' asks Gray. 'I'll come back . . . in an hour or so.'

Suzette sees Nedjar nod to Gray over her shoulder, but by the time she's glanced back herself he's just a shadow, heading down the winding stairs.

Nedjar moves closer as she begins scrolling through her many stored pictures of Timothée and Élodie. She turns the screen towards him so he can see her favourite image of Élodie, describing her children's characters and accomplishments just like the kind of gushing mother she abhors. Nedjar receives everything she says with nods and smiles. He's an expert listener. She remembers that now. He listens. Although you never quite know what he thinks as he does so.

Anyway, small talk about her family only takes them so far. She's not come all this way just to catch up, delightful though it is – unexpectedly so, in fact – to see Nedjar again. He makes mint tea and they sit on rickety chairs either side of his small, cluttered desk. The sunlight casts over it a lengthening shadow of the faded gold lettering on the window that proclaims some long gone secretarial recruitment agency. The past, both personal and general, gathers around them.

'Stephen has told me about your dilemma, Suzette,' says Nedjar, sipping his mint tea pensively. 'My advice to you is simple. Take the compensation the mysterious Monsieur Saidi is offering you. Then you will hear no more of the matter and be able to spend the money on your lovely children. I have known peace since we came here. Most of our customers think I am Moroccan. My past – Algeria's past – is nothing to them. I sell them our special tahini paste, our preserved lemons and our passion fruit jam and they go away happy and Emine balances our books and I am happy too. There is nothing more to ask from life than this. All the rest – justice, retribution, the satisfaction of righting wrongs and correcting untruths – is a mirage. And if you chase a mirage where will you find yourself but the desert, with your feet sinking slowly in the sand?'

There's something horrifying as well as persuasive about Nedjar's argument. Suzette feels she has to protest against it. 'You think it doesn't matter whether Papa wrote the document or not?'

'Chevrette.' He smiles benignly at her. 'I haven't the slightest doubt Nigel wrote it.'

'You haven't?'

'He was tapping away at his typewriter whenever I entered the apartment in those months after you and Monique left. And, besides, he told me he was writing his memoirs. "Time is one commodity I have in abundance now, Riad," he said, "so I may as well put it to good use." The situation grew worse by the day. The GIA were everywhere, with their beards and their shaven heads and their fanatically gleaming eyes. Also their guns and their knives. We were living in the middle of a war between two armies who were so easily confused we had no idea who the enemy really was. Except death. Death was the one constant. I lived every day in dread. For Nigel as well as myself. Le Chélifère was burnt out, but, even if it hadn't been, trying to sell books in the middle of all that madness would have been absurd. Also suicidal. The Islamists were drunk on their suddenly acquired power: to murder, to rape, to terrorize, to dictate. The only thing ordinary people thought about was how to survive. Some families resorted to sending one of their sons to join the GIA and another to join the DRS so favours could be called in from whichever side they had more to fear from at any particular moment. It made sense when nothing else did, especially since it wasn't always clear who was killing who – or why. The only measure of success was making it through from one day to the next.

'Nigel was lost. He had no skills that were any use in such a situation. Except maybe one. It occurred to me his memoirs might be his way of fighting back against the forces he was hemmed in by. You see, your father wasn't just an innocent bookseller, Suzette. He had an arrangement with Zarbi at the DRS that meant he wasn't harassed. In the good times, I mean. In the relatively sane seventies and eighties. All that changed in the nineties. There were no more . . . arrangements. But he and Zarbi went back a long way. To Paris in the sixties. I knew that from odd things Nigel said. So, I started to wonder if he hoped he could use a record of some of the things he'd done for Zarbi as a bargaining chip. For safe passage out of the country. Or just safe passage out of Algiers. Algeria is a big country. Even the Islamists couldn't be everywhere. Sadly, that never happened. He never left Algiers. In fact, he never left the apartment.

'They must have waited in a neighbouring building for him to go out on to the balcony. That gave them a clear shot. And they took it. Killing your father wasn't a random act, Suzette. It was an assassination. Someone ordered it. Zarbi, maybe? It's possible Nigel contacted him through an intermediary to demand help to get out in exchange for handing over his memoir.'

'You really think so?'

'It's what I first thought when I went to the apartment a few hours after he'd been killed. The police were there. They wanted me to identify his body. Before they took me to the mortuary, I checked to see if the memoir was where he normally kept it, in the drawer of his writing desk. It wasn't there. The police officer who was in charge said nothing had been removed. But he would say that, wouldn't he? All I knew was that the memoir wasn't where it should have been.'

'You never mentioned this to us at the time.'

'What would have been the point? It was enough of a burden for you to know he was dead. Would it have helped you to hear he may have been killed because of a document he wrote which had subsequently been taken by those who ordered his killing? No. Who had actually taken it seemed unimportant. Probably the police officer. There would have been many police officers willing to do whatever Zarbi wanted. He was a powerful man then. His fall was still in the future. There is little good to say about le pouvoir, but at least it has a habit of consuming its own in the fullness of time.

'I sent you a few of your father's possessions I thought you would value and disposed of the rest as Monique told me to. Then I did what I would have done sooner if I hadn't felt Nigel would be unable to cope without me. I left Algeria. But Algeria followed me to Paris. The youths of the banlieues reminded me too much of the hitistes of Algiers, waiting for someone to recruit them in the cause of violence. And violence followed. So I came here. Where it did not follow.'

'Papa's typewriter? Did you just throw it away?'

Nedjar doesn't answer at first. He takes a thoughtful sip of mint tea, opens one of the desk drawers and lifts out, of all things Suzette wasn't expecting to see, her father's old Bakelite ashtray. He sets it down carefully in front of her. Her gaze is met by the smirking likeness of Cagayous in his faded outfit of crooked hat, striped jersey, check trousers and short jacket. Some ash from the many cigarettes that have rested in the tray over the years remains embedded in its surface, contriving to add an extra layer of disrepute to Cagayous's mischievous expression.

'Son cendrier,' she murmurs in wonderment.

'I don't have his typewriter to give you, Chevrette, but I do have this.'

'I never thought I would see it again.'

'But here it is. And here's Cagayous. Remember his most famous saying? "Algériens nous sommes." Nigel had a collected edition of his misadventures in the window at Le Chélifère right up to the end. I told him displaying a popular hero of French

Algerians was a provocation to the Islamists – a needless reminder of the country's colonial past. But he couldn't help himself. "Once a bookseller always a bookseller," was his answer. I don't think it actually made any difference. He would have been a marked man whatever he put in the window. He should have left with you and Monique.'

'I've never really understood why he didn't.'

Nedjar sighs. 'I think I understand. It was guilt, Suzette. Guilt for what he had done – and not done.'

'You mean in Paris in 1965?'

'Partly, yes.'

'Has Stephen told you what Papa says about Harriet Gray in his confession?'

'He did not need to tell me. I already knew.'

Suzette frowns. Does Nedjar mean her father confided in him long ago? Or that he read the memoir while her father was writing it? 'How did you know?'

There comes another heavy sigh. 'Nigel kept a carbon copy of what he wrote. I think he anticipated Zarbi would try to steal the document – before or after his death. So, as backup, there was the carbon copy, which he gave to me for safe keeping.'

Suzette gapes at him in astonishment. 'You have it?'

He nods in confirmation. 'I collected extra pages of the carbon copy whenever I went to the apartment. The last time was two days before Nigel was killed. I never read a word of it while he was alive. He asked me not to and I abided by that. Afterwards . . . was a different matter. I considered destroying it unread. Anyone who'd stolen the top copy could easily have come across Nigel's sheaf of carbon paper and realized there must be a second copy somewhere. It seemed to me they were likely to suspect I had it. So, I posted my copy to my uncle in Oran and asked him to store it for me. It was lucky for me I did, because my apartment was broken into and searched a few days after Nigel was killed. They didn't find what they were looking for. The police questioned me closely. I gave them no hint I knew anything about a memoir. If they were keeping Zarbi informed, as I'm sure they were, he must have concluded there was no copy and I posed no threat to him.

'When I eventually left the country, I took the train to Oran, collected the parcel from my uncle, went straight to the port and boarded the ferry to Marseille. Then – and only then – I read what your father had written. And came to understand what he had died for.'

'You never said anything to us about this either.'

'I thought Monique probably knew most of it anyway. And if not . . . It is not a happy story, Suzette. Nigel was not a hero. He did bad things. Some of them he did to protect you and Monique, but still . . . I saw no need to inflict on you the truth of his life – and death.'

'I think you need to inflict it on me now. Otherwise, how can I decide what the best thing to do is?'

'I've told you what I think the best thing to do is. But I understand why you need to read the whole document. I hoped, for your sake, you would never have to. But it seems I hoped in vain.'

Nedjar leans down and starts twisting the knob of a small safe stowed beside the desk. Then he turns the handle and pulls the door open. He lifts out a well-filled crumpled manilla envelope and slides it across the desk to her. The envelope itself dates from the years when Le Chélifère was in business. The name and address of the shop is scrawled on it in faded brown ink. The stamp is still on it, partially obscured by a badly smudged postmark.

'Before you read it, Suzette, I ought to tell you there is no Nazim Haddad anywhere in its pages. His name has been substituted in the extract Monsieur Saidi sent you for Nadir Laloul.'

'I thought that must be so.'

'As to why, well, perhaps you'll have a better idea when you've read everything your father wrote. I say everything, but I suppose he may have written some more pages after my last visit to the apartment.'

'Has Stephen read this?'

'I showed it to him a long time ago. He came to Algeria twice in search of the truth about his sister. I did not feel I could keep it from him.'

'So, when I showed up at his cottage yesterday and handed him a copy of the extract sent to me by Monsieur Saidi, he already knew for certain it was genuine – and what the full version contained.'

'Yes. But he could hardly tell you that, could he, without speaking to me first? When he did, I decided I should explain to you myself how it came about. And now . . . here is the truth, for you to read yourself.'

Suzette reaches for the envelope. As she touches it, Nedjar lays his hand lightly across hers.

'Try to remember that your father loved you dearly. He would not want you to endanger yourself on his account under any circumstances. He has been dead for twenty-six years. The world has turned – and you have grown and become a parent yourself, without needing to trawl through the darker passages of his life.'

She looks at Nedjar and holds his gaze. 'I think I must, Riad.'

'I understand. But listen to me, Chevrette. Whatever you decide to do, don't go back to Algeria. It consumes its sons and daughters. It shows them no mercy. The day I left, I swore I would never return. I walked down to Agha station for the early train to Oran on a spring morning in 1994 and gazed back across the roofs of Algiers as the sun was rising, casting a dusty golden light on the Martyrs' Memorial that seemed to squat on the city like some giant locust. And the certainty was hard and clear in my mind. Algeria is a quicksand. If you are fortunate enough to escape its sucking grip, as you and I have been, you should never set foot there again. I never will. And you never should either.'

He pats her hand and withdraws his. He gives her a crumpled little smile. Then he sighs and says no more.

TWELVE

THE WORKING DAY IN ALGIERS IS WINDING TO A CAREWORN CLOSE when Taleb reaches Police Headquarters. His drably clad colleagues are wandering out into the clammy, airless early evening. One of them is Megherbi from Vice, whose path Taleb is seemingly doomed to cross all too frequently.

'Trying to rack up some overtime to fund your retirement, Taleb?' comes the predictable jibe.

'Better that than selling confiscated pornography on the black market.'

The riposte hits a nerve. Megherbi bristles. 'You're the only one who laughs at your jokes, Taleb, you know that?'

'Who said I was joking?'

The main door swings shut before Megherbi can devise a further response. Taleb finds Hidouchi waiting for him in the reception area, leaning against the counter, behind which the corpulent and notoriously idle Sergeant Slimani is endeavouring to appear busy, presumably in order to impress Hidouchi, whose expression suggests he isn't succeeding.

'I hope I haven't kept you waiting long, Agent Hidouchi,' says Taleb.

'Long enough.'

'My apologies.'

Hidouchi stretches her long neck, pushes back her hair and frowns ominously. 'Why are we here, Taleb?'

'To follow a hunch.'

'A hunch? Is that all?'

'In my experience, a hunch is not necessarily a small thing. Come with me. We're going to Archives.'

'Azzi's closed up for the night,' says Slimani.

'Then give me the key.'

'You'll have to sign for it.'

Taleb scrawls his signature on the proffered form and takes delivery of the key.

'You'll be careful down there, won't you? Azzi doesn't like things being disturbed.'

Nothing is said as they descend into the shadowy bowels of the building. Everything hinges now on what, if anything, Taleb can unearth from one of the numberless and not always scrupulously catalogued files that hold the details of thousands of crimes, the solved and the unsolved alike, stretching back to the dawn of the republic. In keeping with national tradition, the past at Police HQ, though seldom visited, is never discarded. Everything is there – if you know where to look.

Taleb unlocks the double doors of the Archives department and enters a cavern of darkness, with Hidouchi close behind. He gropes for the light switches. A dozen or so fluorescent tubes flicker reluctantly into life. A fan on the attendant's desk whirs into motion, wafting across to them some of the lingering odour of his cigarette smoke and stirring the pages of his abandoned newspaper, which rustle against the prominently displayed DÉFENSE DE FUMER sign.

'You bring me to all the best places,' says Hidouchi drily.

'This is the best place, if you're looking for what we're looking for.'

'And that is?'

'The truth.' Taleb cocks his head and runs his eye along the yellowing cards stuck on the ends of the file-stacks. The years encompassed by each stack are recorded in none too legible a hand on the cards, some of which, alas, have fallen off and not been replaced.

'What year are we interested in?'

'Nineteen ninety-three. The Islamists were keeping us very busy. And ordinary criminals were naturally trying to benefit from how overstretched we were. In archival terms, it was a bumper year.'

'There.' She points to a distant stack. 'That's where we should look.'

'Thank you. Your eyesight is better than mine.'

'But your memory is longer.'

Taleb wonders as they cross the room if Hidouchi's remark is actually a compliment. He'd like to believe it is, but he's not sure. What is a long memory, after all, but a symptom of age?

They reach the 1993 row of cardboard archive boxes, piled one on top of another on the steel shelves that stretch away towards the distant rear wall of the basement. Taleb takes a moment to gauge the scale of their task. He spoke of it as a bumper year and here is the proof of it in the sheer quantity of preserved records.

'Which month?' Hidouchi prompts him.

'October. Or November. I'm not sure.'

'A pity.' Hidouchi wanders ahead of him, glancing up at the boxes. Motes of dust float around her in the pool of light she moves through. 'This should all have been digitized long ago. Then we could just tap a button and access what you're looking for.'

'We've never had the DSS's resources.'

'Despite your workload? Don't worry. I will never again suggest the police have too little to do. Or had, at any rate. Did you really keep everything back then? The records of every single minor misdemeanour?'

'No. Just the serious stuff. Murder, rape, arson, abduction, extortion, blackmail, robbery, fraud, corruption, smuggling, racketeering. There was plenty, even so.'

'October starts there.' Hidouchi points to a box on the topmost shelf. 'We'll need the steps. I'll get them.'

Hidouchi strides past Taleb. He tries to will his brain to remember the exact date of the record he's looking for. But it won't come. The autumn of 1993 was such a cavalcade of violence that distinguishing one blood-soaked week from another was impossible at the time, let alone now.

There's nothing for it but to make a start. He takes down a couple of boxes from the shelf and heads for the reading table located near the archivist's desk. He hears the rattle of the steps being wheeled round by Hidouchi behind him. 'Just bring a few to start with,' he calls as he plonks the boxes down on the table. 'No sense emptying the shelves unless we have to.'

He opens one of the boxes and is confronted by a bulging file containing the details of a gruesome multiple rape and murder case. His memory of it is jogged by the names of the victims listed on the cover, including that of an off-duty policewoman he remembers as lively and fun-loving and irrepressibly optimistic. He lifts the file out carefully, having no wish to chance upon a photograph of her dismembered body. He draws a deep breath. He knew this was going to be difficult. Now he begins to understand just how difficult.

He has made little further progress when Hidouchi joins him with another two boxes. 'I do need to know what we're looking for,' she says, arching her eyebrows at him. 'With or without a date.'

'The arrest of an Englishman – I can't remember his name – on a train from Annaba. He was found to be travelling with an invalid passport.'

'That doesn't sound like "serious stuff".'

'There were complications.'

'Involving Zarbi?'

Taleb nods. 'As I recall.'

They search on in silence. The only sound is the rustling of paper, the whirring of the fan and a barely audible buzz from the fluorescent tube above them. Taleb tries to concentrate on what he needs to find while blotting out the memories stirred by so many names of so many dead. He finishes one box and starts on another. Hidouchi, unencumbered by his grisly recollections, goes faster, finds nothing and goes to fetch another two boxes.

And so it continues. From one box to another. Partway through a fourth box, Hidouchi stops and looks across at him. 'Did you work with an officer called Dif, Taleb?'

Taleb does not reply at first. He stares down at the file before him. It contains the details of a bracingly old-fashioned bank robbery. In the circumstances, it is positively soothing. He finds some words in the end. 'Why do you ask?'

'Decapitated after being kidnapped. Genitals hacked off and stuffed in his mouth. October tenth, according to this file.'

'Yes. As you say.'

'And the following day, October eleventh—'

'One officer killed and another injured by a sniper at Dif's funeral.'

'You were there, Taleb?'

'I was.'

'It cannot have been . . . easy.'

'How old were you in 1993, Agent Hidouchi?'

'Four. I went through my childhood believing bomb-blasts and gunfire were the normal sounds of city life.'

'As they were, for too many years. Dif wasn't the first we lost to the Islamists. Or the last. We were their favourite target.'

'You may as well tell me what the Englishman with the invalid passport means in all of this. I'm sure you remember, even if you can't remember his name.'

'Yes. I remember. And it could take hours to find the file. So . . . sit down for a moment.'

They pull up chairs either side of the wide wooden table and look at each other between the dusty boxes and their dog-eared contents. Hidouchi's expression is less disdainful than usual. The Dif file – complete with post mortem photographs – has evidently made for sobering reading.

'Foreigners in Algeria at that time were virtually unknown,' Taleb begins. 'The Islamists had issued a fatwa against visiting unbelievers and the world had got the message: Algeria wasn't a healthy place to go. So, when an Englishman was arrested on an overnight train from Annaba following a disturbance of some kind and was found to have no visa in his passport, he was taken in for questioning. It was as much as anything for his own protection. Some other passengers accused him of being drunk, which could easily have been enough in those days for him to end up like Dif. But his luck was in. So he spent the morning in one of our cells and, at some point in the afternoon, I went along to question him.'

'What was your rank then, Taleb?'

'Inspector.'

'Wasn't a visa irregularity beneath you?'

'Ordinarily, it would have been. But, after being arrested, the Englishman had accused a senior DRS staff member and a highly placed executive at Sonatrach of a serious criminal offence, making the issue . . . a delicate one. For some reason, Superintendent Meslem always believed he could entrust such cases to me.'

'The senior DRS staff member and the highly placed executive at Sonatrach were, I assume, Zarbi and Laloul?'

'They were.'

'And the crime levelled against them by the Englishman?'

'An assassination, according to the officer who arrested him, carried out in Paris around the time President Ben Bella was deposed, in 1965. But he was drunk when he said that. He'd sobered up by the time I interviewed him and denied making any such accusations.'

'Sounds like a dead end. What did you do with him?'

'Well, he'd clearly entered the country illegally. Via Tunisia was my guess. As to why, he couldn't give me a satisfactory explanation. Eventually, he named a fellow Englishman living in Algiers who he said could vouch for him. I've forgotten his name as well, but he ran a bookshop called Le Chélifère.' Seeing Hidouchi frown in puzzlement, Taleb continues, 'Named after those tiny spiders you sometimes find in the binding of old books. You know what I mean?'

'I don't spend much time with old books.'

'No. I suppose you don't. Anyway, I went along to Le Chélifère to see what I could learn. Selling books – other than the Koran – was a risky business at that time. The door of the shop was locked and the blinds were down so you couldn't see in, but there was a sign inviting customers to knock for admittance. It took quite a lot of knocking to rouse the Algerian assistant who was minding the premises on behalf of the owner. He said he'd never heard of the Englishman we'd arrested, but I wasn't convinced. I insisted he give me his employer's address. As I recall, he went there with me because he doubted I'd get in without him. His employer was a lock-in. One of the many in those days who never left home because they feared they were on the Islamists' hit list. He told the same story: no knowledge whatever of the man we'd arrested or Zarbi and Laloul. I felt certain he was lying. So I came back here intending to question the Englishman further. But it wasn't to be.'

'Why not?'

'Because he was gone. Taken off our hands by the DRS on the grounds that national security issues were involved. The order, in case you're wondering, came from Zarbi himself. My boss agreed with me it smelt all wrong but told me nevertheless to drop the case. Which I did. Going against your department then, when Toufik was in charge, was tantamount to suicide. And I don't just mean the career kind.'

Hidouchi doesn't like the sound of that. 'You're surely exaggerating.'

'Am I? You were only a child during la décennie noire. You said so yourself. You would not believe some of the things that happened – some of the things humans did to other humans. I would not believe them myself, if I had not seen them with my own eyes. The Islamists were not the only terrorists. I saw evidence that DRS agents provocateurs were responsible for some of the massacres blamed on the GIA. One of those massacres claimed the lives of my—'

Taleb breaks off. He sits back in his chair, letting the familiar wave of grief sweep over him. It will pass, he knows. It will pass and he will still be here, living and breathing. Well, breathing, anyway. Living, he has come to understand since the deaths of his wife and daughter, is a relative term.

He is angrier with himself at this moment than with the malign fate that condemned him to grow old alone. He swore he would not reveal this truth about himself to Hidouchi. Yet now . . . 'I am sorry, Agent Hidouchi. Forget what I just said.'

Hidouchi looks at him intently – and, it seems, compassionately. 'How can I do that?'

'By trying hard – for my sake.'

'You surely don't think I agreed to work with you without first checking your record, Taleb? You were granted six weeks of bereavement leave in 1997 following the killing of your wife and daughter in a GIA raid on a village near Tiaret. There was extreme brutality, according to the report I read. Mutilation; evisceration; decapitation. And doubtless for the female victims violation before death. I cannot imagine how a husband and father could cope in such circumstances.'

'I do not claim to have coped.'

'But you did survive.'

'You speak as if that was a positive achievement on my part. In reality, I simply failed to die.'

'There was no suggestion in the report that anyone other than the GIA were responsible.'

'I take it to be a DRS report. What else would you expect?'

'You mentioned evidence.'

'Survivors spoke of some of the attackers wearing false beards. And calls for help to the local police went unanswered. Draw your own conclusions. I drew mine a long time ago. But to be clear, Agent Hidouchi, I blame myself quite as much as whoever actually attacked the village. My wife's family lived there – her parents and sister were also killed. I sent my wife there with our daughter because I feared they would be targeted on account of my status as a police officer if they remained in Algiers. As it turned out . . . I sent them to their deaths.'

'Their killers are to blame, Taleb, not you.'

'Maybe we share the blame.' Taleb stands and moves across to the archivist's desk, where he hunts for the ashtray he is certain is there somewhere. He discovers it in a drawer. He takes out his cigarettes, lights up and returns to the table, ashtray in hand. 'Excuse me flouting the regulations, but at times such as this my old friend Nassim is my only recourse. You want one?'

Hidouchi shakes her head. 'You have no idea what happened to the Englishman?' she asks, apparently sensing that the kindest thing to do now is to change the subject.

'I made discreet enquiries. He left the country, by plane to Paris, two days after the DRS removed him from our custody.'

'Not eliminated, then? Not found dismembered by the roadside?'

'No. Zarbi seems to have been surprisingly merciful.'

'Perhaps because he posed no real threat.'

'Perhaps. Or perhaps because he foresaw a time might come when the two of them needed to cooperate. I believe that Englishman to be the same Englishman Abderrahmane smuggled into Zarbi's villa. And if we find the file detailing his arrest, we'll find his name. So . . .' Taleb draws deeply on his cigarette. 'I suggest we concentrate on the search.'

And so they continue in resumed silence, as the hands on the clock that hangs high on the wall behind the archivist's desk move slowly round and the evening creeps on.

Forty minutes pass.

Then, delving into yet another box, Hidouchi freezes, a file in her hand, and looks across at Taleb. 'This is it, I think.' She turns the file to show him the name scrawled on the cover. STEPHEN FREDERICK GRAY.

'Yes,' says Taleb quietly. 'That's him.'

Hidouchi lays the file – thinner than most of those they have sifted through – on the table and opens it. 'There's a report by the arresting officer dated October twenty-fifth, 1993, a photocopy of Gray's passport and . . . an interrogation report written by you, plus a transfer document signed by a DRS officer and . . . some notes.'

'Gray's date of birth?'

'May seventeenth, 1955.'

'Yes. He was about my own age. And that was what Abderrahmane said. "About the same age as you." It's him.'

Hidouchi studies the documents. 'It's as you said. Arrested on the Annaba to Algiers train following a complaint of drunkenness. Claimed to be known to the British owner of Le Chélifère bookshop, Nigel Dalby, which Dalby denied. Vague allegations levelled by Gray against Zarbi and Laloul. Allegations withdrawn when questioned by you . . .'

'What do the notes say?'

'They're handwritten. By you?'

'Yes. I'm sorry if they're difficult to read.'

Hidouchi frowns. 'Did you write them with a pen, Taleb, or a stalk of corn?'

'I can decipher them if you want me to.'

'No. I can manage. "Case to be dropped. No further action. AM approved."'

'AM would be Superintendent Meslem. Is there more?'

'Oh yes. Quite a lot more, really, for a dropped case. "Scan of news archives based on Gray's alleged timing and location suggests link with assassination of French presidential aide Tournier, Paris, second of the sixth sixty-five. Store as DNP. SB, asterisked." What do those initials and the asterisk mean, Taleb?'

'DNP means do not pursue. SB means . . .' Taleb smiles. 'SB means Sami Bahlouli. And the asterisk means . . . bear him in mind.'

'I don't understand. Bahlouli the crooner?'

'The same.'

'What's his connection with this?'

'I've only just remembered. It's been hovering at the corner of my mind ever since you said Razane Abderrahmane had visited him in El-Harrach. I took my wife to La Girafe on the twenty-sixth of April, 1988. It was our fifth wedding anniversary, so I can be sure of the date. Zarbi was there, with his latest mistress and various sleazy hangers-on. He was at his peak then, arrogant and strutting. And loud. Yes, very loud. The group were seated close to the stage. Bahlouli went through his usual numbers, accompanying himself on the piano. I paid little attention. Then there was a disturbance. Zarbi was suddenly on the stage, red-faced and shouting. He pulled Bahlouli off his piano stool and took a swing at him, though as I recall he missed. It was mayhem, albeit briefly. I decided I ought to step in to cool things down, but Zarbi's goons told me they had everything under control. Bahlouli disappeared backstage. Razane fluttered about, soothing Zarbi with free champagne, reassuring everyone that a brief misunderstanding had been resolved and we could all get on with the important business of enjoying ourselves. And that was all there was to it.'

'But obviously that wasn't all there was to it.'

'No. Can you look up Tournier on your phone? As a police officer, all I get is a basic dial and text model.'

'Poor you.' Hidouchi takes out her smartphone and taps away. She gets a swift result. 'Here we are. Guy Tournier, aide to President de Gaulle, murdered at his apartment in Paris, June second, 1965.' She reads on, summarizing as she goes. 'His murderers were never caught, but the French authorities believed the FLN were responsible . . . Tournier was born in 1928 . . . Son of an eminent lawyer . . . Followed the usual elite educational route: l'Institut d'études politiques de Paris, then l'École nationale d'administration – a classic énarque . . . Rose rapidly through the civil service . . . Became a trusted aide to de Gaulle, 1958 . . . Rumoured to have . . . Ah. Now that's interesting.'

'What?'

'Rumoured, though never confirmed, to have served on a secret committee coordinating repressive measures against the Algerian community in Paris before and after the 1961 massacre of Algerian demonstrators, which would explain why he was targeted by the FLN.'

'It would, of course. And Zarbi and Laloul were faithful agents of the FLN at that time.'

'You think it was they who murdered Tournier?'

'What I think isn't the point, Agent Hidouchi. I draw your attention to Tournier's first name.'

'Guy.'

'Yes. And that was what my note on Gray's file was intended to remind me of. You see, the song Bahlouli was playing when Zarbi leapt up on the stage at La Girafe was a French version of an Elton John hit: "Une Chanson pour Guy". That was what provoked Zarbi. He must have thought Bahlouli was taunting him, letting him know his role in Tournier's murder wasn't as big a secret as he supposed.'

'But how would someone like Bahlouli be in on it?'

'Perhaps Razane told him. As to how she would know, well, she supplied Zarbi with female company, probably including her own. Believe it or not, back in 1988 she was quite an attractive woman.'

'We need to ask her some more questions.'

'Why not try Bahlouli first? He won't be enjoying imprisonment. He might be keener than her to cooperate.'

'I'll arrange a visit for early tomorrow.'

Hidouchi punches a number into her phone. She begins to look displeased when there isn't an instant answer. Taleb takes note of her impatience, which in his experience can sometimes be an advantage and sometimes a disadvantage. He veers more towards the dogged end of the spectrum himself.

There's an answer. Hidouchi begins speaking. Taleb barely listens, playing in his mind with the frail but tangible connections between Laloul, Zarbi, Abderrahmane, Bahlouli, Stephen Gray, the proprietor of Le Chélifère . . . and a long dead aide to President de Gaulle. Then he notices a change in Hidouchi's tone. She sounds vexed.

She rings off and stares simmeringly at the phone, as if it is responsible for whatever bad news she has just been given. 'What is it?' Taleb asks.

'Bahlouli was released on parole three weeks ago.'

'Well, he isn't a danger to the public, is he? We're only talking about tax evasion. They have an address for him, presumably?'

'Oh yes. They have an address. In fact, you already know what it is.'

'I do?'

'We were there just a few hours ago. Surprising, isn't it, that Abderrahmane didn't mention she'd taken in a lodger?'

on vol. There were no surface. Clear, you already know that

I know

We know there was Jane-Junot de Saint-Simon who is . . . Gray interrupting (?) this conversation, faithful (?) . . .

THIRTEEN

SUZETTE STARTS TO READ THE REMAINDER OF *J'AVOUE* ON THE TRAIN
back to Basingstoke. Gray's hoping she'll be so moved by the
concluding section of her father's confession that she'll resolve
to tell Monsieur Saidi it's definitely genuine. He's more or less
told her as much. And it could be so. Suzette just doesn't know
whether in the end she'll be ruled by her heart or her head. She
has to read her father's words to find that out.

The confession feels as different as it looks, more intimate somehow: the flimsy, translucent paper bearing the faintly blurred
imprint of the carbon-copied original. It takes her closer to her
father to hold the pages in her hands, to imagine him twisting the
carriage of his typewriter as he removes them and separates them
out, with the smoke of his perpetual cigarette drifting around him
and the deep gold late afternoon light of Algiers stretching towards
him through the half-shuttered window of their apartment.

She leafs through the pages, searching for the first of those she
hasn't read. She finds the interrupted passage at the bottom of
the last page Coqblin & Baudouin saw fit to supply. The train
rumbles over the forking tracks as it coasts out of Waterloo

station. Gray says nothing, gazing pointedly out of the window, giving her the space she needs.

✛

God knows how that would have turned out. But at least I wouldn't be here, alone in this crumbling apartment, in this city of heat and hatred, in this present I can't seem to find a way out of: [she turns the page and reads on] my present, the present I brought upon myself. It's nothing less than I deserve, of course. I can hardly complain. I outran fate for a long time, so long I thought it would never catch up with me. But now here it is, whispering in the corner, hovering outside the window, manoeuvring around me until it's ready to strike.

Zarbi was unstintingly generous to me when we arrived in Algiers in the summer of 1965. Ben Bella was gone, ousted from the presidency and replaced by Boumediene, his Defence minister. Zarbi and Laloul were rewarded for their service in Boumediene's cause with plum appointments, Zarbi to the Sécurité Militaire, Laloul to Sonatrach, the national oil and gas company. And I was rewarded for my service to them with a small but centrally located apartment and an undemanding job at ONAT, the national tourist organization, housed in a large house left over from the Ottoman era in the lower Casbah.

Algiers was utterly alien to me, which was in one sense a blessing. There was nothing - absolutely nothing - there to remind me of my past. Algiers's past was a different matter. Many buildings carried visible signs of damage inflicted by snipers and bombers during the War of Independence. The house where the notorious Ali La Pointe had been blown up by French paratroopers survived as a ruin. And numerous large-scale construction projects were under way in areas where the French had demolished parts of the city for redevelopment that had never happened. In the Place des Martyrs, formerly the Place du Gouvernement, the famous statue of the Duc d'Orléans on horseback was gone, but the plinth remained. The colonial era was over, but reminders of it were all around.

By a bizarre coincidence, I soon found myself caught up in another film project. Gillo Pontecorvo, the Italian director, was in town filming The Battle of Algiers, for which he needed an army of extras and the run of the city. ONAT was roped in to assist with the production. I threw myself into the work, as much as anything to stop myself thinking about what I'd left behind in Paris. I never breathed a word to the Italian crew that I'd been involved in Playtime. I was in a new world. I needed to renew myself to match.

The first sign of what Zarbi had in mind for me came when he asked me to report anything vaguely political said by the extras while Pontecorvo kept them busy recreating famous scenes from the War of Independence. I had little to tell him. The extras were ordinary Algerians eager to earn money. Many of them were anxious about the future, not sure what to make of Ben Bella's removal. That was as far as it went.

I contacted my father and told him I was living in Algiers, but I said I couldn't give him an address until I was properly settled and I never actually supplied one, which meant he had no way of contacting me even if he wanted to. As I saw it, that guaranteed no one would be able to trace me through him. I was consciously burning my bridges. Zarbi told me the Paris police believed Harriet had drowned in Amsterdam, a probable suicide, even though the body found in a canal there hadn't been identified as hers. We both knew she'd died in Paris, of course, though I never had the nerve to ask him what he and Laloul had done with her. He wouldn't have told me, anyway. I had to live with my part in her death. I had to live with the knowledge of my own lack of courage. I feel ashamed now that I managed to do that.

Pontecorvo's film crew moved on at the end of 1965 and time began to hang heavy at ONAT. Algerian tourism might have had a future, but it certainly didn't have a present. I made some friends among the staff, who introduced me to the few nightspots of the city, including Cinémathèque, where I saw The Battle of Algiers when it was eventually released. The sixties moved towards the seventies. I slowly reconciled myself to living in Algiers for as far ahead as I could imagine.

Then Zarbi found another role for me, working as a document translator at Sonatrach HQ, which he wanted me to combine with sniffing out discontent among the workforce. There wasn't any that I could detect, though it was clear to me the organization harboured a lot of low-level corruption. I began to wonder if Zarbi had put me there to keep an eye on Laloul. If so, the plan didn't work,

because Laloul spent most of his time out
of town, working on the expansion of the gas
terminal and petrochemical plant at Arzew, near
Oran.

The best thing that came out of working at
Sonatrach was meeting Monique Dirèche, my boss's
secretary. I didn't think anyone knew or cared
about our burgeoning romance, but Zarbi had a
disturbing facility for knowing more about my
life than I thought. He sarcastically gave me
his blessing to marry her if she'd have me and
suggested we should leave Sonatrach and take
over a bookshop whose owner was eager to sell up
and retire. He offered to fund the purchase of
the business, dressing it up as a loan.

Why should he want to give us such an
appealing start to married life? Because, it
transpired, he'd found the perfect use for my
talents. He'd concluded pen-pushers at ONAT and
Sonatrach weren't the problem in Boumediene's
Algeria. The intellectual community was where
dissident thought was likely to take root. And
intellectuals read books. So, who better to feed
him information about what the artists and
teachers of the city were reading and thinking
than the proprietor of a bookshop to which they
all gravitated?

So it was that from the beginning I welcomed
customers to Le Chélifère with mixed motives.
I enjoyed the bookseller's life. I relished
rubbing shoulders with discerning readers. But I
was always on the alert for anything that could
be potentially subversive. Most of what I passed
on to Zarbi was inconsequential. But some people
let their guard down and confided opinions they'd

have been horrified to learn might reach the
ears of a senior SM officer. Did they suffer as
a result of my actions? Some of them, certainly.
Passed over for promotion. Pushed out of their
state-funded job. But nothing worse, Zarbi assured
me. 'We do not need to kill people now we are in
charge, Nigel,' he told me once. 'All we do is
make sure the wrong people do not take our country
in the wrong direction.' But what was the wrong
direction? Or the right one?

The answer was clear to those who chose -
unlike me - to see what was truly happening. I
told myself Algeria was too young a country for
its government not to feel the need to protect
itself against the enemy within. But I know now
that wasn't the reality of the situation. I was
a pawn of le pouvoir: the controlling force that
determined every fundamental issue. I was a cog
in the wheel of repression.

How much of this my sole employee, the former
owner's assistant, Riad Nedjar, appreciated I
can only guess. We've never spoken openly of it.
But he's always understood more than he's given
credit for. I have little doubt he knew what was
going on behind the scenes. But he was grateful
to me for keeping him on and for teaching him
English in my spare time. And the customers,
though they liked me, loved Riad. He was
invaluable to me. The shop would never have
been as successful without him.

I believed I'd put my past decisively behind
me, but I discovered that wasn't so easily done.
A French tourist who'd worked at Tativille came
into the shop one day and claimed to recognize
me, though I genuinely didn't recognize her. It

was through her that Harriet's brother Stephen
Gray tracked me down in 1975, appearing out of
nowhere to ask questions about Harriet - and
Zarbi, who'd been mentioned to him by Viviane
Labbé. I stonewalled as best I could, peddled
the Amsterdam story as the probable truth of
what had happened to her and detailed Riad to
give him a friendly warning off. Riad didn't
need much persuading. He was genuinely concerned
for Stephen's safety. So was I. If I'd reported
his visit to Zarbi, there's no telling what
might have happened to him. But I said nothing
and I hoped, when he left, that I'd never hear
from him again.

1978 was a big year for me. Suzette came into
my life. Having a daughter altered my sense of
my place in the world. It made me determined
that Le Chélifère would still be operating
successfully when she was old enough to consider
working there herself and eventually taking it
over from me. And then President Boumediene
died - a rare cancer, it was said, though there
were rumours of poisoning, as there were bound
to be in the hothouse of Algerian politics.
Whatever accounted for his death, I was glad he
was gone, because I thought it likely Zarbi
would be sidelined by the new regime. Then he'd
be off my back. The future suddenly looked
inviting.

It didn't turn out like that, though. Zarbi
actually wanted more from me to help him impress
President Bendjedid's underlings - people he
didn't know and who didn't owe him any favours.
But I didn't have more to give. Zarbi was
unimpressed. He implied he'd call in his loan

to me, which previously he'd said would never happen. I needed to give him something. But I didn't have anything.

Arezki Tidjani, a history lecturer at the university and a regular customer over the years, came to my rescue when he asked me a few questions about Sonatrach, where he knew Monique and I had both worked. Tidjani revealed he was working on a history of the Algerian oil industry, starting from the first French strikes in the Sahara back in the fifties. 'You'd be surprised by some of the things I've found out,' he said. It was just a throwaway remark. Maybe he was trying to impress me. That's certainly what Monique thought. But I passed it on to Zarbi. And he stopped pressurizing me for a while.

About a month later, Tidjani was killed in a car accident when he drove off a cliff on the corniche road between Algiers and Oran. His death chilled me to the bone. It surely couldn't be coincidental I'd reported his oil industry research to Zarbi. 'No one gets killed for writing about Sonatrach,' Monique airily assured me. She'd long known I worked as an informant for Zarbi. Growing up in Algeria had taught her that many accommodations had to be made with le pouvoir. She regarded the arrangement as a regrettable necessity and not something I should reproach myself for. 'We all have to take our chances.'

Monique's insouciance on the issue ate away at me over time. I'd idealized her when we first met. Now I realized she was entirely pragmatic about such things, even if they might have led

in this case to someone being killed. But who
was I fooling? This was Algeria. And these were
the rules of the game. As she'd said, 'We all
have to take our chances.'

Which is what I continued to do, uneasily
though it sat with my conscience. Stephen Gray
returned twice more over the following years,
using a supposed interest in Roman archaeology
as the reason. He was accompanied on the second
occasion by his wife, which gave me some cause
to hope marriage would blunt his determination
to discover the truth about Harriet. He learned
nothing from me, though he never stopped trying
to unpick the story I kept on telling: Harriet
had vanished inexplicably from my life in Paris
in 1965 and that was all I knew for certain. I
didn't breathe a word to Zarbi about his visits.
The one thing I was determined to do for
Harriet, having failed her so comprehensively
when she was alive, was to protect her brother
to the best of my ability.

My own life, for all its compromises, would
probably have continued on a largely uneventful
course but for the chaos Algeria began to
descend into in the late eighties. Bendjedid, it
turned out, was unable to impose himself on the
country as Boumediene had. I've always felt,
looking back, that the rot began to set in with
the construction of the Martyrs' Memorial.
Vastly expensive and massively tasteless, this
towering chunk of grandiosity incorporated, as
well as an Islamic-style crypt, a glitzy
shopping centre, complete with nightclub: a
standing insult to Islamists, who dubbed it

Hubal - the name of an idol destroyed by the
Prophet in Mecca. And soon enough Hubal was more
than the memorial. It was everything Algeria had
become and they abhorred.

Then the price of oil started to fall, sapping
the state's finances. Inflation, food shortages
and unemployment eroded support for the FLN.
Protests multiplied. Ordinary people had had
enough of being governed by self-serving
veterans of the independence struggle. Their
frustration exploded in the famous mass
demonstrations that began on 4 October 1988.
I felt at the time that the chanting of sexual
jibes against Bendjedid and other members of the
government was the provocation le pouvoir wasn't
willing to tolerate. Resentment was one thing,
ridicule quite another. The army came on to the
streets, fired on the demonstrators and killed
several hundred.

There was no way back from there. As Riad said
to me when it was all over, 'The FLN have turned
into le gouvernement général.' The massacre was
something the French might easily have carried
out. But this was Algerians killing Algerians.
And there was destined to be more of it. Much
more of it. Until, seemingly, there was no end
to it.

I can't bring myself to recount in any detail
the grisly sequence of events that followed: the
electoral victories of the Islamist FIS; the dread
harboured by those - like me - who suspected an
Islamist government would be many times worse
than the bunch of crooks and incompetents we
had at the head of our affairs; the removal
of Bendjedid by the military décideurs; the

declaration of a state of emergency to avert a triumph by the FIS at the polls; the assassination during a televised address of the new president, Boudiaf - some people's last frail hope for stability - just five months into his term; and the creeping appreciation by the summer of 1992 that a ferocious struggle for mastery was the course the country was set on.

From then on violence began to escalate on all sides. And there were more sides than just the government and the FIS. There was the GIA, set on the forcible Islamization of Algeria. There were militias with scores to settle. There were gangsters who saw the chance to carve out territory for themselves. If you ran into a roadblock, you had no idea who'd actually be manning it. All you knew was that they might kill you for no obvious reason. The violence attained an identity of its own. Boudiaf's assassination turned out to be more than the start of it. It was also a demonstration of the terrifying nature of it. The bodyguard who'd shot him was either a closet Islamist or a tool of le pouvoir eliminating one of its own for reasons of its own. But no one knew which. No one could be sure of anything. Qui tue? was the universally asked question. Who was doing the killing? And why?

For me and people like me, that wasn't the most important question, though. Journalists, academics, intellectuals, foreigners and women in western dress became the target. An English bookseller, his French wife and their teenage daughter had to be on the list as well. That was clear. And the police, who were also targeted - along with their families - couldn't give us any protection. After the novelist Tahar Djaout, whose books we stocked at Le Chélifère, was gunned down as he left his apartment one morning, it was impossible to ignore the danger we were in. What were we to do? Eventually, Monique and I took the decision that she and Suzette would move to Marseille, where so many of the pieds noirs had taken refuge.

I stayed on initially because I wasn't willing to abandon Le Chélifère. We'd worked hard to make a success of it and I thought it could be nursed through this desperate time, which surely couldn't last long.

I was wrong on both counts. The violence only grew worse, claiming more victims every day. The Islamists who gave me the evil eye in the street were obviously going to strike at some point. I stopped going to the shop and left Riad to cope with the pitiful trickle of customers. Then, at Riad's urging, I stopped leaving the apartment altogether. 'They will kill you if they see your face,' he warned me. 'It has come to that, my friend.'

So, having left it too late to arrange a safe departure from the country, I became a recluse, staring at the walls of the apartment and at the bleak reality of my situation. I contacted Zarbi in the hope he'd be able to help me, but he said he had his own safety and that of his wife to worry about: there was nothing he could do for me. But he urged me to stick it out. 'There will come a better time, Nigel.'

There seemed scant prospect of that. And just when I thought the situation couldn't in all seriousness get any worse, my past came back to haunt me.

One day Riad showed up at the apartment accompanied by a plain clothes police officer. For a crazy second, I thought Riad had in some way betrayed me. But it wasn't that. The police officer - Taleb was his name - wanted information about Stephen Gray, who I was horrified to hear had been arrested drunk on an overnight train from Annaba. More horrifyingly still, Stephen had accused Zarbi and Laloul of carrying out an assassination in Paris in 1965 and had said I could vouch for him.

What Stephen can have been thinking of I couldn't imagine. Making such an accusation to the police bordered on the suicidal, though I got the impression he'd struck lucky with Taleb: he seemed to be that rarity in those days, an honest detective. As to what had prompted Stephen to travel to Algeria at such a dangerous time, my fear was that he'd found out the truth about what had happened to Harriet and wanted to confront me with it.

All I could do in the circumstances was deny all knowledge of him - and of Zarbi and Laloul. I suggested Stephen Gray might be one of our postal customers and had named me because there was literally no one else he could name in Algiers. Taleb looked unconvinced. He said he'd be back if he needed to ask me any more questions.

Several days passed without word from Taleb. It looked as if I was off the hook. But I was worried about what would happen to Stephen. So was Riad. As far as he was concerned, 'Stephen is mad to have said such things.' And he was right. Yet what could we do to help him without antagonizing Zarbi and Laloul?

Riad did at least have a contact at Police HQ, so he was able to make some discreet enquiries and we learned Stephen had been deported from the country at the DRS's direction a couple of days after his arrest. I didn't doubt this was Zarbi's doing and I was relieved he hadn't dealt with the problem in some more drastic way.

I hoped that was the end of the matter. But no. When Riad next came to deliver supplies to me, he also brought disturbing news. Zarbi had visited the shop and instructed him to pass a message to me. A car would collect me from outside the apartment building at eight the following morning and take me to meet him.

It sounded like a trap to me. But Zarbi had apparently anticipated my reaction. 'Tell Nigel this,' he had said to Riad. 'If I wanted to kill him, I wouldn't do it myself. I'd contract the job out to Napoli.' Napoli was a notorious Algiers gangster, real name Yacine, nicknamed Napoli because he'd supposedly expressed a desire to earn enough money to retire to Naples. 'All we're going to do tomorrow is talk.'

I wasn't reassured. On the other hand, I had no choice but to obey. And so I was loitering in the street doorway of the apartment block next morning when a black Range Rover drew up and a shaven-headed heavy in reflective sunglasses told me to climb in.

Our destination was a pull-in overlooking the sea out on the Cherchell road. If I'd been driving, I'd have been scared stiff of

encountering a roadblock round every bend, with
potentially fatal consequences. We encountered
two, but were waved through both with a cursory
exchange of nods and single-fingered salutes.
Those manning the roadblocks wore military
uniforms of some description, but I couldn't have
said with any certainty what their affiliation
was. We were OK, though. We weren't to be messed
with.

To my surprise, Laloul was waiting for me as
well as Zarbi. They were reclining on the rear
seat of a silver grey limousine, surveying
the sparkling blue of the Mediterranean in the
shade of a small grove of Aleppo pines. It was
a beautiful autumn morning. The air, which
I breathed in deeply as I walked across to
join them, was clear and warm, scented by the
pines. But for its human inhabitants and their
killing frenzy, I reflected, Algeria would be
paradise.

The driver climbed out of the car as I climbed
into the passenger seat. I'd already been searched,
absurd though the idea was that I'd try to bring
a gun with me, even supposing I had a gun or
knew how to use one. As the driver's departure
confirmed, I represented no physical threat to
Wassim Zarbi and Nadir Laloul. I never had. The
sharing of that knowledge between us reinforced
their superiority. I was in their power. I had
been since Paris. For nearly thirty years,
they'd had me under their thumbs, even though,
for long periods of self-delusion, I'd persuaded
myself it wasn't so. But there, that morning, as
I looked round at them - older and fatter but
more dominating than ever - I realized all

pretence on the issue was futile. I was their creature, no better than some pet macaque whose neck they could wring as and when he ceased to amuse or be of service to them.

'Like old times, hey, Nigel?' said Zarbi with a smile. 'Just the three of us.'

'Why am I here, Wassim?' I asked, unsure if I really wanted an answer to my question.

'We need to come to an understanding,' said Laloul, removing a toothpick from his mouth as he spoke. 'Wassim has told me of the visit from Stephen Gray.'

'He's gone now. I'm sure you made it clear to him he'd be crazy to come back.'

'Oh yes,' said Zarbi. 'But maybe he is crazy. A brother seeking justice for a dead sister. You cannot always reason with such a man.'

'Yet you let him go.'

'The British make a lot of noise when their citizens get into trouble. We would have had the embassy on the case. And we do not want some London newspaper leading a campaign to rescue Stephen Gray, innocent tourist, from the snakepit of Algeria, do we?'

Laloul chuckled. 'You should offer to write an editorial for them, Wassim. You have it off just so.'

'We let you send Monique and Suzette to Marseille, Nigel,' said Zarbi. 'And this is how you reward us.'

'I had no idea Gray was coming to Algeria.'

'I questioned him before we put him on a plane to Paris. He has learned a great deal about what happened there with you and us and Guy Tournier . . . and Harriet. You should have warned us.'

'I don't know what he's learned.'

'Too much. And what he hasn't learned he has guessed. He knows what we did. To Tournier and to Harriet. He can't prove it, of course. He could only do that with your help.'

'I'm not going to help him.'

'No. You are not. Because you are not going to leave Algeria.'

'I have no plans to leave.'

'You must be the only foreigner who doesn't. But we need to make it clear to you, Nigel. You are one foreigner who isn't leaving. You have a bookshop to run, after all.'

'How is business?' asked Laloul with an undertow of sarcasm.

Before I could think of a response, Zarbi said, 'You have your passport with you?'

'Yes.'

'Give it to me.'

Refusal wasn't an option. I took out my passport and glanced for a moment at the gilded lion and unicorn coat of arms, then handed it to Zarbi. 'When will I get it back?'

'When things quieten down and it is safe for Monique and Suzette to return to Algiers. A family should be together. And your family belongs here.'

'You really think things will quieten down?'

'Eventually.'

'Can we rely on you, Nigel?' asked Laloul. It was clear from his tone that he doubted it.

'Yes,' I said, stubbornly and self-servingly. 'You can.'

'We're not sure that's true. Remember Tidjani?'

'Of course I remember him.'

'You waited three days before telling us about his research plans.'

It was a strange and disturbing remark by Laloul, because it was true: I had waited several days to tell Zarbi Tidjani was delving into the history of the Algerian hydrocarbons industry. I didn't want to get him into trouble, though in the end I realized I'd get myself into trouble if they found out I knew and had said nothing. But . . .

'And how do we know you waited three days?' Laloul continued. 'Because your wife only waited two.'

'What?'

He gave me a sickening smile. 'No young pied-noir woman could get a secretarial post at Sonatrach without supplying something more than . . . la dactylographie au toucher.'

'What is that in English, Nigel?' asked Zarbi, as if he genuinely wanted to know.

'Touch-typing,' I replied numbly.

'Yes. That is it. Touch-typing. The word sounds . . . prettier than the French.'

For some reason, I felt ashamed by the revelation that Monique had also been acting as an informant. Why hadn't I realized? Why hadn't she told me? I'd told her about what I did for Zarbi, after all. Hadn't she trusted me enough to admit what she did for Laloul? What that said about our marriage gouged at my innards.

Zarbi gave me a consoling look that only made me feel worse. 'You cannot live in this country without compromising, Nigel. We all have to do it. Don't be hard on Monique.'

'Why did you kill Tidjani?' I asked, suddenly
eager to know the truth where previously I'd
preferred not to.

'The police were certain his death was due to
careless driving.'

I held Zarbi's gaze. 'It would be refreshing
if just for once you didn't lie to me.'

He looked at me for a long time in silence.
Then he turned to Laloul. 'Do you want to
explain, Nadir?'

Laloul chewed his toothpick as he weighed the
question. Finally, he said, 'This country's
greatest sources of wealth are oil and natural
gas. The details of how they are managed - the
financial details - are complex. It is necessary,
in order to protect the nation's future, to
maintain . . . certain channels of capital . . .
that would look to some like . . . improper uses
of revenue. These arrangements have been in place
since the French left, in some cases . . . since
before they left. And they will remain in place
long after the current insurgency is ended.
Indirectly, you and Monique have benefited from
them, Nigel. That also will continue, if you
are wise enough to understand your place in
the world.'

'Are you saying Tidjani found out about
these . . . channels of capital?'

'I am saying only a fool would try to bring
them to public attention. You might think this
would be a bad time for attracting investment
into this country. You would be wrong. The price
of oil is rising again. We have new oil and gas
fields ready for development deep in the Sahara.
And we have foreign companies willing to sign

multibillion-dollar contracts for access to
those fields. That is more important than
anything else happening in Algeria today.
Nothing - and no one - will be allowed to
obstruct the process. Not a moralizing
university lecturer. Not even a moralizing
president.'

He was talking about Boudiaf. He had to be.
He was claiming his share of the credit for
the assassination of the president - and by
implication for pinning responsibility for it
on the Islamists.

'Warning us of Tidjani's activities was good
work, Nigel,' said Zarbi hurriedly, as if
embarrassed by Laloul's frankness. 'And there
will be more good work for you to do when
normality returns.'

Laloul murmured something in Tamazight I
couldn't understand. I looked at him
quizzically, then at Zarbi, who smiled back.
'It is an old Kabyle saying. If you share a
secret with a man, you share his soul.'

The intimacy of the thought repelled me. But
what repelled me most of all was the truth of
it. I was part of something bigger and more
dreadful than I'd ever realized. 'Those men on
the roadblocks we passed to get here,' I said.
'Who do they represent? The GIA? The DRS? Both?
Neither?'

'Arrangements are made that serve le pouvoir's
objectives,' said Laloul impatiently. 'In the
desert, water is gold. And he who measures the
water weighs the gold. That is the rule of life
in this land. Which is all you need to know. All
we need to know is do we have an understanding?'

He stared at me pointedly. 'We must have one to guarantee your safe return to Algiers.'

It had come to that: a threat to my life, plain and simple, in a context where little else was either. I was helpless. I had no recourse. I was complicit in the web of corruption woven by people like them - and by people who used people like them. I couldn't complain about what my complicity had brought me to. It was my own fault. I nodded. 'We have an understanding.'

'You will not try to leave Algeria?' Zarbi pressed.

I shook my head. 'No.'

'You will not try to cause either of us any problem?'

'No.'

'Remember we have contacts in Marseille. We know where Monique and Suzette live.'

'I'll remember.'

He reached out and patted me on the shoulder. 'Don't worry, Nigel. After it's got worse, it'll get better. It's a rule of life.'

And so I returned under safe escort to these rooms where I can hide from the Islamists but not from the hard truths Zarbi and Laloul laid before me that morning in the brittle autumn sunshine above the heedless blue of the Mediterranean. I wonder how many other inhabitants of this city have come to such a bleak moment of understanding: that le pouvoir is not something apart from them; that they are themselves part of the state of things - that they cannot escape it because it is always within them.

A week or so later, frustrated perhaps by their inability to kill me on the street, the local Islamist youths set fire to Le Chélifère. All the books and shelves and records and hopes and plans contained within its walls were consumed by the flames. No one tried to put them out. They watched - or didn't, according to choice - as the life I'd carefully built in Algiers was reduced to ashes.

Which leaves me only with whatever kind of life Zarbi and Laloul are prepared to allow me - when normality returns. Which will be, as Zarbi said . . . eventually.

1993 has become 1994. Nothing has changed. The killings continue. The madness holds us in its grip. Unless, which is what I don't want to believe but increasingly do, it isn't madness at all.

Eventually has become worse than never in my mind.

I'm not sure I can wait for normality to return.

No. I am sure. I'm sure I can't.

Because normality is only another set of lies. And I need to stop lying. Especially to myself.

I need to walk out into the sunshine and breathe the fresh air. One last time.

It's a good idea.

It's the best idea I've ever had.

FOURTEEN

TALEB AND HIDOUCHI AGREE TO TRAVEL TOGETHER TO Abderrahmane's apartment building, so they can discuss tactics on the way. Hidouchi has conceded this is the most economical use of their time, but being driven by Taleb seems to cause her almost physical pain, as she sighs and grimaces at his various manoeuvres.

'Is there something wrong with the steering?' she asks at one point. 'Or do you normally take corners as if you're at the wheel of an articulated lorry?'

'I like to see as much of where I'm going as I can.'

'Seeing where we're going is one thing. Getting there is what counts.'

'And we are getting there.'

Hidouchi mutters something under her breath. Then she says, 'Why do we think Stephen Gray is helping Zarbi – if that's what he's doing?'

'Because they both have a grudge against Laloul. Zarbi for being left in the lurch when Laloul fled the country, Gray for some reason connected to the Tournier assassination in Paris in 1965.'

176

'But he accused Zarbi along with Laloul of involvement in that. Why team up with him?'

'Perhaps he thinks Zarbi has been punished enough. Perhaps this is the only way he can get to Laloul.'

'Which implies Zarbi knows where Laloul is.'

'It seems likely.'

'But it's surely less likely that Abderrahmane and Bahlouli know.'

'I agree. But they're here, in Algiers. Zarbi isn't. And nor is Gray.'

'At some point, we'll have to go after Zarbi and Gray, Taleb. You realize that, don't you?'

'Go after them where?'

'What about the English bookseller – Dalby? Would he know anything?'

'Le Chélifère is long gone. And Dalby with it, I expect. Hold on, though.' Taleb grows thoughtful.

'What?'

Taleb takes one hand off the wheel and taps himself reproachfully on the forehead. 'My memory's not as sharp as it used to be, I'm afraid. Dalby was killed, in a presumed Islamist attack, a few months after I spoke to him. Nothing strange about that. He was an obvious target. But . . . there was something unusual about it, if I remember correctly. I'll have to look it up in the records.'

'You can do that without me. I've had enough of Police HQ's dusty archives.'

'Dusty or not, they've served us well so far.'

Astonishingly, Hidouchi seems to concede the point. 'I'll give you this, Taleb. Where the past is concerned, you're an expert.' Then, as if worried he may take the remark for a compliment, she adds, 'It's almost as if you live in it.'

They arrive at the apartment block. Most of the windows they stare up at are lit, the occupants doubtless slumped in front of whatever their televisions are tuned to on the satellite dishes sprouting from virtually every balcony. The coronavirus lockdown has stilled the customary ferment of the city. Traffic noise would normally drown out the hum of air-conditioning units, but now it's quite noticeable. Loitering youths are nowhere to be seen, though there's shouting in a distant courtyard and the barking of a dog. And over and around them, cicadas are sawing away in the sticky warmth of the night.

They start up the stairs, Taleb trailing behind, as before, from the second landing upwards. He assesses their findings so far as he climbs, concluding that everything they've learned has been superficial. It fails to take them closer to Zarbi and Laloul, not to mention the dark secret he senses they share. Laloul took a lot of money with him when he vanished in 1999. And he'd taken a lot before that, siphoned off from Sonatrach dealings he'd had a hand in over the years. Somehow, though, Taleb doesn't think money is really what this is all about. It goes beyond that. It goes deeper into the past and the history of the country he serves. And uncovering it, if he succeeds in doing so, could be the stupidest thing he's ever done.

He reaches the top floor, where Hidouchi is waiting for him. She waits some more while he recovers his breath. It appears she too has been thinking about Laloul's flight from justice twenty-one years ago. 'How did Laloul leave the country, Taleb?' she asks.

'Ah . . .' He supports himself against the balustrade, chest heaving. 'He was . . . er . . . at a gas production facility . . . near the Libyan border. He was . . . er . . . due to meet the . . . Energy Minister . . . when he got back to Algiers, but . . .'

'He never got back?'

'Exactly. He may have crossed . . . into Libya . . . or gone north and crossed into Tunisia. We were never sure. But . . . he certainly didn't want to keep that appointment.'

'They were on to him?'

'Bouteflika had only been president . . . for a few weeks. But long enough, I suppose . . . for Laloul to realize the game was up.'

'And Zarbi? How soon was he arrested?'

'Quite soon. By your department, Agent Hidouchi. He was a known close associate of Laloul. And he was registered as a signatory for the account Laloul used to move the money.' Taleb coughs his way through to reasonably smooth breathing and pushes himself upright. 'Zarbi denied all knowledge of the account. No one believed him. And with Laloul gone . . . someone had to be seen to pay. Zarbi was suddenly friendless. It's amazing how quickly you can lose it all . . . in our glorious republic.'

She looks at him seriously. 'You should be careful who you say things like that to.'

'I am.'

She regards him steadily for a moment. 'Ready now?' She nods at Abderrahmane's door.

He coughs again and nods. 'Ready.'

Hidouchi stabs the bell several times, then gives it one long press. Predictably, there's no response. A couple of minutes of repeated pressing follows, then Hidouchi stands close to the door and shouts, 'Agent Hidouchi, DSS. Open the door or I'll break it down.'

The threat comes as a surprise to Taleb. Is she really prepared to break the door down? It looks quite solid to him. But, when there's still no response, Hidouchi shouts, 'Last warning.' And Taleb is slightly disappointed when the door opens by about twenty centimetres before catching on a chain. Razane Abderrahmane glares out at them.

'Haven't you finished with me?' she rasps.

'Can we come in, Razane?' Taleb asks with a smile he intends to be ingratiating.

'Do I have the option of saying no?'

179

'Say what you like,' Hidouchi cuts in. 'We are coming in.'

Abderrahmane curls her lip. 'Yes. Of course you are. Because I am old and powerless and too poor to bribe you to go away.' She releases the chain and steps away.

As they enter, she's waddling ahead of them. They follow her into a lounge that would be spacious but for the size of the furniture and the quantity of decorations. Beaten copper trays and framed black and white photographs cover most of the walls. Taleb glimpses flash-lit scenes from evenings at La Girafe during the 1980s. He recognizes several of the faces. He's pleasantly surprised by the absence from the room of the parrot and wonders if the bird lacks his mistress's enthusiasm for game shows, one of which is playing, with the sound turned down, on the giant-screened television.

'What do you want?' Abderrahmane asks as she turns and faces them. She emits a weighty sigh as of some creature releasing its hold on life.

'We want to speak to Sami Bahlouli,' Hidouchi announces. She does so from the doorway, which she's blocking in order to control the exit route from the apartment.

'You should try El-Harrach prison,' Abderrahmane brazenly replies.

'He was released three weeks ago.'

'Was he?'

'I think you know he was, Razane,' says Taleb. 'Where is he? By which I mean . . . which room is he hiding in?'

'Which room?'

'Yes. Which room . . . in this apartment.'

'I don't—'

Abderrahmane's denial is cut short by the movement of a shadow from the doorway that leads into the next room. The bead curtain parts and Sami Bahlouli steps through it.

He's a shrunken, hollow-cheeked, patchily bald version of the

180

stylish nightclub crooner he once was, dressed in a shapeless tracksuit and grubby trainers. He's trembling slightly and his eyes are rheumy. He's missing several teeth as well, though whether through poor dental hygiene or falling out with one of his cellmates at El-Harrach is unclear. What is clear is that prison hasn't agreed with him.

'It's all right, Razane,' he says in a hoarse voice. 'You can stop pretending I'm not here.'

'Were you here earlier?' asks Hidouchi.

'Yes. I barely go out. I find the stairs . . . a strain.'

'Failure to come forward then could be deemed a breach of your parole.'

'I suppose anything could. If a DSS agent wanted it to be.'

'We have some questions for you,' says Taleb.

'Of course. Questions. The police always have those.'

'We have questions for you also,' Hidouchi says to Abderrahmane.

Abderrahmane flops down on to the low-slung sofa. 'I don't get a prize for answering them, do I?' she grumbles, gazing at the television.

'There's a penalty for not answering them.'

'There's a penalty for everything in this country.'

'Assisting Wassim Zarbi in his flight from the country was a criminal offence.'

'I didn't know he was planning to leave. And Sami was still in prison then, so you can't drag him into this. I said he could live here when he was released because he had nowhere else to go.'

'That won't be good enough for them, Razane,' sighs Bahlouli. He looks at Taleb. 'Will it, Superintendent?'

Taleb shakes his head. 'No. It won't.'

'Could we talk, you and I? Out on the balcony, perhaps?'

Abderrahmane beetles her brow. 'What are you planning to say to him, Sami?'

181

'Whatever will keep me out of prison. I don't owe Zarbi anything. Neither do you.'

'You owe me something.'

Bahlouli shrugs. 'Sorry.' He looks at Taleb. 'What about it?'

Taleb looks at Hidouchi. She nods. She doesn't like it – this hint by Bahlouli that it would be better for him and Taleb to resolve matters man to man. But, reluctantly, she accepts it.

Taleb follows Bahlouli through another room into the kitchen and then out on to the balcony, where the lights of the city twinkle beneath them. The air is sweet but heavy, the Algiers they look down on not so very different from the Algiers of their younger days. For all its travails, it has aged better than them.

'Do you have a cigarette, Superintendent?' Bahlouli asks. Out here, in the shadows, he looks slightly better, a little more like his old self.

'Sure.' Taleb gives him one of his Nassims and a light. Then he lights one for himself.

Bahlouli coughs as he inhales. As smokers' coughs go, it doesn't sound good. 'Razane won't let me smoke in the apartment. Though that doesn't stop her choking me with her joss sticks.'

'Do you still sing, Sami?' Taleb asks.

'What do you think?'

'They put you away for tax evasion. That surprised me.'

'It surprised me too. If anyone was evading tax, it was my accountant, not me.'

'You had a good voice. You released a few records, as I recall. You had some good years. More than most.'

'More than you?'

'You were riding high in eighty-eight, weren't you?'

'I suppose I was.'

'I was at La Girafe the night Zarbi took a swing at you for daring to sing "Une Chanson pour Guy".'

'That was just a stupid misunderstanding.'

'But you know what the misunderstanding was about, don't you? Did you know then?'

'Of course not. Razane suggested I should play that number. She said it was one of Zarbi's favourites. It was her idea of a joke. I had no idea she was setting me up. Do you seriously think I'd have deliberately antagonized someone as powerful as Zarbi?'

'Were you frightened of him?'

'Who wouldn't have been? He could have had me killed if he'd wanted to.'

'But he didn't. And all these years later you end up helping him get out of the country.'

'He didn't need my help.'

'Come on. Razane visited both of you in El-Harrach. Are you going to claim you never talked to him while you were there?'

'We talked.'

'Good. So, what about?'

'I can't go back there, Superintendent. I'm too old and too sick. I don't want to die in prison.'

'Tell me everything you know and you may not need to.'

'May not?'

'I can't give you any guarantees, Sami.'

'No. You can't, of course. You're only a policeman, after all. You don't make the really big decisions.'

'Are you going to tell me about Zarbi or do we have to have this conversation at Police Headquarters?'

Bahlouli has already finished his cigarette. He's been smoking much faster than Taleb. He steps across to the concrete parapet to stub it out, coughing phlegmily. 'Spare me another?' he gasps.

Taleb obliges. In the brief glow of the lighter, Bahlouli's shadow-wreathed face takes on a phantasmal appearance. He takes a spluttering puff on the cigarette.

'Remember how Zarbi was when he was part of le pouvoir,

Superintendent? Inflated, cocksure, arrogant? Well, twenty years in prison has sucked all that out of him. He understands now the horror of the system he was part of. And he's old, of course. Also sick. I met him in the prison hospital. His heart's giving out, like my lungs, only not quite so quickly. He was in the next bed to mine. We played backgammon and talked about the old times, his and mine. It's not for revenge he's gone after Laloul. It's for redemption.' Bahlouli senses Taleb's incredulity in the brief silence that follows. 'You don't have to believe me. You can find out for yourself. He wants to force Laloul to blow it all open.'

'Blow what open?'

'Le pouvoir. The world of the people who decide our fates.'

'How could Laloul do that?'

'I don't know. But Zarbi seems to think he can. He called him kiyal al-ma: the water-measurer. Does that mean anything to you?'

The water-measurer. The phrase brushes across Taleb's memory as if he has walked into a cobweb. It is a half-remembered rumour, more of a myth, really. He first heard of it shortly after his wife and daughter were killed, when his thoughts were so tortured he couldn't distinguish between logical probabilities and the most lurid of conspiracy theories. If almost every outrage during la décennie noire was a false flag operation or the work of agents provocateurs, then there had to be freelancers operating in considerable numbers, paid to do their grisly work and to keep quiet about it. But where did the money come from? And who distributed it? Who was their paymaster? Kiyal al-ma, it was whispered – the water-measurer, named after the local official who in Ottoman times supervised the allocation of water from Saharan oases. In 1990s Algeria, money had become the irrigator of existence, the determinant of who lived and who died, so it pleased some to believe there was a modern water-measurer who doled out the vital resource. Taleb's old boss, Superintendent

Meslem, had dismissed the idea. 'Le pouvoir is collective,' he had said. 'There are no individuals in control.' And so Taleb had eventually convinced himself. The water-measurer did not exist. But if he did . . .

'Have you nothing to say, Superintendent?' Bahlouli asks at last.

'What else did Zarbi tell you . . . about Laloul?'

'He didn't need to tell me anything else. I agreed to help him because I believed he might be able to pressurize Laloul into bringing the truth of all those blood-soaked years into the open. You said I was "riding high" back in eighty-eight and you were right. All I worried about then was whether those damned raï singers with their electronic backing groups would steal my audiences. But the Islamists stole their audiences as well as mine and soon I swapped singing for just . . . surviving. But was it really the Islamists who did that to me and many like me, Superintendent? Or was it le pouvoir all along?'

'How did you help Zarbi?'

'He knew Razane visited me regularly. He asked me to persuade her to visit him as well. This was last summer. Bouteflika had finally resigned and Zarbi had been told he was being seriously considered for parole. He wanted someone he could trust to contact an Englishman who'd—'

'Stephen Gray?'

'I never knew his name. And I never met him. He'd visited Zarbi some time before – I'm not sure when – with a scheme that would enable Zarbi to take revenge on Laloul. But Zarbi wasn't interested while he was in prison. It was only with his release looming that he wanted to take up the offer. And he needed Razane's help to contact this . . . Stephen Gray. Exactly what he asked her to do I don't know. She's never told me. But his flight from the country was obviously part of the plan. He's going after Laloul. And I for one wish him luck.'

'So, all you did was ask Razane to visit Zarbi?'

'Yes. That's all. A small thing, really. You're surely not going to arrest me for that.'

Taleb lights a second cigarette for himself and offers Bahlouli a third, which he accepts with apparent eagerness. 'What's wrong with your lungs, Sami?'

'Oh, cancer,' comes the casually phrased reply. 'Terminal, naturally.'

'I'm sorry.'

'Are you? I'm not sure I am. I can't see old age working out well for me. Or you, if I'm honest, Superintendent. You have family?'

'No.'

'There you are then. I bet a police pension won't fund a lavish lifestyle. Your future doesn't sound much brighter than mine, just longer.'

'Well, your immediate future's all I know about, Sami. You and Razane will both be coming to Police Headquarters with me when we leave here. I'm doing you a favour, really. If I don't take you in, Agent Hidouchi will. And you won't like how the DSS treats you.'

'I can't go back to El-Harrach. I told you that.'

'I'm afraid you may have to. I'll do my best for you, if you cooperate fully, but even so . . .'

'I hope Zarbi succeeds. You should hope for that too. Bring down the water-measurer, I say. Bring them all down. I'm with the demonstrators. Yatnahaw ga!'

That was the cry heard on the streets before coronavirus closed the protests down. 'Yatnahaw ga!' 'Get rid of them all!' Taleb believed – he still believes – such aspirations to be a delusion. You can never be rid of all of them. Le pouvoir is a self-replicating organism in the body politic of Algeria. 'You sound surprisingly idealistic, Sami.'

'That's the effect of imprisonment and terminal illness. I recommend them for clearing the mind.'

'Let's go inside now, shall we?'

'I'd rather not.'

'Well, I'm afraid I'm going to have to insist.'

'I used to be terribly nervous before singing in front of an audience. I was sometimes physically sick. You know what the problem was? The waiting. When you decide to do something, you shouldn't hesitate. That's the lesson. Just do it.'

'Very interesting. But—'

Bahlouli moves suddenly and at speed. He turns and lunges forwards over the parapet of the balcony, diving into the darkness that separates them from the lights of the city. Taleb makes a desperate grab to restrain him, manages to grab one of his ankles and is almost carried over the parapet with him.

'Let me go,' Bahlouli shouts, writhing as he dangles in Taleb's grasp. 'Let me go.'

The strain on Taleb's arms is more, he realizes, than he can bear for long. His teeth are clenched, the pain in his shoulder muscles is mounting and his hands seem to lack the strength to keep a tight grip on Bahlouli. Far below he can see, lit by the lights of lower apartments, the roofs of parked cars and the unforgiving weed-pocked concrete of a side street. And he knows Bahlouli can see that too. What is he thinking? Is he terrified now? Has Taleb forced upon him the very hesitation he claimed was so disastrous? Is he having second thoughts about what he's done?

'Hidouchi!' Taleb shouts. 'Hidouchi!'

It's no use. His words drift away into the night air. Bahlouli has stopped squirming. He's not moving at all now, just hanging beneath him. There's a wide split in the heel of his trainer. Taleb notices it as he feels his grip loosening.

'I can't hold you much longer,' Taleb shouts.

Bahlouli doesn't respond. Has he blacked out? Is he praying? Or is he just waiting for the moment they both know will soon come?

And then it does come. Taleb's fingers slip. And Bahlouli plummets away from him through the alternating stretches of darkness between the splashes of light from apartment windows.

Taleb steps back. Just before Bahlouli hits the concrete. But he hears the impact.

He looks down at his hands. And realizes he's still holding the split-heeled trainer. He sets it down carefully at his feet, then moves to the parapet.

He knows he has to look down. He has to see what has happened. He's a policeman. He can take nothing for granted. He has to see for himself.

FIFTEEN

SUZETTE CAN'T AT FIRST FIND ANY WORDS TO DESCRIBE HER reaction to reading her father's final words. It takes all her effort not to cry. She knows he had much to be ashamed of. He probably couldn't have saved Harriet, but he could have gone to the Paris police and helped them bring her murderers – and those of Guy Tournier – to book. But he would have suffered too, so he'd fled to Algeria. And once there he'd been sucked deeper and deeper into Zarbi's corrupt world.

It surprises Suzette that she can readily forgive Papa all the wrongs he did. He loved her and she still loves him. He wasn't strong enough to break free when it counted. That doesn't make him an evil man or a bad father. For some reason, she's more appalled by what she's discovered about her mother, who passed information to Laloul that led to a man's death yet has never once given the impression of having a guilty conscience. She's always implied Papa lacked determination, but now it seems to Suzette that what he actually lacked was ruthlessness. Whereas her mother . . .

'I'm sorry I wasn't honest with you about all this yesterday,' says Gray softly, leaning across the table between them as the train speeds through the deepening darkness of the Hampshire countryside. 'And I'm sorry you had to find out so much about your parents that you might have preferred not to know.'

'I don't blame you for anything, Stephen,' Suzette replies. There are no other passengers within earshot, but, even so, they speak in the low tones of people sharing disturbing secrets.

'I didn't feel I could tell you about my last visit to Algiers without telling you what it led to. And I needed Riad's agreement for that.'

'I understand that. What I don't understand is why you decided to travel there at such a dangerous time.'

'I'd better come clean with you. I never stopped looking for clues about what had happened to Harriet. Eventually, I tracked down a former scene-shifter at Tativille, who told me he'd seen Zarbi and another man he reckoned was also Algerian – Laloul, presumably – leaving a remote area of the site late one night in June of sixty-five carrying crowbars and shovels. He couldn't be sure, but he thought it was probably the night of the eighth. And the eighth was the last day Harriet was seen alive.'

'You think . . . they buried her there?'

Gray nods. 'I do. The area's under the Autoroute de l'Est now. No body was found when construction work began on the road, which was straight after filming finished, but that would have been a matter of chance. Parts of the site remained unexcavated. I'm sure that's where Harriet is. I'm also sure I'll never be able to prove it. It's just too late now. But I didn't think it was then. I wanted very badly to confront Nigel, to force him to admit what he'd done. Algeria was basically a no-go zone, but I contacted one of the guides from our Roman ruins tours and he put me in touch with a man who was willing to smuggle me across the border. Still, I hadn't appreciated just how much Algeria had changed since my previous visit. The lunatics had taken over the asylum. I realized as soon as I reached Annaba that I'd put myself in a whole load of danger, running the gauntlet of Islamist extremists with every move I made. I'd drunk quite a bit when I was arrested on the train to Algiers, it's true, but that was mostly to settle my nerves. Big mistake. Nigel was right about the policeman who questioned me. He was actually quite reasonable. But I was pretty soon taken off his hands by the DRS. And that's how I came to meet Zarbi.'

'You must have been terrified he'd have you killed.'

'I was. Those two days in DRS custody were the worst two days of my life. I already knew Zarbi was something senior in the organization, of course. He wore a ridiculously smart suit and had this air of swollen self-satisfaction about him that was actually more frightening than any strong-arm stuff. "Coming here was foolish, Mr Gray," he kept saying to me. "Very foolish." They didn't torture me, as I'd feared. In fact, they didn't lay a finger on me. But then they didn't need to. I never said what I believed Zarbi had done to my sister and he never said he'd known her in Paris, but the acknowledgement that he'd murdered her hung between us in that interrogation room. He'd murdered her and would never have to answer for it. It was as simple and as certain as that.

'I've wondered since: why did he let me go? Well, your father's confession goes some way to clearing that up. Zarbi told Nigel I'd revealed to him how much I knew about his role in Harriet's death – and Guy Tournier's – but that wasn't true. What was true was that Zarbi assured me that if I ever returned to Algeria he'd make sure I never left. And I believed him. When I got on that plane to Paris, I swore I'd never go back. I decided I had to abandon the search for the absolute truth of what happened to Harriet. She was nearly thirty years dead and it was time to let it go. Now she's been gone more than fifty. Yet strangely, here we are, still talking about her, still wondering where the consequences of her murder will eventually lead us.'

'Do you think Zarbi had my father killed?'

'It's more likely he was killed by the Islamists. But by forcing him to remain in Algiers, Zarbi and Laloul went a long way to guaranteeing he wouldn't survive.'

'And Saidi? You think he's Laloul?'

'Laloul. Or someone close to him. It was only his name that was altered in the version they sent you. As I see it, he has to be behind the offer you've been made.'

'Time I gave him my answer, then, I suppose.'

'What's that going to be?'

'I'm working on it.'

Suzette picks up her smartphone and begins an email to Coqblin & Baudouin. She's angry now, as well as sad. In particular, she's angry that these slick Swiss lawyers and their deep-pocketed client have tried to bribe her to deny that the confession her father wrote was actually written by him. In her present mood, that's not something she's willing to do.

The lights of Basingstoke appear as the words form on the screen in front of her. She nods as Gray indicates they should get ready to leave the train. 'I'm nearly done,' she says.

A few minutes later, they're off the train, making their way through the underpass to exit the station. 'I've decided,' she announces, as much to herself as to Gray.

'Was that your answer to Saidi?' he responds.

'Yes. I'm telling him I've reached a conclusion but I need to meet him face to face to explain it.'

Gray whistles. 'That's bold.'

'Not really. If Saidi really is Laloul, he'll refuse to meet me, won't he?'

'I imagine he will, yes.'

'Then at least we'll know who we're dealing with.'

It takes Taleb a couple of hours to deal with the immediate consequences of Bahlouli's suicide. He summons uniformed officers to seal off the scene. A pathologist who's known to him and can be relied on not to make a fuss arrives around the same time as the mortuary van. There's a delay in removing the body while they await a photographer, but otherwise all goes smoothly, at least beyond the confines of the apartment.

Abderrahmane receives the news with dry-eyed realism. It appears she foresaw some such move on her lodger's part. 'He was a dying man, Mouloud. You think he was going to let you put him back in prison?' Taleb denies he had any such intention, but she is dismissive. 'That's where he would have ended up. You know it. I know it. He knew it.'

She's rather less composed when he explains the need to take her in for questioning. 'I told you everything I could last time you were here. If you'd left it there, Sami would still be alive.' Taleb brushes the accusation off. He knows from the little Bahlouli told him that Abderrahmane hasn't revealed all she can. She will, though. With a little encouragement.

Much time and effort is then expended in persuading Abderrahmane's neighbour to take charge of the parrot, who squawks manically when Taleb carries his cage round to the next door flat. Taleb had hoped Hidouchi would agree to do that for him, but she seems annoyed with him and says little until they've seen Abderrahmane off in the police van and are standing by his car in the sallow light of the lamp above the entrance to the apartment building.

'Something on your mind, Agent Hidouchi?' he asks, as he works his way through another Nassim.

She looks at him narrowly. 'If we'd questioned Bahlouli together, this wouldn't have happened.'

'Maybe not.'

'You should have been between him and the parapet.'

'You're probably right. It never occurred to me he might jump.'

'Nothing in your long experience prepared you for such a possibility?'

193

'To be honest, no.'

She rolls her eyes. 'Incredible.'

'He told me everything he knew,' Taleb insists, knowing of course that he can't actually be sure of that. 'All he did was put Zarbi in touch with Abderrahmane.'

'Then I suggest we do what we should have done earlier. Squeeze the old bitch. Until we're certain she's keeping nothing back.'

'I agree. But we should leave it till the morning. Let her mull over her options. She'll be more cooperative after a night in one of our cells. Besides . . .'

'You're tired, Taleb? Is that the problem?'

'I am tired, yes. Since you ask.'

'I could question her on my own.'

'But you don't have the authority, Agent Hidouchi. She's in police custody.'

'That could change.'

'Aren't we supposed to be working together on this?'

'Yes. We are supposed to be.'

Taleb wonders for a moment if Hidouchi senses he's held something back in his account of what Bahlouli told him. On balance, he thinks not, even though, in fact, he has. He's made no mention of the water-measurer. Which in truth is partly to protect Hidouchi. He can't burden her with the knowledge that they might actually be on the track of one of le pouvoir's most important members – the one who could tell them who was paid, how much and for what, over all the years of the nation's worst trauma. She's too young. She has too much life ahead of her. It wouldn't be fair. But he's quite certain she wouldn't see it that way.

'If treating Abderrahmane gently doesn't produce results tomorrow morning, Taleb, I will take her off your hands.'

Hidouchi's statement sounds high-handed. But Taleb realizes it actually represents a concession to him. She may even have taken pity on him, which he's not sure he welcomes. He takes a last drag on his cigarette, flicks it into the gutter and nods. 'Understood.'

'Now you can drive me back to DSS HQ. Then we can both go home.'

Hidouchi seems happier with Taleb's driving style on the way back into the city centre. Either that, Taleb concludes, or she's simply resigned to it. She asks him again what Bahlouli told him and listens to his crucially edited version of their discussion without comment. Then she says, 'That tallies with the information I got from the DSS database on Stephen Gray. He's visited Algeria twice since Immigration digitized its records: in February of last year and again in March of this year.'

'So, deportation in ninety-three didn't block a visa being issued to him?'

'No. There's no record of his deportation then. Either because it didn't make it through the digitization process or because Zarbi never recorded it officially.'

'Is there anything else on him?'

'Just his place and date of birth, which we already know, and his current UK address.'

'Thinking of flying over to see him?'

'If necessary, yes. And you'll be flying with me.'

'I've never been to England.'

'And maybe you never will. It depends on what Abderrahmane tells us.'

'Did you get anything out of her while I was with Bahlouli?'

'I couldn't shut her up long enough to ask her any questions. She demanded to know why I wasn't married with children.'

'What did you say to that?'

'That she was a sexist dinosaur.'

'She's never been married herself. Though I think there might be a child somewhere.'

'So, hypocritical as well as sexist.'

'What else did she want to know about you?'

'My taste in music. When I said I'd never heard of Cheikha Rimitti, she started searching for one of her records to play me.'

'Ah, Rimitti,' says Taleb nostalgically. 'What a woman. Ben Bella banned her from the airwaves after independence for singing what he called "folklore perverted by colonialism". Did she find the record?'

'Yes. It was booming out when you came back in from the balcony. Otherwise I might have heard you calling for help. Don't you remember?'

Taleb honestly does not remember. He can only assume he was too shocked by Bahlouli's suicide to notice, which isn't something he wants to admit. 'Have you really never heard of Cheikha Rimitti, Agent Hidouchi?' he asks. It seems inconceivable to him that this could be true.

And it isn't. 'Of course I've heard of her,' Hidouchi snaps back. 'I just didn't want to discuss her with Abderrahmane. I certainly don't intend to tomorrow morning.'

'There's no need to worry about that,' says Taleb, half-regretfully. 'Music isn't allowed at Police Headquarters.'

Suzette has to concentrate hard during the drive back to Litster's Cot. Once they're out of Basingstoke, the lanes are high-hedged and inkily dark. As it is, Gray notices the light ahead of them before she does. 'What the hell's that?' he murmurs.

Looking ahead, Suzette sees a yellow glow beyond the crest of the hill they're climbing. Gray lowers his window and leans out. 'Jesus,' she hears him say.

'What's wrong?' she asks. Even as she does so, she catches the smell of burning that drifts in through the window and hears – or thinks she hears – a crackling in the distance.

'Something's on fire,' Gray replies. 'Just keep going.'

Suzette speeds up. They reach the crest. Round the next bend, they see, as if suspended in the surrounding darkness, a building ablaze, the roof engulfed, the windows filled with flame, smoke rising in thick, red-tinged clouds. The smell of the smoke is stronger now, the crackle of burning timbers louder. She brakes to a halt. She's not sure, but she thinks—

'That's Litster's Cot,' says Gray.

SIXTEEN

THE SUN IS WARM ON TALEB'S BACK, EVEN THOUGH IT'S SO EARLY IN the morning. A couple of fishermen are trying their luck on the harbour wall, but otherwise he has this finger of the city jutting out into the sea all to himself. He's soon to be joined, though, by the figure heading towards him at a determined pace – the bustling, portly figure of his boss, Farid Bouras.

Taleb has time to finish one cigarette and start another before Bouras reaches him. The Director is already sweating despite the earliness of the hour. It's hard to judge his mood without being able to see the look in his eyes, which are concealed by sunglasses, but his posture suggests he isn't happy, which is no surprise to Taleb. He didn't sound happy when Taleb spoke to him last night on the emergency-use-only mobile and it's unlikely he will have woken this morning suffused with optimism.

'Well, Taleb?' he begins, without preamble. 'What is it I need to know but doubtless would rather not?'

'The case has taken a disturbing turn, Director.'

'You've been working on it less than forty-eight hours. And I specifically instructed you not to do anything I wouldn't approve of, did I not?'

'You did. I assure you the disturbing turn was not of my making.'

'Is it related to the suicide of a suspect you were questioning last night – and the arrest of former nightclub proprietress Razane Abderrahmane?'

'It is.'

'The suspect was Sami Bahlouli?'

'Yes.'

'My mother will be saddened to hear of his death. She called him Algeria's Frank Sinatra. What shall I tell her? That one of my officers hounded him into jumping from the top floor balcony of an apartment block?'

'I'll be filing a full report on Bahlouli's death after questioning Abderrahmane, Director. I did not "hound" him. But something he said to me – which will not feature in my report – is why I felt obliged to contact you . . . as instructed in such circumstances.'

'This, then, is an extreme emergency?'

'Potentially, yes.'

'Which is why I find myself here, at this hour of the morning?'

'I thought you would prefer to discuss the subject out of the office and . . . face to face.'

'And what exactly is the subject, Taleb?'

There is no one within earshot, but nevertheless Taleb drops his voice as he replies. 'The water-measurer.'

Silence reigns for a moment. Bouras looks past Taleb, out to sea, where the sunlight sparkles on the gentle swell. Then he says quietly, 'Speak.'

'Bahlouli said Zarbi told him Laloul was the water-measurer.'

Bouras takes a deep breath and lets it out slowly. 'Are those Nassims you're smoking?'

'Yes, Director.'

'I'll have one anyway.'

199

Taleb proffers the pack. Bouras takes a cigarette. Taleb lights it for him. They start walking slowly along the breakwater, towards the lighthouse at the far end.

'Do you regard yourself as a lucky man, Taleb?' Bouras asks in a philosophical tone.

'No, Director, I don't.'

'Yet it's true, is it not, that you only survived the car bomb attack on our headquarters in 1995 because you turned back as you were leaving the building when you remembered you had left your beloved Nassims in your office?'

'It is true, yes.'

'And how many died in that explosion?'

'Forty-two, Director.'

'Which would have been forty-three, but for your addiction to smoking. An addiction which hasn't killed you yet. You sound lucky to me.'

'It is a question of perspective, Director. If I had died that day, my wife and daughter would not have had to leave Algiers because they were close relatives of a serving police officer. Then they would not have died in the massacre at my wife's home village. She would have a widow's pension to support her now, and grandchildren, I expect, to delight her. That would sound lucky to me.'

'Mmm. Well, you are right, of course. It is all a matter of perspective. And my perspective on the myth of the water-measurer is that since 2006 we have been specifically forbidden to inquire into such matters.'

Bouras is referring to the amnesties granted by Bouteflika's government covering most atrocities committed during the years of terror. He knows – and Taleb knows he knows – that this legalistic argument won't matter if the search for Laloul turns sour on them. 'I could not keep this development from you, Director. I do not welcome it. And I know you don't either.

The water-measurer a myth? Who can say? I learned long ago that what is unbelievable is often true in this country. If Laloul was more than just an embezzler – if he was a facilitator of some of the bloodiest unsolved murders in our history – then there will be many powerful people determined to prevent him speaking out, amnesty or no amnesty. And Bouteflika is gone. Can such people rely on the new administration as they did on the old?'

'We are police officers, Taleb, not politicians.'

'If you say so, Director.'

Bouras shoots him a glare. 'I cannot call off the pursuit of Zarbi or Laloul. I look to you to ensure it has no . . . wider ramifications.'

'I will do my best, Director.'

'The DSS must not hear of this . . . potential complication.'

'They will not, from me.'

'Agent Hidouchi knows nothing of what Bahlouli told you?'

'Nothing relating to the water-measurer.'

'But you are due to question Abderrahmane with her this morning.'

'I am.'

'What if Abderrahmane mentions the water-measurer?'

'I don't believe she'll do so willingly. Obviously, I won't encourage her to. And Agent Hidouchi is too young to know of such matters.'

They reach the lighthouse and walk round it to the end of the breakwater, where they stand gazing out towards the uncertain horizon. Bouras finishes his cigarette and pitches the butt into the water. 'You are treading a fine line, Taleb,' he says quietly.

This is neither praise nor condemnation, Taleb realizes. It is simply a statement of fact. 'Why was Zarbi released, Director?'

'He is old. He is sick. It was assumed he no longer posed any kind of threat.'

'I think that was a false assumption.'

'Well, I am happy we can agree about that.'

'I regret any . . . difficulty this may cause you.'

'Your regret gives me no comfort whatever. But I suppose . . . there is no one else I would prefer to be handling such a case.'

'Thank you, Director.'

'You have nothing to thank me for, Taleb. If this goes wrong, I will do everything in my power to avoid going down with you.'

'I quite understand that,' says Taleb unreproachfully, almost neutrally.

'Perhaps you were right.' Bouras takes a deep draught of sea air. 'Perhaps it would have been better if you hadn't gone back for your cigarettes.'

Wendy is roused by the sound of movement down in the kitchen. She hoped to sleep in after the disruption of last night, but the bedside clock tells her it's only just gone seven. Fortunately, Oliver is still sound asleep, so it has to be Stephen who's already up and about. She slides reluctantly out of bed.

Much was left unsaid last night in the general turmoil. She for one is still processing the implications of what has happened. Litster's Cot burnt to the ground; her father's remaining possessions destroyed in the fire. It was a shock when Stephen phoned late in the evening. The fire brigade were on the scene, but it was already clear nothing was going to be salvaged.

Stephen's car, parked next to the house, was burnt out as well. He wasn't there when the fire started and claims to have no idea what caused it. 'The electrics, maybe' is the only suggestion he's come up with so far. 'They were always dodgy.' Which, as it happens, is news to Wendy.

Stephen, it appears, travelled to London earlier in the day, with Suzette Fontaine. What took them up to town together hasn't been explained. Suzette drove him over after his phone call, before heading back to her hotel. The fire seemed to have had more of an impact on her than on Stephen, which was odd. 'Such a terrible thing,' she kept saying, lapsing into the French pronunciation of terrible, as if stress had undermined her mastery of English, though why a fire in which no one was injured destroying a house she had no personal connection with should seem so very terrible to her also went unexplained. Yet there was no doubt it had affected her deeply. 'My God, I never expected anything like that.'

Stephen appeared keen Suzette should leave as soon as she dropped him off. 'Go and get some rest. Thanks for everything. We'll talk in the morning.' He kept repeating himself until she drove away.

For the hour or so they remained up after Suzette's departure, Stephen lamented the loss of his clothes, his computer and his car and the futility of all the work he had done on the house, while emphasizing too often for Wendy's suspicions not to be aroused that it was all just a dreadful accident.

Wendy never liked Litster's Cot, or its remote location, so her sense of loss is focused on the family keepsakes that have been destroyed: photographs, pictures, ornaments and the like. She would never have imagined how hard it is to adjust to the knowledge of just how many small, apparently inconsequential things she associates with her father she'll never see again. He had some snaps of them all as children that are gone now. It's another flaking away of the memory of Harriet as well as her parents.

She and Stephen agreed last night that they'd drive over this morning to see what was left of the cottage, although Stephen's already warned her it'll just be the walls. She feels she's about as well prepared for the scene that will greet them as she can be. But she's not ready to set off yet and heads down to the kitchen intent on making that clear to him.

She finds Stephen seated fully dressed at the table, most of the way through a bowl of cornflakes. He looks up as she enters and gives her a rumpled smile. 'Hi,' he says. 'Sorry if I woke you.'

'Trouble sleeping?'

'Took me a long time to get off. I guess I was more shaken up than I thought.'

'I'm not surprised. You want some coffee?'

'Please.'

He finishes the cornflakes while she's brewing the coffee and carries the empty bowl to the sink. 'I'm sorry about all of this, Wendy,' he says wearily.

'It's not your fault.'

'No, but . . . an unexpected guest is the last thing you need.'

'I can't quite believe the cottage isn't still there.'

'You'll believe it when you see it. We really should have had the place rewired. I suppose it's a blessing this didn't happen while Dad was still alive.'

'You think an electrical fault is what caused the fire?'

'What else could it be?' He sounds faintly defensive on the point.

'I don't know. Youths messing about.'

'What youths? I haven't see any.'

'What exactly did the fire brigade say?'

'That it was too soon to know. They'll be back later. We'll have to contact the insurance company, of course.'

Wendy pours the coffee. 'Why did you go to London yesterday with Suzette?' she asks as she takes a first sip.

'I thought she ought to meet Riad Nedjar. Hear what he makes of her father's memoir.'

'The man who used to work for Nigel Dalby and now runs a shop in Soho?'

'That's him.'

'So, he's already read the memoir? Before me?'

'Ah . . .' Stephen looks sheepish. 'It turns out he's had a copy for years.'

'What?'

'Look, it's . . . complicated.'

'When am I going to see this memoir, Stephen?' She looks at him sternly.

'Ah, I'll have to . . . get another copy from Suzette. She dropped one off to me yesterday, but of course it . . . went up with everything else.'

Stephen's evasiveness where Nigel Dalby's memoir is concerned is becoming palpable. He's hiding something, possibly a lot of somethings. Wendy doesn't believe an electrical fault caused the fire. And she doesn't believe local hooligans were responsible either. But that only leaves more questions to trouble her. And one in particular that she doesn't dare to put to her brother. What did he hide in their garage yesterday?

Stephen has already finished his coffee. He sets the mug down. 'I'm thinking of going up to Litster's now,' he announces.

'I'm not ready,' Wendy objects. 'I need a shower. And I have to give Oliver his breakfast.'

'Actually, I thought I'd walk. It's a fine morning.'

'You're going to walk all that way?'

'I need some air, Wendy. You can join me when you're done here.' He smiles, hoping no doubt to reassure her. Which he utterly fails to do. 'There's no hurry.'

Suzette paces her room at Tylney Hall, turning over in her mind the choices that confront her. She slept badly, unable to stop thinking about what the fire at Litster's Cot means. An electrical fault, as Gray desperately suggested? She doesn't believe that for a moment. And she doubts he does either. It's just too big a coincidence that this should follow her reluctance to give Monsieur Saidi what he obviously wants.

What troubles her even more than the suspicion that burning down the cottage is intended as a warning is the thought that she's been followed to England. It's hard to see otherwise how anyone could have made the connection with Litster's Cot. But, if that's true, then they know she's staying at Tylney Hall as well. And probably that she and Gray went to see Nedjar yesterday. They know altogether too much for her to feel remotely safe.

Which makes her wonder if she should have sent the email to Coqblin & Baudouin after all.

There was something comfortingly theoretical about her discussions with Gray and Nedjar. Laloul's record as a dangerous man is undeniable, but somehow it never occurred to her he could still be dangerous – to her, in the here and now. But staring at the smoke and flames that consumed Litster's Cot last night changed everything. She suddenly realized her misgivings about saying her father could ever have written *J'avoue* counted for very little compared with ensuring her safety – and that of her children.

Thinking about Timothée and Élodie only alarmed her further. If Laloul could have her followed to England, he's quite capable of discovering her children's whereabouts. She texted them both early this morning and has so far received an answer only from Élodie, who's continuing to enjoy her holiday on Mykonos in carefree fashion. Timothée hasn't responded. That isn't surprising in itself, considering how badly they've been getting on recently. But Suzette's finding it difficult to convince herself there's nothing more to be made of his silence.

She goes into the bathroom and douches her face with cold water. She clasps the rim of the basin and stares at herself in the mirror. The strain she's under is apparent in the hollowness of her eyes. This can't go on. That much is obvious. She's starting to believe things are actually worse than they really are. Timothée and Élodie aren't in any danger. Nor is she, if she follows the line of least resistance. That's all she has to do.

The decision is made. She'll go and see Stephen Gray. They'll talk this through until the nonsense about electrical faults is stripped away and they can reach an agreement about what has to be done, like it or not, to let them both get on with their lives safely and securely. It's the only course of action open to them. And the sooner they embark on it the better.

Taleb reaches Police HQ with about forty minutes to spare before he and Hidouchi are due to question Abderrahmane. He checks with Slimani on the desk that all is well with the prisoner, as indeed it is, which is a relief but no great surprise: Abderrahmane is made of sterner stuff than Bahlouli. Then he heads down to Archives, where the lugubrious Azzi greets him with an unfounded complaint that he left the records in chaos after his visit of the previous afternoon.

This Taleb ignores. He literally has no time to waste arguing with Azzi. He's interested only in seeing whatever the files hold on the murder of Nigel Dalby, proprietor of Le Chélifère bookshop, and Azzi, much as he'd like to, can't stop him.

His search reveals that Dalby was shot through the head on the balcony of his apartment some time on Monday 21 February 1994. His body was discovered late that afternoon by his former employee at the bookshop, Riad Nedjar, who regularly delivered food and supplies to him. Ballistic evidence suggested a rifle shot from a neighbouring apartment block. The investigating officer was a notorious slacker called Djillali, who concluded it was probably an Islamist killing, despite the fact that a murder such as this required planning, patience and precision, none of which was the norm for Islamist groups in those days. The question Taleb would have asked was why anyone should have gone to such lengths to kill Dalby. And he finds himself asking the question still, twenty-six years later.

'You're going to put that file back properly, aren't you?' shouts

Azzi from his desk. 'I don't like having to clear up after you and your DSS houri.'

Taleb doesn't give Azzi the encouragement of a reply. He jots down Riad Nedjar's address as it was in 1994 with no great optimism that he'll still be living there and closes the file. He already doubts Dalby was murdered by Islamists. Even in Djillali's slap-dash account it reads more like a professional hit. Ordered by Zarbi, maybe? It's possible Nedjar knows.

Taleb returns the file to the shelf and sets off for the door, determinedly avoiding Azzi's gaze. Still he says nothing. He's actually quite proud of his self-restraint.

'They tell me you lost a suspect last night, Taleb. Did he fall? Or did you push him to save—'

The door closes. And Taleb starts up the stairs, relieved he has to hear no more. Until the next time.

'Delightful though it is to be served breakfast in bed,' says Oliver as he sits up, 'I think I'm beginning to feel equal to eating it down in the kitchen.'

'That's really good news,' says Wendy. She smiles broadly and sets the tray down on the bedside table, then kisses him on the forehead.

'You haven't brought any coffee for yourself?' Oliver asks as he picks up his glass of orange juice.

'No. I have to be off shortly.'

Oliver sighs. 'Ah yes. Litster's Cot. It's not going to be a pretty sight. Stephen's impatient to leave, I imagine.'

'Actually, he's already gone.'

'He has?'

'Yes. On foot. I'll drive him back, obviously.'

'Do you want me to come with you?'

'No, no. There's no need for that.'

He gives her a concerned frown. 'It could be quite a shock for you, Wen.'

'It'll be a blackened, smoking ruin,' she says briskly. 'I'm prepared for that.'

'Are you sure?'

'Don't worry, darling. I'll cope.'

'As you always do. By the way, was there something wrong with the wiring?' Oliver seems to have placed more reliance on Stephen's theory than she has. 'Did your father ever report any problems?'

'Not that I can recall. But that'll be for the insurance company to work out. I must dash.'

'I'll see you later, then.'

Wendy reaches the doorway, where she pauses and looks back at her husband. 'I'm sorry my brother keeps complicating our lives, darling, really I am.'

'It's not your fault, Wen.' Oliver smiles. 'It's not really his either.'

Not Stephen's fault? Wendy isn't sure. Oliver doesn't know about the box he stowed in their garage yesterday. She decided not to worry him with the information. But she knows. And she can't help suspecting a connection with the fire, though what the connection might be she can't imagine.

A few minutes later, she calls a goodbye to Oliver up the stairs and heads out to the garage. She opens the door, climbs into the Subaru and starts up.

At that moment her eye is taken once again by the box Stephen added to one of the piles of his boxed-up possessions. She'd like very much to open it and see what's inside, but she knows she can't do that without his discovering it's been tampered with, because he's written his name across the tape sealing the lid.

Suddenly, an idea occurs to her that appeals to her instantly, so much so that she acts on it without further thought. Stephen would be justified in reproaching her if she opened the box without his permission, but if the box opened accidentally – if it opened itself, as it were – that would be a different matter.

She engages forward rather than reverse and presses down on the accelerator.

The car nudges into the stacks of boxes, dislodging several of them, including the one she's interested in, which lands on the floor with a heavy thump.

Wendy turns off the engine and jumps out. The box is lying on its side, but is annoyingly intact, though the contents – whatever they are – have pushed out a bulge in the lid. The tape is still holding it closed. But that doesn't trouble her. It'll be easy to claim it didn't hold when she explains what happened. She crouches by the box and prises the tape free, releasing one flap of the lid and pulling it down flat with the floor.

Some sheets of paper, some covered with type, some blank, slide out. Something else, dark and metallic, is wedged inside the box. Wendy yanks it out, unconcerned for niceties now.

It's an old manual Olivetti typewriter. How old Wendy wouldn't like to say. It looks to her as if it dates from the middle of the previous century. And it's had a lot of use, judging by the chips to the paintwork and some of the keys. She's never seen it before. It certainly didn't belong to her father.

A shadow falls across her as she crouches by the box, holding the typewriter in her hands. She looks round and sees Suzette Fontaine standing a few feet away.

'I called, but you didn't hear,' Suzette explains. 'I'm—' Then she stops. And stares in obvious amazement at the typewriter.

'What's wrong?' asks Wendy, standing up slowly, still holding the typewriter.

'Mon Dieu,' Suzette gasps. 'La machine à écrire.'

210

'You look like you've seen a ghost.' For once this is literally true. That's exactly how Suzette looks. Like she's seen a ghost.

'The typewriter.' Suzette points a wavering finger at the machine.

'Yes? What about it?'

'It's my father's.'

SEVENTEEN

THE WALLS OF LITSTER'S COT STILL STAND, BLACKENED AND BATTERED. But the rest of the cottage and its contents are a jumble of sodden ashes. It's hard to distinguish between roof trusses, floorboards, carpets and furniture. The larger objects – oven, fridge, washing machine – are carbonized hulks. The smell of smoke still hangs in the air. The garden is a scorched blank, the bushes and shrubs reduced to stumps, the oak tree a skeleton, the wrought-iron table and chairs standing so thin that the slightest touch would surely see them crumble to dust.

Gray walks solemnly round the taped-off perimeter of the property, passing at one corner the tiles he had yet to put on the roof, coated in soot. He doesn't know what the fire brigade are ultimately going to determine as the cause of the blaze, but he hasn't much doubt in his own mind that it wasn't an accident, or the work of local youths. He wonders whether, if he sifted through the debris, he'd find his laptop anywhere, or whether that was removed by those who did this.

He walks back out to the lane past the wreck of his car and leans against the bank on the opposite side. A few branch-ends on the tree above him are burnt, but otherwise the damage is confined to Litster's Cot itself. And there the damage amounts to complete destruction.

Laloul must have had Suzette followed when she travelled here from France, he reasons. It was what he feared as soon as she turned up, though there was nothing he could do then to deflect the threat. They must have waited until the cottage was empty before breaking in under cover of darkness. What were they looking for? The typewriter? The original of the confession? Well, at least they didn't find either of those. And Gray took extreme care when he drove to Wendy and Oliver's yesterday to ensure no one was tailing him.

He was worried at first about a physical attack. He supposes he should be grateful, in a way, that they preferred to strike when he wasn't there. He needs to alert Nedjar to what's happened, of course. He knows he does. He hasn't quite brought himself to do so yet, largely because Nedjar warned him moving against Laloul was dangerous. But he can't delay much longer. When his phone pings, he wonders if it might be him. Then he realizes it's his A phone, as he calls it, not his B phone – the one Nedjar insisted he buy and use exclusively for communications between them and with Zarbi's intermediary.

As he pulls the phone out of his pocket, he sees the message-received alert. A message from Wendy, maybe, telling him she's set off. No. It's from an unknown number. That instantly troubles him. He opens it.

And sees only an array of Arabic characters: وعش الآن توقف

That troubles him even more. He needs to speak to Nedjar, no question about it.

He swaps phones and makes the call.

No reply. Gray curses silently and leaves a voicemail message. He can do nothing now. Except wait.

Oliver enters the kitchen to find Wendy sitting at the table, staring bemusedly at Suzette Fontaine, who's sitting opposite her.

213

On the table between them stands an old and somewhat battered manual typewriter and a strew of sheets of paper, some typed on, some blank.

Neither of them reacts to his arrival at first. Then Wendy looks up at him. 'Oh, darling, there you are,' she says. 'You remember Suzette?'

'Of course.'

'Hello again,' says Suzette, nodding to him. She sounds slightly dazed.

'What's going on?' he asks, pointing to the table.

'You should sit down,' says Wendy. 'This has been . . . quite a shock.'

Oliver's worried now. Since his illness, he finds he craves tranquillity. Shocks have never been less welcome.

'Why don't you explain, Suzette?' Wendy asks, looking towards her. 'I think I'd like to hear it again myself anyway.'

'I am sorry for it all,' Suzette says quietly, her eyes downcast. She picks at a thread on the sleeve of her top.

'We're past that,' says Wendy, reaching out and patting her on the wrist. 'Just tell Oliver what you know.'

'Yes.' Suzette sighs. 'I will.' She swallows hard and begins. 'My father wrote a memoir he called "J'avoue" during his last months alone in Algiers. In it he confessed to involvement in the murder in Paris of a presidential aide, Guy Tournier, while he and Harriet were working at Tativille in the spring of 1965. The murder was carried out by two Algerians, Wassim Zarbi and Nadir Laloul, in revenge for Tournier's part in a massacre of Algerian demonstrators in Paris in 1961. Papa witnessed that massacre, which is what led him to help them. Zarbi also worked at Tativille. That's how they met. Harriet discovered what they'd done and told Zarbi she'd go to the police unless he left Paris straight away. He was a hardened FLN fighter: the last man she should have threatened in such a way. He killed her. Or Laloul did. Or both of them. I am sorry, but that is how her life ended. He and Laloul disposed of her body and took Papa back to Algeria with them. And so . . .'

She sighs again. 'He never left. He ran a bookshop. He married my mother. I was born. Zarbi became something big in the Sécurité Militaire. He used Papa as an informant about members of the intelligentsia who bought books from him. It is not a happy story. Not much from those days in Algeria is. Stephen visited him several times, looking for information about what had happened to Harriet. Papa did his best to block his investigations. Eventually, after Stephen's visit in 1993, Zarbi decided – I think – to have Papa killed. And that is what happened, early in 1994.'

She falls silent. 'Tell Oliver about the confession, Suzette,' Wendy prompts her. 'Explain how it reached you.'

'A man calling himself Saidi contacted me recently through a firm of Swiss lawyers, claiming the confession had been discovered hidden in our old apartment in Algiers. He wanted me to say, based on an extract he sent me, whether I thought it was genuine before exploring the possibility of having it published as some kind of . . . document of the period. That is why I came to see Stephen. To ask his opinion before I gave an answer. But I didn't understand what was really going on. I didn't understand that this was all . . . part of a battle.'

Oliver frowns at her. 'A battle?'

'I believe Saidi is actually Nadir Laloul. He left Algeria in 1999 with a fortune embezzled from the national oil and gas company. Zarbi was arrested and imprisoned for corruption shortly afterwards. He was given a thirty-year sentence. I don't know whether he's been released or not. But I believe Stephen found out where Laloul has been living and sent him a copy of the confession in order to . . . I'm not exactly sure . . . blackmail him, I guess, into admitting the truth about Harriet's murder.'

215

'So, Stephen . . . knew all about this before you contacted him?'

'Yes. He and Riad Nedjar, who used to work for Papa and now runs a shop in London. Stephen took me to see him yesterday. He gave me a complete copy of the confession: a carbon copy, entrusted to him by Papa. That showed Laloul's name had been changed to Haddad in the extract Saidi sent me. Saidi is also Laloul, of course. That seems obvious. He altered his name to Haddad in the extract to conceal his role in Harriet's death. His lawyers offered me money – a lot of it – if I would say the confession was a fake. I guess that would mean it couldn't be used to blackmail him. And I guess Stephen and Riad showed me the carbon copy so I'd be convinced it really was Papa's work and would be less inclined to . . . take the money. It worked. But now . . .'

'Now what?'

'This is my father's typewriter, Oliver. And these papers . . . are the original confession. Hidden in your garage yesterday by Stephen, Wendy tells me.'

'I didn't want to worry you, darling.' Wendy smiles apologetically at him. 'He didn't come here to look for something. He came to hide something. I think Suzette's visit made him question whether it was safe to keep the typewriter and the confession at Litster's Cot.'

'Good God.' A terrible thought has struck Oliver. 'Does this have something to do with the fire?'

'It's possible.'

'Then his damned stirring up of trouble may have put us in danger as well.'

'I hope not,' says Suzette. 'But there is something more you need to know.'

'More?'

'When I look at these pages . . . I wonder if they were really all written by my father.'

'What are you suggesting?'

'These are the last three pages.' Suzette slides three sheets of paper across the table to him.

Oliver looks. And sees nothing extraordinary.

'And here are the three pages before those.'

There's an obvious difference. The print is considerably fainter. Though to Oliver's mind there's an obvious – and innocent – explanation for that. 'Well, it looks as if your father simply changed the ribbon.'

'Why would he? It was still printing quite well.'

'I don't know. But—'

'I think Stephen typed the last three pages. Using a new ribbon. The one in the machine had probably rotted over the years, so he had to buy a new one. Because he wanted to rewrite those pages. He wanted to alter them.'

'Why?'

'To make Laloul's guilt more obvious, maybe. If the confession is authentic, which basically it is – I have no doubt about that – no one will question the highly incriminating little speech Papa quotes Laloul giving close to the end. You'll see what I mean when you read it. He reveals far more than he needs to about how the corruption he was involved in worked. I think they added that to put more pressure on him. If I'm right, they created new carbon copies as well.'

'They?'

'Riad Nedjar must have gone along with it. He denied knowing what happened to the typewriter. But I think he kept it, along with the top copy and the carbon copy of Papa's confession. That's how Stephen got hold of them. Riad probably still has the original last few pages. I think he'll admit that when I confront him.'

'We should confront Stephen first,' says Wendy. 'If he really has been involved in trying to blackmail this man Laloul . . .'

'Yes?' Oliver looks at her, silently reminding her of the many allowances she's made for her brother over the years. 'What are we going to do if he really has?'

Wendy sighs. 'I don't know. It's appalling. It's worse than I ever imagined. But he's waiting for me at Litster's Cot. And he has no idea we've found this. So . . .'

'We should go there now,' says Suzette. 'I don't want him to have the chance to make up some other story. I want the truth this time.'

Wendy nods. 'So do I.' And with that she stands up. The decision, it seems clear to Oliver, has been taken.

Gray has fallen into a gloomy reverie when his phone rings, making him jump. He nearly drops it while trying to answer.

'Stephen?' It's Nedjar's voice.

'Riad. Thanks for calling back.'

'Your message said it was urgent.'

'Well, I'm looking at the burnt-out remains of my home. I think that makes it urgent.'

'There's been a fire?'

'The cottage has been gutted. Everything's gone.'

'Everything?'

'If you mean the confession, no, I moved that elsewhere. Just in time, as it turned out.'

He can hear Nedjar sigh. 'When did this happen?'

'While we were with you last night.'

'So, they waited for the cottage to be empty.'

'Apparently so. Do you reckon I should be grateful for that?'

'You have no reason to think the fire could have . . . started accidentally?'

'It wasn't accidental. You know that. I know that. It was a message.'

'Like when they set fire to Le Chélifère. That was a message also. I warned you, Stephen, that going after Laloul was danger-ous. He's a clever man.'

Gray rubs his forehead. 'How closely do you think I'm being watched?'

'Maybe not so close as you fear. He would not have men he could send personally to this country to handle something like this. It would be contracted to people in London who would know none of the details. I guess they judged burning the cottage down was the likeliest way to destroy the evidence and make you stop without . . .'

'Without what?'

'Without killing anyone.'

The word killing sinks into Gray's psyche. Nedjar waits while it does its work. Eventually, Gray says, 'Laloul may have told me exactly what he wants from me.'

'How so?'

'I received a text message earlier on my other phone from an unidentified caller. It's a phrase in Arabic. Can I send it to you? I don't know anyone else who can read Arabic.'

'And you would be unwise to ask them to translate it if you did. Yes. Send it.'

Wendy sets off for what's left of Litster's Cot with Suzette follow-ing in her own car. They both have good reason to be angry with Stephen. He's put them in danger thanks to his crazy attempt to extort the truth out of one of Harriet's murderers. Wendy has lived for fifty-five years without knowing how and why her sister died and could happily have gone on doing so. The truth her brother has sought for so long is now little more than a historical curiosity. Weighed against her welfare and Oliver's and that of Suzette and her family it simply doesn't matter. She's quite certain Harriet would agree with her on that. Stephen has, as usual, put the service of his obsessions beyond everything – and everyone – else. It's the

219

story of his life. But she's determined it's not going to be the story of hers.

Stephen is going to call off his campaign. She and Suzette are going to insist on it. Nigel Dalby's confession is back where Stephen hid it, in her garage, along with the typewriter. If they offer to send the original, albeit doctored, confession – along with the carbon copy now in Suzette's possession – to Laloul's Swiss lawyers, the whole terrible thing will surely go away. There will be nothing left to contest. And nothing for Laloul or Saidi or whatever he wants to call himself to fear. Then the truth – and Harriet – will be laid to rest.

Wendy intends to extract Stephen's consent to this course of action. But she intends to do it even without his consent. It's actually, as far as she and Suzette can see, the only sane thing to do. And since they have the original and the carbon copy, there will be nothing he can do to stop them. For once, Wendy is going to lay down the law to her brother.

As she should have done a long time ago.

Gray's phone rings.

'"Stop now and live,"' Nedjar says without preamble. 'That is what the message says, Stephen.'

Gray swears silently. 'Much as you surmised.'

'I do not enjoy being proved right, my friend. Laloul could not have accomplished what he has in this world without being cunning as well as ruthless.'

'Why send the message in Arabic? He must know I can't read the language.'

'That was the point. You had to ask me to translate it. As he calculated you would. So, I receive the message also. Two birds, one stone.'

'How did he get my phone number?'

'Such things are not as difficult as you would like to believe. It's possible he hacked Suzette's phone.'

220

'I suppose you think I should do as he demands: stop.'

'Do you have a choice?'

'Zarbi won't give up.'

'How can he continue without the original of the confession?'

'Who says he won't have it? Maybe I could hand it all over to him and step out of the picture.'

'Maybe you should have done that right at the start.'

'But then I'd have no say in what happens to Laloul.'

'Haven't you just lost your say? Listen to me, Stephen. If you leave Laloul alone, he will leave you alone. That is really what his message means. "Stop now and live." So why not do that? Stop. And live a life that doesn't involve chasing your sister's ghost. Find some peace. It's worth more in the end than any portion of revenge. Believe me, you will not win this now.'

EIGHTEEN

HQ when Hidouchi arrives. She is in the process of concluding a telephone conversation and, after signalling for Taleb to bear with her, prowls in a slow circle, doing much more listening than speaking. Taleb wonders if it's her boss on the line.

Sergeant Slimani, meanwhile, slouched behind the reception desk, ogles Hidouchi whenever her back is turned to him. And winks at Taleb when he catches his eye. Taleb doesn't wink back.

The telephone conversation ends. The impression floats in and out of Taleb's mind that Hidouchi is troubled by what she has heard, though she composes herself so swiftly he can't be sure he hasn't imagined it. 'Your prisoner is still alive, I hope, Taleb,' she says by way of opening pleasantry.

Slimani chuckles. Taleb does his best to ignore him. 'Last time I checked, Agent Hidouchi, Razane Abderrahmane was still breathing, despite eating one of our breakfasts.'

'Shall we go and talk to her, then?'

'Certainly. This way.'

They set off.

'I checked the files on Nigel Dalby's murder earlier,' Taleb

222

informs her. 'It looked more like a professional hit than your average Islamist slaying. I have an address for his bookshop assistant, Riad Nedjar, who was a frequent visitor to his apartment. He may know something.'

'This is a current address?'

'No. But it's all I have on him.'

'Perhaps Abderrahmane will give us more.'

'Perhaps.'

'You won't allow her to swat away questions as you did yesterday, will you?'

'Is that what you think I did?'

'You and I need to make progress with this case, Taleb. That is what I think.'

She is clearly not happy. Taleb reckons the telephone conversation probably was with her boss. And he reckons her boss isn't happy either. Which is something he and she have in common.

They reach interrogation room three. It's small and grimly painted in battleship grey. But at least there are no hooks in the ceiling.

Razane Abderrahmane, clad in the oversized olive-toned shift dress and matching turban she insisted on donning before leaving her apartment the night before, sits at the table in the middle of the room. She greets their arrival with a scowl. The policewoman in attendance looks relieved to see them.

'Ah,' Abderrahmane croaks. 'The tortoise and the gazelle.'

There are chairs drawn up ready for their use: standard issue tubular steel and plastic. Taleb sits down on one of them. Hidouchi remains standing. She clasps the back of her chair and rests her weight on it, raising its front two feet from the floor.

There's a recording device on the table. Taleb switches it on and introduces himself and Hidouchi for the record. 'Questioning of Razane Abderrahmane commences at' – he glances at the clock on the wall – 'zero nine hours and zero eight minutes, Wednesday July twenty-second, 2020.'

'Can I have a cigarette?' drawls Abderrahmane.

'Can we have some information?' Hidouchi responds.

'I told you everything I know yesterday.'

'My conversation with Sami Bahlouli suggested otherwise,' says Taleb.

'You must have misunderstood. It's a pity you can't ask him to clear up the confusion.'

'He agreed to help Zarbi take revenge on Laloul when he came out of prison. Specifically, he agreed to persuade you to visit Zarbi so that he could ask you to contact an Englishman called Stephen Gray on his behalf.'

'Is that what Sami said?'

'Do you deny it?'

Abderrahmane shrugs massively. 'It's my word against a dead man's.'

'But a dead man you liked and took in as a lodger when he was released. You surely aren't going to tell me you think he lied to me.'

'There are white lies and black lies and many shades of grey between. You know the rules of life in Algeria as well as I do, Mouloud. The absolute truth is a suicide note.'

'Well, Sami did commit suicide, didn't he?'

'Did he? I wasn't there when it happened.'

'We know the Englishman's name, Razane. Stephen Frederick Gray. And we know he accused Zarbi and Laloul of assassinating a French presidential aide in Paris in 1965. What we don't know is how that explains his apparent cooperation with Zarbi in the revenge plot against Laloul that Bahlouli told me about. As their go-between, however, you should be able to enlighten us.'

'You're asking the wrong person. If Wassim had any dealings

with the Englishman you say is called Gray, it would have been through his lawyer, Ibrahim Boukhatem. Have you questioned him, Mouloud? Or is he too well connected for you to risk making an enemy of him?'

'He is currently out of the country.'

'Lucky man.'

'You spoke longingly of going to live in Sardinia yesterday,' Hidouchi cuts in. 'You obviously have little regard for your country.'

Abderrahmane looks contemptuously at her. 'It has little regard for me.'

'Why did you help Zarbi? You have already admitted smuggling Gray into his villa, which you must have realized was a breach of his parole. And Bahlouli's statements to Superintendent Taleb indicate your help went well beyond that. So, why take such risks?'

'What is life without a few risks?'

'Safer and more secure. For you . . . and your son.'

Abderrahmane's face drops. The colour drains from her cheeks. Taleb has difficulty disguising his surprise. Her son? What is it Hidouchi knows that he doesn't?

'Born August fifth, 1979. Registered surname at birth later altered from Abderrahmane to Aberkane. Forename Zakaria. Father not identified. But you were the mother. And the choice of Zakaria as a forename hints at Zarbi as the father.'

Of course. It's obvious to Taleb now Hidouchi has said it. The rumoured child was Abderrahmane's . . . and Zarbi's. That is why she helped him. Bahlouli's motive was to strike at le pouvoir. Abderrahmane, on the other hand, was rendering assistance to the father of her son.

'Do you admit Zarbi is Zakaria's father?' Hidouchi presses.

Fear and anger squirm beneath Abderrahmane's features like some subcutaneous creature. 'No,' she says.

'It does not matter. We know it is so.'

We? Taleb assumes Hidouchi is referring to the DSS, rather than herself and her hapless police co-investigator. Still, on one level he is relieved. It is less likely now he will need to step in to prevent Abderrahmane mentioning the water-measurer. Hidouchi's revelation will surely have cowed her sufficiently.

And so it seems. 'Give me a cigarette, Mouloud.' She looks sorrowfully at him. 'Please. For the sake of old times.'

Taleb relents. There is an ashtray tucked behind the recorder. He slides it out into a position halfway between them and lights two cigarettes, one for Abderrahmane, one for himself.

'A child is a woman's greatest strength,' she laments through her first puff. 'And also her greatest weakness.'

'Where is he?' Taleb asks gently.

'She knows.' Abderrahmane jerks her head towards Hidouchi, who walks slowly round her chair and sits down beside Taleb.

'Egypt,' Hidouchi says, coolly and quietly. 'He is the manager of a hotel in Sharm el Sheikh.'

'You see?' Abderrahmane smiles mirthlessly. 'The DSS knows everything, Mouloud. You know . . . as much as they allow you to.'

The situation, Taleb knows, is more complicated than that. But he is in no position to argue. 'Did you raise the boy yourself?' he asks, guessing not.

'My mother looked after him. I was busy getting into the nightclub business.'

'Did Zarbi set you up at La Girafe?'

'He helped. Not as much as he should have, though. And it was always a loan from him, never a gift.'

'Did you hope he'd marry you?'

'I was never that naive.'

No. Taleb doesn't suppose she was. 'You never visited him in prison before Bahlouli passed on his message?'

226

'We lost touch after I was forced to close La Girafe. He went on paying for Zakaria's education, though. After he was arrested, I thought it was safer for Zakaria if I stayed away from him.'

'But you responded to the message.'

'Bahlouli told me how ill he'd been. I have a soft heart.' She permits herself a twitch of a smile.

'And you agreed to help him . . . why? Simply because he is the father of your son?'

'You make that sound like a bad reason.'

'Just tell us what you did for him,' says Hidouchi.

'And if I don't?'

'Relations with Egypt are good. A request for the repatriation of an Algerian citizen would almost certainly be granted.'

'Zakaria is a good boy.' The boy, Taleb reflects, is actually a forty-year-old man. 'He deserves to be left alone.'

'Then make sure he is.'

Abderrahmane takes several long draws on the cigarette while they wait for her to acknowledge the invidiousness of her position. Eventually, she begins talking, slowly and almost expressionlessly. 'Stephen Gray has a memoir written by a man called Nigel Dalby. He used to run a bookshop here in Algiers – Le Chélifère. The memoir gives details of how Zarbi and Laloul murdered an aide to de Gaulle, Guy Tournier, in Paris in 1965. Dalby helped them. The murder was ordered by Boumediene, to undermine the Ben Bella government. The French have always wanted to catch the people who killed Tournier. Our new leader wants to improve relations with France. So, identifying the killers would be useful to him. Wassim knows where Laloul is hiding and he's threatening to hand over the memoir. It would take them both down, which he's willing to risk. He doesn't have much to lose. But Laloul has a luxurious life to lose, funded by the money he stole from Sonatrach. No one is seriously looking for him. I'm not sure they ever were under

Bouteflika. But with the French on his trail, it would be a different matter. Wassim is betting he will pay a lot of money to keep him and Gray quiet.'

'It comes down to blackmail, then,' Taleb says.

Abderrahmane shrugs. 'Call it what you like.'

'How did the memoir end up in Gray's possession?'

'I don't know. But he had dealings with Dalby. And he's English, like Dalby. There must be some connection.'

'What exactly did Zarbi want you to do?'

'Contact Gray. Tell him to make preparations for using the memoir against Laloul as soon as Wassim was released.'

'So, they'd already discussed the idea?'

'Gray had visited Wassim some months earlier.'

'The prison have no record of such a visit,' Hidouchi intervenes.

'Sami told me Gray came in with Wassim's lawyer, posing as his clerk.'

'Incredible,' Hidouchi sighs.

'Why didn't Zarbi use Boukhatem for further contact with Gray?' Taleb asks.

'The lawyer started to suspect the DSS were tapping his phone. Maybe some of Wassim's old colleagues started to get nervous when they heard he was going to be released.'

'Why should they be nervous?' asks Hidouchi.

Abderrahmane gives her a scornful glance. 'Why do you think? Anyway, Wassim needed a go-between unknown to the authorities. When he discovered Sami knew me, I went to the top of his very short list of candidates.'

'And how were you supposed to contact Gray?' Taleb asks.

'Through Dalby's former assistant at the bookshop, Riad Nedjar. He runs a deli. In London.'

Taleb raises an eyebrow. 'Sounds like he's done well for himself.'

'Some people do, Mouloud. Others just . . . moulder. Can I have another cigarette?'

Silently, Taleb hands one over and lights it for her.

'So,' says Hidouchi, 'you called Nedjar, he called Gray, Gray called you and you took the message to Zarbi, then passed his response back. Correct?'

Abderrahmane savours her cigarette for a moment, then nods in confirmation.

'How many messages were exchanged?'

'Two or three. They were never about the details of what they planned to do. They only discussed those face to face, when Gray came to Algiers.'

'And you smuggled him into Zarbi's villa – but never heard a word of what they said?'

Abderrahmane smiles. 'I didn't want to hear. Wassim told me the less I knew the safer I was.'

Hidouchi smiles back at her. 'Look how that's turned out.'

'He wasn't trying to protect me from the likes of you.'

'Who, then?'

'Use your imagination. You have one, don't you? Or is that trained out of you at the DSS? Mouloud here, he has imagination. He knows who I mean.'

Taleb does know. But he has no intention of pursuing the subject. 'Where is Zarbi now, Razane?'

'I don't know. Marseille would be my guess. He has connections there.'

'Marseille is a big city.'

'So they tell me.'

'What about Gray? Do you have a number for him?'

'I never called him. He called me. If I needed to speak to him, I called Nedjar.'

'So, you have a number for Nedjar?'

229

'Yes. But he has a website for his deli. He isn't hard to find. Even for you.'

'Do you think trying to antagonize us is a good idea?' asks Hidouchi.

Abderrahmane leans her head back and sends a column of cigarette smoke towards the ceiling. 'A girl has to have some fun.'

'We'll need all the numbers you have. Including for your son.'

'They're on my phone. Which you confiscated. But there isn't a number for Wassim on it. And Zakaria won't have one for him either. Wassim cannot be called. He can only be hunted. And he's ex-DRS, remember. The people who trained you were trained by him. Ask yourself what your chances are of finding him.'

'You can let us worry about that.'

'I intend to.'

'You shouldn't have agreed to contact Gray for him, Razane,' Taleb observes mildly.

'You're probably right. The problem is . . . I loved him once. I don't any more. But the memory of love is . . . hard to shake off. Am I going to be sent to prison because of that?'

'I'm afraid so.'

Abderrahmane nods bleakly. 'If only my mother was still alive. She always said getting mixed up with him would end badly. And she always liked to be proved right.'

The policewoman handcuffs Abderrahmane and leads her out of the room, bound for her cell. Taleb ends the recording and takes the disc out of the machine.

'I'll need a copy of that,' says Hidouchi.

'Of course.'

'I'm sorry I didn't warn you beforehand that I had information on her son.'

Taleb looks at her curiously. Why didn't she tell him? He isn't going to ask. After all, he hasn't told her everything he knows. 'Where did you get the information from?'

'A DRS file on Zarbi I wouldn't normally have access to. Under Toufik everyone, however senior, was vetted for blackmail vulnerability. Zakaria Aberkane is what they found on Zarbi. I went into the system and turned up Abderrahmane's name on his birth registration. The father's name was unrecorded. But the intelligence was clear. He's Zarbi's son. I should actually thank you. I'd never have thought to look if you hadn't told me there was a rumour she had a child.'

'Well, I'm glad I was some help.'

'There just wasn't time to explain all of that before we started questioning her.'

'Right.'

'We did well, though, didn't we? We have a trail to follow. I think you and I may be going to London, Taleb.'

'I'll have to report to my boss on these developments, Agent Hidouchi. I can't say what he'll decide we should do.'

'He'll liaise with my boss, Taleb, who I will have briefed myself. But Nedjar should be our first target, don't you think? He can lead us to Gray. And then . . .'

'You sound confident. That's a good thing to be.'

'But you're not?'

'I'm cautious. As Abderrahmane said, Zarbi isn't going to be easy to find. And neither is Laloul.'

Hidouchi treats him to a rare smile. 'My confidence and your caution should get the job done, Taleb. I have a good feeling about this.'

Her smile is magnificent. He basks for a moment in its radiance. It makes him wish he could believe her. And he's going to try to. He really is.

NINETEEN

STEPHEN GRAY HEARS THE CARS COMING BEFORE HE SEES THEM. Then they appear, nosing along the narrow lane. Wendy is in the lead in her Subaru, with Suzette following in her Renault. He wasn't expecting to see Suzette so soon and assumes she showed up, looking for him, before Wendy set off. Which only makes the situation more delicate. What is he going to say to them?

As they climb out of their cars, he senses tension even before he notices their tight, drawn expressions. Something's wrong. Something's already wrong, of course. But this is something else. This is more.

'What a terrible sight,' says Wendy glumly, turning to confront the blackened wreckage of Litster's Cot.

'I'm afraid it is,' he agrees.

'But it's your fault,' she says, looking straight at him as he approaches her. 'Isn't it, Stephen?'

'I'm not sure I—'

'We know what you hid in the box in the garage.'

'Box?' The ground feels as if it's opened beneath him.

'The one you put there yesterday morning.'

'Saidi – Laloul – doesn't have the original of my father's

232

confession,' says Suzette, moving to Wendy's elbow. 'You had it all along. I think you're trying to blackmail him with it. And I think this fire is the answer he's given you.'

'How could you be so stupidly reckless, Stephen?' Wendy demands. 'You may have put us all in danger.'

He looks from Wendy to Suzette and back again. He has no immediate response to offer them. If they've looked in the box, they know the truth – or at least the essence of it. He transferred the box to Wendy's garage because he feared what Suzette's arrival portended. About that he was right. But the precaution he took has led only to this moment of exposure. He's been caught in more lies than he can count. 'You don't understand,' he says haltingly. It sounds inadequate even to him.

'Help us understand.' Wendy spreads her hands. 'Explain how you got us into this situation. And why.'

'You wanted revenge for Harriet's murder,' says Suzette. 'Was that it?'

'I suppose . . .' He can hardly deny it. 'Yes. That's basically what it was all for.'

'Oh, Stephen.' Wendy's look of profound disappointment is somehow worse to confront than her anger. 'You surely can't believe Harriet would want you to waste your life seeking justice for her more than fifty years after her death.'

'Well, if you know what's in the box, Wendy, then presumably you know who killed her and why. Which is more than you knew yesterday.' He's regained a little composure now – a little strength of mind. 'Isn't that worth something?'

'It's not worth this.' Wendy waves an arm towards the ruins of the cottage. 'And it's not worth us having to live in fear of what Laloul might do next.'

'His argument is with me, not you.'

'Does he know that?' Suzette snaps. 'He may think I'm in league with you.'

'Why would he? You obligingly led him straight to me. Without your journey here he'd never have realized I might be the source of the confession. Then the plan would have worked.'

'And what was the plan?'

'To make him suffer for what he did to Harriet.'

'By blackmailing him?'

'You can call it that if you want.'

'How much are you demanding?'

'It doesn't matter. The money's not really the point. The point is forcing him to pay enough to hurt – really hurt.'

'And Riad's helping you do this?'

'Don't blame him. It was my idea, not his.'

'But he supplied you with the confession?'

'No. He only had the typewriter, which he'd kept as a memento. I found the confession. The original and the carbon copy. Hidden in your old apartment in Algiers. Riad told me he'd seen your father typing it, but there was no sign of it after his death. I reckoned it had to be there somewhere. And I was right.'

'Where? Where exactly did you find it?'

'In a void under the boards at the base of one of the kitchen cupboards.' He recalls the elation he felt when he discovered the hiding place. He didn't know what he would do with Dalby's confession. But he knew finding it was his biggest achievement in his long struggle to bring the truth to light.

She lets out a sigh of exasperation. 'How did you get access to the apartment?'

Stephen hesitates. He's not sure how much of this story he wants to tell. It all goes back so far and strays into so many areas of his life he's conditioned himself to keep secret. Besides, a full explanation would require him to admit his collaboration with Zarbi. And to account for that he'd have to go back to his interrogation by him at DRS HQ in Algiers in 1993.

He remembers the stale, sweaty air in the room where the slick young lawyer Zarbi had supplied came to him: Ibrahim Boukhatem. 'There will be no record of your deportation, Monsieur Gray, and therefore no report to the French or British authorities. That's a good deal for you. That's a very good deal.' He took the deal, but still he didn't dare return to Algeria until Laloul had fled the country and Zarbi was in prison, even after Riad piqued his curiosity with tales of the memoir Nigel Dalby had written before his death. The occupant of the apartment was a tetchy recluse who couldn't be induced to give Stephen access. So he hired Boukhatem to solve the problem. It took a long time and a ridiculously large payment to the tetchy recluse, but in the end Stephen was able to search the apartment. And find the confession.

He could only use it against Laloul if he could find him, of course. And the only person likely to be able to do that was Zarbi. True, he was as guilty as Laloul where Harriet's murder was concerned, but he'd suffered and Laloul hadn't. And Stephen couldn't get to Laloul without his help. So, with Boukhatem's assistance, he paid Zarbi an incognito visit and outlined his idea. Zarbi wasn't interested until and unless he got out of prison and could benefit from the blackmail plot. Yes, he wanted revenge too, but he also wanted money – as much as he could get. Bouteflika's hold on power was faltering by then. Zarbi was optimistic that under new leadership he'd be paroled. Then they could go after Laloul. He would send word to Nedjar when the time was ripe.

'Are you going to tell us how you were able to search the apartment?' Suzette presses.

He looks at her. Where to begin? Where to end? He suspects it will make no difference. 'It doesn't matter how I got into the apartment,' he says at last. 'The fact is I did. And the fact is I found your father's confession. You'd have preferred me to do nothing with it, I suppose.'

'I would have preferred you to give it to me. As his daughter, it rightfully belongs to me.'

'Does it?'

'Obviously it does, Stephen,' says Wendy. Her gaze is full of reproach.

'And you altered part of the confession, didn't you?' says Suzette. 'The last three pages are new. Written by you, I assume.'

What was bad has now become worse. The alterations Stephen made at Zarbi's insistence to Dalby's account of his last meeting with him and Laloul have always troubled him. He sensed he was being used to send a coded message to Laloul from Zarbi. 'He who measures the water weighs the gold.' What did that mean? Surely something beyond the merely figurative. But Stephen doesn't know. So all he can do is deny that he altered anything. 'I don't know what you're talking about. The confession is as I found it.'

'I don't think that's true.'

'Are you calling me a liar?'

The question hangs between them as a dare. Is she going to come out and say yes, he is lying? If she does, neither will have anywhere left to turn.

'There's no sense throwing words like that around,' says Wendy, seeking to find a middle path.

Then Stephen's phone rings. He answers it eagerly, grateful for the interruption, though the caller is unidentified. 'Hello?'

'Stephen Gray?'

'Speaking.'

'Detective Constable Foulds here, Hampshire Police. I've received a fire service report about a suspicious fire at your property, Litster's Cot. Extensive damage, apparently.'

'It was completely gutted.'

'Well, I'm sorry to hear that. This happened while you were away from the property?'

'Yes. I came back to find the blaze well under way.'

Stephen notices Suzette checking her phone as he speaks to Foulds. He wonders about the email she sent to Laloul's lawyers last night. Last night? It seems much longer ago. He reckons she must wish now she hadn't sent it. Has she had an answer yet? And if she has . . .

'I'm at Litster's Cot now, as a matter of fact,' he continues. 'What's left of it.'

'Oh, you're there, are you? Perhaps I could come and take a look. Can you hold on for half an hour?'

'Well, I . . . suppose so.'

'There's been a spate of farm thefts and acts of vandalism over the past month. If this was arson, it would be a worrying escalation.'

Suzette's talking to Wendy. Stephen can't catch what they're saying, especially not with Foulds jabbering in his ear.

'Have you seen anyone suspicious hanging around the area lately, Mr Gray?'

'No, I don't think so. Look, officer, could we talk about this when you get here?'

To Stephen's dismay, Suzette is walking smartly towards her car. 'Hold on,' he calls, which confuses Foulds but gets no response from Suzette. She climbs into the Renault and starts up.

'See you in half an hour,' Stephen gabbles into the phone before ending the call. 'What's going on?' he asks Wendy.

She shrugs. 'Suzette's decided to leave. She told me she didn't think we were getting anywhere. And I have to say I agree with her.'

Suzette pulls out into the lane, then reverses into the entrance to the cottage in order to turn round. Stephen rushes across to stop her. They haven't said all there is to be said. Most important of all, they haven't agreed what they're going to do next.

'Wait, Suzette,' he shouts. But she pays him no heed. All he manages to do is thump the front passenger window as she swings out into the lane.

He runs a few paces after her. But the car speeds away. And vanishes round the next bend.

Only when Wendy speaks does he realize she's standing right behind him. 'I don't think I'm ever going to be able to forgive you for this, Stephen,' she says, quietly but firmly.

He turns and looks at her. 'I've found out who killed Harriet and why. You should be grateful.'

'But somehow I'm not. Why do you think that is?'

'Because the truth about Harriet doesn't matter as much to you as it does to me, I suppose.'

'You've turned looking for that truth into a substitute for leading a normal, fulfilled life.'

'Making Laloul pay for what he did is fulfilment enough for me.'

'And to hell with Suzette? To hell with Oliver and me?'

'I never intended to involve any of you.'

'You never intended. Well, bully for you. You've always had the best of intentions. And the worst of outcomes. It's just bad luck, I suppose. Our bad luck.'

'Look, I'm sorry if—'

'You being sorry doesn't make any difference. We are where we are. In a mess. Of your making.'

'You shouldn't have opened the box.'

'It was on my property. I have the right to know what risks you're running that might involve me. So does Suzette. And she's right. Her father's confession belongs to her, not you. And she can do whatever she likes with it.'

'Has she told you what she plans to do?'

'I think she's going to phone the Swiss lawyers and come to some arrangement that gets us all – you included – out of the

238

hole you've dug us into. It's certainly what I hope she does. But it's her decision, not mine. And definitely not yours.'

'You don't think she might . . . hand the confession over to them?'

'Possibly.'

'But that would wreck everything I've achieved.'

'And what exactly is it that you've achieved, Stephen – apart from antagonizing a dangerous old man?'

'For God's sake, Wendy, we're talking about one of the men who murdered our sister.'

'Fifty-five years ago, Stephen. Fifty-five years. You were ten. The Harriet you think you remember never really existed anyway. And your fixation on her memory wrecked your marriage and quite a lot else besides. You need to let her go.'

'Well, I'm not going to.'

'I'm not sure Suzette will give you any choice in the matter.'

'We need to go after her. Right now.'

'Didn't you just make some kind of appointment? Who was that on the phone? The police?'

'Yes, but that doesn't matter. I can call him and reschedule while we're on the road.'

'I'm not going anywhere. I'll wait here with you and we'll speak to the officer together. The cottage belonged to me as well as you, after all.'

'Call Oliver, then. Tell him not to let Suzette take the box away until I've spoken to her.'

'I'm not going to tell him any such thing. The contents of the box are rightfully hers.'

'I'll call him if you won't.' Stephen pulls his phone out of his pocket.

'I don't want Oliver upset. And he won't take any notice of you anyway. He agrees with me. It's for Suzette to decide what to do with her father's confession.'

'Where does that leave me?'

'In the wrong.' Wendy stares hard at him. 'You're my brother and I love you. But this has to stop. This has to stop now.'

Stephen stalks away along the lane. He punches a number into his phone. Then he pulls up and cancels the call. Wendy's right. Oliver won't intervene. If Suzette plans to remove the box, there's nothing he can do to prevent it. Then she'll have the original of the confession as well as the carbon copy. And if she delivers them both to Coqblin & Baudouin, there'll be nothing to black-mail Laloul with. The game will be up.

He looks back at Wendy. He can't find anything to say to her. She spreads her arms in a gesture of exasperation. He shakes his head. He raises his arm, the palm of his hand towards her, as if pushing her physically away.

Then he turns and starts walking.

TWENTY

BOURAS EXPRESSES CAUTIOUS SATISFACTION AT THE OUTCOME OF Taleb and Hidouchi's interrogation of Abderrahmane. This extends to asking his secretary to arrange a coffee for Taleb when she serves the Director his, which her reaction suggests is a rare honour for a mere superintendent. It does not spare him a comfortless perch on the slippery leather sofa, but he appreciates the gesture nonetheless.

'So, nothing was said about . . . the matter we discussed earlier?' Bouras comes close to winking conspiratorially at Taleb.

'No, Director. Abderrahmane and Zarbi are former lovers and he is the father of her child. That appears to account completely for her agreement to help him.'

'And this child . . .'

'Manages a hotel in Egypt, apparently.'

'Hidouchi proposes to pursue the matter by going after . . . what was his name?'

'Riad Nedjar.'

'Yes. Nedjar. Settled in London?'

Taleb nods. 'He is.'

'Well, if a trip to London can't be avoided, you'll have to go. I

241

shall press for the DSS to cover your costs. You'll have no official status. Arranging formal recognition with the British would take too long and raise more questions than we would wish to answer. So, you will maintain as low a profile as possible. Understood?'

'Yes, Director.'

'You've done well so far.' Bouras sips his coffee and beams at Taleb. 'I rely on you to keep it up. I'm not necessarily expecting you to deliver Zarbi and Laloul in chains. In fact, a conclusion that causes no . . . controversy . . . is more important than bringing them to justice, however gratifying that might be. Is that clear?'

'Absolutely, Director.'

'No doubt I'll hear soon enough from my opposite number at the DSS. Until then—'

Bouras's telephone rings, the tone signifying it is his secretary on the line from the adjoining room. He frowns and picks up the receiver.

'Yes?' The frown remains in place as he listens. Taleb can just detect the secretary's voice, transformed at this distance into a whine like that of a distant mosquito. 'I see.' The mosquito continues. 'Yes. Thank you.' Bouras rings off.

'Abderrahmane wants to speak to you, Taleb,' he announces. 'Evidently she did not say all she wanted to say when you and Hidouchi questioned her. I'm told she's most . . . insistent. I think you'd better go and hear what she has to say, don't you? But be careful. We require no complications – no amended testimonies – at this stage.'

'I'll see what she wants.'

'Do that. And whatever it is . . . make sure it doesn't cause us a problem.'

'The avoidance of problems is my guiding purpose in life, Director.'

Bouras eyes him suspiciously. 'A sense of humour is not necessarily desirable in a police officer, Taleb. Your sense of humour is of course so dry it can easily be missed. As we will agree to pretend it has been on this occasion. Now, go and deal with the Abderrahmane woman. Preferably in a way I don't need to hear about.'

Stephen Gray reaches Wendy and Oliver's house hot, weary and depressed. The long walk from Litster's Cot has given him plenty of time to turn over in his mind the mistakes he's made. He doesn't know what to do now. Telling Zarbi their blackmail plot may just have collapsed around their ears isn't something he's either ready or willing to contemplate. But what alternative does he have?

Oliver greets him with the news he's feared and foreseen. Suzette has been and gone, taking with her the box containing her father's confession and the typewriter he wrote it on. Stephen reacts with a resigned shrug. 'I thought she would have,' is all he manages to say.

'Wen called and gave me the gist of what happened up at the cottage,' Oliver goes on, choosing his words with palpable care. He clearly doesn't want to be caught up in a rerun of the argument Wendy's already had with Stephen. He could level his own complaints about his brother-in-law's conduct. But he isn't about to. 'A DC Foulds turned up at her end while we were talking. She told me to tell you she's got that covered.'

'Good,' mumbles Stephen. He's even less sure of what to do now than of what to say.

'There's a message for you from Suzette as well.'

'Oh yeah?'

'She wants you to call her. She should be back at her hotel by now.'

'She wants me to call her?'

'It's what she asked me to tell you, Stephen. What you do about it is up to you.'

'OK. Thanks. Look . . .' He considers Nedjar's warning that Laloul may have hacked Suzette's phone. 'My mobile's lost its charge. Can I use your landline?'

'Be my guest,' Oliver sighs, stalking away and leaving Stephen to find his own way to the kitchen.

He closes the door behind him and uses his mobile to find the number for Tylney Hall before calling it on the landline.

The hotel receptionist puts him through to Suzette's room. She answers straight away. She's obviously been expecting to hear from him. But not quite like this. 'Stephen? Why are you using the hotel number?'

'I'm not sure your mobile is secure.'

'Why do you say that?' She sounds worried by the thought.

But he can't answer her question properly without mentioning the text message in Arabic, which he has no intention of doing. 'I have a suspicious nature,' he replies. 'You should certainly choose your words carefully when you use your mobile, though.'

'OK. I . . .'

'What did you want to say to me?'

'Well . . . All right.' She pauses. 'What my father wrote belongs to me, Stephen, not you, morally as well as legally. You should have told me the truth when I came to you seeking your help. I'm going back to France tonight. I don't know what I'm going to do about Laloul – Saidi. His lawyers have been lying to me, obviously. But what I'm going to say to them . . . I'm not sure. I'll think about it. I'll make a decision. That's all you need to know.'

'Will you tell me what the decision is . . . when you make it?'

'Maybe. I'm not sure about that either.'

'Don't just hand the confession over to them, Suzette. Please. You're right. I should have told you the truth. But I was afraid you'd do . . . something like what you are doing. Don't give Laloul what he wants.'

'Still hoping to blackmail him, are you?'

'Blackmail was never the point. You know that.'

'How did you find him, Stephen? How did you track him down?'

Is this the moment to tell her about his deal with Zarbi? He wants to. But something holds him back. She's taken the confession. All that leaves him with are a few secrets he doesn't have to share. 'Finding Laloul certainly wasn't easy. It took me a long time. Don't let all my efforts go to waste. I'm begging you. He wrecked your father's life and he ended my sister's. He doesn't deserve to be let off the hook.'

'It's the hook I'm on that bothers me.'

'Well, whatever you do, be careful. I'm trying to reason with you. Laloul won't. He'll just act in what he sees as his best interests.'

'I know that. And I know you had every right to seek justice for your sister. But not like this. Not this way.'

'We could have talked this through, Suzette. We could have come to an agreement on . . . what to do.'

'Maybe. But you made that impossible by deceiving me. So I'm afraid . . . I'm going to deal with this on my own. And you'll just have to accept that. Goodbye, Stephen.'

The line goes dead. Stephen holds the phone in his hand for several long moments before replacing it in its cradle. He can't decide what to do or where to go. He can't see, in fact, what the immediate future might hold for him.

As he heads out of the kitchen and makes for the front door, Oliver shuffles into view in the drawing room doorway. 'How did that go?' he asks.

'It went.'

'Where are you going now?'

'For a walk.'

'Haven't you done enough walking for one morning?'

'Apparently not.'

The clammy fetor of Abderrahmane's ill-ventilated cell comes as a shock after the air-conditioned splendour of the Director's office. For once Taleb's glad he's wearing a mask.

245

Abderrahmane appears resigned to her situation, smiling wearily up at him from the narrow bed on which she's slumped. 'So,' she says with the ghost of a smile, 'you came.'

'What can I do for you, Razane?'

'Drop all charges?'

'Not my decision.'

'But if it were?'

'I'd offer to go easy on you in exchange for detailed information that led us to Zarbi. That's your best option anyway. It's Zarbi we want. And Laloul. You've just . . . come up in the net. Maybe we'll throw you back if you can land us the bigger fish.'

Abderrahmane sighs heavily. 'Like I told you, I think Wassim is in Marseille. But I've no information about his contacts there. Your DSS girlfriend probably knows more about them than I do. On the other hand, Wassim isn't really your problem, is he, Mouloud? Not your biggest problem. That would be Nadir Laloul.' She stares meaningfully at Taleb. 'You know what I mean, I think.'

'We are looking for both of them,' he responds, disingenuously, for there's little doubt in his mind what Abderrahmane is hinting at.

'We could not speak of him and his . . . importance . . . when Agent Hidouchi was with us, could we? But now, here, Mouloud, we can deal frankly.'

'Can we?'

'Sami told you, didn't he? What Laloul was – before he fled. So you know who you're chasing. And the danger that puts you in. Le pouvoir is watching you.'

'I doubt I'm of any interest to le pouvoir.'

Taleb is unconvinced by his words. And clearly so is Abderrahmane. 'I can help you, Mouloud,' she whispers.

'You can help me?'

'We can help each other. I am too old to go to prison. And you are outmatched by your enemies. So, we do a deal. You protect me. I protect you.'

'How do you propose to protect me, Razane?'

'By tipping the odds in your favour . . . just a little. By giving you . . . something to bargain with.'

'And what might that be?'

'Will you do me a favour, Mouloud?'

'It depends what it is.'

'Well, I am worried. About Barbarossa.'

Barbarossa, Taleb recalls from the chaos of the previous evening, is the name of Abderrahmane's parrot. 'Your neighbour is looking after him. I think he is probably more comfortably accommodated than you are.'

'Houda Ghanem has no understanding of parrots. He will not be happy with her. He will not thrive.'

'Then I suppose he will have to do as the rest of us do: simply survive.'

'I forgot to give Houda Barbarossa's favourite seed mix. I keep it for those times when he needs rousing from depression.' The bird had not struck Taleb as being prone to depression, but he lets the point pass. 'Can you go to my apartment and fetch the box, Mouloud? Take it in to Houda and explain she should give Barbarossa a scoop of it every other evening until I return.' The improbability of Barbarossa seeing her again soon Taleb also disregards. 'You will need to borrow my key from her, of course.'

'We have your key, Razane.'

Abderrahmane reaches up and grasps Taleb's wrist. 'Use Houda's spare, Mouloud. Then there will be nothing . . . official . . . to record your visit.'

'Why should that concern me?'

'I store the box flat on top of the cupboards facing the window in the kitchen. That way Barbarossa cannot see it from his cage and start demanding to be given some.'

'Why don't we just phone . . . Houda . . . and ask her to fetch it herself?'

'You forbade her to enter my apartment when you took me away.'

It's a good point, which Taleb has to concede. 'So we did.'

'Also, she suffers from vertigo. You will need to use the step-ladder I keep in the cupboard near the front door to reach the box. Houda could easily break her neck trying to do that. Then somebody else – such as you – would have to look after Barba-rossa. So, will you do it?'

He will, of course, but not out of concern for the wretched bird that tried only last night to amputate one of his fingers. Whatever Abderrahmane is sending him to her apartment for, it isn't a box of mixed seed.

'Le Perroquet au Paradis.'

'What?'

'That's the brand. Printed on the box.'

'I see.'

'Open it, won't you?'

'Is it important I open it?'

She nods emphatically, but says nothing.

'Then I will.'

She lets go of him, swings her legs off the floor and lies full length on the bed. 'Why do flies fly only in straight lines, Mouloud?'

'Do they?'

'The one I'm watching now does. See him up there?'

Taleb looks up and sees the fly in question, tracing a series of aimless but undeniably sharp-angled diagonals close to the ceiling. 'It's a good question. I don't know. Do you?'

'Because they don't live long. You have to live as long as you and me to realize there are no straight lines in this world. Only circles so wide it takes years – many years – to understand that what you thought you were escaping . . . you're actually heading towards. All the time, without knowing it. I have to stay here. You can leave. But which of us is actually the freer?'

'You're full of good questions today, Razane. I don't know the answer to that one either.'

But in truth he does know. As far as freedom goes, there is very little between them. In every sense bar the physical fact of Abderrahmane's detention, they are both prisoners – of the past, theirs and Algeria's; of the choices they've made and the choices others have made for them; of the stark historical realities that govern their lives and the lives of everyone around them. They both know this. Even though they can't help behaving as if they don't.

Gray sits at a table in the sun outside the Bell Inn, Odiham, working his way steadily through a second pint of beer while the outline of the disaster that has overtaken him grows marginally more blurred – and more bearable.

When his phone – his B phone – rings, it is for the third time since he arrived at the pub and for the third time it is of course Riad Nedjar. He feels ready to speak to his friend now. He feels equal to describing what has happened and debating what might happen next. And he knows he cannot put off the discussion much longer. It has to be faced. He answers the call.

'Hi, Riad.'

'You sound sorrowful, Stephen.'

'Well, I am.'

'What has happened?'

'Suzette and my sister Wendy have both denounced me for lying to them and putting them in danger. Suzette has taken possession of the original of her father's confession and is going back to France with it. Along with the carbon copy we gave her, of course. Which leaves me empty-handed. Oh, and homeless, by the way, just to fill my cup of joy to overflowing.'

'It couldn't be much worse, then.'

'No. I don't think it could.'

'The confession rightfully belongs to Suzette. I always said that.'

'Yes, you did. And I can't argue with you. Or with her. Altogether, there's nothing I can do about any of it.'

'But what is she going to do?'

'I don't know. I don't think she knows either.'

'You've been unlucky, Stephen. I did not foresee Laloul would try to bribe Suzette to say the confession was a fake. Because she came to you for help, he realized you might be Zarbi's source. He would never have thought of you otherwise, I am sure of it.'

'It doesn't matter now. He hopes the confession was destroyed in the fire. Failing that, he hopes his message to me will frighten me off.'

'And will it?'

'Would it, you mean. Without the confession, I can't back up Zarbi's threat. So there's nothing to frighten me off of.'

'Will you tell Zarbi what has happened?'

'Not yet. Suzette may decide to let us use the confession once she's thought it all through.'

'Unlikely, I fear.'

'As long as she doesn't actually deliver it to his lawyers, there's some hope.'

'Not much.'

'But not none either.'

'Where will you go – now the cottage has been destroyed?'

'A hotel, I suppose. Staying at my sister's isn't really an option considering what she thinks of me. I'm going to have to buy some clothes as well. Currently all I possess is what I'm wearing.'

'You will stay in contact?'

'I'm sure Emine would rather I didn't.'

'She understands.'

'You have a wonderful wife, Riad.'

250

'I know. So, I will hear from you soon?'

'You can count on it.'

Taleb sits on a bench amidst the stepped greenery of the Monument aux Morts, eating his snack lunch of merguez ficelle in leisurely fashion, enjoying the palm-dappled sunshine and the tranquillity of his surroundings. The relative emptiness of central Algiers is one of the few benefits conferred by coronavirus. In normal times he would have found bench space here hard to come by in the middle of the day.

This is one of his favourite spots in the city, as much because of its historical associations as its proximity to Police HQ. He remembers the old French war memorial, of which he was unpatriotically fond for aesthetic reasons. It was covered over in the late seventies with a concrete sarcophagus, to which he was unpatriotically averse, also for aesthetic reasons. About ten years ago, the sarcophagus began to fall apart, allowing the memorial to make a sneak reappearance before it was obscured by scaffolding while repairs were undertaken. The irony of Algeria's past breaking out physically into the present appealed to Taleb. It seemed to him to sum up so much about his country.

Dabbling personally in one of the most troubled reaches of that past, on the other hand, does not appeal to him at all. Yet it seems to him, as he lets himself be lulled by the warmth of the sun and the sweetness of the air, that he is powerless to prevent himself doing just that. He and Agent Hidouchi are pursuing two veterans of some of the worst misdeeds in the nation's history. It is a pursuit that holds more hazards than someone as young as Hidouchi is capable of imagining. But Taleb is not young. And his imagination is already constructing dire possibilities arising from whatever it is Abderrahmane has pointed him towards.

He cannot fail to act on what Abderrahmane has told him. It would be a dereliction of duty as well as a personal betrayal of the trust she has infuriatingly insisted on placing in him. In his own best interests, however, he should step aside. He should remove himself from the path of the dark historical horror that is thundering towards him. But he can't. He is a serving police officer. He has a job to do. And if he doesn't do it . . . what does he amount to? What has his life been worth?

His phone burrs in the pocket of his jacket, which he's removed and slung over the back of the bench. It goes on burring while he reaches into the wrong pocket. Eventually, he finds the phone. The caller, as he expected, is Bouras's secretary.

'Superintendent Taleb?'

'Yes?'

'You are not in the building.'

He ignores the implied rebuke. 'Does the Director want to see me?'

'As soon as possible.'

'Then I'll be there.'

'When?'

'As soon as possible.'

Twenty minutes later, Taleb heads breathlessly into the Director's office. He is instantly grateful for the cool breeze of air conditioning that greets him. And Bouras doesn't appear to resent being made to wait for him to hurry back to HQ. He is actually smiling.

'What would you do if you had to chase a criminal on foot, Taleb?' he asks, still smiling. 'I wouldn't back you to beat my mother-in-law over a hundred metres.'

'I suppose . . . I would . . . have to shoot them.'

'Mmm. Maybe I should arrange a race for you with my mother-in-law. Now, sit down before you fall down.'

Taleb descends into the slithery maw of the couch. 'News from the DSS, Director?'

'Yes. I've spoken to Deputy Director Kadri. A decision has been taken on how to proceed. A joint decision, obviously.'

It seems likelier to Taleb that Kadri simply told Bouras what they were going to do. The power structure does not allow Bouras much – if any – room for manoeuvre when the DSS has made its wishes known. 'Are Hidouchi and I going to London, then?' he asks.

'No. Paris. The DSS feels it is necessary to brief the DGSE on this matter before any further action is taken.' So, the Algerian secret service defers to the French secret service. Perhaps Taleb should have anticipated such a development. There is a power structure. And there is a power structure above that. 'If Zarbi and Laloul are in France, delicate issues of Franco-Algerian cooperation will inevitably arise if we seek to apprehend them. And these are sensitive times, Taleb. You are aware of the recent improvement in relations between our countries?'

How could Taleb not be aware, in view of the general hoopla in the media, that a few weeks ago the skulls of twenty-four rebels beheaded by the French after an uprising in 1849 were returned as a gesture of goodwill to Algeria for burial with full military honours? President Tebboune shed tears as he presided over the ceremony. President Macron spoke of 'l'espoir d'un apaisement des mémoires'. A new era was evoked. Let the healing begin. Taleb, of course, has heard it all before. So has Bouras. But now isn't the time to point that out. 'Does that complicate the situation, Director?'

'Perhaps. You will have to judge for yourself after you have heard what the DGSE's position is. You and Hidouchi will fly to Paris tomorrow and meet Assistant Director of Intelligence Ménard at their headquarters. You will inform me of the outcome as soon as possible. Use our secure phone for the purpose.'

'Yes, Director.'

'Remember, we do not know what the French know.'

'That is an eternal truth.'

Bouras gives him a cautionary glare. 'My point, Taleb, is that they may – may – already have knowledge of Laloul's where-abouts. And they will certainly have a view on the desirability or otherwise of digging into an unsolved murder of a presidential aide dating back some fifty-five years. It is not your job to antag-onize any part of the French establishment. You understand?'

'I do, Director. But my understanding of exactly what you want me to accomplish is . . . fraying a little. Are we still trying to bring Laloul to justice?'

'If circumstances permit, yes. But Hidouchi will have been given her own instructions by Kadri. Be guided by her.'

'If this all comes to nothing . . .'

'There could be worse outcomes. As you and I both know. As we have . . . discussed.' Bouras gives Taleb a look that is strangely intimate. They are obliged to trust one another, which is congen-ial to neither.

'Working with the intelligence service is not a comfortable experience for me, Director.'

'You think I enjoy it? Bring Zarbi back if you can. Laloul too, ideally. If the French will let you. If doing so doesn't . . . re-open old wounds . . . or put me in an impossible position. Is all of that clear to you?'

'It is, Director.'

'You're to be at Blida Air Base at eight tomorrow morning. Don't be late.'

'I won't be.'

'Don't let me down, Taleb.'

'I will do my very best, Director.' Taleb struggles to his feet. 'You have my word on that.'

TWENTY-ONE

SUZETTE IS HALFWAY DOWN THE M20 WHEN SHE REALIZES SHE'S GOING to be far too early for her Eurotunnel slot, so she leaves the motorway near Ashford and pulls into a pub car park. She winds down the window and smokes a cigarette. The evening air is soft and clear. There are drinkers and diners in the pub garden. It's a scene as close to normal as the times permit.

She checks her phone, hoping there'll be a message from Timothée. Still nothing. There's a text from her mother, though, which, to her surprise, brings her news of her son. *It is lovely having Timmy here. We are spoiling him. When will you be going home?*

She phones Maman immediately, irritated but also relieved. At least the boy is all right, though still doing his infuriating best to ice her out of his life.

'Suzette, ma chérie. Where are you?'

'On my way to Folkestone. For le Shuttle.'

'Ah. So, you are done in England?'

'Yes. I'm done.'

'Good. That is very good.'

'Why is Timothée with you?'

'Ah, he came down yesterday. He said Paris was boring him. Well, it is July. The city empties. So, he came to us.'

'He didn't tell me he was going to do that.'

'Does it matter? He has no college. He is free and young. He wants fun.'

Exactly why he should suppose fun is to be had with his grandmother and step-grandfather in Marseille rather than his friends in Paris Suzette forces herself not to ask. It is almost as if he chooses to do whatever will annoy her most. 'Can I speak to him?'

'He is out with Gérard. They have gone to the casino.'

'The casino? He's too young.'

'Don't worry. Gérard will make sure he doesn't lose much money.'

Suzette has to take a deep breath to calm herself. What has she done to deserve this? Gérard Kermadec is a man of almost limitless vulgarity who makes no secret of having voted for Le Pen in the 2017 presidential election. Timothée should hate everything about him. Instead, he's unaccountably fond of him. Le Coquin, he calls him – the Rogue. And a rogue – a real one – Suzette has always believed Kermadec to be, with his Corsican roots and his rackety amusement arcade business and his generally obscure sources of finance.

'Are you going to tell Monsieur Saidi now that you recognize the confession is a fake?' Maman continues.

'No.'

'But surely . . .'

'Monsieur Saidi has been lying to me, Maman. That isn't even his real name.'

'Does it matter what his name is? He is offering you good money.'

'He doesn't have the confession in his possession. He never did have it.'

'Nonsense. He sent you an extract. How could he send you an extract of something he didn't have?'

'He has a copy. Not the original.'

'How can you know that? You have been in England. His lawyers are in Switzerland.'

'I'm not going to argue with you, Maman. The story Saidi's lawyers told me is a pack of lies. I have the original to—' She breaks off. She shouldn't have said that. Suddenly she remembers Gray's warning that Laloul may have hacked her phone. And confiding in her mother means confiding in her stepfather, which is something she's never happy to do. 'I mean . . . I have seen the original, and . . .'

'Where have you seen it?'

'I will call from home tomorrow. We can talk about it all then.'

'Listen to me, Suzette. The money is there for you to take. Saidi has the original of the document or someone else does. What difference does that make if all you have to say is your father did not write it?'

'It makes a difference to me.'

'You are being stupid. You are not . . . you are not . . . thinking about this with a clear head.' Maman is beginning to lose her temper.

And so is Suzette. They never fail to bring out the worst in each other. 'Do you remember a regular customer at Le Chélifère called Tidjani, Maman? He was a lecturer at the university.'

'No. I do not think so.'

'He died in a car crash.'

'So? Algerians are crazy drivers.'

'Sure you don't remember him?'

'Very sure.' She's lying, of course. Suzette knows she remembers him. In fact, remembers betraying him. The proof of this is that she doesn't ask why Suzette has mentioned him.

'I have to go.'

257

'But we will speak tomorrow?'

'Yes.'

'By then I hope you will be thinking about this in the right way, Suzette – the sensible way. Perhaps I will ask Gérard to give you his advice. You know how well he understands the world.' Suzette fumes inwardly. Kermadec understands his world, not hers. She doesn't need his advice about anything. 'You have Timothée and Élodie to consider,' Maman continues. 'You cannot afford to be . . . self-indulgent.'

'Is the truth a self-indulgence, Maman?'

'Sometimes.'

'And you think this is one of those times?'

'You know what I think.'

'Yes. I do.'

Houda Ghanem doesn't look pleased to see Taleb. In common with most Algerians, she has a well-founded dread of policemen presenting themselves at the door.

'Don't worry,' Taleb says, anxious to put her at her ease. 'I'm only here about the parrot.'

'The parrot? What do you want with him?'

'Razane is concerned he might be . . . pining for her.'

'If shitting on my rugs is a symptom, then, yes, he is pining.' The woman is definitely more irascible than when Taleb last met her. Barbarossa has obviously worked his magic.

'Has he said anything?'

' "God forbid." Over and over. Like a broken record.'

'Well, he's probably under stress.'

'He's not the only one.'

'Razane thinks some special seed mix will help. I've come to fetch it from her apartment.'

'So, she has a senior police officer running errands for her now, does she?'

'I just need the key. This could make the parrot more . . . manageable.'

'More manageable would be good.' There follows a deep sigh. 'I'll get the key.'

A few minutes later, Taleb unlocks the door of Abderrahmane's apartment and, stooping under the line of DÉFENSE D'ENTRER police tape, lets himself in.

The apartment has been unventilated all day, so the atmosphere is hot and fusty, laden with scent memories of spicy food, joss sticks and parrot. Banishing as best he can the fear that the dead Bahlouli is about to appear in a doorway in the eerie twilight, Taleb hunts down the stepladder in the hall cupboard and carries it into the kitchen. He has no wish to switch on any lights and can see adequately enough.

The stepladder is wooden and rickety. He erects it with care and clambers up to the level of the tops of the cupboards facing the window. He can't see anything that might have been put up there, thanks to a raised cornice, so he has to reach over the cornice and run his hand along to left and right, encountering only thick layers of dust . . . until he meets something more solid.

It's a large cardboard packet. Taleb lifts it down. His eyes are met by a faded artist's impression of a happy parrot beneath the brand name Le Perroquet au Paradis. His immediate impression is that it's too heavy to contain just birdseed.

He descends carefully from the ladder before opening it. Inside is an inner pack of seed, held closed with a peg, and a square cardboard box almost as wide as the packet itself. He slides the box out on to the kitchen table. The lid of the box is flat and full-width, held on by a rubber band. As he removes the band, it snaps, perished, he suspects, from being stretched round the box for a long time.

He finds himself paranoiacally checking over his shoulder to confirm he's still alone before he removes the lid. Inside is a large old-fashioned audio tape – the kind played on reel-to-reel recorders before they were superseded by audio cassettes about forty years ago.

There's a label stuck on the reel, peeling at the edges, with something written on it in faded black ink. He has to peer closely to make out what it says.

2 juin '65.

The second of June 1965. The date Guy Tournier was murdered in Paris. Zarbi was one of the murderers. Taleb knows that. And Zarbi entrusted Abderrahmane with many of his secrets. Taleb knows that as well.

And here's one of those secrets. Right in front of him.

At that moment his phone rings, causing him to start violently. He drops the phone as he pulls it out of his pocket, bends down to pick it up and bangs his head on the underside of the table as he stands up. By the time he's recovered from that, the phone has stopped ringing.

He checks for a message. There is one: from Hidouchi.

'I'll see you at Blida tomorrow morning for our flight, Taleb. O eight hundred hours. Don't be late. Wear your smartest suit. The French are impressed by that sort of thing. And please don't tell me the one you've been wearing for the past two days is it.'

Taleb closes the message, finds a chair and sits down at the table. He lights a cigarette and smokes it slowly through, gazing at the tape. What's on it he cannot begin to imagine. But it matters. Oh yes, it assuredly matters.

His most immediate problem is that he has no machine on which to play the tape. There might be one buried away at Police HQ, but he fears locating it would attract attention and he's quite sure he shouldn't be doing that. He could probably buy one somewhere in Algiers, but he's leaving before he'll have the chance. He'll just have to take the tape with him. He certainly

260

can't leave it here, especially since he has no idea when he'll be back.

He extinguishes the cigarette under the tap and screws it up in a tissue. Then he puts the tape back in its box, replaces the step-ladder in the hall cupboard and prepares to deliver the pack of birdseed to Ghanem. She can know nothing of the tape. The same goes for everybody, including Hidouchi.

'Thank you so much for making my life even more compli-cated than it already is, Razane,' he mutters under his breath as he heads for the door.

Agent Souad Hidouchi emerges from the lift into the dimly lit cavern of DSS HQ's underground car park and strides towards the bay where she keeps her motorbike. She is not happy about the diversion to Paris she has been required to take. Briefing the DGSE strikes her as unduly obliging, bordering on the obse-quious. She sees no reason why the French have to be kept informed of her activities. She and Taleb should be going to London to question Riad Nedjar, not Paris to ply some DGSE bigwig with intelligence his own organization has done noth-ing to gather. But orders are orders, however much she chafes against them.

As she approaches her motorbike, the headlights of a car occupying a nearby bay flash twice. She recognizes the vehicle as Deputy Director Meschac Kadri's sleek black Mercedes. And Kadri is at the wheel, beckoning her to join him. Clearly, he has been waiting for her.

Two possible explanations present themselves to Hidouchi more or less simultaneously. One is that Kadri, who has always believed himself to be irresistible to women, is intent upon renew-ing the advances Hidouchi subtly rebuffed on a previous occasion. The other, more disturbing in its way, is that he wishes to discuss something with her that could not be broached in his office, where they met earlier to lay the ground for her visit to Paris. She will soon enough know which it is.

Kadri pushes the passenger door open as she approaches. She slides into the seat to be met by an aroma of expensive leather overlaid with an oily cologne that Kadri favours.

'I wanted to have a last word with you before you fly to Paris tomorrow, Souad,' says Kadri.

'Was there something we didn't cover earlier, Deputy Director?' Hidouchi asks.

'Please, we don't need to be so formal. Call me Meschac. It's more a case of there being something we didn't emphasize earlier, Souad. Or rather I didn't. Do you feel your collaboration with Superintendent Taleb has been successful?'

'His experience has been useful. And we've made quite rapid progress.'

'His "experience" is what concerns me. It may hamper you at a later stage if he views dealing with Zarbi and Laloul through the prism of the past.'

'But Zarbi and Laloul are very much of the past.'

'Indeed. But it's a past our superiors wish to put behind them, for the sake of the nation's progress. The youths protesting on our streets earlier this year weren't interested in scandals dating from la décennie noire. Most of them were born in this century, not the last. So, it would be best if Zarbi and Laloul . . . did not return.'

'You made that clear when you gave me this mission . . . Meschac. Zarbi and Laloul either stay missing . . . or are terminated.'

'Quite so.'

A brief silence falls. Hidouchi wonders what point Kadri is trying to make. She understands the government has no wish to see Laloul in court. An unmarked grave, somewhere in Europe, is where she has been explicitly instructed to put him if she is able to track him down. And she has no compunction about that. Nadir Laloul is a traitor to his country as well as a common criminal. She would have no objection to serving as the instrument of his well-merited extinction. It is, after all, her professional duty to carry out such acts.

Thus far in her career, she has not been ordered to kill someone she knows to be innocent. And this is fortunate, because she is well aware of what she would and would not be capable of doing in such circumstances. The DSS has its priorities, which she is required to observe. But she has her principles, which her nature dictates she must also observe.

Kadri sighs and pats Hidouchi's knee, a gesture she tolerates because she knows she must. 'I'm thinking of your future, Souad. It could be brighter than that of any woman who has ever joined the service if you manage this affair with the sensitivity I've come to expect from you. Taleb was involved in the original investigation of Laloul's embezzlement of funds from Sonatrach, was he not?'

'He was.'

'It's therefore possible he knows more about Laloul's activities than we do.'

'It is possible, yes.'

'And we don't know exactly what this man Bahlouli said to him before he jumped off that balcony, do we?'

'Well, I wasn't there, certainly.'

'We don't even know beyond doubt that Bahlouli did jump off . . . rather than being pushed.'

Hidouchi is unflappable by nature as well as training. Even so, she's relieved it's too dark inside the car for Kadri to see her expression as she registers his suggestion that Taleb may have murdered Bahlouli. 'I personally have no doubt on the point. Taleb did not murder Bahlouli.'

'How can you be sure?'

'He had no reason to.'

'His reasons may date back twenty years, perhaps longer. He presents himself to you as a conscientious police officer. But his relations with people close to this case – Zarbi, Abderrahmane, Bahlouli, not to mention the English bookseller, Dalby – render him suspect. He cannot be allowed to obstruct a clean resolution of the Laloul problem. You cannot allow him to.'

'I won't.'

'Good.' Kadri turns to look at her. All she can see of his face in the shadows is the pale curve of his smile. 'That is good.'

'May I ask . . .'

'Yes?'

'What exactly is the Laloul problem? If I knew more about it, my task might be simpler.'

'I sympathize. I would tell you more if I were able to. As it is, I know no more than I have told you. Laloul is a smouldering fire that must be extinguished. And Taleb . . . may need to be extinguished also.'

'That would be . . . a drastic step.'

'The DSS exists to take drastic steps when they are necessary, Souad. And in this case they are deemed to be necessary. If and when the moment comes, you will recognize it and act accordingly, I'm sure.' He is no longer smiling. 'You are equal to this task, aren't you?'

'Of course.'

'Then see it through. To the end.'

Taleb returns to his apartment weighed down by anxiety. He has a vital piece of evidence in his possession, but no way of learning what it signifies. He also has obligations to report this discovery to both Bouras and, arguably, Hidouchi. But his every instinct tells him not to breathe a word to either of them until he has heard what is on the tape himself. It could amount to nothing.

Or it could amount to everything. While the tape remains unplayed, it is an open question – as open as a chasm yawning beneath his feet.

His apartment is furnished and decorated in a style thirty years behind the times, for the very good reason that nothing has been changed in all that time. The rugs are frayed and faded, the originally orange velvet three-piece suite has turned beige with age and, atop the ancient Sonelec push-button-controlled television, there still stands the silverplate oasis scene of a camel and two palm trees. He has not actively sought to preserve the apartment as a shrine to Serene and Lili's memory, though he does find it comforting to reflect that they would recognize more or less everything if they were to walk back in.

This they are not about to do, of course. The finality of death has long since cut him off from them. It has also cut him off from the consolations of religion. He secretly renounced God the day after their funerals and he and the Almighty have not been reconciled since. Oddly, he did not blame God for what happened to them. But his repugnance for so many of the humans he was required to worship God with – humans who were capable of the kind of unimaginable violence that claimed his loved ones – drove him to renounce their beliefs. And in that renunciation he has found a form of peace.

He prepares a frugal supper and mulls over his options as he eats. Neither the eating nor the mulling takes long. He will have to take the tape with him to Paris and create an opportunity while he is there to beg, borrow or steal a machine on which to play it. How he is to manage that he cannot imagine, but it will have to be done. Until he knows what is on the tape, he is perilously placed, though it's quite possible he'll be even more perilously placed when he's listened to it. Ignorance is dangerous. But knowledge may be still more dangerous.

He packs his suitcase with clothes for a few days, though how long he's to be away is just another of the uncertainties he's beset by. He swathes the box containing the tape in assorted papers and crams the whole lot in a dog-eared folder, which he stows in his shoulder bag. Now he's just about ready for an early departure in the morning.

He turns out all the lights, opens the blinds and sits down in his favourite armchair, facing the window and the night beyond. He lights a cigarette and studies the velvety blackness of the sky that looms over the city. It occurs to him that it's possible this is his last night in Algiers, considering the many unknown hazards that are surely waiting for him on the journey that will begin tomorrow. All the thousands of nights he's passed in the city of his birth – and this could feasibly be the very last.

It hardly seems possible. But death never seems possible, as he knows from his own experience – until it becomes a fact.

Hidouchi returns to her apartment also weighed down by anxiety. A mission she initially saw as an opportunity to impress her superiors and enhance her prospects within the DSS has now become something wreathed in so many sinister possibilities she's aware it may become a battle for her own survival.

She is paid well by Algerian standards and enjoys the material trappings of a privileged existence. Her apartment is large, stylishly decorated in tasteful hues of grey and silver, with a balconied lounge commanding a broad view of the harbour and a kitchen absurdly over-equipped with hobs, ovens, freezers and storage units. It all came as a package with the latest technological extravagances, including smartphone-controlled air conditioning and music of her choosing to follow her from room to room.

She sheds her clothes with relief and gazes out at the lights of the harbour as she drinks a chilled passionfruit juice from a tall glass in which cubes of ice clunk at every tilt. Then she takes a long bath, listening to her favourite Souad Massi album and trying not to think about the choice laid before her by Kadri. Death is nothing less than a predatory schemer like Laloul deserves. Taleb, on the other hand, is an honest and diligent detective. And she's grown fond of him. She likes his self-deprecating humour. Extinguishing him – Kadri's chosen euphemism for killing – is something she finds it hard to believe she will be capable of.

Unless Taleb isn't as honest and diligent as she thinks. Perhaps Kadri is right. Taleb may have a hidden agenda, wrapped up in the murder of his wife and daughter by Islamist terrorists and his strange dealings with Stephen Gray and Nigel Dalby. Is it possible – is it conceivable – that he threw Bahlouli off Abder-rahmane's balcony? If he did, then she has misjudged him completely. And in her profession misjudgements can have fatal consequences.

But Taleb is not the only one in all this who may have a hidden agenda. Kadri was far more explicit about what he required of her when they spoke in his car than when they met earlier in his office. Clearly, he didn't want there to be any record of their discussion. Whose objectives is he serving? His own, or those of nameless power brokers above him? It is impossible for her to say. She simply doesn't know enough about the many secrets buried in Zarbi and Laloul's past to grasp what is at stake.

She resents, on behalf of her whole generation, the way in which their lives are still governed by conflicts and power struggles that took place before they were even born. The War of Independence is a piece of dusty history to her. Yet those legendary freedom fighters who expelled the French sixty years ago have become the grandfathers of a fractured present. And their determination to deny the Algerian people the freedom they claimed they were fighting for has soured every decade since. Le pouvoir still keeps its foot clamped on the citizens' necks. And she, however she cares to pretend otherwise, is a servant of that system.

But her service comes with conditions attached. And Kadri, though he may not know it, has violated one of those conditions. Hidouchi is not prepared to allow herself to be pushed around. And she will not be a slave to anyone's hidden agenda.

Who is there who knows what she needs to know and might be willing to tell her? And who can she trust? There seems to be only one man who qualifies, which is better, she supposes, than none. And Kadri wants that man dead.

She toes the plug from the horizontal to the vertical and rises from the bath as the water begins to drain out. Reaching for her towel, she sees a condensation-blurred reflection of herself in the floor-to-ceiling mirror.

She steps out of the bath and moves across the room in leisurely strides, enjoying the looseness of her limbs and the sensation of the water drying on her skin. She wipes just enough of the condensation from the mirror to meet her own gaze clearly in the glass.

The eyes of the woman who looks at her project strength and confidence. Only if you know her better than anyone else in the world does or can is a tiny trace of fear also evident. Strength can be overborne, confidence misplaced. The immediate future for Souad Hidouchi has become a treacherous place.

TWENTY-TWO

THE HOLLOW-EYED REFLECTION THAT GREETS STEPHEN GRAY IN THE bathroom mirror in his room at the Premier Inn, Basingstoke, early the following morning, is a grim sight. He washes his face and smears some toothpaste round his teeth, the closest he can come to brushing them after forgetting to buy a toothbrush yesterday. He rinses his mouth under the tap, grateful at least to have banished the lingering taste of the half-bottle of whisky he drank last night. Then he returns to the bedroom and opens the curtains as wide as his eyes can bear.

His throat is like sandpaper. His head aches. He can't go on like this. That much is obvious. He has to do something to retrieve the situation. He is homeless, Suzette has departed with the confession and he has managed to fall out seriously with his only surviving sibling. He can't simply wait for Suzette to decide what she's going to do. He has to act. He remembers reaching that conclusion before the Scotch kicked in last night.

He locates his B phone in the jumble of clothes draped over the chair by the table, sits down on the bed and punches in Riad Nedjar's number.

'No answer. He leaves the briefest of messages. 'It's me. Call me as soon as you can.'

In Algiers, Akram is just opening the gate of the garage when Taleb arrives, bleary-eyed from lack of sleep. It is uncommonly early – but not too early for Akram to proffer some badinage.

'They are working you too hard, Inspector.'

'You may be right. But what about you? Where's that idle brother of yours?'

'Still in bed, I expect. Are you going away?' Akram nods at the suitcase Taleb is carrying.

'For a day or two, yes.'

'Business or pleasure?'

'What do you think?'

'I think you should go carefully. It's a mad world out there.'

'You don't need to tell me that.'

'Oh, I'm not telling you, Inspector. You already know it, I'm sure. I'm just reminding you.' Akram smiles. 'It's part of the service.'

Gray is still sitting on the bed in his hotel room, trying to summon the energy to get dressed, when the phone rings.

'Hi, Riad. Thanks for calling back.'

'You sound rough, my friend.'

'Do I really?'

'What can I do for you at this hour?'

'It's early, I know. Sorry if I've woken you.'

'You haven't. A shopkeeper's day begins before dawn.'

'I need to ask you a favour.'

'What is it?'

'When Suzette and you parted on Tuesday evening, she gave you her address in France, didn't she?'

'Yes. So that we could stay in touch.'

'Can you give it to me?'

'Why would you want her address, Stephen? Are you proposing to write to her?'

'No.'

'To visit, then?'

'I can't let it end like this, Riad. I've worked too long and too hard to punish Laloul to allow the plan just to fall apart.'

'Do you have a choice?'

'I can try to persuade Suzette, now we've both been able to reflect on the situation, that we should . . . go on.'

'But she no longer trusts you, Stephen. And she's frightened of Laloul. For good reason. You will surely fail.'

'I have to try.'

'Call her, then. You'll know from her reaction whether you stand a chance.'

'You warned me yourself her phone might have been hacked. It has to be face to face.'

'That's a neat argument. But it does not convince me.'

'OK. But will you give me her address anyway?'

'This is a mistake, my friend.'

'Maybe. But it's my mistake to make.'

Little is said between Hidouchi and Taleb during the flight from Blida to Paris, partly because of noise levels in the transport plane, on which they are the only passengers, and partly because Taleb, overtaken by exhaustion after his largely sleepless night, falls into a deep slumber shortly after take-off. Turbulence over the Mediterranean rouses him only briefly.

On landing at Vélizy-Villacoublay Air Base in Paris, Hidouchi welcomes him back to the wide awake world. 'When were you last in Paris, Taleb?'

'A conference twelve years ago,' he replies, rubbing his eyes and squinting out at the runway. 'I barely left the hotel.'

'And before that?'

'Nineteen eighty-three. With my wife. It was our honeymoon. This time of the year, actually. It rained a lot.' He smiles. 'We didn't care.'

'How old were you in 1983, Taleb?'

'Oh . . . twenty-eight.'

'Hard to imagine.'

'Harder for me than you, I suspect.'

'The embassy will have a car waiting for us. We're to go straight to the Swimming Pool.'

He frowns in puzzlement. 'You are joking, aren't you?'

'It's the nickname for DGSE HQ.'

'Why?'

'Easy to drown there if you don't know the strokes, I suppose.'

'But you must know the strokes, Agent Hidouchi. The DGSE are your kind of people.'

'I'm not sure about that.'

'No?'

'We need to be careful while we're in Paris, Taleb.'

'You think so?'

'Don't you?'

'Me? I'm always careful. Haven't you noticed?'

The driver of the embassy car seems to have acquired quite a lot of Parisian reserve during his posting there. He displays a very un-Algerian level of taciturnity as he drives them round the autoroute system to their destination on the eastern side of the city. Glimpsing a sign reading *Piscine des Tourelles* as they arrive, Taleb realizes an adjacent swimming pool is the mundane explanation for DGSE HQ's nickname, as Hidouchi must be aware.

'I preferred your version,' he says to her in an undertone.

'Names are never just names, Taleb,' she responds. 'They breed their own symbolism.'

The driver announces he's been instructed to take their cases on to the hotel the embassy has booked and will return to collect them later. Taleb keeps his bulging shoulder bag with him. Hidouchi carries something predictably slimmer and smarter. There's a security gate just inside the building, where they're patted down and deprived of their guns for the duration of their visit.

'Don't worry,' the burly guard presiding tells them. 'You won't need to shoot your way out.' Taleb manages a smile. Hidouchi doesn't.

They're ushered to an upper floor office to meet Assistant Director of Intelligence Ménard. The initial E before the Assistant Director's name on the door turns out to stand for Erica. Taleb tries hard not to look surprised when he discovers this. He suspects Hidouchi already knew but chose not to tell him.

Erica Ménard, as it turns out, isn't in her office. She's been delayed by 'an operational emergency', according to her assistant, a small, wiry, curly-haired young man with a disconcertingly rapid blink who introduces himself as Gilles Réau and invites them to share the conference table with him while they await her arrival.

The table forms the vertical to a T completed by Ménard's desk, on which a telephone and PC do not have to jostle for space with anything as personal as framed family photographs. Réau starts tapping away at his laptop, leaving Taleb and Hidouchi to study their surroundings and guard their tongues.

As the minutes tick by and the abstract paintings on the walls fail to yield stimulation, Taleb begins to pay closer attention to Réau. He notices a number of long grey hairs on the young man's jacket – cat hairs, he suspects. They remind him of the hairs he used to find on his clothes after visits to his great aunt Lunca, who kept a veritable colony of Persian cats.

Nearly half an hour slowly elapses before Erica Ménard enters the room with the slightly breathless air of a busy woman. She's slim and elegant, dressed in a black trouser suit. Taleb's eye is caught by a glittering brooch on her lapel in the likeness of a scorpion. Her smile of greeting has a chilly edge to it and her eyes a predatory gleam.

'Welcome to Paris,' she says, seating herself at her desk and opening a file she brought with her. 'We are grateful to the DSS for proposing this meeting.' She addresses the remark to Hidouchi. The Algerian police apparently warrant no thanks for sending Taleb along for the ride. 'I must say I was surprised to hear the issue of the Tournier murder had been revived. It was fifty-five years ago. That is not so much a cold case as a frozen one.'

'But sensitive, even so,' says Hidouchi, 'at this time of improving relations between our governments.'

'True,' concedes Ménard. 'So, are you able to give me details of what has come to light – after such a very long time?'

Hidouchi nods to Taleb. 'Superintendent?'

'Thank you, Agent Hidouchi.' Taleb clears his throat. He would very much like a cigarette, but they have passed several DÉFENSE DE FUMER signs on their way through the building and the room they are in is spotlessly clean. He might as well think of spitting on the floor. 'Wassim Zarbi, formerly with the DRS, left Algeria four months ago in breach of his parole conditions following release after serving twenty years of a thirty-year prison sentence for complicity in the embezzlement of funds from our national oil and gas company, Sonatrach. The embezzler-in-chief, Nadir Laloul, who worked in a senior capacity at Sonatrach, has never been caught. We believe Zarbi may be looking for him in order to take revenge for being left to face prosecution alone.'

'Where do you believe Laloul is?' Ménard asks.

'We don't know. Switzerland, possibly. France, conceivably.'

Ménard arches a sceptical eyebrow. 'France? Really?'

'As I say, we don't know. But French is his first language.'

'And what is the connection with Guy Tournier?'

'It's possible Zarbi and Laloul murdered him. They seem to have been in Paris at the time of his death and were active FLN operatives, although in 1965 they were working to help Boumediene replace Ben Bella. The coup that deposed Ben Bella took place just a few weeks after Tournier's death.'

'And what is that except a coincidence of timing?'

'We're aware of the rumours that Tournier was a member of a secret committee that may have approved the seventeenth of October 1961 massacre,' Hidouchi cuts in. 'The date was daubed on the wall of his apartment, was it not?'

'It was,' says Ménard. 'According to the file I studied before you arrived. A nasty business, in which Tournier's predilection for young male company was exploited to gain access to his apartment. He was propositioned by a young Englishman at a nearby restaurant.'

Taleb and Hidouchi exchange a glance. 'We may know who the Englishman was,' says Taleb. 'Nigel Dalby. He ran a bookshop in Algiers for many years. We think Zarbi helped him establish the business.'

'Is Dalby still alive?'

'No. He was murdered by Islamist extremists in 1994.'

'So, you have two elderly fugitives and a dead man to back up all this speculation?'

'Was Tournier a member of a secret government committee?' Hidouchi asks, undercutting Ménard's sarcasm.

She is rewarded with a wintry stare. 'Obviously I can't, by definition, confirm the existence of a secret government committee, even from many presidential administrations ago. But I don't deny it's widely rumoured such a committee existed. And that Tournier served on it.'

'Would your government like to see his murderers brought to justice?'

'Naturally. And I'm sure assistance from your side to achieve that would be warmly welcomed by my government.'

'We don't know where Laloul is,' says Taleb, 'but it seems likely Zarbi is in Marseille. Whether that means Laloul is also in Marseille . . .'

'The city is a sump for Muslim malcontents, so either might have found refuge there.' Ménard doesn't appear to be troubled by the harshness of her language. 'This country is in a state of undeclared war against Islamist extremists who are unwilling to respect our traditions. They would probably regard Tournier's murderers as heroes.'

'Well, we don't.' Taleb feels angry at having to say as much, but he is no stranger to suppressing his emotions. 'Zarbi and Laloul are enemies of Algeria just as much as they are of France.'

Ménard gives him her attention for what seems to be the first time. 'I am pleased to hear it, Superintendent. How can we help you in your pursuit of these elderly murderers?'

'Give us official clearance to conduct inquiries wherever they need to be conducted.'

'Official clearance? That would tie us all up in paperwork. Unofficial clearance is a different matter.'

'Can we have that, then?' asks Hidouchi.

'Subject to being kept informed on a regular basis as your inquiries proceed, yes.' Ménard smiles icily.

'I wonder . . . if you have any information about either man.' Taleb notices a slight stiffening of Hidouchi's posture as she says this. She evidently believes Ménard's response will be the acid test of her cooperativeness.

'I instituted a system-wide trawl as soon as Deputy Director Kadri gave me their names. The results were . . . meagre. Gilles?' Ménard turns to Réau, whose blink rate instantly increases.

'There's no recent intelligence at all,' he reports, speaking so quietly Taleb has to concentrate hard to catch his words. 'For both men there are alleged links with underworld figures in Marseille, but nothing definite.'

'If you can supply us with the names of known current associates of the two men,' says Ménard, 'we may be able to dig up more.'

'There's a former nightclub owner called Razane Abderrahmane,' says Hidouchi. 'Zarbi had a son by her. And a friend of hers who was in prison with Zarbi called Sami Bahlouli.'

'Abderrahmane is in custody,' says Taleb. 'And Bahlouli committed suicide when about to be arrested.'

Ménard looks unimpressed – as well she might, Taleb admits to himself. 'Where is the son?'

'Managing a hotel in Egypt.'

'No obvious links with France, then.'

'No. But there is also . . . Zarbi's well-travelled lawyer, Ibrahim Boukhatem. Perhaps—'

'Boukhatem?' Ménard is suddenly animated. 'Why didn't you mention him sooner?'

'You know of him?'

'Only too well. Ibrahim Boukhatem is a roving associate of Coqblin and Baudouin, a Franco-Swiss law firm that's given us much trouble by mounting mysteriously well-funded defences for Islamist extremists threatened with deportation. We suspect Boukhatem is their principal fundraiser in Arab states.'

'That's interesting. He happens to be in Bahrain at present.'

'Not so, Superintendent. He's here, in Paris. Gilles?' Ménard turns once more to Réau, who taps away at the keys on his laptop.

'Boukhatem flew in from Bahrain yesterday and booked into the Horizon Hotel at Charles de Gaulle airport,' he reports. 'He's still there, according to the latest tracking report.'

'Taking meetings before flying out again, perhaps,' says Ménard. 'He's always on the move.'

'Boukhatem is at the airport?' Hidouchi checks. 'Right now?'

'We can't be certain of his present location, but . . .' Réau squints at the screen in front of him, 'he definitely hasn't checked out.'

'You have his room number?'

'Thinking of paying him a visit, Agent Hidouchi?' Ménard asks.

'Why not?'

'No reason. In fact, it's a good idea. Particularly for us.'

'Why for you?'

'Because Coqblin and Baudouin will allege harassment if we knock on Boukhatem's door. And they have enough politicians in their pocket to cause us problems. But we can't be held responsible for the actions of Algerian agents operating in France without official sanction, can we?' Ménard smiles at them, then points a strikingly long index finger at Réau. 'I haven't discussed Boukhatem's whereabouts with Agent Hidouchi and Superintendent Taleb, Gilles. Is that clear?'

Réau nods emphatically, which has the effect of slowing his blinking.

'But they have undertaken to notify us of all interactions they have with French citizens while they are in this country.'

Réau nods again and taps away on his laptop.

'Boukhatem is not a French citizen,' Hidouchi remarks.

Ménard shrugs. 'I believe you're right. So . . . we will not expect to be notified of any interactions you have with him.' And to the shrug she adds a smile.

Suzette is relieved to be home. Les Fringillidés is a converted farmhouse west of Versailles, bought by her and Vincent when his art gallery business was thriving in the spendthrift days before the 2008 crash. Keeping it has stretched her financial resources to the limit, but she's pleased to have been able to give Timothée and Élodie a semi-rural childhood. They're seldom there now and Vincent's long gone, but the memories of family life it holds are precious to her.

Above all, Les Fringillidés represents peace, which is what she needs after her trip to England. She reached the house just as dawn was breaking, exhausted after the drive from Calais. Angélique, her cleaner, has left it in good order, as ever. All she had to do was drop her bags, close the curtains and go to bed in the hope of catching up on some sleep.

She managed five solid hours before waking to a sunny late morning. She showered and unpacked, then had breakfast and took her coffee out on to the terrace facing the fields that stretch away north towards the Forêt de Beynes.

As she sits at the garden table, she feels the tranquillity of her surroundings seep into her soul. It's still not clear to her how she's going to extricate herself from the problems posed by her father's confession, but she's calmer than she was and senses the answer will present itself to her if she has the patience to let it.

She hasn't turned on her phone since arriving and she's unplugged the landline as well. She needs to think things through without interruption and certainly without the advice her mother is doubtless eager to give her.

But the phone isn't the only source of interruption. As she sips her coffee and watches the fat cattle moving slowly in one of Farmer Pépy's fields, she becomes aware of the sound of a car engine, growing ever louder as it approaches along the poplar-lined lane. It's not the postman, whose van makes a distinctive put-put noise. It's the throaty growl of a high-powered saloon.

Turning, she sees a plume of dust moving along the lane. Then the car itself appears: grey and low-slung. It slows as it approaches the yard in front of the house. Suzette can see nothing of the driver thanks to the angle of the sun. But the appearance of a car she doesn't recognize in the middle of the day is concerning enough. She stands up, wondering what to do.

The car draws to a halt. The engine dies. Quietude is restored. The driver's door swings open and a large man in a blazer and chinos climbs out. He's fair-haired and jowly. He waves to her, the sunlight flashing on the lenses of his sunglasses. 'Madame Fontaine?' he calls.

She doesn't actually confirm her identity, but calls back, 'What can I do for you?'

'I am sorry to arrive unannounced. I tried telephoning you earlier, but . . .' He spreads his hands.

'Who are you?'

'Lionel Baudouin.' He leans into the car to fetch a briefcase, then starts walking slowly towards her, smiling broadly. 'I hope you don't mind me . . . calling by like this.'

The sunlight catches the heavy gold bracelet of Baudouin's wristwatch and the unnatural whiteness of his teeth. He's wearing a cravat, which gives him an old-fashioned, slightly raffish appearance. This certainly isn't how she unconsciously pictured the writer of the letters she's received from Coqblin & Baudouin. Besides, the writer of those letters is supposed to be in Geneva, not the Île de France.

'As I'm sure you can imagine, Madame Fontaine, our client, Monsieur Saidi, is anxious to hear what you have concluded about the, ah . . . document.'

'Have you come all the way from Geneva to ask me what I've decided?'

'No, no. We have an office in Paris. I divide my time between here and Geneva so as to . . . address the needs of all our clients.'

'How nice for them.'

His smile stiffens. 'Indeed.'

'Do you want to sit down?'

'Thank you.' He arranges himself in one of the chairs spaced around the table. 'I must say your coffee smells . . . superb.'

'Would you like a cup?' There seems no way out of offering him one.

'That would be very nice.'

Suzette goes to fetch a cup for her visitor. She resents being invaded by him. It strikes her as most unlawyerly behaviour. But at least the trip to the kitchen gives her a chance to collect her thoughts. What does he want? What does he really want?

He's talking on his phone when she returns. At the sight of her, he says, 'I will call you back,' and ends the conversation.

She pours him coffee and some more for herself. He sips his and gives a sigh of satisfaction.

'I had understood, monsieur,' says Suzette as she sits down, 'that your client was content to wait for me to reach a decision in my own time.'

'Oh, he is. It was simply that, so long having elapsed, and finding myself in the area . . .'

'You found yourself in the area?' Suzette can't help sounding sceptical. She's also increasingly apprehensive. She's only been home for a matter of hours. Does this visit suggest he knew she was back? She remembers Stephen Gray warning her that her phone might not be secure. She had tried to dismiss that as paranoia on his part. Suddenly, she's not so sure.

'We have an elderly client who lives near Dreux,' claims Baudouin, quite shamelessly. 'I have to visit her periodically.'

'You obviously believe in personal service.'

'It's our watchword.' He takes another sip of coffee. 'So, may I ask if you have, in fact . . . reached a decision?'

She has, though she was planning to dwell on it for a while before contacting him. But she recoils inwardly from further prevarication. 'I have.'

281

'And that is?'

'I have decided it's impossible to be certain whether the confession is genuine . . . or not.'

Baudouin leans back in his chair and studies her. 'Impossible to be certain?'

'Yes. Exactly so.'

'Well, I confess, madame . . . you surprise me.'

'I would need to see the original before I could . . . say for sure.' She meets his gaze unflinchingly.

'My client only asks that you reach a determination based on the copy supplied to you.'

'Then, based on that, you have my answer.'

'His instructions to me do not allow for the possibility of your examining the original.'

'May I ask why not, monsieur?'

'It is a question of confidentiality. The original is not available for inspection.'

'Could that be, perhaps, because your client . . . does not have it?'

Baudouin frowns. 'That is a strange question. He approached you in good faith. He hopes – I hope – you will respond in the same fashion.'

'Well, you have my answer. And it is in good faith.'

'And if that is your answer – your final answer – it will of course rule out the payment of compensation.'

'Compensation for what?'

'I believe I set out the details in my letter.'

'Yes. You did.'

Neither speaks for several moments. Baudouin sips his coffee thoughtfully. Suzette holds her nerve. She senses a negotiation is taking place. But the parameters are uncertain. She cannot guess what he will say next.

Baudouin looks across the table at her. 'If the original was recently destroyed,' he says slowly, 'there would be nothing for us to discuss.'

'Yet here we sit.'

'If the original was not recently destroyed, it would be possible to attach a monetary value to it, whether we categorize that as compensation or simply . . .' His voice trails away.

'Simply what?' she prompts him.

He smiles his ready, gleaming smile. 'Payment on delivery, madame. If that is what you have in mind.'

'Perhaps it is.'

'Then perhaps we have the basis for a deal.'

Another tactical silence falls, which Suzette decides to break. 'Such an exchange would bring an end to all contact between me and your client?'

Baudouin nods. 'Of course.'

'I would never hear from him again?'

'Never. Nor he from you. Those would be the terms.'

'And what payment would you propose?'

'For the verifiable original, a little more than we envisaged as compensation for loss of commercial proceeds.'

'Which amounts to?'

Baudouin takes a carefully timed sip of coffee, then says, 'Two hundred and fifty thousand euros.'

Suzette can hardly believe he has set it out so blatantly, though it didn't sound blatant in his velvety phraseology. He is offering her €250,000 for the surrender of her father's confession. For the surrender of the original of the confession, that is. Nothing else has any value. Except the carbon copy, which she guesses Baudouin knows nothing about.

She's guessed too soon. 'A few further points, however, before you give me your answer,' he goes on. 'We are speaking of a document produced on a manual typewriter twenty-seven years ago. You should be aware that a modern imitation will be immediately apparent to us when our expert examines it. There is also the possibility that your father used carbon paper to produce a copy. We would need that copy as well. If we discovered such a copy existed but was withheld, the consequences for you would be . . . severe.' He smiles as he uses the word severe, but that doesn't make it sound any less threatening.

Suzette takes a slow, calming breath. Baudouin has thought of everything. But what he's proposing is nonetheless attractive. She wants Laloul out of her life. And for that she has to give up her father's confession. Perhaps she can retain a photocopy, though perhaps it would be better not to. Either way, the original – the real thing – has to be given up. Or rather sold. That is the sugar on the pill.

'I would suggest we fix the exchange for five o'clock tomorrow afternoon at our Paris office,' Baudouin continues. 'That will allow our client time to travel to the city. He will need to see the document with his own eyes. And at that hour we can be sure of conducting the transaction without interruption. Do you agree?'

An answer has finally to be given. So she gives it. 'Yes.'

'And the sum I proposed is also acceptable to you?'

'Yes.'

'Then only one issue remains to be settled.'

'Which is?'

'Whether you prefer a banker's draft . . . or cash.'

TWENTY-THREE

THE EMBASSY DRIVER MUTTERS SOME OBJECTIONS TO THE CHANGE OF destination and Hidouchi pulls him into line in a way Taleb is undeniably impressed by. They're soon on the autoroute, heading for Charles de Gaulle airport.

Neither says much on the journey. Taleb doesn't entirely trust the driver and it seems Hidouchi doesn't either. They direct him to drop them at the entrance to the Horizon Hotel, find somewhere to park and await further instructions.

Both take their shoulder bags with them when they climb out. 'Not happy to leave your bag with him?' Taleb asks as the car pulls away.

'Neither are you, apparently,' Hidouchi replies.

'He certainly doesn't fill me with confidence.'

'Does anything that's happened since we landed?'

'You don't think Ménard is telling us everything she could, then?'

Hidouchi looks at him solemnly. 'What do you think?'

'I'll let you know after we've spoken to Boukhatem.'

'OK. Let's go and find out if he's in his room. And eager to talk.'

*

The hotel lobby is an expanse of gleaming marble, adorned with Paris-themed cityscapes. The lighting is low, the muzak sophisticated. They drift through the space like two regular guests, attracting no attention whatever from the distant reception desk, and take the lift to the executive floor, where all is hushed and still. Looking through a window as they head along the corridor, Taleb glimpses a plane taking off in what seems, within the hotel's soundproofed cocoon, like utter silence. He hears the slight squeak of a distant chambermaid's trolley wheel without actually seeing the chambermaid at all.

They reach Boukhatem's room. A red light signals he does not wish to be disturbed. Hidouchi taps delicately on the door. There's no response. She taps again, more energetically.

'Maybe we should have checked at reception,' says Taleb, though he wasn't in favour of checking. The haziness of their status, particularly his, suggests to him the fewer people they interact with the better. 'He might be luxuriating in the spa.'

'Then we can have a look around in his absence,' says Hidouchi. She opens her bag and takes out a small device that she holds over the keycard recognition panel on the door handle. Lights flash as it goes to work. Then the red light on the panel turns obligingly to green and she opens the door.

'I think you've just broken several laws in the Algerian criminal code, Agent Hidouchi,' says Taleb.

'The DSS are exempt, Taleb. Obviously, I wouldn't have let you use this device. Also, we are not in Algeria.' She leads the way into the room.

She pulls up sharply after no more than a few strides, so sharply Taleb collides with her. He is about to apologize when he sees what has caused her to stop.

A balding middle-aged man is lying on his back in the open doorway of the bathroom, wearing a white towelling bathrobe and rubber-soled mules. There are several dark red patches of blood on the robe and a pool of blood beneath him on the marble floor. There's not much doubt that he's dead. And not much doubt either, in Taleb's mind at least, that the dead man is Ibrahim Boukhatem.

Hidouchi moves cautiously towards the body. She peers down at the face, swollen and frozen in shock, with blank, staring eyes. 'I saw a photograph of Boukhatem when I went to his office in Algiers,' she says quietly. 'This is him.' She presses two fingers under his jaw. 'This was him, I should say.'

Taleb casts his expert eye over the deceased. 'Not long dead, judging by the blood,' he remarks.

'I agree.' Hidouchi looks past Taleb and points. 'Shell casings. There.'

The casings are lying on the carpeted floor of the bedroom. Taleb bends down to examine one. 'Nine millimetre.'

'What gun do you use, Taleb?' Hidouchi asks.

'Beretta. Nine millimetre.'

'Interesting.'

'Why?' He has the sense he's not going to like her answer.

'Because I would guess, when they dig the bullets out of him, ballistics will prove they were fired from your gun.'

'How can that be?'

'Isn't it obvious? This was the "operational emergency" that delayed Ménard. They needed enough time to bring your gun here and kill Boukhatem with it before taking it back to DGSE for you to collect on your way out. They must have been holding him captive.' Hidouchi reaches behind her, draws her gun from its waistband holster and fires three shots into the dead man. The detonations echo deafeningly from the marble walls of the bathroom. And there are three more bloody holes in Boukhatem's bathrobe.

Taleb stares at her in stupefaction. 'Why did you do that?'

'It'll complicate the ballistics. Two guns; two shooters: not quite what they've bargained for. We should leave now. They'll probably have despatched an armed police squad already. This is all one big set-up. I intend to find out who ordered it. And why.'

'I may know why.' Taleb opens his bag and pulls out the tape box.

'What is that?'

'An old reel-to-reel tape recording. Made, according to the label, on the second of June, 1965. Zarbi and Laloul in conversation with Guy Tournier before they murdered him, I suspect.'

'Don't you know?'

'I don't have a machine to play it on. I only got hold of it last night.'

'Then we'd better find one. Now, let's get out of here. We have no allies from this point on.' She holsters her gun. 'Except each other.'

'Any ideas about where we should go?' Taleb asks as they hurry along the corridor from Boukhatem's room.

'A few,' Hidouchi replies. 'But they can wait until we're out of the hotel. We'll go down by the fire escape in case they're already here and are monitoring the elevators.'

Taleb hears a ping from the direction of the lift shaft just as they slip through the door marked ESCALIER DE SECOURS. They start down the stairs.

'Why would the DGSE want Boukhatem dead?' he asks breathlessly as they descend.

'Because dead men can't talk. The same goes for Zarbi and Laloul. I was ordered to terminate both of them.'

'So what was my role supposed to be?'

'Working with your department was intended to make it look as if we really wanted to bring them in. I don't think my boss bargained for me being partnered with a competent detective.'

'"A competent detective". Is that right?'

They reach the ground floor, but Hidouchi heads on down,

following the GARAGE sign. 'We need a car,' she explains. 'Even if we ditch our driver, the embassy vehicle's too easy to trace.'

'How's your car-stealing technique, Agent Hidouchi?'

'Better than yours.' She pauses as they pass a sagging cardboard box full of assorted drawer panels and coat hangers that's been left on one of the landings. She grabs one of the hangers and carries on, bending the hook straight as she goes. 'As you'll see.'

The parking garage is deserted. Hidouchi takes a fast prowl round the cars before selecting an aged Lancia. She opens its door using the coat hanger, so deftly Taleb suspects there's a wild adolescence lurking in her past. Then she takes a small screwdriver out of her bag, unscrews a panel beneath the steering wheel and pulls it off, revealing a bunch of wires. After she's used a penknife she's also carrying to strip the insulation off a couple of the wires, she twists them together and the car starts. 'I'll drive,' she announces.

There's a barrier at the top of the exit ramp that looks as if it might prove a problem until Taleb spots a plastic card with the hotel's logo on it lying in the well between the front seats.

Hidouchi slides the card into a slot and the barrier obligingly rises. They turn out on to the road at the front of the hotel. As Hidouchi predicted, there are a couple of cars with flashing blue lights near the main entrance. She accelerates gently past them and heads for the autoroute.

'Open my bag and take out the grey phone,' she instructs Taleb. 'Not the black.'

'You have two phones?'

'One is for emergency use. HQ don't know the number.'

'That sounds like the kind of precaution someone would take if they expected to be double-crossed at some point.'

'Just get the grey phone out, Taleb. The user code is twenty-two zero three.'

'Who am I phoning?'

'Source retail outlets for used and vintage audio equipment. Then start calling them. We need to hear what's on that tape.'

Taleb finds the grey phone and turns it on. He starts the online hunt as they speed along the slip road on to the A1. Hidouchi doesn't interrupt as they join the southbound traffic, though it's clear to Taleb she thinks he's making heavy weather of it. Eventually, he comes upon a promising candidate: L'Électronique d'Époque, with an address in the tenth arrondissement. He calls the number.

The man who answers sounds gruff but knowledgeable. As for reel-to-reel tape recorders, 'You will find nothing in the whole of Paris to match my range, monsieur. They start at fifty euros. Pricey, you may say, but they come with my personal guarantee. Ask anyone and they will tell you: Hervo is the prince of reel-to-reel reconditioning.' Taleb swallows the patter without quibbling and asks to reserve one. But Hervo will only say, 'If I still have one when you get here, monsieur, it will be yours for sixty-five euros.' Inflation, it seems, is rampant in the vintage electronics market, but Taleb doesn't argue. 'We'll be there within the hour,' he says, ending the call.

'Aim for the city centre,' he tells Hidouchi. 'Gare du Nord, Gare de l'Est – that's the right direction.'

'This guy definitely has what we want?'

'So he says. And he sounds like an expert. It'll cost us sixty-five euros.'

'Have you got that?'

'In cash?'

'Well, it'll have to be. I won't be using my credit card and neither will you.'

'I only have dinars.'

'It's lucky you're with someone who thinks ahead, Taleb. Now, since there'll be no need for you to navigate until we get off the autoroute, there's nothing to stop you from filling me in on how you came by that tape. It's time you told me everything. Then I'll do the same for you.'

Taleb was sure, before leaving Algiers, that he would never inflict the truth on Hidouchi – that one of the two men they are pursuing is the keeper of many of le pouvoir's darkest secrets. Now he finds himself doing just that. The time has come for her to know. After which there will be no turning back for either of them.

To learn, as he then does, that Hidouchi has been authorized, if not encouraged, to terminate him along with Zarbi and Laloul is both shocking and yet unsurprising. Abderrahmane was right. He was in their sights as soon as he took the case on. And he needed her help more than he knew.

There can be no evasions now, only artful accommodations. It is to be a fight for survival: his and Hidouchi's – and Abderrahmane's as well.

Parking is impossible outside L'Électronique d'Époque, so Hidouchi drops Taleb off and heads for the nearest less congested street. The facade of the shop has a faded Art Deco look to it, while the interior is crammed with TVs, hi-fis, video recorders, record players, loudspeakers and empty cabinets of assorted vintages. There doesn't appear to have been a rush of customers since Taleb called. The portly proprietor is partly obscured by a stack of audio cassette recorders and greets his entrance with a weary glance up from the magazine he's reading.

'Monsieur Hervo?' Taleb ventures.

'Monsieur reel-to-reel?' Hervo doesn't smile, but regards Taleb coolly over his half-moon reading glasses. 'You are in luck. I still have a machine for you.'

He hoicks a mask over his mouth and nose, stands, with evident difficulty, and emerges into the chaos on Taleb's side of the counter. 'Audio cassettes just don't have the reproduction quality of reel-to-reel, do they?' he remarks, to which Taleb manages no response beyond a smile and a nod.

Hervo lumbers to a corner of the shop, then lumbers back with the promised tape recorder: a substantial machine of some age but apparently in good condition. He deposits it carefully on the counter. 'Here we are. Philips. Made with loving attention to detail in Eindhoven when you and I were still at school. Restored to full working order by my magical hand.' He lifts the lid to reveal the reel heads. 'You won't do better for the price.'

'Sixty-five euros?'

'Sixty for cash.'

'Can I try it?'

'All right.' Hervo locates the flex and stretches across the counter to plug the machine in. 'Now, where do I have a tape for you to play on it?' He gazes around, scratching his second chin thoughtfully.

Taleb is about to take the 2 June 1965 tape out of his bag when the door opens to a jangle of the bell and Hidouchi strides in.

Hervo turns and gazes at her with admiring eyes. 'Welcome to L'Électronique d'Époque, madame. Claude Hervo at your service.'

'Is that the machine?' she asks, nodding to the Philips on the counter.

'Ah, you're together.' He turns to Taleb. 'Your daughter, monsieur?'

'We are not related,' snaps Hidouchi, advancing towards them.

'No matter, madame.' Taleb senses Hervo is smiling ingratiatingly beneath his mask, though the mask is not the only reason why the effort is futile. 'Your . . . friend . . . was about to try out this wonderful piece of twentieth-century technology. Now you can both hear how well it performs.'

'It works?' queries Hidouchi.

'Most certainly.'

'We need somewhere to use it.'

'Well, I was just looking for a tape to—'

'We have a tape, Monsieur Hervo. And I have your sixty-five euros.'

'Sixty for cash,' puts in Taleb.

'Do you have a private room where we can use the machine after paying you for it?' Hidouchi poses the question to Hervo with an accompanying tilt of the head. She is clearly impatient.

This induces in Hervo a bristle of professional pride. 'This is a shop, madame, not a studio for hire.'

Hidouchi pulls out a wad of euro notes. 'A hundred for the machine plus the room.'

Hervo eyes the money. Pride has its price. And it's not a high one. 'Well, there is a storage room upstairs which you could use, I suppose.' He extends a greedy hand. Hidouchi counts out a hundred and passes it to him. He pockets it immediately, then nods in the direction of a door behind the counter. 'This way.'

The storage room is low-ceilinged and narrow-windowed, the air stale and dusty. The contents comprise an assortment of equipment similar to that of the shop, but in shabbier condition. Hervo huffs and puffs around, clearing a space on a table piled with old catalogues and tracking down a socket obscured by a stack of video cassettes, where he plugs in the tape recorder. Then he wanders off to a corner filled with display boards for what might have been appearances at trade fairs in times gone by.

'You can leave us to it,' says Hidouchi, hands on hips.

'I'm looking for a chair,' Hervo explains. 'So you can both sit down.'

'That won't be necessary.'

'I thought there was a stool up here somewhere.' He has by now vanished from sight behind one of the boards.

'Monsieur Hervo!'

He reappears. 'Madame?'

'We would like you to leave now. We will come down to the shop when we've finished.'

'You don't need . . . the stool?'

'What we need is privacy.'

'Ah. I see. Very well.'

With a flounce of irritation, Hervo makes a shambling exit.

Only when they've heard his footsteps reach the foot of the stairs does Hidouchi close the door behind him.

'Well?' she says, turning to Taleb. 'What are you waiting for? You must know how to use these things better than I do.'

There's no disputing that. Similar machines were used to record interrogations when Taleb began his police career in the 1970s. He switches the Philips on and loads the tape.

'I think we're ready,' he announces.

Hidouchi returns from opening a couple of windows as wide as she can and sits up on the edge of the table. She nods to him. 'Let's hear it.'

Despite Hervo's claims of superior sound reproduction, there's some crackle on the playback. There are background noises too – muffled thumps, rustlings, inaudible mutterings. Taleb was expecting to hear three voices – Zarbi's, Laloul's and Tournier's. In the event, he hears only one voice, quite high-pitched and tremulous. The accent is educated French, with an anxious edge to it that drains out most but not all of the super-ciliousness. Guy Tournier was a frightened man on the evening of 2 June 1965, but he hadn't abandoned all his assumptions about where he stood in relation to the two Algerians holding him captive.

Unfortunately for him, they didn't share those assumptions. The War of Independence was only three years over. The griefs and grudges of the long campaign were still fresh in their minds, as they were in his. They were still Tournier's enemies and, as far as they were concerned, he was still theirs. But he was also their prisoner.

'A forced confession is worth nothing in law, my friends,' is Tournier's opening statement. 'How will anyone know I'm not just saying what you require me to say? Besides, this ugly business between your country and mine has been going on so long no one's really interested in the truth any more. We're all merciless oppressors to you and you're all bloodthirsty murderers to us. You surely don't suppose a single French man or woman will change how they think about Algeria because they hear me admit to a few dirty tricks we played – tricks we only resorted to because you dragged us down to your own uncivilized level and—'

Tournier screams then, so loudly Taleb lunges for the volume control.

Before he reaches it, there is suddenly silence. A few seconds pass. Then Tournier resumes speaking, gasping for breath between his words. 'I suppose . . . this is how—'

Hidouchi reaches across and presses the Stop button. 'What happened there?' she asks.

'The gap, you mean? They stopped recording, then started again. My guess is they didn't want their voices on the tape.'

'What are they doing to him?'

'Something designed to persuade him to be more forthcoming.'

'Well, we'll find out if it worked, won't we? Play the rest.'

Taleb presses the Play button. Tournier's voice resumes once more. '. . . how you dealt with any French soldiers who were unlucky enough to fall into your hands during the struggle. It only proves . . . you weren't fit to govern yourselves. You won the war. You got us out . . . of your rotten country. But how does victory taste to you? Eh? How does it actually taste?'

Another pause, then, slightly slurred: 'All right, all right.

There's no need for that. I understand . . . You'll have what you want. I'll say it, OK? I'll tell all the truths. My name is Guy Albert Tournier. Date of birth fifth April 1928. I have worked for the past seven years . . . as a special aide to President de Gaulle. I am speaking in my apartment in Paris on the second of June, 1965. OK? I am sworn.'

Pause.

'The Algerian committee was set up early in 1959. Its purpose was to advise the Chief – de Gaulle – on all matters relating to what was called the Algerian problem. He never . . . attended our meetings. And all our proceedings were secret. He gave us objectives and we gave him options for achieving those objectives. We communicated on his behalf . . . with whoever we needed to in order to accomplish what he required. Deniability was our watchword. We had to ensure no decision could ever be explicitly traced to the Chief.'

Pause.

'I'm not sure every member of the committee understood the Chief's Algerian policy. We never explicitly discussed it. He never spelt it out. I understood, because I was his closest adviser on the subject. Remember what he said to the crowd outside the Gouvernement-Général in Algiers on that famous day in June of fifty-eight? It was his first visit to Algeria. Mine too. I don't think . . . I've ever seen such a blue sky before or since. Or such hope . . . as on the faces of the people gazing up at him on the balcony. Not just the pieds noirs. The Muslims too. Everyone wanted him to be their saviour. And he told them he would be. "Je vous ai compris!"

'They went crazy. They wept. They cheered. They lapped up every word. He held them in the palm of his hand. He persuaded them to believe . . . in an illusion. Because what he didn't say was more important than what he did. And what he didn't say was "Vive l'Algérie française!" Yes, he understood them. He understood all of them. And because he understood them . . . he knew how to deceive them.'

Pause.

Tournier resumes, but he's breathing heavily now. 'The Chief knew from the outset . . . we had to leave Algeria. Nothing could stop independence . . . But he had to appear to promise the pieds noirs he would not abandon them . . . And at the same time he had to convince the FLN he would not capitulate. It had to seem that letting Algeria go was forced on him by circumstances. But he intended to manipulate those circumstances . . . to secure an independent Algeria that was good for France. One of his original objectives . . . was to grant independence only to the populated coastal strip between the Mediterranean and the Atlas Mountains, on the grounds that the Algerian Sahara was not genuinely Algerian at all. He was only interested in the Sahara because of the oil and gas reserves under it, of course, and because it could be used for nuclear weapons tests. When peace talks began in May of sixty-one . . . he was optimistic we could hold on to the desert as part of an eventual deal. But your lot wouldn't give any ground – literally – and the talks collapsed a month in.'

Pause.

'When talks restarted, your side was immovable on more or less every issue. That put paid . . . to the Saharan project. The Chief realized then that you didn't intend to give him . . . an honourable exit from Algeria. You were aiming to humiliate him and France. Well, two can play at that— Aaah!'

Pause.

Tournier resumes, sounding groggy. 'He needed an excuse . . . to crack down on you – a pretext . . . for a show of strength that would force your negotiators to be reasonable. Our committee recommended an event on French soil for maximum impact. The problem . . . was the truce on terrorist actions in France the FLN had observed since peace talks began. That truce . . . had to be broken. And if the FLN wouldn't break it of their own accord . . . it would have to be broken for them. Our double agents inside the FLN provoked you into violence by setting up victims for police beatings. You didn't know it, but we'd corrupted many of your supposedly faithful brothers-in-arms. Well, I'm sorry to disillusion you, but we had—'

Pause.

'Oh, blackmail, bribery, coercion – the usual ploys. By the summer of sixty-one our agents were threaded through your ranks like veins of blue in a Roquefort cheese. That had always been the Chief's final line of defence: fight the enemy from within.'

Pause.

'Provocation breeds provocation, all right? That was . . . that was the plan. You started murdering police officers. And the police started taking revenge for those murders. We knew what they were going to do and we let them do it. In fact, we wanted them to do it. We needed them to do it. Algerians routinely stopped and searched on the street; mass arrests; deportations back to Algeria; Z squads and harki auxiliaries demolishing shanty dwellings and hauling people into cellars to be tortured; those who died from their injuries trussed up in sacks and thrown into the Seine: it was open season. And then a strictly enforced night-time curfew for all Algerians. We made sure it wasn't easy being an Algerian in Paris that summer and autumn. It's no wonder . . . so many of you joined the protest marches on the seventeenth of October.'

Pause.

'I don't know . . . I don't know how many were killed . . . that night . . . and during the nights that followed. A hundred? Two hundred? No one will ever know for sure . . . A lot of the bodies floated down the Seine all the way to the sea . . . Others were sealed in concrete in large oil drums . . . and dropped into the Mediterranean from planes flying to Algeria . . . All those killings . . . every one of them . . . here, in Paris.' Tournier sighs. 'Most Parisians approved of what was done . . . Some of them even helped the police do it . . . I heard a story that at one of the bridges . . . where corpses were being thrown into the river . . . a bus stopped and the driver and all his passengers got off and joined in . . . A couple of days later, I went to the Palais des Sports . . . where several thousand Algerians . . . were being held . . . to check what was going on . . . in case the Chief wanted to know. It was . . . bad. It was . . . too much, I . . . have to admit.'

Pause.

'You really want it all . . . don't you? Well, at the Palais des Sports . . . a police officer took me to a room where rubbish bins were stored and . . . there were bodies piled in the bins, legs and arms sticking out and . . . on the floor . . . pools of blood and urine . . . He was actually proud to show me . . . what they'd done . . . As for the Chief . . . he never did want to know.'

Pause.

Tournier's voice is hoarse now, but still there's no trace in it of remorse. 'From our point of view it all worked . . . as it was intended to . . . Negotiations restarted, this time in earnest . . . We'd shown you the horror we could unleash if we set our minds to it. The Chief had his way out. We'd bought it for him with your blood.'

Pause.

'All right, all right. I'm going to tell you . . . Nine months later, you were waving flags and blaring car horns on the streets of Algiers to celebrate independence. Vive l'Algérie algérienne! You'd won. Or you thought you had. But Ben Bella needed our help to rebuild the country after eight years of war. We couldn't have the Sahara. But maybe we could still have the resources under it. Our companies are building your pipelines and refineries. Our ships are carrying your oil. We are making the money. And we're letting a select few of you steal most of what's left from the poor misgoverned people of Algeria.'

Pause.

'You see? The Chief never loses, even when you think you've beaten him, even if he says you've beaten him. The Chief always prevails.'

Pause.

'We gave you your country, my friends, but it came with a condition we were determined to impose. You can't prosper. Independence can't be allowed to work. Algeria – your Algeria – must be a failure. You think Ben Bella's difficulties have just been the republic's teething problems? Think again. They're merely the start. We're going to fuck you up for the next fifty years. No, wait! You should hear this. Our agents still take our francs and our favours. They still do our bidding. And your government has no idea who they are, because there are so many of them inside your government making sure they have no idea. If one of you was one of ours – for the sake of argument – the other wouldn't know, wouldn't suspect, wouldn't see the traitor standing beside him. Under the guise of independence, we've imprisoned you in a hall of mirrors. So, take a good long look at what's staring back at you from the glass. In the moment of your victory . . . you lost everything.'

A silence falls, rendering the background hiss of the tape clearly audible. Taleb has the impression Tournier is pausing for effect, letting the full meaning of his words sink in.

Then, for the first time, another voice is heard. Not Zarbi's, Taleb feels sure, so it must be Laloul's, low-pitched and flat-toned. 'Turn it off.'

And there is only silence after that.

Taleb presses Stop, then Rewind. The tape winds back on to its spool. Neither he nor Hidouchi speaks until it's reached the end.

Hidouchi pushes herself upright. 'I did not know they hated us so much,' she says quietly.

'It seems hizb fransa may have been real after all,' Taleb muses. 'A myth become history. Just like the water-measurer. When I told you about him, you didn't want to believe me, did you? You didn't really want to believe any of it. But now you have to. We both do.' He shakes his head in wonderment – and dismay. 'Perhaps we should be pleased to discover that not all our woes since independence have been self-inflicted.'

Hidouchi rounds on him. 'Why didn't Zarbi and Laloul use that tape against de Gaulle, Taleb? Why did they let him get away with it?'

'I'll be sure to ask them. If I get the chance.'

'And does it explain Boukhatem's murder?'

'Not to me. But maybe the DGSE is still playing Tournier's game.'

'Well, we know who to ask about that, don't we? Ménard.'

'It could be difficult to have a frank conversation with her in our present situation.' Taleb sighs thoughtfully. 'But . . .'

'What?'

'Maybe it's easier to engineer some time alone with her assistant, the cat-loving Réau. Yes. I think I have an idea.'

'Make it a good one.'

He looks up at her. 'Well, that's the thing with ideas, Agent Hidouchi. You never know whether they're good or bad . . . until you try them out.'

TWENTY-FOUR

LATE AFTERNOON. AND THE BOULEVARD MORTIER IS QUIET, ALMOST sleepy. Traffic levels have not regained the normal Parisian frenzy, despite the virus abating over the summer. Hidouchi and Taleb loiter in the Lancia, which they're gambling hasn't been reported stolen yet, taking periodic slow drives round the block so as to avoid attracting any attention from the guardposts at the entrance to DGSE.

Several hours have passed since they listened to the tape and they're no closer to understanding how – or if – it explains Boukhatem's murder. They've tuned in at intervals to local news broadcasts on the car radio and heard nothing about a body at the Charles de Gaulle Horizon, though they've no doubt it has been found, along with the incriminating evidence against them.

Hidouchi's best guess is that the DGSE knew what was expected of her – that she was expected to arrest Taleb herself or maybe shoot him at the scene. Now she's failed to act as anticipated, a news blackout has been ordered while Ménard considers her options. She's undoubtedly circulated their identities and photographs to the airports and main railway stations. And facial identification systems are probably tracking the autoroutes. Their chances of leaving France undetected aren't good.

On the other hand, Ménard may not have considered the sort of counterattack they've decided to attempt. Staking out DGSE is riddled with hazards and there's no guarantee Gilles Réau won't leave the building by some route unknown to them or make his exit while they're on one of their circuits of the block. The odds of spotting him aren't a lot better than fifty-fifty.

As it is, though, those odds don't seem so unattractive when their other options are so limited. Taleb has rejected phoning Bouras and asking for his help because, in the circumstances, it's unclear what help the Director could actually give him. He's on his own. Or he would be, but for Hidouchi. She's thrown in her lot with him and must live – or die – with the consequences. Taleb wonders, as they wait and watch the comings and goings at the entrance to DGSE, if she regrets doing that, though he decides not to ask her. He's not sure he really wants to know whether she does or not.

Hidouchi seems to be developing a sixth sense for his trains of thought, however. Despite having a small pair of binoculars raised to her eyes, with her attention apparently fixed on the DGSE compound, she suddenly says, in a thoughtful tone, 'You can't fight your own nature, Taleb. I wouldn't have been able to live with myself if I'd gone along with framing you for killing Boukhatem. Not because I'd have felt guilty for what happened to you. But because I'd have known that I'd been given an opportunity to expose a hard truth about my country's past and present – and thrown it away.'

'It's a relief I don't have to feel indebted to you, Agent Hidouchi,' Taleb says drily. 'Although this opportunity you speak of . . . would be regarded by most people as a curse.'

'Just as well I'm not most people, then.'

'Oh, I don't think anyone will ever accuse you of being that.'

'What about you, Taleb? Are you glad our enemies have finally stepped into the light?'

'When you're my age, Agent Hidouchi, you'll find a quiet life much more attractive than confronting any number of enemies – personal or national.'

'Yet here we are. Preparing to take the fight to them.'

'Sometimes—'

'Wait!' The sudden tension in Hidouchi's posture tells Taleb she's spotted something. He sees her slender fingers adjust the focus ring on the binoculars. 'Yes. It's him. Réau. On foot.'

Taleb squints into the middle distance and recognizes the figure emerging from DGSE. It's definitely Réau. He's carrying a shoulder bag and moving with a short, hurried stride Taleb could almost have predicted. He turns left, away from them.

'Heading for the Métro is my guess,' says Hidouchi as she drops the binoculars in Taleb's lap and starts the car. She's using the screwdriver as an ignition key now. To Taleb's surprise, it has served the purpose perfectly after her adjustments to the wiring. 'If I'm right, I'll get out and follow him into the station. You'll have to drive from there. We'll meet wherever he exits the system and grab him at that point.'

'You're a better driver than me,' Taleb objects as they accelerate away from the kerb. 'Wouldn't it make more se—'

'If Réau realizes I'm following him, he may make a run for it.' Hidouchi has reduced the chances of his recognizing her by tying her hair up and putting on a baseball cap, but her next point is unanswerable. 'Who would you back to keep up with him – you or me?'

'OK. You win.'

They've closed most of the gap between them and Réau by now. Hidouchi slows. He's approaching one of the entrances to Porte des Lilas station. They'll soon know if he's going in. 'I'll keep you updated on where we are as much as I can,' says Hidouchi. 'I'll need you to stay as close as possible.'

'I will. But that's not going to be easy.'

Réau enters the station. Hidouchi pulls over and stops.

'I'm counting on you,' she says, glancing at him as she jumps out of the car.

He's about to say he's counting on her as well, but she's already gone, slamming the door behind her. And by the time he's scrambled out of the car and hurried round to the driver's side, she's vanished into the station.

Taleb moves off and takes a slow left into the next street, where he pulls in again. Hidouchi will report soon on the direction Réau's taking on the Métro. From his bag he pulls out the map of Paris he brought with him from Algiers: an old Michelin pocket street atlas dating from 1983, the year he and Serene came to the city on their honeymoon.

He's looking for the diagram of the Métro network near the back, which will give him some idea where to aim for once Hidouchi starts reporting progress. But the book falls open at a page inside the back cover, where Serene jotted down the names and addresses of restaurants and tea rooms they particularly enjoyed while they were here, in preparation for a return visit that never happened: La Flore en l'Île; Angelina; Le Pantruche – all in her fondly remembered handwriting. Taleb freezes in a long moment of recollected loss.

Then his phone beeps. There's a text from Hidouchi. *Line 11 towards Châtelet.* That's good. He knows where Châtelet is. He flicks his way through the pages to the map of his current location. The stations on line 11 appear to track south-west from Porte des Lilas along rue de Belleville, which he's just turned on to. All he has to do is follow the route from there. He puts the car into gear and moves off.

*

He's just passing Goncourt station when the second text comes in. *Off at République stand by.* He accelerates, shocked to realize how far behind he's fallen. He's only covered half the distance to République when another text comes in. *Line 9 towards Pont de Sèvres.* He flattens the book open on the steering wheel in front of him. He's in luck. Line 9 tracks another major route. From the Place de la République he swings west and follows signs for Opéra and the Gare St-Lazare.

He's at a red light on Boulevard Haussmann, with the frontage of the Gare St-Lazare visible along the street to his right, when the next text comes in. *Off at St Augustin no change of line here so must be leaving stand by.* The map tells him the Place St-Augustin is dead ahead. But he isn't there yet. The red light stays stubbornly, perversely red. He drums his thumbs on the wheel. If only he was still in Algiers. He could switch on the flashing blue light and run the junction. But he's not in Algiers. He has to wait.

Green at last. He floors the accelerator and takes off.

Another text. He glances down to read it. *Exiting station Boulevard Haussmann are you there?* He can't stop to answer. He just drives, scanning ahead for a glimpse of her.

There she is, moving towards him, a few metres behind Réau. Réau's got his head down, attention fixed, his posture suggests, on his phone. Taleb risks a flash of the headlamps. Hidouchi raises a hand discreetly in acknowledgement. She starts closing on Réau as Taleb closes on both of them.

Hidouchi falls in behind Réau, matching him stride for stride. A trio of youths passes by, heading in the opposite direction. One of the youths brushes against Réau, who is knocked marginally off balance and glances irritably after them.

In that second, Taleb guesses, Réau sees Hidouchi. He looks momentarily dumbstruck. Maybe the baseball cap fools him. But not for long. He turns away, as if to run.

But Hidouchi is already on him, one hand clasping his shoulder. Something in her posture tells Taleb she is pressing a gun into Réau's back. The Frenchman freezes.

Taleb pulls in beside them and stretches over to open the near-side rear door. He can see Hidouchi's gun now, jammed against Réau's jacket about halfway down his spine. Réau looks frightened, his face white with shock. Hidouchi pushes him towards the open door.

He half-falls, half-climbs into the car, his bag slipping off his shoulder and tumbling to the floor. Hidouchi climbs in beside him. 'Go,' she says, glancing at Taleb as she pulls the door shut behind her.

Taleb pulls away. 'Wh-what . . . what do you think you're doing?' stammers Réau.

'We're taking you for a drive, Gilles,' says Hidouchi. 'And a talk. We have a lot we want to talk to you about.'

'This . . . this is a mistake.'

'No. No mistake. Except the one you and your boss made by underestimating us.'

Taleb speeds out into the Place St-Augustin and chooses an exit more or less at random, heading north-west along Boulevard Malesherbes. He tells himself to slow down. He's fairly sure there was no one close enough when they grabbed Réau to realize what was happening and therefore there's no reason to fear pursuit.

'Where are you taking me?' Réau asks, his voice wavering.

'We only want answers,' says Taleb, 'not questions.' Which is as well, since this is one question he certainly can't answer.

'Tell us about Ibrahim Boukhatem, Gilles,' says Hidouchi firmly. 'Was he on the DGSE payroll?'

'I can't . . . tell you that.'

'You're going to have to.'

'No. I—'

'Gilles, if you don't tell me I'm going to shoot you in the knee.

Understand? And you really aren't paid enough to have to limp for the rest of your life. So . . . was Boukhatem one of yours?'

Réau sighs. He can see no way out of this. 'Not . . . not officially,' he finally admits.

'But unofficially?'

'We used him . . . from time to time.'

'For what?'

'Manipulating dissidents . . . in the Algerian community.'

'So, killing him lost you a valuable asset. What made him expendable?'

'We realized . . . he couldn't be trusted.'

'In what way?'

'Look, among other things, he . . . kept an eye on Laloul for us. And—'

'Is Laloul part of hizb fransa?' Taleb cuts in.

Réau sounds genuinely puzzled. 'I don't know . . . what that is.'

'What did Laloul do for you, Gilles?' Hidouchi asks.

'I don't know. It was all way before I joined the service. Whatever it was, it earned him lifelong protection.'

'And Boukhatem was part of the protection package?'

'Sort of. Until he . . . stopped playing by the rules.'

'Meaning?'

'He's been blackmailing Laloul. On behalf of a former associate of his.'

'Wassim Zarbi?'

'Yes.'

'So, you decided to eliminate him. And saddle us with responsibility?'

'I didn't decide anything. Boukhatem had become a problem. And your investigations were another problem. How to solve those problems was settled at a higher level.'

'How high?'

'Look, the Assistant Director—'

'Ménard?'

'Yes. Erica. She held discussions. A decision was taken. Implementation was an operational matter. I'm just . . . administrative.'

'In this case, administering a frame-up,' Taleb growls. He stops at a set of lights and glances at his map. Straight on, he reckons. At least for now. 'What were you afraid we'd unearth?'

'Our connection with Laloul, I guess.'

'How long have you been protecting Laloul?' Hidouchi asks.

'Since he left Algeria. And before, I suppose. It's nothing heavy. Just . . . money and a couple of bodyguards. Plus guarantees of immunity from prosecution and extradition.'

'Where is he?'

'A villa just this side of the Swiss border, near Geneva.' The lights change. They start moving again. 'There's nothing more I can tell you.'

'Oh, I think there is.' Taleb hears a grunt from Réau as Hidouchi prods him with the gun again. 'What do you think Laloul did for DGSE that earned him such gratitude?' she demands.

'I don't know.'

'I didn't ask what you know. I asked what you think.'

'Well, it must have been . . . pretty important . . . and over quite a period of time . . . to warrant how he's been treated since.'

'Haven't you ever asked?'

'You don't get far with a career at DGSE by asking questions like that.'

No, Taleb silently agrees, of course you don't. Any more than Hidouchi has thrived at the DSS by nosing into the case histories of double agents recruited by Toufik and his predecessors. The past is carefully guarded territory in the intelligence game. 'Who would know?' he asks. 'Ménard?'

'I suppose . . . Erica knows, yes. She'll have been briefed on Laloul's career.'

'Maybe we need to speak to her, then.'

'What did she expect to happen when we got to the hotel, Gilles?' asks Hidouchi.

'You were supposed to hold Taleb until the police arrived. Then he'd have been arrested and you . . . would have been sent back to Algiers.'

'How did she react when it didn't go according to plan?'

'She's been in touch with your boss at the DSS. Kadri. We're expecting him to arrange for you to be . . . formally disowned. In the interests of . . . good relations between our governments. Then you and Taleb can both be . . . left to us to deal with.'

'Sounds bad for us.' Taleb concedes to himself the stark accuracy of his remark.

There's a heavy pause before Réau responds. 'It is.'

'What was my motive for killing Boukhatem supposed to be?'

'We planted a file on his laptop that suggested you'd been selling him information about police investigations into some of his clients' activities.'

'And what? He and I fell out over terms? I was afraid he'd betray me?'

'Whatever seemed the best fit.'

'And how will my actions be explained?' asks Hidouchi.

'I don't know. We'll think of something.'

They're stopped by another set of lights. Taleb stares at the red light, waiting for it to change. He feels saddened almost as much as he's frightened by what his future holds. Decades of honest toil as a police officer have ended in a casual fit-up by French Intelligence. None of his colleagues will believe the cover story, of course. But their disbelief won't make any difference. Some kind of deal has been done between DGSE and DSS and there's an end of it. Le pouvoir doesn't require credibility, only observance.

The light changes to green and they're moving again. Taleb

turns right, alongside a railway line he suspects leads back to the Gare St-Lazare. Aimless circling is the best he can do until he's certain where this is leading – though, in his own mind, it's already clear.

And Hidouchi's next question confirms it's clear in her mind too. 'Where does Erica live, Gilles?'

'I can't tell you that.'

'You must.'

'That's if you ever want to see your cat again,' says Taleb. 'Or hear her purr contentedly when you stroke her. Persian, isn't she?'

'How do you know . . . about my cat?'

'I'm a detective. At least, I was. But now you and Erica have turned me into something else. A desperate man, with nothing to lose. You used my gun to shoot Boukhatem, so I'm wanted for his murder – a corrupt policeman who's killed a corrupt lawyer and gone on the run. A peaceful retirement is off the agenda for me now. What are my options? Rotting away the rest of my life in a French prison – or gunned down in a shoot-out with the Paris police? They're not exactly appetizing choices, are they? So, tell me, how would they be any worse if I murdered you as well?'

'You wouldn't.' Réau doesn't sound convinced on the point.

'I won't have to. Because you're going to tell us where Erica lives. And then, later this evening, when we can be sure she's home . . .'

'You're going to take us there,' says Hidouchi.

TWENTY-FIVE

THE REST OF SUZETTE'S DAY IS TAKEN UP WITH UNPACKING AND answering emails she let pile up while she was away. She fails to make the promised phone call to her mother, but does exchange a few texts with Élodie either side of a trip to the supermarket. Tonight she intends to grill a salmon steak, open a bottle of Sauvignon Blanc and try her very best to enjoy a quiet evening. She doesn't regret striking a deal with Lionel Baudouin, galling though it is to be required to surrender her father's confession. Handing over the original and the carbon copy will end her dealings with Nadir Laloul, however. That has to be a good thing, in this case made more palatable by the small sum of €250,000. She'll explain what she's done to her mother after the event. As for her father, she's certain Papa would want her to hand the documents over. 'It's for the best,' was something he often said, usually accompanied by a shrug and a smile. His years in Algeria had taught him that pragmatism was in the end the only viable philosophy to live by. And he had taught her the same in turn. He was a romantic at heart and so is she. But if there was ever a time to be ruled not by the heart but the head, this is surely it.

She takes a long, cool bath before dinner and has only just

come back down to the kitchen when the doorbell rings. Callers at the house are few at the best of times. It's too late for any kind of delivery. Besides, she's heard no vehicle on the drive. She wonders if she can pretend there's no one at home. But it's a warm evening and many of the windows are open, along with the doors on to the terrace. It's obvious someone's there.

The doorbell rings a second time before she answers it. Standing outside is more or less the last person she expected to see: Stephen Gray.

He looks rumpled and travel-weary. He's carrying a light rucksack, slung over one shoulder. He smiles at her, half-apologetically. 'Hello, Suzette.'

'What . . . what are you doing here?' she responds uneasily.

'Can I come in?'

'What do you want?'

'To talk. Just to talk. About the . . . situation.'

'I've nothing more to say to you.'

'I've come a long way. Can't you spare me a few minutes?'

She looks past him. 'Did you travel by car?'

'I came over on the Eurostar and took a taxi here.'

But how did he know where to take the taxi to? 'I never gave you my address, Stephen.'

'I got it from Riad.'

Silence falls, amplified by the stillness of the rural evening. She wants to turn him away. She thinks she should turn him away. But she can't bring herself to.

'Can I come in?'

'All right. But nothing you can say will change my mind.'

He doesn't disagree, although, if he believed that, he would never have come all this way. Suzette leads him through to the kitchen. He murmurs something vaguely complimentary about the house while they're en route. He's trying to establish an ordinariness to their exchanges, she senses, a base of understanding

313

he can build on. But it won't work. It's over for Suzette. It's settled.

But not done. Not yet. There's the snag.

She's already poured herself a glass of wine. It's standing waiting for her on the worktop. It would be churlish not to offer Gray a glass as well. He accepts.

They stand looking at each other, glasses in hands. It's only three days since they first met as adults, though it feels longer to Suzette – far longer. 'Where are you staying?' she asks, trying hard to sound unflustered.

'I'm booked into a hotel in Versailles.'

'You've gone to a lot of bother and expense to say what could just as easily have been said over the phone.'

'Face to face is better – and safer.'

'Even so, I'm afraid you've had a wasted journey.' She takes a deep swallow of wine. 'I've arranged to surrender the original and the carbon copy of the confession to Laloul's lawyers tomorrow. I won't be altering the arrangement under any circumstances.'

'All I'm asking you to do is listen to me.'

'Very well. I'm listening.'

'Laloul is a murderer and an embezzler. My sister and your father are among his victims. This is our chance to make him pay for what he did to them. It's probably our only chance. I'm pleading with you to—'

'What was that?' Suzette holds up a hand to silence Gray. She's heard something: the growl of a car engine on the drive. She almost feels she recognizes the sound – and the car. She hurries out through the open doors on to the terrace to see if she's right.

And she is, though she can hardly believe it. The car is Kermadec's black vintage Citroën. She looks back at Gray, who's followed her out of the kitchen. Suspicion suddenly flares in her mind. 'Did you come with him?' she demands.

Gray frowns. 'With who?'

'My stepfather.'

'I don't know what you're talking about.'

'No? Well, he's here. See for yourself.'

The Citroën draws to a halt. The expensively reconditioned engine dies. Kermadec's at the wheel. He sees Suzette looking towards him and nods to her. Beside him is a man she's met a few times before: a 'business associate' of Kermadec's called Franco Storza – an Italian whose particular line of business, according to Suzette's mother, is debt collection.

Kermadec climbs out of the car. He's wearing one of his tailor-made cream linen suits that can't disguise his muscle-bound build. He sweeps back his grey-streaked black hair, of which he's inordinately proud, and strides towards her, his pock-marked face creased by one of his trademark grins, which never convey the slightest warmth, at least in her perception.

Storza emerges into view from the other side of the car, a few steps behind Kermadec, more casually dressed, in nondescript shirt and chinos. He's a taller, leaner, slightly younger man, shaven-headed but with a moustache he's given to fondling, which is about his only distinguishing feature, since he generally maintains a poker face and says little. He has large eyes so dark they could almost be black, creating the disturbing impression that he has no irises.

Suzette has always loathed Kermadec – Storza too, as some-one cut from the same cloth. Her loathing conceals something worse, however. She fears Kermadec. It's a fear she's hidden away inside herself since the first day she met him, when he came to the apartment in Marseille to introduce himself as their land-lord, so smartly dressed in his uncouth way, so ingratiating, but also so threatening. 'You will like me,' he never said but suc-ceeded in conveying. 'You will like me or you will pretend to like me. Those are your only choices.'

Maman did no pretending. She saw Kermadec as the

protector they needed and the kind of man her husband had never been: virile, dominating, powerful. She encouraged him in every way she could. And then, conveniently and obligingly, Papa was killed. Hey presto, she was a widow and soon – indecently soon – she was Madame Kermadec. And Suzette became Kermadec's stepdaughter.

He has never struck her. He has never raised his hand to her. Yet still, now, as a woman in her early forties, she knows he could. She knows he might. She remembers the slyly lascivious glances he gave her when she was a teenager – and the simmeringly angry ones on those rare occasions when she chose to defy him. The only consistent point on which her defiance won out was her refusal to call him Papa as her mother urged her to. Papa lay in an unmarked grave in Algiers and no one – certainly not the hulking Kermadec – could replace him. She insisted on the formal Beau-père and so it has been ever since.

Suzette doesn't manage much more than a flicker of a smile as Kermadec approaches. 'What are you doing here, Beau-père?' she asks.

'Is that my greeting after driving nearly eight hundred kilometres to see you?' He pinches her cheek in what would appear to others an affectionate gesture but feels to her anything but. 'Or have we interrupted something?' He swings round and trains his grin on Gray. 'I am Gérard Kermadec, monsieur. Perhaps Suzette has told you about me.'

Gray summons a smile from somewhere. 'Her stepfather, I believe.'

'That's right.' Kermadec has moved seamlessly into English on hearing Gray's accent. Intellectually shallow though he may be, his wide-ranging business interests have made him fluent in English and Italian in addition to French and his native Corsican. 'And you are?'

'Stephen Gray. A friend.'

'Ah, the man you went to see in England, Suzette.'

She can't deny that. And she doesn't. She's not sure how much her mother has told him.

'Pleased to meet you, Mr Gray,' Kermadec continues. 'This is my . . . associate, Franco Storza.'

Gray and Storza exchange nods. Storza does not speak, though he spares Suzette a nod as well. The introductions, such as they were, are complete.

'I didn't know you were coming, Beau-père,' says Suzette.

'Didn't your mother call you? I told her to.'

'Well, she may have done. I've been rather busy since I . . . got back.'

'Entertaining your new friend. Of course. I understand. The glass of wine in his hand looks very inviting after such a long drive.'

'Why don't you come into the kitchen?' Suzette can see no way round ushering them indoors. 'I'll pour you both a glass.'

'Just for me. Franco doesn't drink.'

Suzette glances at Storza. 'Water, perhaps?'

Storza gives her a nod of consent. It seems as if he considers verbal communication a last resort. She wonders what kind of a journey it can have been from Marseille. Not a chatty one, presumably.

They all go into the kitchen. Suzette fetches a wine glass and a tumbler. 'How was England?' asks Kermadec.

She doesn't know how to answer and, for the moment, as she pours some Sauvignon for him, she says nothing.

'Good to be home, I expect.'

'Yes,' she responds awkwardly, handing him the glass.

'Did you travel together?' Kermadec directs the question at Gray.

His response is evasive. 'Not exactly.'

'Your bag?' Kermadec nods in the direction of the rucksack.

'Er . . . yes.'

'Just arrived, then?'

'Yes. Not long before you.'

'You are popular today, Suzette.' Kermadec beams at her and samples his wine. 'Nice. Very nice. Very . . . crisp.'

Suzette fetches a bottle of Evian from the fridge and fills the tumbler for Storza. She's actually grateful to these small acts of hospitality for supplying her with time and space in which to wrestle with the question her stepfather has signally failed to answer. Why is he here?

'Your mother's been worried about you,' he says, leaning back against the worktop.

'Unnecessarily,' Suzette replies.

'Ah well, that's what mothers do, isn't it? Worry about their children, sometimes unnecessarily. As you do about Timmy.' His use of Timothée's pet name always grates with her, as perhaps it's meant to. 'But I'm not sure Monique's concern about you is unnecessary, Suzette, really I'm not.'

'Is that why you came all this way?'

'Partly, yes. Your phone conversation last night left her . . . uneasy.'

'Why?'

'I'll go into the garden,' Gray offers. 'Give you some privacy.' He heads for the terrace. But to Suzette's astonishment Storza steps into his path, blocking the doorway.

'Actually, you should stay . . . Stephen,' says Kermadec. 'After all, this involves you as well as Suzette, doesn't it?'

Gray turns and looks at him. 'Does it?'

'I know everything, all right? There's no point either of you pretending you don't know why I'm here. When I say everything, by the way, I mean that. Everything.'

Gray looks at Suzette, hoping, she supposes, that she can cut them both loose from a situation that's suddenly acquired an edge of menace. But there's nothing she can do. Kermadec is in control. And now she realizes he's brought Storza with him to ensure his control goes unchallenged.

'You've returned here with your father's confession, haven't you, Suzette? The original of your father's confession. What are you planning to do with it?'

She should have chosen her words more carefully when she spoke to her mother, knowing they'd probably be passed on to Kermadec. But she was tired and out of patience with all the people who'd deceived her. 'It's none of your business what I'm planning to do,' she says stubbornly.

'I'm afraid you're wrong. I have a big stake in the outcome.'

'What do you mean?' She stares at him in bemusement and mounting apprehension.

'I'm acting for Zarbi, Suzette. I've been acting for him all along.'

'That's . . . not possible.'

'No,' Gray cuts in. 'It isn't. You don't have anything to—'

'You both need to shut your mouths.' Kermadec's fixed grin only makes his words sound harsher. 'Listen. Then you'll understand. Zarbi's a sick old man. Sicker than ever with the strain of getting himself out of Algeria. I'm looking after him in Marseille.'

'He's never mentioned you to me,' Gray objects.

Kermadec gives him a silencing glare. 'Zarbi told you as much as you needed to know. Most of the instructions you got through Boukhatem came from me. We go back a long way, Wassim and me. I regularly arranged jobs and accommodation for Algerians he knew who emigrated to France. So it was only natural he'd ask me to keep an eye on you and Monique, Suzette, when you first arrived in Marseille back in ninety-three. He was riding high then and I was happy to manage his French interests for him. Including Monique. She'd been one of his informants. An important one. I think you found that out while you were in England. Marrying her got me even closer to Zarbi. And to Laloul and his conveyor belt of cash stolen from Algerian state enterprises. They were good payers. I did whatever they wanted me to do. And my family – which includes you, Suzette, as well as your children – gained from that. You've always reckoned you're somehow superior to me. The truth is you'd be in the gutter without me. I made you.'

Suzette can't speak. She has no doubt the impact of his words is written on her face. She's always scorned him and his crude circle of friends. She convinced herself Monique chose him because she thought he could make her new life in France easier. Now she has to confront a more disturbing truth: that he chose her, at Zarbi's bidding.

'This must be a nasty surprise for you,' he goes on, 'but since you've always been sure to keep your distance from me you can hardly complain when the realities of how I put food on the table and clothes on your back go right over your haughty little head. Now, it was obviously a setback for me when Laloul vanished and Zarbi was sent to prison. A lot of lucrative business dried up overnight. And I've had my share of reverses since. Life has never been as easy as it was then – or as easy as I made it seem. But blackmailing Laloul with Nigel Dalby's confession? That'll set me up nicely for my retirement. Very nicely. It'll set up Monique too, of course, and I'll be able to treat her grandchildren generously. Which is just as well, considering their father left them high and dry and you, Suzette, don't actually know how to earn a centime.'

He suddenly strides over to her and pinches her cheek, a little harder than before. 'This ploy with the confession was supposed to go smoothly, Suzette. You weren't supposed to involve your morally sensitive self in it at all. Well, Laloul's no fool. I'll give him that. I suppose he reckoned if he could persuade you to say the confession's a fake he could hold us off, or at least force us to drop our price. I couldn't tell Monique to stop encouraging you to do what he was asking without showing my hand. I had to rely on Stephen here to convince you the confession was genuine and tell Laloul to go screw himself. Zarbi went along with that. He's so sick he was glad to let me handle things. But Stephen was stupid enough to let you lay your hands on the original of the confession. And then Laloul got to you, didn't he? He hired some thugs to torch Stephen's cottage. I guess we're lucky the confession didn't go up with it. But that must have frightened you. So, what then? A deal with Laloul, I suppose. The original of the confession in return for . . . how much?' His hold on her begins to tighten painfully. 'How much is he paying you for it?'

'Let her go,' cuts in Gray, moving across the room.

Storza pounces. He catches up, grabs Gray by the shoulder, swings him round and punches him hard in the midriff. The breath shoots out of Gray. He groans and falls to his knees. Storza pats him condescendingly on the head, as if instructing a dog to stay where he is. And Gray topples slowly against the nearest leg of the table.

'Don't worry, Stephen,' says Kermadec. 'I'm not going to hurt my darling stepdaughter.' He releases her. 'As long as she tells me exactly what she's agreed with Laloul. Well, Suzette?' He cocks his head enquiringly at her.

She can hear from Gray's breathing that he's in pain. And the very lack of expression on Storza's face suggests it could be made a lot worse for him in the near future if she doesn't cooperate. 'All right,' she says. 'Just . . . leave Stephen alone.' She's not sure what to do for the best. But she knows that in the short term defying Kermadec isn't an option. 'I've agreed to deliver the original to the Paris office of Laloul's lawyers tomorrow afternoon.'

'What time?'

'Five o'clock.'

'Will Laloul be there?'

'According to Lionel Baudouin, yes.'

'And how much is he going to pay you?'

'Once Laloul is satisfied the document's genuine, I get two hundred and fifty thousand euros.'

'Two hundred and fifty thousand? From the man who embezzled tens of millions over the years from Sonatrach? It's peanuts, Suzette. You're letting them make a fool of you. And that would make a fool of me too. If I let it happen. Where's the confession?'

'Upstairs.'

'Go and get it.'

Refusing is out of the question. Suzette understands that very clearly. The consequences of Kermadec's intervention are too far-reaching to gauge. All she knows is that she has no choice about what happens next. She starts moving towards the hallway.

'Hold on,' says Kermadec. She stops. 'Your father made a carbon copy of his confession, didn't he?'

'Yes,' she says quietly.

'And you have it, don't you?'

'Yes.'

'Be sure you bring that back with you as well.'

Suzette nods and leaves the room.

She heads along the hall, toying with the notion, now she's out of Kermadec's sight, of running out to her car and driving away. But Kermadec's car is blocking the driveway. And what would she do if she succeeded in escaping anyway? Laloul knows she has the original. So does Kermadec. They're two jaws of a vice closing around her.

She climbs the stairs and goes into her bedroom. She slides the box containing the original and the carbon copy as well as her father's typewriter out from beneath her bed. She removes the lid and looks down at the old machine and the sheaves of paper. She thinks of her father and the hours he spent producing those pages, despite what she's learned about him from them. They're his words, his story, which she's about to give away – and never see again.

But she has no choice in the matter. Kermadec's made that very clear. This is her only way out.

She picks up the box and goes downstairs.

The scene in the kitchen hasn't changed much. Kermadec is pouring himself a second glass of wine. Storza is standing exactly where he was when she left. Gray has hauled himself up on to one of the chairs and is sitting hunched forward over the table, breathing more easily now.

He catches her eye as she puts the box down on the table. He looks defeated, weary of the struggle that has brought him – has brought them – to this.

Kermadec advances to the table and peers into the box. He leafs through some of the pages and nods in satisfaction. 'Good,' he says. 'It all seems to be there.' He glances down at Gray. 'I suppose you were planning to split the two hundred and fifty thousand between you. Betraying us was a big mistake, Stephen. Suzette I can forgive. But you? Zarbi had a deal with you. Which means I had a deal with you. You don't walk away from people like us.'

'It wasn't like that,' Gray says in an undertone.

'This was all my doing, Beau-père,' says Suzette, looking directly at her stepfather to make sure he understands. 'Stephen had nothing to do with my arrangement with Coqblin and Baudouin. I was going to keep the money for myself. All of it.'

'So, it's just a coincidence he's here, is it?'

'He was trying to talk me out of it.'

'Persuasive, was he?'

'I just want to end this, Beau-père.'

'Good news, then. That's what we're going to do. Tomorrow, when you go to Coqblin and Baudouin's offices.'

'You still want me to go there?'

'Oh yes. You won't just be delivering your father's confession, though. You'll also be delivering Zarbi's final terms. You'll be telling Laloul the price has gone up. It was ten million euros. Now it's twelve.'

Suzette stares at him in astonishment. 'Twelve million euros?'

'He's got it. And he'll pay it to get Zarbi off his back. Otherwise the French media will be fed a juicy story about the brutal killing of one of de Gaulle's aides back in sixty-five. That'll force the authorities to charge Laloul with the aide's murder, though my guess – and Laloul's too, I reckon – is that they'll make sure he doesn't live long enough to stand trial. They'll want to head off the full-scale scandal that would follow if it emerged they've been protecting Laloul ever since he fled Algeria in ninety-nine. You see? He has to pay.'

'Why don't you go yourself? Why leave it to me?'

'Because it's better for me – and you – if no one knows I'm involved. You don't mention my name? OK? Not a word about me.'

Suzette nods. 'OK.'

'As far as Laloul's to know, this is all Zarbi's doing. Franco will go with you, but he'll wait outside. The confession stays with him. Laloul only gets it when he pays the twelve million euros. That's the deal. You give him the name of a bank in the Cayman Islands and an account number – I'll supply you with the details – and he wires the money to that account. Once the deposit's been confirmed, I phone Franco, he delivers both copies of the confession to Coqblin and Baudouin's reception desk and you both leave. Simple.'

'I hope so.'

'Me too. You can keep the typewriter.' Kermadec smiles. 'Something to remember your father by.'

'I want Timothée back here. As soon as this is over.'

His smile broadens. 'That'll be up to him. All I can promise you, Suzette, is that he'll have a much better life if you do what I've told you to do. So will you. And so will your mother.'

All Suzette can think of at the moment is how to extricate Timothée from Kermadec's influence. It's not going to be easy. But it will have to be done. Somehow.

That lies in the future, however. The next twenty-four hours have to be navigated first. 'All right,' she says, lowering her head slightly to let Kermadec see she has no intention of disobeying him. 'I'll do it.'

'I'm glad to hear that.'

'I don't think there's anything left to say, is there?' She hopes he'll leave now. She badly wants him out of her house, though she knows solitude won't bring her any peace.

'We'll take the box with us when we go. Franco will bring it with him when he meets you tomorrow afternoon. That's when you get the bank information. We'll take Stephen with us as well and make sure he's on the first train to London in the morning. I don't want him trying to talk you into doing something stupid.'

'I told you, Beau-père. I'm going to do exactly what you've told me to do. Nothing more. Nothing less.'

'In that case . . .' Kermadec drains his glass and grins at her. 'None of us has anything to worry about.'

TWENTY-SIX

SINCE HIS PROMOTION TO SUPERINTENDENT, TALEB HAS BEEN LESS active in the field and can't recall breaking into anyone's home, gun in hand, for many years. It's a novelty, therefore – and not a welcome one – to find himself outside a stylish apartment building in Paris's sixteenth arrondissement, activities cloaked by a soft summer night, preparing for a raid on the home of DGSE Assistant Director Erica Ménard. And this raid doesn't even carry with it the imprimatur of the Algerian police, never mind the French. Legally speaking, he's no different from an armed housebreaker.

He tries to bury that thought as he stands just out of range of the security camera above the brass-mounted bell pushes, left arm stretched to accommodate the handcuffs by which he's attached to Gilles Réau, while, in his right hand, he holds his gun and keeps it trained on Réau. Agent Hidouchi is on the other side of the doorway, gun also at the ready. The pavement's empty. The square where Ménard's weekday apartment is located – weekends, according to Réau, would find her at her country residence near Fontainebleau with her husband and her dogs – is quiet and for the moment deserted. But that may not last. They need to enter the building as swiftly as possible.

Réau's terror of being killed has ebbed into a resigned state of low-level fear. Hidouchi has convinced him she'll put a bullet through his head if he fails to cooperate. He's cooperating fully now. His loyalty to Ménard has not survived a close encounter with the human survival instinct.

Several seconds have passed since he pressed the button corresponding to Ménard's apartment. Taleb is just beginning to worry that she isn't going to respond when . . . 'Gilles?' Her voice sounds echoey through the microphone. She can obviously see Réau, but nothing, if they've calculated their positions correctly, to alarm her. 'What are you doing here?'

'Something very important has come up, Assistant Director,' Réau replies. He looks nervous. But Taleb suspects he's often nervous when talking to Ménard. 'Can I speak to you? It won't take long.'

'You could just have called me.'

'This is a . . . sensitive matter. I think you'd prefer it to be . . . face to face.'

'Now you're worrying me, Gilles.'

'It's a serious problem. But . . . I have a solution. If I could come in . . . and explain.'

'All right.'

The door-release buzzes and there's a click from the microphone as Ménard ends the connection. Réau pushes at the door and steps inside, with Taleb following him.

Hidouchi dodges in after them and closes the door. The conventional layout of a high-end Paris apartment building presents itself before them: a white-marbled hallway, with red-carpeted marble stairs curving upwards round the cage of a lift shaft. Ménard's apartment is on the fourth floor. Taleb and Réau are to go up in the lift, while Hidouchi takes the stairs. There are no signs of other residents. The building is heavy with silence.

Taleb and Réau enter the lift. Réau presses the button. It

starts an ascent that's so slow Hidouchi keeps pace with it as she climbs the stairs. 'Don't worry,' says Taleb, sensing Réau requires reassurance. 'No one's going to get hurt.'

'Even if that's true, my career will go nowhere after this. Erica will blame me for bringing you to her.'

'I've had lots of career reverses. Believe me, there are many worse things.'

'You don't understand. Erica's used to getting her own way.'

'We'll see about that.'

The lift reaches the fourth floor. They emerge slowly on to the landing. Ménard's apartment is to the left, the door standing ajar, open in readiness for Réau's arrival. Hidouchi is on the next half-landing down. She gives Taleb a cautioning glance. He nods and signals for Réau to move, stretching his arm to maximize the gap between them.

Réau pushes the door fully open and steps inside. Taleb follows. They're in an empty hallway, with a drawing room visible through an open door at the end. An exotically patterned runner and apricot-hued walls lead them on. For the moment, Ménard is nowhere to be seen.

'Erica?' Réau calls in an uneven voice.

No answer. They move slowly towards the drawing room, where lamplight falls on black and white Art Deco furnishings. Guitar music is playing softly somewhere. It creates a disarmingly tranquil impression.

They've passed several closed doors and Réau has called Erica's name again, without response. When Taleb looks over his shoulder to see where Hidouchi is, he finds one of the doors is open now and Ménard is right behind him, holding a gun that's pointing straight at him. She isn't smiling.

'Put down your gun, Superintendent,' she says.

Taleb places his gun carefully on the floor and stands slowly upright. He doesn't say anything.

'Where's Hidouchi?'

'I came without her. We didn't . . .' He smiles tentatively. 'We didn't agree on tactics.'

'If that's so—'

She breaks off. Hidouchi has snaked in through the open door of the apartment and pressed the barrel of her gun into the back of Ménard's neck. 'Why don't you put your gun down, Erica?'

'Shit,' says Ménard quietly, closing her eyes for a second or so before she glares past Taleb at Réau. 'Idiot,' she murmurs, though it's not clear to Taleb whether she's describing Réau or herself.

'The gun,' Hidouchi reminds her.

Ménard bends down and puts her gun on the floor.

'Take them into the drawing room, Taleb.'

He waves for Ménard to lead the way and follows her in with Réau. He hears the front door close firmly. Then Hidouchi joins them.

They stand a few metres from Ménard in the middle of the room. The lamps are on, but the windows are uncurtained. The illuminated column of the Eiffel Tower soars into the night sky beyond the glass. The music plays peacefully on.

Ménard frowns at Hidouchi as if mystified. 'I'm surprised to see you here, Agent Hidouchi.'

'Evidently.'

'I never thought you would be so crazy as to help Superintendent Taleb.' Ménard's tone suggests she is awarding Hidouchi a demerit in some performance appraisal exercise.

'Is that so?'

'You had the chance to detach yourself and resolve this matter neatly. Why didn't you take it?'

'Because betraying a partner isn't in my code. Whereas shooting someone who tried to frame him is. You should be in no doubt of that.'

'You're not going to shoot me.'

'Give me an excuse to and, believe me, I won't hesitate. You've already betrayed us.' Taleb believes her.

'There's nothing I can do for you,' Ménard responds. 'Taleb is wanted for the murder of Ibrahim Boukhatem and now you'll be wanted for aiding and abetting him. Not to mention abducting a DGSE member of staff. Have they hurt you, Gilles?'

The enquiry sounds disingenuous. Taleb doubts Réau believes she's genuinely concerned about him. 'No,' he murmurs.

'He had no choice but to bring us here,' says Taleb.

Ménard smiles. 'What is this, Superintendent? An effort to make me treat him sympathetically when this charade is over?'

'That's up to you. But it's no charade.'

'What else is it? Kill me and you only make it more certain you'll end up dead yourselves. There's no escape route for you.'

'You could create one if you wanted to,' says Hidouchi.

'I'd need a compelling strategic reason. And there isn't one.'

'Oh, but there is.' Hidouchi holds up the memory stick, to which, for an extra fifty euros, Claude Hervo transferred a recording of the 2 June 1965 tape.

'What is that?'

'A recording of a statement made by Guy Tournier under questioning by Zarbi and Laloul the night they murdered him. It's not the original, of course. We have that.'

'With you?'

'Its whereabouts needn't concern you. What should concern you is what Tournier says on it. Want to hear?'

'I imagine I'm going to have to. I'll fetch my laptop.'

'No. Just tell me where it is. I'll fetch it.'

Ménard points back along the hall. 'Second door on the left. My study.'

Hidouchi leaves the room. In the brief interval that follows, Réau looks at Ménard and says quietly, 'I'm sorry.' Which he certainly sounds.

Now, Taleb feels, would be the moment for Ménard to say something to suggest she understands the invidiousness of the situation her assistant found himself in. Instead, she directs her gaze at Taleb. 'I guess Agent Hidouchi is just biding her time, Superintendent. She will betray you. She has her future to think of. You won't be much use to her in that, will you?'

'You miscalculated what would happen at the Horizon Hotel because, I imagine, you always assume people will behave as you would,' Taleb replies. 'But not everybody is wholly self-serving. Our natures vary. Understanding that will be valuable to Agent Hidouchi in the future.'

Hidouchi returns to the room at that moment. She gives no sign as to how much she's heard of what he was saying. She places the laptop on a low glass-topped table and inserts the stick into its port. With a wave of her hand she invites Ménard to open it.

Ménard crosses to the sofa facing the table and sits down. She uses a remote that's lying there to stop the music, puts on a pair of horn-rimmed glasses and turns the laptop towards her. A few seconds pass. Then Guy Tournier's words, fuzzy with age, emerge into the room.

'A forced confession is worth nothing in law, my friends . . .'

Taleb gestures for Réau to sit down with him on the other sofa, facing Ménard as they listen. Hidouchi remains standing, gun in hand. Réau flinches when Tournier screams. But Ménard doesn't react. Her gaze is focused on some spot on the ceiling. Within her narrow, emotionless range, Taleb reflects, she's actually a superb performer. She's never heard the recording before, but she registers and assimilates each revelation that comes as if it's entirely normal, as if for every problem posed by the survival of Tournier's admissions she has a ready-made solution.

But she doesn't, of course. It's only an act, though an

accomplished one. There can be no ready-made solutions for problems of this nature.

'The Chief knew from the outset . . . we had to leave Algeria. Nothing could stop independence . . . But he had to appear to promise the pieds noirs he would not abandon them . . . And at the same time he had to convince the FLN he would not capitulate.'

It only gets worse from here, Taleb knows. Much worse.

'By the summer of sixty-one our agents were threaded through your ranks like veins of blue in a Roquefort cheese. That had always been the Chief's final line of defence: fight the enemy from within.'

On Tournier goes. And on. While Ménard's basilisk glare threatens to strip the paint from the plaster.

'I don't know . . . I don't know how many were killed . . . that night . . . and during the nights that followed. A hundred? Two hundred? No one will ever know for sure.'

This is bad, Taleb thinks. This is very bad. For Ménard and the French.

'Nine months later, you were waving flags and blaring car horns on the streets of Algiers to celebrate independence. Vive l'Algérie algérienne! You'd won. Or you thought you had. But Ben Bella needed our help to rebuild the country after eight years of war. We couldn't have the Sahara. But maybe we could still have the resources under it. Our companies are building your pipelines and refineries. Our ships are carrying your oil. We are making the money. And we're letting a select few of you steal most of what's left from the poor misgoverned people of Algeria.

'You see? The Chief never loses, even when you think you've beaten him, even if he says you've beaten him. The Chief always prevails.'

Now comes the finale, when Tournier seemed to lose sight of

whatever frail hope of living to see another day he might have had. It's as if his arrogance defeated his instinct for self-preservation; as if it became supremely important for him to demonstrate his contempt for the two Algerians holding him captive.

'We gave you your country, my friends, but it came with a condition we were determined to impose. You can't prosper. Independence can't be allowed to work. Algeria – your Algeria – must be a failure. You think Ben Bella's difficulties have just been the republic's teething problems? Think again. They're merely the start. We're going to fuck you up for the next fifty years. No, wait! You should hear this. Our agents still take our francs and our favours. They still do our bidding. And your government has no idea who they are, because there are so many of them inside your government making sure they have no idea. If one of you was one of ours – for the sake of argument – the other wouldn't know, wouldn't suspect, wouldn't see the traitor standing beside him. Under the guise of independence, we've imprisoned you in a hall of mirrors. So, take a good long look at what's staring back at you from the glass. In the moment of your victory . . . you lost everything.'

Then, after a pause, come the three words spoken by Laloul that as good as ended Tournier's life. 'Turn it off.' He might as well have said, 'Turn him off.' Because that's what they did. And in that moment Taleb finds it hard to blame them. Even though he knows Laloul wanted to shut Tournier up to protect himself. Because one of them was one of theirs. And Laloul was that one.

Silence follows. Then Hidouchi says, 'You can keep the stick. In case you need to remind yourself of some of the details.'

'Thank you so much,' Ménard responds, with undisguised sarcasm.

'Do you still have agents "threaded through our ranks like veins of blue in a Roquefort cheese", Erica?' Taleb notices she's switched to using Ménard's first name, as if the nature of what they've heard has deprived the Frenchwoman of the right to be addressed as Assistant Director.

Ménard looks up at her. 'What do you think, Agent Hidouchi?'

'I think this recording is evidence of French interference in Algerian affairs over many decades, extending to widespread corruption and calculated sabotage of our economy and politics. And that's what anyone who hears it will think.'

'Hizb fransa,' Taleb says in an undertone. 'Conspiracy theory become conspiracy fact.'

Ménard glares at him. His remark seems to have hit a nerve. 'The recording proves nothing.'

'Legally, you mean? Probably not. As Tournier said, it's a forced confession. But this isn't likely to play out in a court of law, is it? It's the court of public opinion that should concern you.'

Ménard looks as if she's finding it difficult to swallow. 'What do you want?' she asks at last. It is, of course, fundamentally, the only question that matters to the people in this particular room, at this particular moment. Everyone has their price. The time has come for Taleb and Hidouchi to name theirs.

'We were never at the Horizon,' says Hidouchi. 'Neither of us shot Boukhatem. We're not implicated in his murder in any way.'

'All right.' It's a purely pragmatic decision for Ménard. They've supplied her with the compelling strategic reason she needed. 'The Boukhatem murder goes away. He'll just be . . . a missing person.'

'And we have safe passage back to Algeria.'

'Agreed. Algeria. Or wherever you want to go. Once we have the original of the recording.'

'You don't get the original, Erica. That stays with us.'

Ménard stares at her, taken aback. 'There can be no deal without surrender of the original tape. That must be obvious to you.'

'What's obvious is that if we surrender the tape to you you'll be free to come after us. And if we release it to the media, you'll also come after us. So, the only way we can guarantee our safety is to keep the tape. And our safety guarantees your safety. It's win-win, Erica.'

Ménard offers no immediate response. She's evidently taking Hidouchi's argument seriously. Eventually, she says, 'I have conditions.'

'Yes?' Hidouchi raises her eyebrows as she looks down at Ménard. This is the crux of the negotiation. This is the moment of truth.

'Laloul has become a liability. Your possession of the tape makes him a potential threat. If he ever told all that he knows . . .'

'He was the water-measurer, wasn't he?' Taleb intervenes on cue. 'He paid for all the subversive actions commissioned by your government.'

'He played a crucial – a central – role, yes.'

'The madness and the mayhem we endured. The assassinations and the massacres. That was all your department's doing, Erica?'

'The destabilization programme had its own logic. My superiors – and their predecessors – were satisfied it served its purpose. As for individual actions, the programme was managed indirectly, at second and third hand. Inevitably, once you give . . . sub-contractors . . . discretion about how to achieve their objectives . . . excesses occur.'

'Excesses?' Taleb is genuinely riled now. 'You mean the death squads, the militias, the insurgents, the pseudo-insurgents, the "false flag" mercenaries, the gangsters, the crazies? You mean all of the killings they carried out? How many died to serve your "destabilization programme"? A thousand? More?'

'Once set in motion, such events become self-replicating. No one controls them.'

'Yet the oil and gas industry remained magically untouched by the violence. You managed to control that. The well heads and the refineries and the pipelines kept pumping unmolested, despite being easy targets. And the money kept flowing. Thanks to Laloul.'

Ménard stares hard at him. 'What is your point, Superintendent?'

'I just want you to understand that I understand the scale of what we're offering to conceal.'

'And how does that—'

'Be careful what you say next, Erica,' Hidouchi interrupts. 'Taleb lost his wife and daughter to one of those "self-replicating events". You might be wise to be a little . . . humbler.'

Ménard gives this revelation a few moments' thought. She eyes Taleb warily. 'It's obvious now things went too far – far too far – in the nineteen nineties. That was . . . deeply regrettable. But I wasn't with DGSE then. Since I joined, we've done our best to clean up the programme.'

'But there still is a programme?' Hidouchi asks.

'Yes, but low-key, non-violent, discreet.'

'So, if Laloul were exposed, media investigations could prove highly embarrassing – to say the least – for your government.'

'Yes. Yes, they could.'

'And a problem for you. A big problem. How would you solve it?'

Ménard looks up at her. 'Why don't you solve it for me? Laloul can't die at our hands. It would alarm too many other people who rely on our protection. But if he was believed to be the victim of a DRS operation on French soil, carried out without our knowledge or consent . . .'

'You want us to kill him for you?'

'Your department wants him dead. In the light of this' – she gestures to the laptop – 'so will mine. Arrange it . . . and you can have your guaranteed safety.'

'We'll need to be able to get to him without encountering serious resistance.'

336

'As it happens . . .' Taleb can almost see the pieces falling into place in her mind. '. . . I can arrange for you to "get to him" without leaving Paris. He's due to visit the Paris office of Coqblin and Baudouin tomorrow afternoon. I'll give you the place and time and instruct his bodyguards to let you grab him when he arrives. After that . . . dispose of him as you please.'

'Do you want his body found?'

'Preferably not. The ambiguity of disappearance has many advantages. But his abduction, in a public place, is important. It must be clear he's been seized by a hostile party.'

Hidouchi glances at Taleb, as if checking he's willing to accept Ménard's proposal. In truth, however, they foresaw this conclusion before they even entered the apartment. 'What about Zarbi?'

'He's less important. If you still want to go after him, I'd suggest you let us find him and deport him back to Algeria. It shouldn't be difficult.'

'All right.' Hidouchi gives Taleb another glance and takes a slow prowl round the table. 'We'll need an up-to-date photograph of Laloul.'

'Do we have one on file, Gilles?' Ménard asks.

'It should be . . . in your dormant assets folder, Assistant Director,' Réau replies, his voice thick with accumulated anxiety. 'Laloul's code number is zero one nine one.'

Ménard taps at her laptop, then swings it round for Taleb and Hidouchi to see. 'One of several taken a few months ago,' she tells them matter-of-factly.

So, there he is. Taleb squints at the grainy image of their quarry: Nadir Laloul, now in his mid-eighties, a shrunken, balder, greyer version of the corpulent, sleek-suited power broker who fled his homeland in 1999 and never changed or aged in the photographs the police were left to work with. His skin has sagged since, his eyes have lost their intensity, his bearing has collapsed in on itself. But his arrogance remains, his sense of entitlement to special treatment, his assumption that he cannot be touched.

'You need to manage this neatly and efficiently,' says Ménard. 'That will give me confidence that our . . . agreement . . . is sustainable for the long term.'

'Neat and efficient?' Hidouchi looks at Ménard without smiling. 'We will be those things, won't we, Taleb?'

He nods. 'Oh yes.'

TWENTY-SEVEN

STEPHEN GRAY IS CONTENT TO BE DRIVEN TO HIS HOTEL IN VERSAILLES after leaving Les Fringillidés. On one level he should feel satisfied, since the blackmail plot against Laloul he concocted with Zarbi will come to fruition after all. But he isn't going to share in the proceeds. Kermadec told him as they sped away from Suzette's home that his bungling had so nearly wrecked the whole scheme he'd forfeited his cut. 'I'm taking your percentage, Stephen,' the Corsican informed him, 'as the man who's repaired the damage you caused.'

Gray had neither the energy nor the will to argue. His ribs are sore where Storza hit him. He suddenly feels old – and altogether outmatched. He was never motivated by the money anyway, hard though Zarbi found that to believe. The sum they demanded was so vast as to seem unreal. He was determined to make Laloul suffer for what he'd done to Harriet. Zarbi had suffered – a twenty-year stretch in jail that had ruined his health. And without Zarbi, he couldn't get to Laloul. Also, according to Zarbi, it was Laloul who actually killed Harriet. But that could have been a self-serving lie, of course, which it suited Gray not to challenge. Zarbi wanted money as well as revenge. And Gray supplied him

339

with Nigel Dalby's doctored confession as the means to achieve their shared objective: hurting Laloul.

And that's still going to happen, even though Gray has so conclusively lost the trust and respect of both his sister and Suzette Fontaine that he feels bruised and defeated by the turn of events. He's spent years looking forward to the moment when he could turn the tables on Laloul and now that moment is imminent. But he isn't going to be able to savour it. He can already taste the despondency that lies in wait for him once the struggle is truly over and he has nothing to show for it beyond the knowledge that Nadir Laloul has ceased to be a rich man and Wassim Zarbi has become one instead – along with Kermadec. As consolations go, it's not much.

His mind drifts into a memory of the last time he saw Harriet, in late December 1964, when their father drove her and Nigel Dalby to the station at the end of their Christmas visit. Stephen ran down the road as they set off, waving to Harriet, who smiled and waved back through the rear window. He stopped at the corner and watched the car pull away from him. He couldn't see Harriet by then. She was gone.

He's spent much of his life since that day pursuing his lost sister. But he can never bring her back, can never reverse time and force the car to stop. Harriet never steps out and walks back towards him. She was gone then. And she's still gone now.

Night has fallen in the present. Gray glances out into the deepening darkness. He glimpses a road sign: Chartres 47km. It takes a few seconds for it to register with him that they're not going in the right direction for Versailles. Then, before he can say anything, the car slows and they turn off the main road.

'Where are we going?' he asks.

'We're taking a diversion,' Kermadec replies from the front seat without turning round.

'Why?'

'There's been a change of plan.'

'What do you mean? I want to go to my hotel in Versailles.'

'I'll explain when we arrive.'

'Arrive where?'

Now Kermadec does look round at him, though there are no street lamps on the road they've turned on to and Gray can't see the expression on his face. 'Shut up, Stephen. I don't want to hear anything from you, OK? Not a word.'

'You can't—'

'Whatever you think I can't do I can. You nearly wrecked everything. I'm not going to let you interfere any more.'

'I told you I—'

'Shut up!'

The car slows as it takes another turn. Impulsively, Gray tries to open the door, but it's locked on some central control. Then the car speeds up again. The going's rougher. The tyres thud and thump over ruts and through potholes. Ahead is a track winding through thick woodland. Beyond the glare of the headlamps the darkness is total. Gray is suddenly fearful. Where in God's name are they taking him?

'Listen, I—'

Kermadec swings his arm. In his hand he's holding something heavy and metallic. It strikes Gray on his jaw, just as he's jolted to one side by the motion of the car. He's thrown flat across the back seat. As the car jolts again, he slides down off the seat on to the floor, stunned by the force of the blow.

He thinks he may have blacked out briefly, because when he's able to reassemble his thoughts and scramble back up to the seat, the car has stopped. He hears one of the front doors slam. Then the rear door on the driver's side is yanked open. Everything's a jumble of shadows, with no light beyond the beams of the headlamps. A figure looms in front of him. Storza, he senses. He's grabbed by the shoulders and hauled out of the car.

He smells the cool woodiness of forest air. His jaw aches and his head's spinning. Storza swings him round and slams him against the side of the car. His arms are twisted behind his back. He feels a narrow cord being wound round his wrists, then tied off with a sharp jerk. Before he can even summon the breath to protest, Storza slaps a strip of duct tape across his mouth and pulls his head back by his hair.

'We go.' The words – the first Gray's actually heard from Storza – rasp in his ear. He's turned back round. Storza switches his grasp to the collar of Gray's shirt and presses what has to be the barrel of a gun against the back of his neck. He kicks Gray's heels and marches him forward, switching on a head torch he's wearing as they start off along a rough trail that leads away from the track into the woods.

The light moves unsteadily between tree trunks as they advance. Gray tries to speak, but can't move his lips enough to form any words. Storza's grip is strong and any attempt by Gray to slow his pace is met with a shove that would carry him off his feet if Storza weren't there to hold him upright. 'Keep walking,' comes the instruction.

Hope has drained out of Gray. He isn't going to survive the night. This is Kermadec's way of ensuring he doesn't interfere in the handover of the confession. A walk deeper into the woods. Then a single shot to the head. And a burial, like Harriet, in an unknown spot far from home, never found, never located.

But for the moment they just keep walking. Gray has lost all sense of how far they've come when Storza swings him away from the trail and into the tussocky, thorn-tangled undergrowth beneath the trees. Then he tells him to stop.

They're standing beneath the low canopy of a tree. The gun barrel is pressed harder against Gray's neck. 'You run, I shoot,' says Storza. He releases the cord binding Gray's wrists. 'Sit down and put your arms behind you . . . round the tree.'

Gray does as he's told. The cord is wound round his wrists again and tied off. He can't move now, with his back hard against the trunk of the tree.

The gun's no longer pressing against Gray's neck. He braces himself for the shot he truly expects will end his life within the next few seconds. There doesn't seem to be space in his head for all the regrets that should be there. He isn't even frightened any more. He's moved beyond fear, into a place of fatalistic acceptance of the inevitable.

Then Storza switches off the torch.

And Gray waits to be swallowed by the darkness that follows.

Taleb and Hidouchi sit facing one another on the two beds that have been crammed into a small room of a seedy hotel in the Goutte d'Or district of Paris. The primary attraction for them of Le Trèfle is that it operates on a cash basis, with no requests made for passports or credit cards. They've struck a deal with Erica Ménard, but they don't trust her. The Tournier tape is not in some obscure place of safety, but in Taleb's bag, and the possibility that Ménard might send some people to take it from them can't be ruled out. This she can't do, however, if she doesn't know where they are. And the Goutte d'Or is an area where two Algerians among so many other Algerians are wholly inconspicuous.

Taleb has just finished a call on his emergency phone to Director Bouras, which Bouras has left him in no doubt he would have preferred to be spared in the middle of what he hoped would be a peaceful evening. But the call has gone well from Taleb's point of view. His proposals have not been dismissed out of hand. Bouras sounded reluctantly convinced, indeed, that they should proceed as Taleb suggested. His instructions to Taleb before he left Algiers to avoid doing anything that would offend

343

the French have been overborne by the implications of the Tournier tape. The evidence that hizb fransa is real has stirred patriotic outrage in his soul and he has agreed to do all he can to help Taleb bring about a successful outcome.

'I want Laloul here, answering questions on the record, whatever those DGSE shits think,' Bouras went so far as to say, sounding riled by the prospect of the French covering their tracks at his expense. 'Are you sure you can rely on Agent Hidouchi, Taleb? Ménard has more friends in the DSS than I do and they may include most of Hidouchi's bosses.'

'We're both out of patience with the back-scratchers, Director. It would be good to get something out of this.'

'All right. But this can only work if I'm able to arrange transport. I'll call you tomorrow with a yes or no.'

'Thank you, Director.'

'And if it's no, Taleb . . .'

'Then we'll do what has to be done.'

The call ended there, leaving Taleb to grimace at Hidouchi, whose presence in the room he judged it best not to mention to Bouras. 'I think we're on,' he says, wishing he could sound a little more confident.

'We're banking a lot on your boss, Taleb,' says Hidouchi.

Taleb shrugs. 'We have to.'

'If you've misread him and he's already on the phone to Kadri . . .'

'There are risks whatever we do.'

'The risks are fewer if I simply execute Laloul.'

'But you don't want to do that, do you?'

'No.' The faint suspicion of a smile hovers on Hidouchi's lips. 'I don't.'

The darkness is unbroken. The sky clouded over as night fell, so there's no moonlight. Gray is effectively blindfolded as well as gagged. As his wait to be killed stretches on, minute by minute, he wonders why Storza is delaying the coup de grâce. What game is he playing? Is he even still there?

More time passes, unmeasurable to Gray. An owl hoots somewhere. A fox barks. The owl hoots again. A small animal – a shrew, a mouse? – scurries through the undergrowth close by. Where is Storza? What is he doing?

Then Gray sees a distant light: the glimmer of a torch. And he hears Kermadec's voice. 'Franco,' he calls. 'Dove sei?'

There's no response from Storza. Kermadec calls again. 'Franco!'

Still nothing. Gray tries to scrabble his way round the trunk of the tree he's tied to, to make it less likely Kermadec will see him. But all he succeeds in doing is scratching his arms on the rough bark without moving very far at all.

Then the torchbeam flashes in his eyes. And Kermadec closes in.

He stops a few yards from Gray. 'Where's Franco?' he demands suspiciously, forgetting, apparently, that Gray can't reply even if he wants to.

The fact eventually registers with him. He bends over Gray and pulls the tape away, leaving the skin around Gray's mouth burning. 'Where's Franco?' he repeats, clearly as baffled as Gray by the turn of events.

'How should I know?' Gray manages to reply.

'This is crazy. Where—'

The crack of a gunshot splits the darkness. And Kermadec goes straight down, crashing to the ground at Gray's feet. The torch lands a little way off. Its beam silhouettes Kermadec's prone figure. He doesn't move or make a sound.

There's movement behind Gray, though: cautious footsteps through the undergrowth. Torchlight gleams over Gray's shoulder. Storza glides past him and stoops over the fallen man. He trains his torch on the back of Kermadec's head. Gray can see a neat round hole, from which blood is oozing. 'Morto,' Storza murmurs in a neutral tone.

'I . . . I don't understand . . .' Gray begins.

Storza looks at him. 'Sta' zitto,' he responds. Then it occurs to him that Gray probably doesn't speak Italian. 'Quiet,' he adds. 'Stay quiet.'

'But—'

'We go now.' Storza retrieves Kermadec's torch, then moves round the tree and releases the cord fastening Gray's wrists. Gray's arms ache as he slowly straightens them and relaxes his shoulders. Storza pulls him bodily to his feet. 'Move.'

They start back the way they came, Storza urging Gray on a little more gently than before. Gray's thoughts are still trying to catch up with what's happened. But he's alive. He's alive and Kermadec's dead. They're wonders enough for him to cope with.

When they reach the car Storza opens the front passenger door. Gray hesitates. Is this a trap? Is he still marked for death? Storza seems to read his mind. He nods for Gray to get in. 'Zarbi says you live.'

Zarbi says you live. It doesn't explain much, but it's enough. Gray climbs into the car. Storza reaches past him and pulls a phone from the shelf under the dashboard. He presses a button and the call logo lights up. A number is being automatically dialled. He hands the phone to Gray. 'Speak while I sort out . . .' He gestures towards the woodland trail. Then he heads round to the back of the car.

By the time Gray's raised the phone to his ear there's already an answer to the call. 'Are you there, Stephen?' comes Zarbi's slow, gravelly, old man's voice. Gray hears the boot being raised. There's a clunk of something heavy.

'I'm here,' he says. The car rocks slightly as Storza slams the boot shut and strides away, carrying a shovel in his hand.

'So, Kermadec is dead?'

'Yes. He's dead.'

'Where's Franco?'

'Gone to bury him, I think.'

'Good. We can talk, then.'

'Why . . .' Gray can't form the question he really wants to ask. Why Kermadec and not me?

But Zarbi seems to understand him well enough. 'Kermadec tried to take the money for himself, Stephen. He thought I was too ill to stop him. You had to be disappeared so I would think you took it. He promised to pay Franco your share. But Franco is loyal to me. And he isn't greedy. You aren't greedy either. Stupid, yes. But not greedy. So, you live . . . and Kermadec dies.'

'And . . . now what? I go back to London?'

'Not yet. I predict, some time tomorrow, Suzette will wonder if you are OK. We need you close by . . . to reassure her. Kermadec never thought of that. Or maybe he thought he could talk her into going ahead without speaking to you. Franco will give her the correct account number to use when she meets my old friend Nadir, of course, not Kermadec's account number. And you will get your share, as agreed.'

'I don't want it.'

'But you will have it. It implicates you, Stephen. It stops you saying the wrong thing to the wrong people. So, you must have your share.'

'I won't take it.'

'Yes you will. Because, if you don't, we really will have to kill you. You don't want that, do you?'

There always is a trap, of one kind or another. Gray has escaped Kermadec's trap, only to fall into Zarbi's. He forces out the only answer he can give. 'No.'

'You will say nothing to Suzette about her stepfather's death.

347

Or anything that has happened since you left her house. Understood?'

'Understood.'

'This will be our secret. It will make you rich. And it will make Nadir poor. Which is the best I can do for you.'

'Where are you now?'

'Marseille. But I will be in Paris tomorrow. I want to see Nadir one last time. You will see him with me. You will see him crushed. That . . . is a promise.'

Taleb lies on the narrow bed in the small hotel room, with the lights and sounds of the city drifting in through the open window: headlamps; street lamps; car engines; the mosquito whine of mopeds; raised voices, in French and Arabic and occasionally English. He would very much like a cigarette. It might help him sleep. But Hidouchi, who is lying on the other bed, has expressly forbidden smoking.

They are sharing a room simply because there is safety in numbers, even if the number is only two. Their current plan, to leave with Laloul as their prisoner, breaks their deal with Ménard and is riddled with hazards. It also depends on Bouras sending a plane to fetch them. All in all, there's a lot to lose sleep over.

'I give up,' says Hidouchi suddenly, surprising Taleb, who thought she was asleep.

He clears his throat, something he's been trying not to do for some time, for fear of waking her. 'What do you give up, Agent Hidouchi?'

'The hope of sleep.'

'Ah. Did I disturb you?'

'Your unexpressed but obvious longing for a cigarette certainly hasn't relaxed me. You may as well light one.'

'You're sure?'

'Just do it.'

He heaves himself off the bed and fetches from the table by the window a chipped saucer to serve as an ashtray. Along with another saucer, a couple of cups, a small kettle and a tub of tea and coffee sachets, it makes up Le Trèfle's meagre display of in-room refreshment possibilities. He reaches into one of the pockets of his jacket, which is hanging on the back of the bed-side chair, and takes out his pack of Nassims and his lighter.

He arranges his two lumpy pillows into a back-support and sits up against them on the bed. Then he lights up. And can't repress a sigh of contentment at the first draw of smoke, fol-lowed by a stifled cough.

'Better?' asks Hidouchi.

'Not so bad, certainly.'

'You're killing yourself. You know that, don't you? I think it's ungrateful of you, considering I was told to get rid of you as well as Zarbi and Laloul. I'm doing my career no good by helping you stay alive, you know.'

'I appreciate that. But smoking isn't the most immediate threat to my life. If Ménard double-crosses us . . .'

'We may have to fight our way out. Is that what you mean?'

'I suppose it is. With which in mind, you probably ought to know I've never actually shot anyone. I've fired my gun at people a few times. But I've always missed.'

'Lucky for you you're with a DSS agent, then.'

'Have you ever killed anyone in the course of your duty, Agent Hidouchi?'

'If you want me to confide information of that nature, Taleb, I think you should start calling me Souad.'

Taleb senses the suggestion he start using her first name hasn't been made lightly. He feels strangely moved. 'I may have diffi-culty getting used to that.'

'It's not compulsory.'

349

'I appreciate that. Thank you . . . Souad.'

'No thanks are necessary. And the answer to your previous question is yes. I have shot six people dead in the course of my duty. So far.'

'Does that keep you awake at night?'

'No. I generally sleep very well.'

'But not tonight?'

'I think we can agree the circumstances are unusual. Besides . . . I've been unable to stop myself wondering why the French hate us so much.'

'Ah. The eternal question. If you're Algerian. Actually, it's not just the French. Being Algerian doesn't make you popular anywhere.'

'Maybe not. But unpopularity isn't hatred. On the tape, Tournier boasts about the Paris police killing a hundred or more Algerians in one night. He glories in revealing his government's plans to wreck our country after independence. That's hatred.'

Taleb draws thoughtfully on his cigarette. It's a good question. He's not sure he has an answer. 'That was long ago.'

'It hasn't gone away, though, has it?'

'Not yet, no.' He takes another drag. 'The problem, I think, is that we're their conscience. And their conscience isn't clear. We keep reminding them, even if we don't want to, of the sins they committed in Algeria. We committed many of our own as well. We inspired the worst in each other. But they were the invader. Which makes their guilt greater than ours. And so they see us as a standing reproach.'

Silence follows. Then Hidouchi says quietly, 'It's hopeless, then.'

'Not quite. It's slowly getting better. The next generation – and the one after that – will see things differently. Time heals everything.'

'How much time? To heal this?'

350

'More than I have left. But you are young, Souad. The future will be bright. Eventually.'

Hidouchi laughs softly.

'I have amused you?'

'I think, Taleb, you may be the most depressing optimist I have ever met.'

Gray takes a long shower once he reaches his hotel room in Versailles. The night porter who let him in didn't seem to notice anything amiss in his appearance, though Gray feels as if he's been put through a wringer. One side of his jaw is swollen. There are cuts and scrapes on the insides of his arms. And there are specks of blood – Kermadec's blood – on his shoes and trousers. He's tried to wash them off, with limited success. But he's weak and shaky and good for little, after his shower, beyond lying on the soft bed, willing sleep to come.

But it won't. His thoughts refuse to stop revolving around the folly of his pursuit of justice for Harriet. He's wasted his life chasing retribution on her behalf. And now – now that some form of retribution is actually within his grasp – he can no longer hold at bay the recognition of that waste. It's cost him his marriage, a family of his own, a settled and contented existence. It's cost him far more than it was ever worth.

It must end tomorrow. He can't go on with this. What happens next for him he can't begin to imagine. But it has to be different. It has to be what it should have been long before.

It must end.

Tomorrow.

351

TWENTY-EIGHT

SUZETTE LAY AWAKE LONG INTO THE SMALL HOURS OF THE NIGHT, willing herself to believe her visit to Coqblin & Baudouin's offices would bring her troubles to a close. Once Laloul had paid off Zarbi and Kermadec and received in return the original of her father's confession, there would be nothing that could come back to haunt her and her family. It would truly be over. She would distrust her mother and hate her stepfather, of course. But she'd done that for a long time. Distrusting and hating them even more was only a matter of degree. She would devote herself to Timothée and Élodie. She would have no dealings with Stephen Gray. The past would fall away. The future would be a serene and hopeful place.

So went her reasoning.

And when she wakes, after a few hours' sleep, to the full glare of a summer morning, it's still intact in her mind. It can be as she wants it to be. All she has to do is hold her nerve. The day will go well. She cannot allow herself to think otherwise.

The day will go well.

It has to.

*

Taleb and Hidouchi linger at Le Trèfle as the morning advances, awaiting the promised phone call from Bouras. They haven't ventured beyond the immediate neighbourhood and they've agreed they won't use the Lancia until they head for Coqblin & Baudouin's offices, in case by now the car has been reported stolen. Time hangs heavy. Hidouchi checks her gun, then rechecks it. She even checks Taleb's gun as well. He smokes several more cigarettes, thankful, unlike Hidouchi, to have discovered that the local tabac stocks Nassims. The hours slowly pass.

Gray walks the streets of Versailles. He avoids the tourist-plagued palace and gardens. As it happens, he's never visited them. His trips to Paris have always been geared to investigating what happened to Harriet. He was dragged up the Eiffel Tower by Catherine during their long weekend in the city in 1983, but that's the limit of his sightseeing. He feels guilty now about how neglectful of Catherine he was. He doesn't blame her for leaving him. In fact, he wishes he hadn't given her such ample cause. The future would be a happier place for him if she was still in his life. The idea crosses his mind that he could contact her when this is all over, sound out the possibilities of some kind of reunion. It's a fantasy, of course. He feels sure she's found someone much more companionable to share her life with. He's alone. Not because he wants to be, but because he didn't work hard enough to prevent it happening. For that to change, he'll have to change.

And maybe – just maybe – that's starting to happen. It's the most cheering thought that's crossed his mind in a very long time.

Suzette is sitting in the garden, trying hard to enjoy the sunshine, the birdsong and the freshly brewed coffee, when her phone rings. The caller, she sees, is her mother. She doesn't want to talk to Maman. But, in the circumstances, she feels she must.

'Maman?'

'Suzette, ma chérie. I hoped you would call me yesterday.'

'Sorry. A lot of things . . . happened. How is Timothée?'

'He is fine. But . . . have you heard from Gérard?'

The question surprises Suzette. It also wrong-foots her. Kermadec wouldn't want her mother to know anything of their dealings. What is she supposed to tell her? 'Er . . . why do you ask?'

'He had to travel to Paris yesterday. On business. It was . . . unexpected. I thought he might contact you . . . while he's there.'

'He hasn't called me, Maman.' Which is technically true.

'I was hoping he might have. I haven't heard from him, you see. And he's not answering his phone.'

'That's odd.' And so it is. Kermadec should have made sure she had no cause for concern.

'Yes. It is. But I suppose he'll be in touch soon. He can be a little thoughtless sometimes.'

A little thoughtless. As character summations go, it hardly does justice to the arrogant bully Gérard Kermadec truly is. 'Well, I don't know where he is, I'm afraid.' Again, this is technically true. 'Can I speak to Timothée?'

'He's not here at the moment. Actually, I called you while he was out so he wouldn't worry about Gérard.' How considerate of her. 'This thing with the Swiss lawyers, ma chérie. You should do what their client wants, you know. You should take the money he's offering you. For Timothée's sake. And Élodie's, of course.'

'I agree.'

'What did you say?'

'I agree. I'm going to tell Monsieur Saidi what he wants to hear and let him pay me off.'

'You are?'

'Yes, Maman. So, you see? Sometimes I really do take your advice.'

*

354

The call comes shortly before noon.

'Taleb?'

'Director?'

'I have made arrangements. It has not been easy.'

'We are grateful for whatever you have been able to do, Director.'

'You are still ready to go ahead?'

'We are.'

'Very well. There is an airfield at Chaubuisson, approximately fifty kilometres south-east of Paris. A four-seater plane will be there at eighteen hundred hours. It will wait for you until twenty hundred hours. If you do not arrive by then . . .'

'I understand.'

'The pilot's name is Moussa Hafsi. I will send you his photo ID. I know his father. He can be trusted.'

'Thank you, Director.'

'In your place, I would delay thanking me until you are safely back in Algeria and Laloul is in our custody. Because, if anything goes wrong . . .'

'You will disown me.'

'Exactly. Which I would regret. But . . .'

'You would have no alternative.'

'If you had a wife and child, Taleb, I wouldn't allow you to take this risk. As it is . . .'

'It's only my neck.'

'Whatever happens, you and I will know the truth.'

'You and I and Agent Hidouchi.'

'I would recommend you pray for good fortune, especially since today is Friday. But I have a suspicion you are not a prayerful man.'

'Your suspicion is correct, Director. The Almighty and I have not been on speaking terms for many years.'

'Then I can only wish you luck.'

'Which I will gladly accept. As will Agent Hidouchi.'

'You are welcome.'

And with that Bouras ends the call.

Gray is back at his hotel when Suzette calls. He acknowledges to himself that Zarbi's judgement has been vindicated. Now it's for him to reassure Suzette he's well and so, should she ask, is Kermadec.

'Hi, Suzette.'

'Stephen. You're back in England?'

'No. Actually . . . I'm still here. In Versailles.'

'But I thought—'

'I decided to stay on . . . until your business with Laloul was settled.'

'And Kermadec didn't object?'

'Short of manhandling me on to a train, what could he do? I'm not going to cause any kind of problem. I made that very clear.' So he did, though to Zarbi, of course, rather than Kermadec.

'I'm surprised Kermadec went along with that. Where is he now?'

'Not sure. Why do you ask?'

'My mother's concerned she hasn't heard from him.'

'It hasn't been long, surely.'

'Not really, no.'

'You should just go ahead as planned, Suzette. You really should. I'm . . . resigned to it.'

'You are?'

'Yes. Truly.' And that is true. 'Will you call me when it's done?'

'Do you want me to?'

'I'd be grateful. It's time we drew a line under this. I see that now.'

'I'm glad to hear you say that, Stephen. And yes. I'll call you. When it's done.'

*

356

Suzette is left puzzled by her conversation with Gray. She had felt sure Kermadec would send him back to England. She's forced to assume Gray was indeed able to convince her stepfather he posed no threat to the execution of the blackmail plan against Laloul. Which leaves everything resting on her doing as she's been told. So, maybe there's nothing to be puzzled by at all. Kermadec is confident his scheme is going to work and is certain she'll play her part in it. He's right about her, of course. His domination of her mother and his increasing influence over Timothée leaves her no choice. She has to do what Kermadec wants. And hope the best for her son will somehow emerge from that.

The afternoon advances slowly. She waits. And watches the clock. Then, exactly on schedule, she hears the crunch of car tyres on the drive. Storza has come for her.

He stops the Citroën and climbs out, but doesn't approach the house. Instead, he stands by the car, smoking a cigarette, waiting for her to appear.

She doesn't keep him waiting long. He opens the passenger door for her as she emerges and heads towards him.

'Where's my stepfather?' she asks. 'My mother's been asking.'

'Not here,' Storza replies. His gaze is unreadable. She can't tell whether he's being deliberately obtuse or genuinely so. He waves her into the car. 'We go now.'

She climbs in and notices at once a briefcase sitting in the footwell. She prises it open. Inside are the familiar dog-eared pages of her father's confession. Soon, very soon, she'll be relinquishing them for ever. And with them a segment of her father's memory. It can't be helped. It can't be altered. She has to lose this part of him.

Storza slides into the driving seat and nods down at the case. 'All there.' His statement hovers halfway between a question and an assertion. Then he hands her a slip of paper. 'For the money.'

The name of a bank and an account number are printed on

the slip. But it's not quite what Kermadec led her to expect. The bank is in Liechtenstein. She looks at Storza. 'Not the Cayman Islands?'

He shrugs. 'I know nothing.' He starts the engine, reverses and sets off along the drive.

As they pull out on to the road and head for the N12, she wonders if she'll gain anything by asking why Kermadec didn't send Gray back to London. She concludes not. Storza clearly isn't about to reveal anything of his boss's reasoning.

Maybe it doesn't matter anyway. This is really all about what she's going to do when they reach Coqblin & Baudouin's offices. And what Laloul is going to do when Zarbi's terms are put to him.

Nothing else counts.

It's a relief when the time comes for Taleb and Hidouchi to check out of Le Trèfle. They make their way cautiously to the car park where they left the Lancia, next to the railway tracks into the Gare du Nord. Hidouchi shows Taleb the route to the airfield on her phone. 'A straight run south-east. A4, D4, N4 and off on to the D402. Easy.'

'Easy sounds good,' says Taleb.

'Think you could get there without me?'

'Why would I need to do that?'

'We need to be ready for every contingency.'

Taleb squints at the phone as Hidouchi maximizes and minimizes the route. 'Looks straightforward. But we're all getting on that plane. You, me and Nadir Laloul.'

She smiles at him, which isn't something she's done often. 'I believe you. Shall we go?'

Gray gets off the train from Versailles at Pont de l'Alma and walks out on to the eastern side of the bridge. The Seine is sparkling in the summer sunshine. Looking down into it, he thinks for a moment about the bodies of all those Algerians thrown off the Pont St-Michel, half a dozen bridges upstream, one October night in 1961. It's hard to believe it actually happened. And yet it did, though most of the people walking past him probably have no conception that such a horror could have unfolded in the centre of Paris in the relatively recent past.

A car horn beeps. He turns from the railings and sees a grey Mercedes has pulled up by the kerb, as arranged. The nearside rear window slides open. Glancing in, Gray comes eye to eye with Wassim Zarbi, who looks even more haggard and shrunken than when they last met, in Algiers, four months ago. He waves feebly for Gray to get in.

The driver, whom Gray doesn't recognize, fails to check he's actually closed the door behind him before starting away and Gray is thrown back against his seat by the foot-to-the-floor take-off. They speed across the junction at the northern end of the bridge and head up Avenue Marceau.

Zarbi turns stiffly and gazes at him through his watery eyes, half-smiling as if in acknowledgement of the pitiful state illness has reduced him to. He's so thin his grey striped suit hangs in loose folds around his limbs. His hair is sparse. His once piratical moustache has been reduced to a line of white stubble.

'It is a good thing, Stephen,' he says, taking gulps of air every few words as he speaks, 'that we do not have to wait many more days to snare my old friend Nadir. I worried I might not live long enough. But I think I will now. Yes. I think I will.'

TWENTY-NINE

THE BROAD AVENUE RUNS NORTH–SOUTH THROUGH THE SEVENTEENTH arrondissement, lined by trees in summer leaf, wide pavements and seven-storey balconied mansions converted into shops, offices and apartments. There is space for parking on both sides of the street. Traffic, both vehicular and pedestrian, is thin. The virus has sapped this district of Paris of much of its normal intensity.

As it is, Hidouchi is able to park the Lancia opposite the offices of Coqblin & Baudouin, on the other side of the road, facing south. From here she and Taleb have an excellent view of the entrance, although the high double wooden doors allow no sight of the interior. A discreet though gleamingly polished brass plaque featuring the intertwined initials C and B is the only indication that the legal practice has its Paris headquarters here.

Coqblin & Baudouin's neighbours comprise a bank and a boutique de mode, whose window is occupied by several trendily dressed mannequins. There are just under ten minutes to go before Laloul is scheduled to arrive, according to the information supplied to them by Ménard. Taleb doesn't expect him to be early. He reckons he certainly has time to smoke a cigarette. He shows Hidouchi the pack and raises his eyebrows, hoping she won't object.

She gives him a look of weary tolerance. 'I'm going over to pretend to look in the shop window while I see if I can spot anyone approaching. Switch to my seat while I'm gone. You'll be the one driving when we leave.'

Hidouchi has assumed it'll be her pushing Laloul into the car, quite possibly with a gun to his head. Taleb has assumed much the same. He nods. 'Be careful,' he says, though he knows being careful isn't compatible with what they've come here to do.

'Don't worry. I'll just be a girl looking at designer dresses.' She slips out of the car and crosses the street. A girl looking at designer dresses? Well, Taleb reflects as he watches her, maybe some would believe it. He lights his cigarette.

An old-style black Citroën growls past at that moment, heading north. Taleb glances at it admiringly – and nostalgically. His old boss, Superintendent Meslem, used to drive the same model. His was black too. Taleb can still remember the biscuity aroma of the seat leather on a hot day, mixed with their cigarette smoke. Like Taleb, Meslem favoured Nassims.

The Citroën reverses into a parking spot and stops. Storza turns off the engine. Suzette checks the time on her phone. Four fifty-three. She glances over her shoulder at the entrance to Coqblin & Baudouin's offices, which they drove past a few moments ago. Her view of it is partially blocked by a young woman dressed in a black leather jacket and jeans who's eyeing the fashions in the window of the shop next door. Suzette wonders if Laloul is already inside, though somehow she doubts it. She also wonders how early she can respectably be for the appointment. She has no wish to sit out here with Storza a minute longer than necessary.

Storza lights a cigarette and offers her one. She declines with an irritable shake of the head, although, in truth, she'd very much like one.

'Advice,' he says, turning his sunglassed gaze upon her. 'Don't act nervous.'

'What if I am nervous?' she snaps, instantly regretting engaging with him.

He pauses. 'Don't act it.'

'I think I'll go in.'

'No. Too soon.'

A grey Mercedes cruises slowly past, heading south. It seems to attract Storza's attention. He inclines his head to follow its progress in the wing mirror. Suzette turns and looks out through the rear window. The young woman is still window-shopping. Twenty metres or so beyond her, the Mercedes pulls in to the kerb and stops. There are two people in the back seat. She can make out the silhouettes of their heads and shoulders. 'Someone you know?' she asks.

But all Storza says is, 'Go in.'

'You just said it was too soon.'

'Now it isn't. My phone will tell me when the money is paid. Then I will bring this.' He reaches down and closes the clasp on the briefcase. 'But first . . . you have to do your thing, signora.'

Gray looks over his shoulder, out through the rear window of the Mercedes, at the entrance to the offices of Coqblin & Baudouin. There's no movement, in or out. He glances at his watch. Four fifty-seven. They're early, though only just.

'Do you think Laloul could already be here?' he asks Zarbi.

The old man shakes his head. 'Nadir will not be here yet,' he murmurs. 'Always make your enemy wait.'

'Why are we here, then?'

'Because I want to see him arrive. I want to watch him enter. I want to know whether old age has treated him better than me.

Then I want to get out of the car and smoke a cigar – against my doctor's strict orders – and wait for him to come back out. And then . . .'

'Then?'

'Then we will really see, won't we? Victory and defeat, Nigel. Victory and—'

'I'm Stephen.'

'What?'

'You called me Nigel.'

'No. I did not.'

'Yes you did. You called me by the name of a man long dead. Nigel Dalby.'

Zarbi's lip curls, but he can't summon much in the way of anger. 'You are here to look and listen, nothing more.'

'Isn't that what we're both here for?'

'It's your revenge as well as mine . . . Stephen. Remember that.'

'I'm not about to forget it. I've spent the past fifty-five years not forgetting.'

'Then for you . . . this is a great day.'

A great day? It should be, yes. But it doesn't feel like it to Gray. There's a bitter taste in his mouth. He looks back through the window at Coqblin & Baudouin's entrance.

And he sees Suzette walking towards the door from further up the street. She's on her way, then. There's no turning back now.

Taleb watches as a chicly dressed middle-aged woman walks past Hidouchi, heading, he senses, for Coqblin & Baudouin. An inclination of Hidouchi's head suggests she's watching her too.

His sense is vindicated. The woman stops by the brass plaque next to the door and presses a button beneath it. She could be an employee or a client calling on some matter wholly unconnected with whatever is expected to draw Laloul here. He reckons it's an even bet whether her arrival is significant or not. Although, according to his watch, it's now five o'clock.

As he watches, she bends forward slightly to speak into a microphone, then dons a mask, pulls open one of the doors and enters.

Hidouchi has her phone in her hand. She's making a call. Who to Taleb has no idea. Until his phone starts to ring.

He answers it with the observation, 'It's nice of you to call.'

'A woman talking on her phone attracts less attention than a woman just standing around. And there's no one else I can call, is there?'

'I suppose that's true.'

'You saw the woman who went in?'

'Yes.'

Two cars, one of them a taxi, pass in quick succession. Hidouchi waits to see if they stop. When they don't, she turns slowly on her heel in the typical fashion of someone absorbed in a phone conversation and says, 'She got out of the black Citroën. It's parked three cars up. You see it?'

'I see it. And it looks like the driver's waiting for her.'

'It seems so.'

'Well, we don't know why exactly Laloul is coming here, do we? Maybe it's to meet this woman.'

'Yes. Maybe it is.'

Coqblin & Baudouin's foyer is a mixture of lustrous wood and modern glass panelling, with up-to-the-minute furnishings. The receptionist, a poised young woman in a black trouser suit and matching mask, greets Suzette with polite formality. 'Bonjour, madame. Monsieur Lionel is on his way down.'

'Thank you.'

Suzette walks slowly in a circle, schooling herself to look and sound calm and composed.

364

Then there are descending footsteps. Lionel Baudouin appears at the corner of the stairs, soberly suited and tied. 'Madame Fontaine,' he declares, spreading his hands in welcome. 'Thank you for coming. Our client is not here yet.' He consults his watch with a flick of his snowy-cuffed wrist. 'Whereas you are admirably prompt. You have brought the document?'

'It's in my car.'

'Ah. You are being careful, I see. Well, that is good. Would you like to come and meet our small team?'

'Certainly.' Moving with calculated slowness, Suzette starts up the stairs towards him.

A dark SUV with tinted windows passes the Mercedes, heading north. It attracts Zarbi's immediate attention. 'Here he is,' he murmurs in a satisfied tone.

'How do you know that's Laloul?' asks Gray.

'It's his kind of transport. And the driver looks like he is also a bodyguard.' Zarbi turns his neck stiffly to follow the car's progress. 'Yes. It's stopping. In a moment, we should see Nadir. The time has nearly come.'

A dark SUV with tinted windows slows to a halt just short of the entrance to Coqblin & Baudouin. Hidouchi walks slowly – and apparently aimlessly – away from it past the window of the boutique de mode. 'This could be him,' she says into her phone.

'We'll soon know,' says Taleb. He places his gun carefully on the seat beside him.

As he watches, the driver of the SUV climbs out. He's a large, thick-necked man with short black hair and a forbidding expression. Something about his girth suggests he's wearing a bulletproof vest, which Taleb doesn't find reassuring.

The driver strides round the front of the car to reach the pavement, where another big, burly man with a shaven head is helping their passenger out of the back. There's a third man from the same gene pool assisting as well, distinguished in his case by ponytailed hair.

Laloul himself – Taleb is certain it is Laloul – is a hunched, shambling figure in a raincoat entirely unsuited to the dry, warm weather. He's grey-faced, his head bowed, his eyes invisible behind wraparound sunglasses. He moves with the aid of a stick. The grand embezzler of state funds and murderer of a French presidential aide who's eluded capture and punishment for his crimes for more than twenty years clearly hasn't been so successful in fending off the ravages of old age.

'I think this is Laloul,' says Hidouchi, who by now is heading slowly back towards the group. 'You agree?'

'Yes.'

The driver of the SUV moves to the door of Coqblin & Baudouin. The other two bodyguards stand next to Laloul as he steadies himself, tugs ineffectually at the tangled collar of his raincoat and starts walking away from the car. But they don't go with him. In fact, they retreat towards the rear of the car, turning their backs on him, although of this he's unaware.

'Start the engine,' says Hidouchi, ending the call.

Taleb turns the screwdriver in the ignition. The Lancia rumbles into life.

Hidouchi walks smartly past the driver of the SUV and intercepts Laloul, who stops and gapes at her, slack-jawed with puzzlement. She says something to him which Taleb can't hear. Whether Laloul responds is unclear. She says something else and shows him her DSS badge. He visibly flinches and looks towards his driver, who's at this moment gazing in the opposite direction. Before he can turn and seek help from the other two, Hidouchi slips her gun out of her waist holster and points it at him. Laloul stares down at the weapon in bemusement.

Hidouchi speaks again, loudly enough this time for Taleb to

catch her words. 'Cross the street to the Lancia, where my colleague is waiting for you, or I will shoot you where you stand.'

'Who . . . are you?' demands Laloul.

'Agent Hidouchi. Département des services de sécurité. Move.' A none too gentle prod with the barrel of the gun achieves the desired effect. Laloul nods nervously and starts shuffling towards the edge of the pavement. He looks round and calls to his men. 'Help me. Stop this.' But they don't move. They don't even seem to hear him.

This is going to be all right, Taleb senses. Ménard is sticking to their agreement. They're going to be allowed to load Laloul into their car and drive away with him. There isn't going to be a problem.

'What's happening?' gasps Zarbi. 'He's not going in. Who's that woman?'

Gray has no answer. Events aren't unfolding as he expected. The same question weighs on his mind. Who is that woman?

Hidouchi and Laloul are crossing the street as quickly as Laloul's unsteady gait will allow, the metal ferrule of his stick tapping on the tarmac as he goes. He casts a look ahead at Taleb and frowns. Then he casts another look back at his bodyguards, who still haven't reacted. He mouths an oath at them. He knows he's been betrayed. And he knows his long evasion of justice is ending, in circumstances he never foresaw.

Hidouchi catches Taleb's eye. She nods faintly to him, signalling that yes, this is going to work. He nods back. She and Laloul are only a couple of metres away now. Laloul tries to turn back, but Hidouchi pushes him forward with the point of her gun. His face squirms with anger, but there's nothing he can do.

Then it happens. Taleb has taken his eye off the SUV driver, who suddenly moves away from the door of Coqblin & Baudouin and swings his arms up, aiming his gun. There are several loud cracks as he fires. The offside tyres of the Lancia burst and sag. And into Taleb's mind comes a clear and terrible thought. First, they stop us driving away. Then . . . they kill us.

Gray starts with alarm at the sound of gunshots.

'What are they doing?' cries Zarbi. He tugs at the handle and pushes his door half open.

Gray tries to restrain him. 'Don't go out there.'

But Zarbi ignores him. 'Get your hands off me,' he rasps, struggling out of the car.

The accelerating staccato of gunfire reverberates in the hushed offices of Coqblin & Baudouin. The small group waiting to welcome Suzette in the street-facing conference room spill out on to the landing, shocked and open-mouthed in alarm. 'Don't go near the windows,' one of them cautions. 'There are people shooting at each other.'

Taleb grabs his gun. The SUV driver is still firing. The other two bodyguards have joined in. Bullets are pinging off the bodywork of the Lancia. Hidouchi winces, as if she's been hit. But, if she has, it doesn't stop her swinging round and firing back.

Laloul staggers in front of Taleb, blocking his view. The shots keep coming. Laloul jolts and groans as bullets that might otherwise have killed Taleb thwack into his chest and stomach. His stick clatters to the ground and he goes down like a paper bag being crushed.

Hidouchi darts round the rear of the car, taking shelter behind the vehicle. The way she's moving and the set grimace on her face confirm to Taleb she's injured. He ducks down as low as he can and fires through the open window towards their attackers, though with little hope of actually hitting them. He and Hidouchi are outnumbered and outgunned and they don't have a bullet-proof vest between them. He glimpses the three bodyguards advancing towards them, still firing. Taleb suddenly remembers another piece of advice Superintendent Meslem once gave him. 'Don't get killed on duty. Retirement's the only luxury an honest policeman knows.'

Gray scrambles out of the Mercedes, ducking his head as gun-shots crackle and ricochet. He glimpses Zarbi moving unsteadily towards the SUV, the direction most of the fire is coming from, aimed, as far as Gray can tell, across the street at Laloul and the woman who appeared to be trying to apprehend him.

'Stop,' Zarbi cries pitifully. 'Stop.' He takes a few hurried steps and breaks into a tottering run. 'Stop!'

And then someone does stop.

With a groan, Zarbi bends almost double and falls to the ground.

More shots now. But they're different, lower-pitched and more powerful. And they're not hitting the car. Taleb pushes himself up gingerly in his seat.

What he sees is incomprehensible in its way. A fourth man, tall, lean, shaven-headed and moustachioed, is marching down the street towards their attackers, firing at them with a short automatic rifle. The SUV driver is already down, spreadeagled in the street. As Taleb watches in disbelief, one of the other two is struck in the throat. He falls straight backwards and out of sight behind their car. But the third bodyguard, the one with the pony-tail, is still firing. Two shots hit the rifleman in the midriff. He staggers, but he doesn't fall. He fires again, but his aim is less accurate. He slumps to his knees.

The ponytailed man walks towards him, firing repeatedly.

Taleb shoots at him, but misses. His eyesight just isn't good enough for marksmanship any more. But a younger pair of eyes is a different matter. Hidouchi has been taking careful aim. Two shots hit the ponytailed man, one in the knee, one in the thigh. He topples sideways. As he does so, he comes within range of the rifleman, who gets off one last blast that blows a hole in the ponytailed man's head. Then the rifleman topples forward on to his face and doesn't move again.

And there are no more shots.

Gray edges out from behind the Mercedes and looks nervously along the street. The shooting has stopped, but the smell of the expended ammunition is hanging in the air. Everything happened so quickly. Yet now time seems suspended. There are four bodies lying near the SUV. One of the dead men is Storza. A fifth body – Laloul's, he assumes – lies next to the car the woman was leading him towards. He can't see the woman. Closer to him, Zarbi is also down, curled on the tarmac and looking from here like little more than a discarded heap of rags. He isn't moving at all.

Suddenly, the Mercedes starts up. The driver, it seems, has decided he wants no part of this. He must reckon his boss is a goner. He pulls out into the road and speeds away. Gray is on his own.

Taleb climbs out of the Lancia and turns to see Hidouchi leaning against the rear wing of the car. She's still grimacing. The lower two thirds of her left jeans leg is dark with blood. He hurries towards her.

'We have to get out of here, Taleb,' she says through clenched teeth. 'Erica planned to kill all of us – you, me and Laloul – and get hold of the tape. We can't risk discovering she has a back-up plan. But we'll have to switch cars now. The guy who saved us came from the Citroën. We can take that.'

'Who was he?'

'No idea. I'm just glad he was here. We'd both be dead otherwise.'

'I'll get the Citroën. But are you really up to travelling to the airfield and getting on that plane?'

'I'll have to be. Just fetch our bags and get the car.'

Zarbi is lying on his side. Gray rolls him gently over on to his back. His face is grey and slack, his eyes blank. Gray finds one of his bony wrists and checks for a pulse. There isn't one. Wassim Zarbi's heart, it seems, has given up on him. He and Laloul are both dead. After all their years of association and the years of separation since, their lives have ended together, on this street in Paris.

Gray glances ahead. A slightly built man with curly grey hair wearing a rumpled suit and open-necked shirt – he could easily be Algerian – has just slammed the boot of the car Laloul's body is lying next to. He sets off at a loping run across and along the street, carrying two bags slung awkwardly over his shoulder.

The woman who accosted Laloul is leaning against the rear wing of the car, breathing heavily. As Gray watches, she slides slowly to the ground until she's sitting with her back resting against the wheel arch. Her chest is heaving.

Gray stands up and runs towards her, slowing as he sees the gun in her hand. There are shell casings scattered around her.

She looks up at him as he approaches and tries to smile. 'Don't worry,' she says in throaty French. 'I'm not going to shoot you.'

Gray notices the blood oozing through the denim of her jeans. 'That looks bad,' he says.

'No kidding,' she says weakly, switching to English.

He pulls out his phone. 'You need an ambulance.'

'No. Taleb and I have to leave. We're in danger if we stay here.'

'Taleb?'

371

'My colleague.' She nods towards a black Citroën that's nosing out of a parking space a little way along the street.

'Inspector Taleb?'

'You know him?'

'From many years ago.'

She smiles weakly. 'Actually, he's been promoted to superintendent . . . since then. Who are you?'

Taleb glimpses several backed-up cars ahead of him as he pulls out. The drivers have obviously stopped at the sight of bodies in the street. Remaining here until the police arrive and phoning for an ambulance in the meantime would make sense in other circumstances. But not now. He and Hidouchi have to go. What seriously worries Taleb, however, is whether Hidouchi is in any condition to go anywhere.

He makes a rapid three-point turn and speeds the short distance back to the Lancia. Worryingly, Hidouchi is no longer standing. She's sitting slumped against the side of the car. A man – a passer-by, maybe? – is crouching beside her, talking into his phone. He looks anxious. And he looks strangely familiar as well. Taleb scrambles out of the Citroën, leaving the engine running.

'I'm sorry, Taleb,' says Hidouchi, smiling weakly. 'I don't think I can . . . leave after all. Go on . . . without me.'

'I'm not doing that.'

'You have to. I'll be safe . . . as long as you make it out of the country.'

'An ambulance is on its way,' says the man. He looks up at Taleb. 'We've met before, Superintendent. Do you remember? My name's Stephen Gray.'

The surprise of encountering Gray here and now scarcely registers amidst Taleb's greater concerns. 'Yes. Yes, I . . . recognize you. You are Stephen Gray. Why are you here?'

'I came with Zarbi.'

'Zarbi's here as well?'

'Back there.' Gray points to the crumpled figure of an old man lying in the street some ten metres or so away. 'Dead.'

'He was shot too?'

'No. I think his heart gave out. He was trying to stop them killing Laloul. The effort was too much for him.'

'Why would he want to save Laloul?'

'Because Laloul was here to pay him a fortune in blackmail money. But we don't have time to talk about that now.' Gray turns to Hidouchi. 'I think we should put a tourniquet on your leg. You're losing a lot of blood.' It's true. Blood is trickling out over her ankle now and slowly spreading across the tarmac. 'Lie flat. That'll reduce the blood flow.'

Gray supports Hidouchi as she slides round and lets him lower her to the ground.

'We'll need a cloth to wrap round your leg,' Gray continues. 'And a stick or something to tighten it with.'

'Hold on.' Taleb flings open the rear door of the Citroën and rummages in his bag. He pulls out one of his spare shirts. Then he spots Laloul's walking stick, lying in a pool of blood beside his body. He grabs it.

'The shirt's perfect,' Gray pronounces. 'But the stick's far too long. Got anything shorter?'

Taleb moves to the front door of the car, swings it open, yanks the screwdriver out of the ignition and hands it to Gray. 'Better?'

Gray nods. 'Better.' He spins the shirt into a band and winds it round the top of Hidouchi's thigh. Then he ties the arms of the shirt round the screwdriver and turns it like a handle, tightening the tourniquet.

A minute or so slowly passes. Then Taleb says, 'I think it's working. The bleeding's begun to slow.'

'That's good ... to hear,' says Hidouchi. Her voice is weak now, her face pale.

Sirens wail in the distance. Police or ambulance. Or both.

'You should leave ... before they get here, Taleb,' says Hidouchi.

'She's going to be all right, Superintendent,' says Gray, holding the screwdriver in place. 'The paramedics will make sure of that.'

'I'll need ... my bag, Taleb,' says Hidouchi, slurring her words.

'Of course.' Taleb fetches it from the Citroën and drops it beside her. 'Don't die, Souad,' he says, looking into her eyes. 'I couldn't bear it if you did.' He realizes how odd a thing he's just said. He and Souad Hidouchi have known one another less than a week. Yet what he has said is nonetheless true.

'Don't worry ... about me. Start driving. Make it to the airfield. Make it home.'

'OK.' He stands up. 'I'll see you ... in Algiers.'

She manages a nod. 'You can count on it.'

Taleb hopes he can. But he doesn't say so. There's no need to say anything else. The sirens are getting closer. It's time to go.

THIRTY

SUZETTE IS PACING AROUND LIONEL BAUDOUIN'S PRIVATE OFFICE, which overlooks an inner courtyard of the building. He ushered her in there for her own protection as the gunfire continued outside. But there's been no gunfire for some little while now and she badly wants to know what's happened. She decides the time has come to leave.

But, just as she moves towards the door, it's opened by Baudouin coming to fetch her.

'It is very . . . bloody . . . out there, madame,' he says. 'Several people have died. There are . . . bodies in the street. There is no threat now, though. The police are on their way. They will have many questions. For everyone.'

'Who was shooting at who?' she asks, suddenly reminded by her own words of the rhetorical Algerian question from la décennie noire: 'Qui tue qui?'

'It is . . . unclear.' Baudouin sounds more than merely hesitant. He sounds evasive. 'I have to tell you that our client appears to be among the dead. His bodyguards also died. And another—'

'Laloul's dead?' There seems nothing to be gained by pretending she doesn't know who Baudouin's client is – or was.

He nods, which is as much of an answer as he apparently deems it prudent to give. 'We should agree – you and I – what it is wise to say to the police,' he continues. 'The transaction we proposed to carry out this afternoon has obviously been ... overtaken by events. In fact, I wonder if we should ... consider the merits ... from your point of view ... of saying nothing more about it ... beyond these walls.'

They exchange a look that is both furtive and conspiratorial. With Laloul dead, there is no blackmail plot. Her father's confession has no monetary value. No one is going to pay her – or anyone else – a cent for it. But, on the other hand, she can have her old life back – free of charge. All she has to do is forget she was ever here. Which, considering Baudouin doesn't know the increased demand she was going to put to Laloul, might be best for her all round. She should be relieved, even though she doesn't feel it. She was safely inside Coqblin & Baudouin's offices when the shooting started, after all, which is something to be grateful for. And Kermadec won't get what he wanted, which has to be good. She wonders whether Storza tried to intervene in the attack on Laloul. Altogether, there is much to wonder about. Yet one question above all troubles her. 'Who can have done this?'

'I cannot speculate about responsibility, madame. As I think you may be aware, our client had some ... controversial connections. In that world violence is not uncommon. We will of course account fully to the authorities for the limited legal services we supplied to him. But you may wish ... in your own best interests ... to avoid involvement. And for my part ... I see no reason why your visit here should ever be officially known.'

'What are you suggesting, Monsieur Baudouin?'

'I am suggesting, madame, that you may wish to leave here before the police arrive. And since their arrival is imminent, I would recommend you leave . . . now.'

Looking up, Gray can see an ambulance steering a path through the traffic. Its light is flashing, though its siren is only intermittent now.

'The ambulance is nearly here,' he says to Hidouchi.

'Thank you,' she murmurs, gazing up woozily at him, the wavering shadows of leaves on a nearby tree moving across her face. 'I think . . . you've saved my life.'

'Let's hope so.'

'If you want it to stay saved . . . don't mention Taleb . . . to the police.'

'Why not?'

She tries to grasp his wrist, but her hand merely flops across it. 'I can't . . . explain. Just . . . don't. OK?'

'All right.'

'I'm . . . serious. Not . . . not a word.'

'OK. I've got it. I won't say anything about Taleb. Or about anything else. I was just passing by and did my best to help. This carnage . . . has nothing to do with me.'

'Good . . . idea,' she says faintly. She's slipping into unconsciousness. But the ambulance crew is here. He's confident she's going to make it.

He glances round at the bodies lying in the street. People have started emerging hesitantly from the nearby shops, offices and apartments. They're quiet, speaking in whispers, shocked by what's happened. So much death, in so short a time, late on a summer's afternoon in Paris.

Among the dead are Laloul and Zarbi. Old and frail as both of them were, they succumbed swiftly. All Gray's long-harboured thoughts of revenge feel foolish to him now he's seen the dismal ends these two men have come to, together, in the city where they murdered his sister, fifty-five years ago. Time was always waiting to close around them. Justice, of a kind, has been served.

And he was there to see it happen. But it was none of his doing. He understands now. He understands it was never going to be.

Suzette steps out of the offices of Coqblin & Baudouin into a street transformed. There are several police cars and ambulances on the scene. Blue lights are flashing, car radios crackling. A cordon's been placed across the pavement as well as the road, blocking access to – and exit from – the immediate area. Operatives in white coveralls are examining the bodies. Suzette counts six dead. Other police officers, some uniformed, some not, are conferring on their phones or quizzing witnesses. The occupants of adjoining offices, shops and apartments are gathered in knots, discussing what's happened. And all the while the late afternoon sun shafts prettily through the bright green leaves of the trees and sparkles perversely on patches of blood.

Suzette doesn't know, now she's emerged, what she should actually do. If she tries to walk away, she'll be turned back pending questioning. The police will probably want the names and addresses of everyone along with their reasons for being there. She's going to have to lie to them about that and exactly how to do so isn't clear to her.

She looks along the street, to where the Citroën was parked, wondering if she'll see Storza. But the car isn't there at all. It's gone. Storza must have left while he still had the chance.

But no. He didn't leave. Suddenly, as an operative moves clear of one of the bodies lying in the street, she sees Storza, sprawled face down on the tarmac. As she watches, his corpse is photographed, swiftly and efficiently, from several angles. But who, if he's dead, drove the Citroën away?

An ambulance pulls off from the other side of the street, heading north. A man is standing on the opposite pavement, next to a Lancia with punctured tyres. Suzette's view of him was blocked by the ambulance. Now their gazes meet in mutual recognition.

Stephen Gray signals for her to wait where she is. He walks slowly across to her, head down, keeping his distance as best he can from the groups of police officers assembled round the bodies.

'What are you doing here?' she whispers to him as soon as he's close enough. Then she notices the blood on his hands and trousers. 'What's happened to you?'

'Don't worry,' he says. 'It's not my blood. I was . . . helping a woman who'd been shot in the leg. That ambulance is taking her to hospital.'

'Is she going to be all right?'

'I think so. As for why I'm here, I came with Zarbi. He wanted to see the look on Laloul's face after he'd been forced to pay him all that money.'

'Where's Zarbi now?'

'He's one of the dead, Suzette.' Gray points towards the most distant body. 'When the shooting began, he tried to intervene. The effort was too much for his heart.'

'My God.' She's still struggling to take it all in. 'Who was doing the shooting?'

'Laloul's bodyguards. The woman in the ambulance is with Algerian Intelligence – I think. She tried to apprehend Laloul. Then the bodyguards started shooting. They nailed Laloul straight away. It was obviously some kind of set-up. They must have been paid to kill him. Storza tried to stop them. That ended with all three of them plus Storza dead. You wouldn't believe how quickly it happened. One minute Zarbi, Laloul, Storza and the bodyguards were alive, the next – so it seemed – they were all dead. I couldn't believe it was happening. I still can't believe it

379

did happen. But there are the bodies. And here are the police.' Gray pushes his hair back from his forehead and surveys the scene. 'This is real.'

'Where's the Citroën – the car Storza brought me here in?'

'Taleb drove away in it.'

'Who?'

'Superintendent Taleb. Inspector, as was. The Algerian policeman who questioned me after I was arrested in Algiers back in ninety-three.'

'He was here?'

'Yes. To arrest Laloul, apparently. I got the impression he and the wounded intelligence agent – Souad, he called her – were intended to die with Laloul. But Storza's intervention saved them. There was a lot of treachery that went into this, Suzette.' Gray shakes his head. 'I don't understand the half of it.'

'But Taleb left in the Citroën?'

'Yes. And I agreed not to mention him to the police. So, could you keep quiet about him as well?'

Suzette barely registers Gray's request. 'He left – with my father's confession?'

'The confession?' Gray smiles ruefully. 'Of course. Yes. It was in the car. It's strange, but that never occurred to me. You're right. He must have it now.'

'Where's he gone?'

'Back to Algeria . . . I think. They were talking about flying out from some airfield.'

'You let him take the confession with him?'

Gray shrugs. 'I never thought about it. And I'm sure he didn't know what was in the car. He was only interested in getting out of the country. I think the French authorities are after them. Somehow it's crucial to Souad's safety that Taleb makes it home. That's why we mustn't mention him to the police.'

'Why would the French be after them?'

'I honestly don't know.'

Gray doesn't know. And looking at him, Suzette has the impression he doesn't really care. Something's changed in him.

'The last firm I worked for before I retired sent me on a first aid course, you know,' he continues, almost cheerfully. 'And today, because of that, I may have saved a human life. Improvising a tourniquet on this street this afternoon . . . is the best thing I've done in longer than I can remember.' He smiles at Suzette. 'I've spent far too many years chasing the dead and forgetting about the living. What was it all for in the end? Justice? Revenge? You could call this both if you wanted to. Zarbi and Laloul are dead. And no one's suddenly got rich. Even Laloul's lawyers will probably miss out on their fee. While your father's confession . . . is on its way back to the city where he wrote it.'

Suzette stares at Gray, amazed by his sudden shedding of the burden of involvement in these dead men's secrets. There's nothing she can do to retrieve her father's confession. And there's nothing she can be made to do either. To her own bemusement, she actually feels relieved. No money's coming her way – or Gray's. But maybe something much more valuable is.

Not yet, though. 'What are you going to tell the police, Stephen?' she asks, aware this may be the most urgent question of all.

'Nothing,' he replies. 'I'm just a tourist . . . passing through.'

'They'll probably believe you. It won't be so easy for me. Even if I fool them, I still have to deal with Kermadec.'

'No.' Gray shakes his head. 'You don't, actually.'

'Why not?'

'Well, that's something else . . . I have to tell you.'

Taleb navigated his way out of Paris based on his memory of Hidouchi's summary of the route: A4, D4, N4, D402. He was surprised it went as well as it did, with most of his problems arising at the beginning, when he struggled to find his way on to the Périphérique.

He had difficulty concentrating, distracted as he was by worrying about Hidouchi, although he'd seen the ambulance approaching the scene of the shootings and knew she'd soon be in expert hands. There was a worry beyond that, however, about what Erica Ménard might do now her plans had gone awry. Hidouchi was no longer in a position to defend herself. It was all down to him.

It was a relief when he spotted the sign pointing to the airfield, set amongst flat farm fields bathed in evening sunlight. Glancing at his watch, he saw it was just gone seven o'clock. All being well, the plane Bouras had sent would be waiting for him. There was surely nothing to stop his flight home going smoothly.

He pulls into the car park next to an aeroclub building, a hangar and some Nissen huts. There are a couple of other cars parked there, but the owners are nowhere to be seen. The runways are directly ahead. There are no planes landing or taking off, but several small aircraft are drawn up in front of the hangar. Silence and soft evening air breeze in through the window.

Taleb climbs out of the car. As he does so, a man in jeans, T-shirt and baseball cap moves into view from behind the wing of one of the parked planes and looks expectantly towards him. Hafsi, he assumes – the pilot. He raises his hand cautiously. Hafsi gives him the thumbs up. Taleb signals for him to stay by the plane.

He goes to fetch his bag from the front passenger seat of the Citroën. As he's rounding the bonnet, he hears the growl of an approaching car engine and spends a couple of seconds trying hard to believe this simply heralds the arrival of an aeroclub member.

But it doesn't. A big black SUV similar to the one in which

Laloul was delivered to Coqblin & Baudouin speeds into the car park and skids to a halt behind the Citroën, blocking it in. Two large men in black military fatigues spring out. They're both carrying automatic pistols at their waists. And they're followed by Erica Ménard, sliding out of one of the rear doors. The driver stays where he is, hands on the wheel, staring at Taleb and chewing gum with mechanical intensity.

Taleb glances over his shoulder towards the plane. So near and yet so far. He signals to Hafsi more emphatically than before that he's to stay where he is. The least Taleb can do is make sure the pilot leaves unharmed. He can't possibly change whatever's about to happen.

'Going somewhere?' Erica asks, pulling off her sunglasses to give Taleb the full benefit of her superior gaze.

'I was hoping to,' he replies, speaking slowly, pitching his voice at a level of calmness he doesn't feel.

'You were never going to get away, Taleb. Did you really think I wouldn't be able to track you?'

'Why let me leave Paris, then?'

'I wanted to see what your plan for Laloul was. The plane's a four-seater, isn't it? You and Hidouchi were going to take him back to Algeria with you.'

'Were we?'

'It's pointless to pretend otherwise.'

'It's certainly pointless for you to pretend you ever meant to honour our agreement. What was your plan? Have Laloul supposedly caught in the crossfire when his bodyguards resisted our attempt to arrest him? Was that it?'

Ménard smiles. 'As far as I'm concerned, that's what happened. The intervention by Zarbi's man was unfortunate and we lost three good agents as a result, but it changes nothing. I'll have the tape now, please.'

'The tape?'

'Don't try to play games with me. Hand it over.'

'I can't do that.'

'Ridiculous.' She signals for her men to start searching the Citroën. One goes for the boot, the other the interior.

'It's not there, Erica.'

She frowns, considering for the first time, apparently, the possibility that she might have misjudged the situation. Taleb still fears for his life. But he's also secretly triumphant. This is the contingency he and Hidouchi agreed they had to take precautions against – even though those precautions carried their own risks.

The search of the boot doesn't take long. Taleb has no idea what's in there. A spare tyre and a jack, maybe. As for the interior of the car, it holds only his bag, in which he knows the tape isn't going to be found. Ménard's man already has it. He unceremoniously dumps Taleb's clothes and toiletries out on to the ground, then returns to the car and ransacks the glove compartment and storage pockets. He turns up nothing.

Except a briefcase, stowed on the floor beneath the passenger seat, which Taleb completely failed to notice when he drove here. The man brings it to Ménard, who rifles through the contents: a large envelope filled with typewritten pages, some of them flimsy carbon copies. Taleb's mind races to deduce what they could be.

Ménard glares at him. 'What are you doing with this?'

'I didn't even know it was there. What is it?'

Ménard doesn't look as if she believes him. And she doesn't look remotely happy either. 'A pile of waste paper, now Laloul and Zarbi are both dead,' she snaps, tossing the envelope aside. It splits as it hits the ground and the pages slide out fanwise across the tarmac. 'Where's the tape?'

She nods to her man, who frisks Taleb aggressively, though it's obvious he isn't concealing a reel-to-reel tape in his pocket. 'It never left Algiers,' Taleb says defiantly.

'That's a lie. Gilles saw it in your bag yesterday.'

384

'Is that what he told you?'

'It's what he saw.'

Yes, Taleb supposes, it must have been. Because that's where the tape was. Yesterday.

'Where is it?'

'I told you. Algiers.'

Ménard's mouth curls. She's about to say something when a smartly dressed middle-aged man wanders into view from the direction of the aeroclub. He has the fussy, frowning manner of a busybody. 'Can I help you?' he calls.

'Get rid of him,' orders Ménard, without taking her eyes off Taleb. Her man marches over to the busybody, flourishing a badge. Words are exchanged. The busybody retreats. Her man marches back.

'Now,' says Ménard quietly, 'let's be clear. If you don't hand over the tape, I doubt Agent Hidouchi will survive her stay in hospital. And I guarantee you won't be getting on that plane. So, where is it?'

'Gilles was mistaken. The tape was never in my bag. He was frightened. He wasn't thinking – or seeing – clearly.'

'You're lying.'

'Am I? You're not thinking or seeing clearly either, Erica. Let me tell you what I can guarantee. If you don't let me get on that plane, or if Agent Hidouchi comes to any harm at your hands, the tape will be released to the media, here as well as in Algeria. What do you think that's going to do for relations between our two governments? Macron and Tebboune have been like two cooing doves these past few months. Do you want to be responsible for wrecking that? Do you want to take the blame – personally?' He pauses, letting his words sink in. 'It's your choice.'

And it's a choice Ménard dwells on at some length, as they stare each other down. A slight flicker of her gaze signals the moment when she swallows a bitter truth. But the recognition of defeat and the admission of it are two very different things. 'We haven't finished with you, Taleb. Yes, you can go home and crawl back to whatever squalid apartment you live in. But remember this. There will be a night we come for you. That's a promise.'

Taleb decides against pointing out to Ménard that she's in the habit of breaking promises rather than keeping them. Silence seems the wisest policy in such a decisive moment.

Ménard barks, 'We're leaving,' and turns on her heel. As she and her men head for the SUV, she leaves a bootprint to remember her by on one of the pages that's spilt out of the envelope. She doesn't look back.

A few moments later, the SUV speeds out of the car park. Silence reasserts itself. Taleb looks towards the plane and sees Hafsi heading in his direction. There's nothing standing in the way of their departure now. He's going to make it.

He gathers up his belongings and loads them back into his bag. Then he starts collecting the scattered pages. They look as if they've been produced on an old-fashioned typewriter. There's a top copy and a carbon. He looks at what seems to be the first page.

✣

```
I'm like a fly trapped in an upturned glass. I
can see out, but I can't leave. I should have
left with Monique and Suzette when I still had
the chance. I'm not sure why I didn't. I said I
had to look after the bookshop. Monique said I
was crazy. She was right. Who was I kidding?
They burnt me out a few weeks later. Le
Chélifère up in flames.
```

✣

Le Chélifère? The writer surely has to have been Nigel Dalby. And the title at the top – *J'avoue* – makes it clear what Taleb has in his hands. It's Nigel Dalby's confession. It's a compendium of his secrets.

'Superintendent Taleb?' asks Hafsi as he approaches. He's a serious-eyed man, with the manner and appearance of someone who prides himself on getting a job done.

Taleb nods. 'That's me.'

'I was told to expect three passengers.'

'The other two aren't coming.'

'I thought you might not be coming either when those people showed up.'

'I persuaded them to go away.'

'You want to leave, then? While we can? It's good flying weather.'

'Yes.' Taleb thrusts the pages into the briefcase and clips it shut. 'I want to leave.'

EPILOGUE

ELEVEN DAYS HAVE PASSED SINCE TALEB'S RETURN TO ALGERIA. A summons to the Director's office was waiting for him when he arrived at Police HQ this blazingly hot morning and he sets off up the stairs straight away to find out what has prompted it. He and Bouras conferred at Bouras's villa the day after Taleb's return and have not met since.

The first indication that he has nothing to worry about – nothing more to worry about, anyway – comes as he enters the Director's outer office, where Bouras's notoriously flint-faced secretary greets him with a smile and an offer of coffee.

Bouras too is smiling, swinging round from contemplation of the view from his window to welcome Taleb. The sofa, however, remains as uncomfortable as ever. It's almost a relief to know some things never change.

'I thought we should . . . review our situation,' Bouras explains with a wave of the hand, 'now I've been able to assess the consequences of your . . . Paris visit.'

'Yes, Director?'

'You achieved more than I asked of you in some ways and less in others. On balance, though, we are well placed as a result of your . . . endeavours.'

'I regret I was not able to bring Laloul back with me.'

'As do I. For twenty-four hours, I dreamt we would record a notable victory. But it wasn't to be.'

Bouras breaks off as his secretary enters with the coffee. It will be far too sweet for Taleb's taste – the Director likes his coffee ziyada – but the honour of having it served to him is compensation enough.

'Still,' Bouras resumes as soon as they are alone again, 'there is much to be said for what we have accomplished. The DSS have made no complaint about your actions in Paris. Our possession of the Tournier tape, unacknowledged though it may be, gives us bargaining power in any difficulties we may encounter in the future. You did well in that regard, Taleb, though until the tape was delivered to my door I admit I had some doubts about your plan.'

'Ménard would never have let me leave with it, Director. By posting it to you before we intercepted Zarbi and Laloul, I hoped something could be salvaged whatever happened to me and Agent Hidouchi. Fortunately, Ménard believed me when I told her the tape had never been in Paris at all.'

'And now we have the DGSE at a permanent disadvantage. With the DSS scratching their heads trying to understand how we outwitted the French. If only I could tell more people how artfully we've performed. But never mind. The tape is gold-plated insurance.'

'Ménard admitted to me there were still elements of hizb fransa operating in this country. Someone still occupies the position of water-measurer.'

'And you want to try to smoke them out? No, Taleb. We will not be making the mistake of trying to do that. Zarbi and Laloul are dead. Also lawyer Boukhatem. The case has been closed for us, on terms much better than any I could have anticipated at the outset.'

'If so, Director . . .'

'Yes, yes.' Bouras flaps a hand. 'Abderrahmane. I know. I passed on your request.'

'Well, if, as you say, the case is closed . . .'

'There's no need to plead any further on her behalf, Taleb.' Bouras smiles. 'The Ministry of Justice has agreed all charges against her should be dropped. She'll be released . . . later today.'

'That, Director, I am glad to hear. And her neighbour will be overjoyed.'

'Really? Abderrahmane must have friendlier relations with her neighbours than I have with mine.'

'She will be overjoyed because she will be able to return Barbarossa the parrot to his mistress. He has not taken their separation well, apparently.'

'Then this is evidently a good day for all concerned. I'm told Agent Hidouchi flew home yesterday.'

'Yes, Director, she did.'

'Have you spoken to her?'

'I have.' And Taleb is planning to speak to Hidouchi again very soon, though he decides not to mention the lunchtime rendezvous they have arranged. 'She is recovering well from her injury.'

'What of her standing within the DSS?'

'They wanted Zarbi and Laloul dead. And they're dead. They can have no complaint.'

'My impression after my most recent conversation with Deputy Director Kadri is that he views her with some suspicion.'

'I believe she views him with some suspicion.'

'Then the progress of their respective careers should be instructive, shouldn't it? On the subject of careers, Taleb . . .'

'Yes, Director?'

'Your retirement is overdue.'

'It is.'

'But your relationship with Agent Hidouchi, which may prove valuable to us in the future, and your considerable experience in so many areas . . . prompts me to ask if you would be willing to postpone it . . . at least for another year.'

'You'd like me to stay on?'

'I would.'

'Well . . .'

'I could even arrange . . . an air-conditioned office.' Bouras gives Taleb an encouraging smile. 'If that would tip the balance.'

Stephen Gray sits at a table outside a café in the old heart of Annecy after a late breakfast. Before him on the table lie two postcards, both picturing a snow-capped Mont Blanc. He picks up the one he's already written and reads it.

Dear Wendy & Oliver, Suzette will have told you what happened in Paris. I've been travelling since, trying to find my bearings. I don't know what the future holds, but I've finally put the past behind me. Sorry for all the trouble I've caused you recently – and not so recently. Whatever you do, don't worry about me. I'm going to be OK now. I'll see you when I get back. Love, S.

Yes, that's about right. He is going to be OK now, though exactly what OK's likely to comprise he's not sure. But it doesn't matter. He can wait to find out.

He leans over the table and writes the second card.

Dear Riad, Suzette will have told you what happened in Paris. I've been travelling since, trying to find my bearings. I should have taken the advice you gave me when we first met, of course. Feel free to say 'I told you so' when we meet again. Anyway, I'm finally done with the past. So, you can stop worrying about me – if you were! I'll see you when I get back. Amitiés, S.

Gray takes a strip of stamps out of his wallet, tears off two and sticks them on the cards. He could have sent text messages, but he prefers old-fashioned postcards, however long they may take to arrive. They're a nod to the past he's left behind.

He stands up, slips the cards into his pocket and sets off in search of a postbox.

At Les Fringillidés Suzette is in the kitchen, with the doors open on to the terrace, scrolling through messages on her phone while she drinks her mid-morning coffee. Her mother has texted her again, reporting that the police have still not turned up any information about Kermadec's whereabouts. Suzette will call her later and offer a few consolatory words. What she won't say is that she knows for a fact Kermadec isn't coming back. She assumes his body will eventually be found, but until then Maman will just have to live with uncertainty about what's happened to her husband. Which isn't so very bad. Uncertainty, Suzette has come to believe, is actually an underrated condition.

The ring of the doorbell draws her away from her phone. She hurries out into the hall and glimpses the post van through the window by the door. When she opens the door, Jacques the regular postman is waiting to hand her a parcel.

They exchange pleasantries, then he's on his way, leaving Suzette to wander back to the kitchen, examining the parcel as she goes. It's quite heavy, wrapped in brown paper and string. Her name and address are handwritten. And the stamps are Algerian.

She puts the parcel on the worktop, unties the string and tears the package open.

Inside is a cardboard box. When she removes the lid, she finds herself looking at the first page of the carbon copy of her father's confession.

'What's wrong, Maman?'

Suzette looks up at the sound of Élodie's voice. She's standing

392

out on the terrace, dressed, as she generally has been since returning from Mykonos, in spaghetti-strapped top, short shorts and flip-flops. Tears have sprung into Suzette's eyes, so she can't see the expression on Élodie's face. 'Nothing's wrong, chérie,' she replies, blinking to clear her vision.

'Are you crying?'

'Oh, just a . . .' Suzette thumbs her tears away. 'Just a little.'

Élodie steps through the doorway. 'Is it news of Grand-père?'

She means Kermadec, of course, understandably enough. 'No.' Suzette smiles. 'And then again yes.'

'What do you mean?'

'This is about your real grandfather, Élodie. This is about my father.'

Taleb wouldn't have chosen Place Emir-Abdelkader for his rendezvous with Hidouchi. The famous – or infamous – Milk Bar is still there, its name preserved so none should forget the FLN bombing of the premises during the War of Independence. To Taleb's mind, a blast that killed and maimed dozens of pieds noirs children enjoying a milkshake on their way home from the beach on a Sunday afternoon was a step that should never have been taken into a world of brutality from which his country has never escaped. It's the world he has dwelt in all his life. But he has no wish to be reminded of the fact.

Fortunately, the sunlight is so bright the letters on the facade of the Milk Bar are virtually illegible and it has no customers anyway thanks to the coronavirus lockdown. There aren't many passers-by either. Place Emir-Abdelkader is enveloped by tranquillity. Taleb is sitting on a stretch of wall shaded by a palm tree next to the steps leading up to the statue of the legendary nineteenth-century freedom fighter Abd al-Qadir, after whom the square is named. He's smoking a cigarette and flicking crumbs from the wrapper of a pastry he's just eaten on to the steps for birds to peck at. He likes to feed birds when he can, on the balcony of his apartment, or in places such as this. He enjoys their skittering movements and cheerful tweets.

A deeper shadow than that of the palm tree falls across him and he looks up to discover that Hidouchi has appeared beside him. She smiles at his surprise. 'You didn't see me coming, did you?'

'I did not,' Taleb admits.

'Good. It suggests I haven't lost my edge.'

'How are you?' To Taleb's eye Hidouchi looks more like someone who's had a holiday than a stay in hospital. She's wearing a dark blue dress patterned with tiny white spots. This is the first time he's seen her in anything but trousers. Her hair is flowing freely, wafted by the slight breeze, and she's holding her chin at that slightly raised, self-confident angle he realizes he identifies with her and no one else. 'Do you want to sit down?'

'No. You brought your car?'

'As instructed.'

'Then take me somewhere with a view. I need air. And wide horizons – Algerian horizons.'

Taleb scrambles to his feet. 'OK. Let's go.'

He drives east, then north past the harbour. Hidouchi asks if he's brought along Nigel Dalby's confession, which she wants to read as soon as possible. He assures her it's on board. He doesn't mention sending the carbon copy to Dalby's daughter. He's afraid Hidouchi will disapprove and accuse him of giving way to sentiment. She is, after all, not a sentimental person.

Nor a self-indulgent one. She describes her spell in hospital – an operation, an infection, a second operation – in matter-of-fact terms. 'I'm rattling with antibiotics, Taleb,' she says. 'And I'm only wearing this dress because I can't bear any pressure on the wound.' She twitches up the hem of the dress to reveal a bandage round her thigh. 'Try to avoid getting shot. It turns out bullets aren't always very clean.'

'I'll remember that.'

'Considering how much blood was shed in the conflict between Algeria and France, it's ironic I only survived because they pumped several litres of French blood into my veins.'

'A hopeful sign, perhaps.'

'I'll try to believe that. Of course, nearly dying meant I could tell Kadri I'd done my best to follow his orders, so there was that to be said for it as well. I arranged for Zarbi and Laloul to be killed and would have gone on to eliminate you, as instructed, if I hadn't been shot.'

'I'm a lucky man, then.'

'You are. Especially since your possession of the tape means Erica will have told Kadri you're to be left alone now.'

'Did he believe your story?'

'Of course not. But he had to pretend he did. I think he knows I don't trust him any more than he trusts me. Now, tell me where the tape is.'

'In a safe-deposit box at Bouras's bank. He and I are joint key holders.'

'I'll need a key as well.'

'In case Bouras and I meet with fatal accidents, you mean?'

'Exactly.'

'Unfortunately, no locksmith can legally supply a copy of a safe-deposit key.'

'I'm sure you know a locksmith who'll supply one, though.'

Taleb gives the point a few moments' thought. 'Well, maybe I do.'

The basilica of Notre-Dame de l'Afrique – Madame l'Afrique, as it is known to locals – stands stolidly on its high terrace above the broad blue Mediterranean, its domes and turrets peach-hued in the strident midday sun, the air sweetly scented by Aleppo pines and eucalyptus.

Taleb and Hidouchi have the esplanade beside the cathedral entirely to themselves. They walk out slowly across it towards the parapet, Taleb puffing at a cigarette, Hidouchi tilting her head back and luxuriating in the warmth of the sun.

'How did you leave matters with Erica?' Hidouchi asks.

'She certainly wasn't happy. She made that very clear to me. But . . . she recognized the force of my argument.'

'So, she won't come after us?'

'She threatened to. But I think she was just venting her frustration.'

'You think?'

'Well, she wouldn't warn us if she was really planning to move against us, would she?'

'Just as we wouldn't warn her if we decided to pursue her remaining undercover operatives.'

'No,' Taleb warily agrees. 'Just as we wouldn't.'

They reach the parapet at the edge of the terrace and gaze out towards the horizon, a distant line of blue, rippling in the heat haze, where sea and sky meet.

'We should leave this alone, Souad,' says Taleb. 'In our own best interests.'

'But what about our country's best interests? Le pouvoir still squats on all our lives. And who is the water-measurer now? Who is he paying? And what is he getting for his money?'

'Maybe some things are better not known.'

'Maybe they are. But I suspect Erica will come after us, sooner or later. It's in her nature. It's inevitable.'

Taleb senses the truth of this, even though he'd prefer to believe it was otherwise. He sighs. 'You could be right.'

'We can't let her choose the moment. We were lucky to get out of Paris alive. We may not be so lucky next time.'

'What do you propose?'

'We start identifying her operatives. We start putting names and faces to hizb fransa. We prepare for the struggle to come.'

'I should be preparing for my retirement.'

'You can't retire. There's too much for you to do.'

'That's more or less what Bouras said to me this morning.'

'There you are, then. So, are we agreed?'

'It sounds like a lot to take on.'

'It is. Which is why it needs to be a joint effort.'

Taleb says nothing. They look at each other in a silence broken only by the shrieks of a wheeling gull. Hidouchi can't be stopped. He knows better than to try. And if she can't be stopped . . .

'Are you with me in this, Taleb?'

And still he says nothing. Because, in truth, he doesn't need to. They both know the answer to her question. They both know what he's going to do.

AFTERWORD

No novelist could contrive the sanguinary horrors of the Algerian War of Independence, far less the carnage of inter-necine strife that afflicted Algeria during the 1990s. We can only believe such things were done by human beings to other human beings because the historical record assures us they were. This is certainly true of the massacre of Algerian protesters by the Paris police on the night of 17 October 1961, by a long way the most lethal action taken by state forces against street demonstrators in western Europe in modern history. In writing this novel, I have tried to do justice to the effect such terrible events had on the people caught up in them – and hence on the characters in this story.

GLOSSARY

Ben Bella – Ahmed Ben Bella (1916–2012), first president of Algeria after independence, deposed in a coup, June 1965

Bendjedid – Chadli Bendjedid (1929–2012), Boumediene's successor as president, forced out of office by the military, January 1992

Beur – French slang word for North African immigrants, no longer in respectable use, derived from the French pronunciation of Arabe

Boudiaf – Mohamed Boudiaf (1919–1992), recalled from exile to become Algerian head of state, February 1992, assassinated 29 June 1992 during a televised speech

Boumediene – Houari Boumediene (1932–1978), Ben Bella's successor as president, died aged 46 of a very rare blood disease amidst rumours of poisoning

Bouteflika – Abdelaziz Bouteflika (1937–2021), president of Algeria from 1999 until he was forced to resign following prolonged street protests, April 2019

Cagayous – Archetypal pied noir braggart and hustler, depicted in cartoon adventures in Algerian and French newspapers and magazines from the 1890s through to the 1920s

Camus – Albert Camus (1913–1960), French–Algerian writer, author of *L'Étranger* and *La Peste*, winner of the Nobel Prize for Literature, 1957

DGSE Direction générale de la sécurité extérieure – France's external intelligence agency, equivalent to MI6 or the CIA, known until 1982 as **SDECE** (Service de documentation extérieure et de contre-espionnage)

DRS Département du renseignement et de la sécurité – Algeria's intelligence and security agency, known until 1990 as **SM** (Sécurité militaire) and after 2016 as **DSS** (Département des services de sécurité)

La décennie noire – the 'dark decade' of terrorist violence that claimed tens of thousands of lives in Algeria during the 1990s, also referred to as the Algerian Civil War

Djaout – Tahar Djaout (1954–1993), Algerian poet and journalist, assassinated by the GIA as he left his apartment in Algiers, 26 May 1993

Énarque – a graduate of France's École nationale d'administration, thereby destined for a senior civil service post

FIS Front islamique du salut – the Islamic Salvation Front, whose likely victory in Algerian elections in January 1992 was blocked by the military, sparking off the Algerian Civil War

FLN Front de libération nationale – Algeria's nationalist political party, founded in 1954 at the outset of the Algerian War of Independence and the dominant party of government since independence from France was achieved in 1962

De Gaulle – Charles de Gaulle (1890–1970), president of France from 1958 to 1969, who brought the Algerian War of Independence to an end in 1962

GIA Groupe islamique armé – Islamist insurgent organization blamed for much of the violence in Algeria during the 1990s

Harkis – Muslims who fought for the French in the Algerian War of Independence, many repatriated to France after independence, many who stayed in Algeria massacred by the FLN

Hirak Movement – Protest movement that began in major Algerian cities in February 2019 campaigning for Bouteflika's removal from office and general liberalization of the state

Hitistes – Slang Algerian word for young idlers who loitered in groups, leaning against walls, during the 1990s, derived from the Arab word for wall, hit, another meaning of which – an interruption of time, a hitting of the wall – may refer to their lack of motivation

Hizb fransa – Literally the 'party of France', a malign secret network dedicated to undermining Algeria believed by some Algerians to have been seeded within their society by de Gaulle at independence to ensure their country could never prosper

Massi – Souad Massi (b. 1972), Algerian folk singer, songwriter and guitarist

ONAT Office national algérien du tourisme – Algerian national tourist organization, established 1962

Papon – Maurice Papon (1910–2007), prefect of police in Paris at the time of the 17 October 1961 massacre of Algerian demonstrators, later imprisoned for crimes against humanity during the Second World War

Pieds noirs – The term generally applied to colonial settlers in Algeria of European descent, the derivation of which is variously attributed to the polished black shoes worn by the French military or the patronizing view of the metropolitan French that the colonists spent too long barefoot in the North African sun

Le pouvoir – The description applied by Algerians to the secret power structure believed to dictate political events in the country

Raï – A form of Algerian popular music blending traditional, modern and protest elements that caught on particularly during the 1980s when electronic instruments were introduced and it became known as pop-raï, whose practitioners were targeted by Islamist terrorists during the 1990s

Rimitti – Cheikha Rimitti (1923–2006), popular Algerian female raï singer, known as la mamie du raï

Sonatrach – Société nationale pour le recherche, la production, le transport, la transformation et la commercialisation des hydrocarbons – Algeria's national oil and gas company, established in 1963, later hit by a massive corruption scandal

Tati – Jacques Tati (1907–1982), legendary French comic filmmaker famous for his accident-prone everyman character Monsieur Hulot, bankrupted by the production costs of his fourth feature film, *Playtime*

Tativille – The vast open-air set south-east of Paris where Jacques Tati filmed *Playtime*

Tebboune – Abdelmadjid Tebboune (b. 1945), Bouteflika's successor as president of Algeria

Toufik – Nickname of Mohamed Mediène (b. 1939), notoriously hard-line director of the DRS from 1990 to 2015

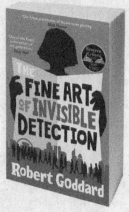

'He's the high priest of plot . . . deftly woven, but also beautifully written . . . I loved it' Mel Giedroyc

Umiko Wada has recently had quite enough excitement in her life. With her husband recently murdered and a mother who seems to want her married again before his body is cold, she just wants to keep her head down.

As a secretary to a private detective, her life is pleasingly uncomplicated, filled with coffee runs, diary management and paperwork.

That is, until her boss takes on a new case. A case which turns out to be dangerous enough to get him killed. A case which means Wada will have to leave Japan for the first time and travel to London.

Following the only lead she has, Wada quickly realizes that being a detective isn't as easy as the television makes out. And that there's a reason why secrets stay buried for a long time. Because people want them to stay secret. And they're prepared to do very bad things to keep them that way . . .

Read on for an extract of *The Fine Art of Invisible Detection*, introducing Umiko Wada

ONE

UMIKO WADA WASN'T A PRIVATE DETECTIVE. SHE JUST WORKED FOR ONE. She answered his phone, managed his accounts, kept his records, talked through problems with him, greeted his visitors, fetched him bento-boxed lunches and made him tea, which he'd taken to drinking virtually all day now he'd supposedly given up smoking.

The sign on the door of the seventh-floor office in the Nihonbashi district of Tokyo where Wada spent her working days described it as the premises of the Kodaka Detective Agency. But there was only one detective in the agency: fifty-eight-year-old Kazuto Kodaka. There'd been several detectives, apparently, when Kodaka senior was in charge. But his son preferred to operate alone. What would happen if and when his body collapsed under the strain of his unhealthy habits and chronic overwork was easy to predict. Wada would need a new job. Which wasn't a happy thought. She liked this job. It suited her.

She always thought of herself as Wada rather than Umiko because that was how Kodaka referred to her. It had seemed disrespectful at first. Now she was rather fond of it. It reinforced an image of herself she'd honed over years of being alone. Simple, strong, independent. That was Wada. Umiko was a girl she'd once been. The Wada she'd become was nearly forty-seven, though she looked younger, probably because, as her mother regularly reminded her, she'd never had children to raise and worry over.

That wasn't Wada's fault, as her mother used to acknowledge but now seemed inclined to forget. She was a widow. Her husband Tomohiko – Hiko, as she'd called him and still did, in the privacy of her own thoughts – had been killed in the sarin gas attack on the Tokyo subway back in 1995, though technically he hadn't actually died until twelve years later. The decade and a bit he'd spent in a coma froze Wada's life. Her mother had still hoped, when he finally expired, that Wada would find somebody else to marry. But it had never happened.

Sometimes, though she'd never have admitted it to anyone, she was glad she hadn't gone on in the world with Hiko, bearing his children, keeping house for him, cooking, cleaning, deferring, conforming. She was as sorry as anyone could be that he'd died as he had. There was a time when she'd been sorry on the same account for herself. But that time had passed. That was why she'd finally dropped his surname and gone back to the one she was born with: Wada.

She'd met Kodaka because of the sarin attack. He was gathering evidence to use against members of Aum Shinrikyo, the murderous cult responsible, on behalf of relatives of other victims and wanted to know if Hiko had said anything to her, before lapsing into his coma, about Yozo Sasada, the cult member who'd released the gas in the train carriage Hiko had been travelling in that fateful spring morning in 1995. No, was the answer. Hiko was already unconscious when she'd reached the hospital. He'd said nothing. To her or anyone else.

She was working as an English translator when Kodaka first contacted her, earning money the only way she knew how. She enjoyed speaking and reading English. It took her to a mental space half removed from the Japanese world she didn't quite have a firm stake in any more. She felt freer there, better able to be herself.

It was a surprise when Kodaka contacted her again a few months later, this time inviting her to apply for a job as his secretary. Her fluency in English was something he reckoned would be valuable in dealing with foreign clients. Not that he actually had any foreign clients. But he was optimistic about expanding the reach of his operations and there were quite a few occasions when an improvement on his halting grasp of the international language was called for.

She took the job, which she described as personal assistant rather than secretary. It often involved working late or at the weekend for no extra pay, but she didn't mind and Kodaka rewarded her with occasional bonuses when business was good.

The business itself was biased towards commercial matters. There was a lot of vetting of potential recruits for companies or identifying which of their employees might be responsible for leaking sensitive information to competitors or the media or the tax authorities. Kodaka senior had sited the agency within easy reach of the Tokyo Stock Exchange to attract such business. Divorce and missing persons, the other staples of the profession, were less significant at the Kodaka Agency, though Wada enjoyed them when they came along. She found the tangled problems of other people's lives grimly fascinating.

Most of the time, her involvement with those lives was confined to putting Kodaka's notes and other records in order and compiling reports to lawyers, which she was much better and quicker at than Kodaka himself, whose talents lay in ferreting out information, staking out addresses and piecing together evidence. More than once, after pulling his bottle of Suntory whisky out of the bottom drawer of the scratched green filing cabinet behind his desk and pouring them both a glass as the lights of the city danced in the night beyond the office windows, he'd say they made a good team.

Sometimes, very rarely, Kodaka asked her to go out into the field and follow someone. This occurred when only a female tail was likely to escape detection. She proved to be rather good at it. Without intending any insult, Kodaka said she had the gift of being invisible. No one noticed her. She was anonymous. She attracted no attention.

Kodaka was unmarried. Wada's mother had suggested, in her desperation for a grandchild that only grew as her daughter progressed into her forties, that he might be a suitable husband, even though she'd never actually met the man. The idea was absurd. Kodaka found all the female company he desired in his late-night forays to assorted bars and clubs. He often arrived at the office in the morning with the rumpled, unshaven, red-eyed look of someone who'd barely slept, let alone in his own bed. He'd never made any kind of overture to her, probably because he valued her services too highly to risk losing them. He was right. The overtures wouldn't have been well received. That would have been unfortunate. Because they were a good team.

Yozo Sasada, the Aum Shinrikyo member responsible for Hiko's death, had finally been executed twenty-three years after the attack, along with the cult's founder, Shoko Asahara, and twelve others. Kodaka made no reference to their hangings, though when the day came Asahara's blank, heavy-lidded face was all over the newspapers and the giant TV screens that Wada passed on her way to work. She interpreted her employer's silence on the subject as an example of his sensitivity, which as

410

ever could only be detected by what he didn't say rather than what he did.

The twenty-fourth anniversary of the attack had passed now as well, again unremarked upon in the offices of the Kodaka Detective Agency. Spring was advancing. Cherry blossom viewing spots in Kitanomaru Park were hard to come by. The world went on its way. It was business as usual.

Until it wasn't.

Wada made most of Kodaka's appointments for him. Most of his office appointments, anyway. He fixed personal rendezvous for himself. An unenthusiastic convert to modern technology, he recorded these in an old-style pocket diary and insisted Wada keep a paper diary for the office as well. He made occasional joking references to his reluctance to embrace paperless procedures, though Wada suspected he was also worried about the security of information committed to the virtual world. And there was no doubt many of his clients valued security so highly that his old-fashioned methods appealed to them.

That Friday, when Wada reached the office, she was mildly surprised to see an afternoon appointment with someone identified only by the hiragana み and た written in the diary in Kodaka's inelegant hand. It must have been made after she'd left the previous evening. She mentioned it to him when he arrived. He was looking far from spruce but by no means unusually dishevelled. All she learnt from him was that み た was one Mimori Takenaga, her name recorded in traditional albeit abbreviated style with the surname first and the forename second.

'She caught me on the telephone just before I left last night,' Kodaka explained.

'Husband trouble?' Wada enquired.

'Not the way you mean.'

411

And that was that. He didn't elaborate. And Wada didn't press him to. That was one of the things that made them a good team.

Mimori Takenaga arrived promptly at four thirty. She was a woman of about Wada's own age, but smaller and more delicately built. She would have looked perfect in a kimono, whereas Wada, on those ever rarer occasions when she wore one, felt lumpy and awkward. In the fashionable western clothes she was actually wearing, Mrs Takenaga looked smart and affluent but somehow ill at ease. There was an impression of someone playing a part she wasn't suited to, which the large, well-filled Mitsukoshi carrier bag she left in the waiting area failed to dispel.

She was closeted with Kodaka for about an hour, their voices reaching Wada as an indistinct murmur often drowned out by the telephone or traffic noise from the street below. The length of the consultation suggested the matter was both delicate and complicated. Kodaka asked for tea halfway through and Wada only caught a brief snatch of the conversation as she delivered it. Her curiosity was aroused, but she had no difficulty hiding it. Hiding her feelings came easily to her.

Eventually, Kodaka showed his new client out. Mrs Takenaga cast Wada a long frowning glance as she collected her Mitsukoshi carrier bag along with her umbrella. It was faintly disquieting. Wada could think of nothing she had done to merit such attention.

It had started to rain during the hour Mrs Takenaga had spent with Kodaka. The sky was unnaturally dark for the time of day and the rain, coursing down the window, appeared from Wada's place behind her desk to be coursing down Kodaka's forehead and cheeks as well as he stood close to the glass, gazing down, waiting, it was soon apparent, to see his visitor emerge on to the street.

'Hasui could have painted this,' he said at length, just as watery sunlight began to wash over his face. His interest in art, whenever it revealed itself, always came as a slight surprise to Wada. She was fond of Hasui's work herself, though she'd never mentioned this to Kodaka. 'He might have called it *Spring rain in Nihonbashi*. Takenaga-san has a traditional umbrella. Did you notice? Dark red.'

'Maroon.'

Kodaka smiled. 'Why do problems always seem simpler when I discuss them with you? I wonder. Perhaps your precision is the reason.' He turned towards her. 'Please lock the outer door and come into my office. Oh, and more tea would be welcome.'

The play of cloud and low sun was casting eerie variations of light across the walls of Kodaka's office when Wada delivered the tea and sat down, facing him across his desk. The green-shaded lamp wasn't on. Shadows were being given free rein, as Kodaka often seemed to prefer. There was cigarette smoke in the air, adding its own layer of haze to the atmosphere.

'Takenaga-san asked if she could smoke,' Kodaka said with an apologetic shrug. 'She was a little . . . nervous.'

Kodaka looked a little nervous himself, which was unlike him. But it was clear to Wada that he wanted to tell her why Mrs Takenaga had come to him. 'What is the nature of the case?' she enquired gently.

'The nature of the case?' Kodaka frowned pensively and took a sip of tea. 'Certainly this is not a normal problem. It is . . . complicated. And not just because of Takenaga-san's position. I will explain. Takenaga-san's father, Shitaro Masafumi, died when she was five. He committed suicide. Officially. She has never believed that. She believes he was murdered.'

'With good reason?'

Kodaka sucked his teeth. 'Hard to say. Masafumi died in Showa fifty-two.' 1977, fifty-second year of the Showa era, was more than forty years ago. Wada realized at once that the statute of limitations ruled out challenging a suicide verdict at such a distance in time.

'Too long ago for criminal or civil redress,' she remarked simply.

Kodaka nodded. 'Takenaga-san wants to know the truth, though. What she will do with the truth . . . I do not know. I am not sure she knows.'

'Can you get it for her?'

'Maybe it is already known. Masafumi was not a respectable man. He lived expensively, but the source of his income was unclear. He was suspected by the police of having sokaiya connections.'

Wada didn't need to be told anything about sokaiya. They were criminals who traded in commercial secrets, threatening to reveal damaging information, often at a company's AGM, unless they were paid off. Some had yakuza affiliations, some not. Kodaka had often been employed by companies to neutralize sokaiya threats.

'To escape arrest, which he is thought to have believed was imminent, Masafumi left the country, supposedly on holiday. He joined a tour party visiting Europe. Other members of the group described him as . . . distracted. He made many telephone calls and often sent telex messages from the hotels they stayed in. He looked worried all the time. He chain-smoked. He did not join in light conversation. They went first to Rome, then Paris, then London. While they were in London, Masafumi hired an English student who spoke good Japanese to act as his translator. He knew very little English himself, it seems. The translator was seen with him a lot. Sometimes they were in

414

telephone boxes together, with the translator talking on the telephone while Masafumi stood beside him. Suspicious behaviour, certainly. The translator said he was "helping Masafumi-san do business".'

'What kind of business?'

'Unknown. But probably not legal. We can guess Masafumi was trying to raise money to get himself out of trouble. The translator could tell us. But he disappeared straight after Masafumi's death.'

'That is also suspicious.'

Kodaka nodded. 'I agree.'

'How did Masafumi die?'

'He used a plastic laundry bag in his hotel room to suffocate himself. Or . . .'

'Someone else used it to suffocate him.'

'Takenaga-san believes the translator killed him. Or knows who killed him. That was also her late mother's belief. Other members of the family believe he killed himself because he knew he would go to prison if he came home and may have wished to avoid bringing shame on them.'

'What do we know about the translator?'

'Very little. His name: Peter Evans. Estimated age: mid-twenties. A student, perhaps. Never traced. There was also a photograph.'

'Of Evans?'

'Of the tour party, standing in a group near St Paul's Cathedral. Masafumi was in the back row, with Evans standing beside him. But Evans moved just as the photograph was taken, so he was . . . blurred.'

'Takenaga-san showed you the photograph?'

'No. She no longer has it. It was sent to her mother by the member of the party who took it after they returned to Japan. It was later destroyed by Takenaga-san's uncle because . . .'

Kodaka paused to assemble his thoughts, then continued. 'Her mother gave her the photograph shortly before her death from cancer twenty-seven years ago. After her death, Takenaga-san, who was still unmarried then, arranged for a cropped portion of the photograph, with only Evans in it, to be printed in the personal advertisements page of the London evening newspaper, offering a reward of one thousand pounds to anyone who could identify him. The notice stated that this person had worked for her father in London in late August and early September of 1977. Anyone who *could* identify him was asked to write to her. This outraged her uncle, who was at that time supporting her financially and considered the matter of her father's death, *his* brother, best forgotten. So, he destroyed the photograph and forbade her to reply to any letters she received.'

'Did she receive any?'

'It was not likely she would, was it? A blurred photograph. Fifteen years after the event. With scant information. And all on the chance that someone who might know something would read that particular newspaper.'

'On that particular day.'

Kodaka smiled. 'Actually, the notice ran twice a week for a month.'

'But, still, she heard nothing?'

'Not at the time.'

'Nor since?'

Kodaka's smile broadened. He couldn't stop himself taking pleasure from such twists of fate as his clients sometimes brought him. And clearly there'd been such a twist in the matter of Mimori Takenaga. 'She had a letter . . . last week.'

'After twenty-seven years?'

'Remarkable, no?'

'Very.'

'The letter was sent on to Takenaga-san at her current address by the occupant of the house the Masafumi family had lived in back then. It was from an Englishman called Martin Caldwell. He said he had only recently seen the advertisement and believed he knew who Peter Evans was. That was not his real name, apparently. Caldwell did not say who Evans really was, but he implied there was a mystery surrounding him. Caldwell was willing to meet Takenaga-san to discuss the matter. Could she come to London for the purpose? He was not interested in the reward, but he *was* interested in helping her discover the truth, if she still wanted to pursue the matter.'

'As she does.'

'Oh yes. But she cannot go to London. Her husband takes the same view as her uncle of her father's long-ago supposed suicide. He would not allow her to go. She can contact Caldwell and arrange a meeting, since he has supplied her with his email address, but *she* cannot meet him. Even coming here had to be done under the cover of a shopping expedition. However, since Caldwell has never met her, there is no reason why someone claiming to be her – a woman of about her own age, suitably briefed and fluent in English – could not go instead.'

Silence fell. The implication was obvious. Kodaka had a mission for Wada. One more challenging than anything he'd previously asked her to do. She waited for him to make the request specific, but he seemed reluctant to do so. He sipped his tea and smiled weakly at her. Eventually, she took pity on him. 'You want me to go?'

He nodded. 'If you are willing.'

ROBERT
GODDARD

WHERE WILL HE
TAKE YOU NEXT?

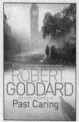

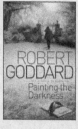

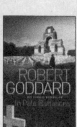

SEA CHANGE   What are the contents of a mysterious package that could spark a revolution in England?

1720

PAINTING THE DARKNESS
The arrival in London of a stranger claiming to be a man long thought dead uncovers dark family secrets.

1880

1910

PAST CARING   Why did cabinet minister Edwin Strafford resign at the height of his career and retreat into obscurity on the island of Madeira?

IN PALE BATTALIONS   Loss, greed and deception during the First World War – and a murder left unsolved for more than half a century.

1920

TAKE NO FAREWELL   A murder trial forces Geoffrey Staddon to return to the Herefordshire country house that launched his architectural career – and to the dark secret it holds.

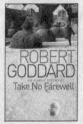

1930

CLOSED CIRCLE   On board a grand cruise liner, a pair of chancers are plunged deep into a dark conspiracy.

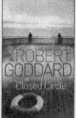

1960

DYING TO TELL   What happened in Somerset in the summer of 1963 that holds the key to a devastating secret?

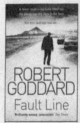

FAULT LINE   A father dead in his fume-filled car. His young son alive in the boot. Not your average suicide . . .

1970

LONG TIME COMING   For thirty-six years they thought he was dead. They were wrong.

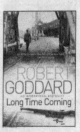

1980

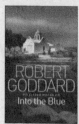

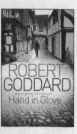

INTO THE BLUE   When a guest goes missing from his friend's villa on the island of Rhodes, Harry Barnett becomes prime suspect and must find her if he is to prove himself innocent.

HAND IN GLOVE   What long-buried secret connects the murder of a dead poet's elderly sister with the Spanish Civil War?

BEYOND RECALL   Dark family secrets are unlocked when a man seeks the truth behind the suicide in Truro of a childhood friend.

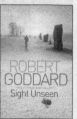

SIGHT UNSEEN   A trail of dangerous deceits connects eighteenth century political writer Junius with the abduction of a child at Avebury more than two hundred years later.

1990

BORROWED TIME   A chance meeting. A brutal murder. How far will one man go to gain justice?

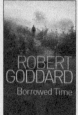

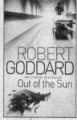

OUT OF THE SUN   Harry Barnett must unravel a web of conspiracies if he is to save the son he never knew he had.

CAUGHT IN THE LIGHT
A photographer is drawn into a complex web of deception and revenge following an encounter with a beautiful woman in Vienna.

2000

SET IN STONE A house steeped in a history of murder and treason exerts an eerie and potentially fatal influence over its present inhabitants.

DAYS WITHOUT NUMBER
Five Cornish siblings are dragged into a deadly conflict with an unseen enemy as they confront their family's mysterious past.

PLAY TO THE END An estranged husband becomes caught up in a dangerous tangle of family rivalries and murderous intentions while appearing in a play in Brighton.

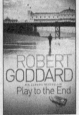

NEVER GO BACK A group of ex-RAF comrades, Harry Barnett among them, uncover an extraordinary secret during a reunion in Scotland, which puts them all in mortal danger.

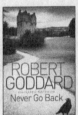

NAME TO A FACE When an ancient ring is stolen in Penzance, a centuries old mystery begins to unravel.

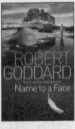

FOUND WANTING What connects a dying man's grandfather with the tragic fate of the Russian Royal Family, murdered ninety years earlier?

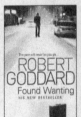

BLOOD COUNT There's no such thing as easy money, as surgeon Edward Hammond is about to find out.

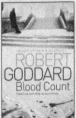

2010

PANIC ROOM

Robert Goddard

High on a Cornish cliff sits a vast uninhabited mansion. Uninhabited except for Blake, a young woman of mysterious background, currently acting as house-sitter.

The house has a panic room. Cunningly concealed, steel lined, impregnable – and apparently closed from within. Even Blake doesn't know it's there. She's too busy being on the run from life, from a story she thinks she's escaped.

But her remote existence is going to be threatened when people come looking for the house's owner, rogue pharma entrepreneur Jack Harkness. Soon people with questionable motives will be asking Blake the sort of questions she can't – or won't – answer.

WILL THE PANIC ROOM EVER GIVE UP ITS SECRETS?

'Is this his best yet? . . . Full of sinister menace and propulsive pace with twisty plotting'
LEE CHILD

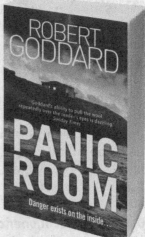

ONE FALSE MOVE

Robert Goddard

What value can be put on a human mind?

How Joe Roberts does what he does is a mystery. He has a brain that seems able to outperform a computer. To a games company like Venstrom, that promises big profits if his abilities can be properly exploited. So they send Nicole Nevinson to track him down and make him an offer too good to refuse.

But Venstrom aren't the only people interested in Joe. His current boss is already making serious money out of Joe's talents and isn't going to let him go without a fight. And then there are other forces, with still darker intentions, that have their own plans for him.

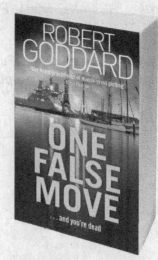

Unwittingly, Joe and Nicole cross an invisible line into a world where the game being played has rules they don't understand. And the battle now isn't just for Joe's mind. It's for Nicole's life.

'Our finest practitioner of double-cross plotting'
MICK HERRON